MW00622463

The Best
AMERICAN
SCIENCE
FICTION &
FANTASY
2024

The Best
AMERICAN
SCIENCE
FICTION &
FANTASY™
2024

Edited and with an Introduction
by HUGH HOWEY

JOHN JOSEPH ADAMS, *Series Editor*

MARINER BOOKS
New York   Boston

FIRST EDITION

ISBN 978-0-06-331578-5
ISSN 2573-0797

24 25 26 27 28 LBC 5 4 3 2 1

Contents

Foreword

WELCOME TO YEAR ten of *Best American Science Fiction and Fantasy*! This volume presents the best science fiction and fantasy (SF/F) short stories published during the 2023 calendar year as selected by myself and guest editor Hugh Howey.

About This Year's Guest Editor

#1 *New York Times* bestselling author Hugh Howey took the publishing world by storm in 2011 with the publication of *Wool*, which was originally self-published (or indie-published, as we'd say now) on Amazon's Kindle Direct Publishing platform as five novellas—and later was collectively republished as the *Wool Omnibus*. Over the next couple of years, *Wool* became such a phenomenon that coverage of it appeared everywhere from the *New York Times* to the *Wall Street Journal* to *Forbes*—not about the book itself but about the incredible success story of the book's publication. *But everyone loved the book too*, readers and critics alike. If you somehow hadn't heard about any of that, you might know Hugh's work from the hit Apple+ show *Silo*, which is an adaptation of *Wool* and the whole Silo series (which includes *Shift* and *Dust*). There's also a TV show based on his deep-space science fiction novel *Beacon 23* currently airing on MGM+, and other novels of his—such as the incredible *Sand*—are also in development for adaptation.

Although Hugh's first big success was *Wool*, before that he published four books in the young adult Bern Saga, starting with *Molly Fyde and the Parsona Rescue*, and the "I'd shelve it in the science fiction/fantasy section, but is also kind of a YA novel" novel *Half Way Home*. (Hugh has something to say too about where books are shelved in his introduction that follows.) Other books include *I, Zombie*; *The Shell Collector*; and a collection of his short fiction, *Machine Learning*. His latest books are the *Sand* sequel *Across the Sand* and *The Balloon Hunter*.

Hugh and I hit it off when we met at the 70th annual Worldcon in Chicago in 2012, and afterward we ended up co-editing The Apocalypse Triptych anthology series and then several years later (with Christie Yant) edited The Dystopia Triptych; then—with Christie and screenwriter Gary Whitta (*Rogue One, The Book of Eli*)—Hugh edited *Resist: Tales from a Future Worth Fighting Against*.

Aside from writing, Hugh has worked as a bookseller, a computer-repair technician, a roofer, a yacht captain, and for a long time he lived on a catamaran on which he sailed across the world . . . alone. He also was at Ground Zero in New York on 9/11 and had been inside the World Trade Center the night before; many of the autobiographical details of that experience were depicted in his absolutely astonishing short story "Peace in Amber." If you'd like to learn more about Hugh, I highly recommend the "Who I Am" page on his website (hughhowey.com/who-i-am), which is perhaps the best "behind the page" author bio I've ever seen—and, honestly, just a damn fine piece of writing.

Selection Criteria and Process

The stories chosen for this anthology were originally published between January 1, 2023, and December 31, 2023. The technical criteria for consideration are (1) original publication in a nationally distributed North American publication (i.e., periodicals, collections, or anthologies, in print, online, or ebook); (2) publication in English by writers who are North American, or who have made North America their home; (3) publication as text (audiobook, podcast, dramatized, interactive, and other forms of fiction are not considered); (4) original publication as short fiction (excerpts of novels are not knowingly considered); (5) story length of 17,499 words or less; (6) at least loosely categorized as science fiction or fantasy; (7) publication by someone other than the author (i.e., self-published works are not eligible); and (8) publication as an original work of the author (i.e., not part of a media tie-in/licensed fiction program).

As series editor, I attempted to read everything I could find that meets the above selection criteria. After doing all of my reading, I created a list of what I felt were the top eighty stories (forty science fiction and forty fantasy) published in the genre. Those eighty stories—hereinafter referred to as the "Top 80"—were sent to the guest editor, who read them and then chose the best twenty (ten science fiction, ten fantasy) for inclusion in the anthology. The guest editor reads all of the stories anonymously—with no bylines attached to them, nor any information about where the story originally appeared.

The guest editor's top twenty selections appear in this volume; the remaining sixty stories that did not make it into the anthology are listed in the back of this book as "Other Notable Stories of 2023."

2023 Selections

One author this year performed the very rare feat of having not one, but *two* stories selected for inclusion in the anthology: Rebecca Roanhorse, with her stories "Falling Bodies" and "Eye & Tooth." Five authors selected for this volume previously appeared in *BASFF*: P. Djèlí Clark (2), Kel Coleman (1), Isabel J. Kim (1), Sam J. Miller (3), and Rebecca Roanhorse (1). Thus, V. M. Ayala, A. R. Capetta, James S. A. Corey, P. A. Cornell, Jonathan Louis Duckworth, Amal El-Mohtar, Andrew Sean Greer, Thomas Ha, Grady Hendrix, Alex Irvine, Ann Leckie, Hana Lee, Sloane Leong, and Christopher Rowe are all appearing in *BASFF* for the first time.

The selections were chosen from fifteen different publications: *Beneath Ceaseless Skies* (2), *Clarkesworld* (2), *Fantasy Magazine* (2), *The Far Reaches* from Amazon Original Stories (3), and the following, which all had one selection each: *Asimov's*; *The Book of Witches* edited by Jonathan Strahan; *Creature Feature* from Amazon Original Stories; *The Dark*; *Escape Pod*; *Lightspeed*; *Out There Screaming* edited by Jordan Peele and John Joseph Adams; *Reactor* (formerly

Tor.com); *The Sunday Morning Transport*; *Uncanny*; and one single-story digital chapbook from Amazon Original Stories.

Several of our selections this year were winners of (or finalists for) some of the field's awards[1]: "How to Raise a Kraken in Your Bathtub" by P. Djèlí Clark (Locus winner, Hugo finalist); "Once Upon a Time at The Oakmont" by P. A. Cornell (Nebula and Aurora finalist); "John Hollowback and the Witch" by Amal El-Mohtar (Locus finalist); "Window Boy" by Thomas Ha (Locus and Nebula finalist); and "If Someone You Love Has Become a Vurdalak" by Sam J. Miller (Stoker finalist).

2023 Top 80

In order to select the Top 80 stories published in the SF/F genres in 2023, I considered several thousand stories from a wide array of anthologies, collections, and magazines.

The Top 80 this year were drawn from thirty-two different publications: seventeen periodicals, twelve anthologies, two single-story chapbooks, and one single-author collection.

Tochi Onyebuchi had the most stories in the Top 80 this year, with three; several authors were tied for second most, with two each: Violet Allen, P. Djèlí Clark, Jonathan Louis Duckworth, Andrea Kriz, Yoon Ha Lee, Sam J. Miller, Nnedi Okorafor, Malka Older, Rebecca Roanhorse, and Daniel H. Wilson. Overall, seventy-one different authors are represented in the Top 80.

In addition to the selections that were nominated for awards, several Notable Stories were winners of (or finalists for) various awards as well: "A Soul in the World" by Charlie Jane Anders (Locus finalist); "What I Remember of Oresha Moon Dragon Devshrata" by P. Djèlí Clark (Locus finalist); "Tantie Merle and the Farmhand 4200" by R. S. A. Garcia (Nebula winner); "The Most Strongest Obeah Woman of the World" by Nalo Hopkinson (Aurora finalist); "Reckless Eyeballing" by N. K. Jemisin (Locus finalist); "I Am AI" by Ai Jiang (Aurora, Hugo, Locus, and Nebula finalist); "The

---

[1] At the time of this writing, several genre awards had not yet announced their lists of finalists, and the final results of some of the awards mentioned above won't be known until after this text is locked for production, but will be known by the time the book is published.

Sound of Children Screaming" by Rachael K. Jones (Hugo, Locus, Nebula, and Stoker finalist); "The Year Without Sunshine" by Naomi Kritzer (Nebula winner, Hugo and Locus finalist); "Prince Hat Underground" by Kelly Link (Locus finalist); and "Stones" by Nnedi Okorafor (Locus finalist).

Outside of my Top 80, I had around one hundred additional stories this year that were in the running, and the difference in quality between the stories on the inside and the ones on the outside looking in was often imperceptible—thus the choice came down to pure editorial instinct.

Anthologies

The following anthologies had stories in our Top 80 this year: *Out There Screaming**² edited by Jordan Peele and John Joseph Adams (6); *The Far Reaches** from Amazon Original Stories (6); *The Book of Witches** edited by Jonathan Strahan (4); *Life Beyond Us* edited by Julie Nováková, Lucas K. Law, and Susan Forest (4); *New Suns 2* edited by Nisi Shawl (3); *Creature Feature** from Amazon Original Stories (2); *All These Sunken Souls* edited by Circe Moskowitz (1); *Communications Breakdown* edited by Jonathan Strahan (1); *A Darker Shade of Noir* edited by Joyce Carol Oates (1); *Fit for the Gods* edited by Jenn Northington and S. Zainab Williams (1); *Luminescent Machinations* edited by Rhiannon Rasmussen and dave ring (1); and *Qualia Nous, Vol. 2* edited by Michael Bailey (1). Anthologies marked with an asterisk had stories selected for inclusion in this volume.

Other anthologies that published fine work in 2023 that didn't manage to crack the Top 80 include: *Adventures in Bodily Autonomy* edited by Raven Belasco; *Christmas and Other Horrors* edited by Ellen Datlow; *Dark Matter Presents: Human Monsters* edited by Sadie Hartmann and Ashley Saywers; *Dark Matter Presents: Monstrous Futures* edited by Alex Woodroe; *The Digital Aesthete* edited by Alex Shvartsman; *Fourteen Days* edited by Margaret Atwood; *The Good, the Bad, and the Uncanny* edited by Jonathan Maberry; *Jewish Futures* edited by Michael A. Burstein; *Mermaids Never Drown* edited by Zoraida Córdova and Natalie C. Parker; *Mothersound* edited by Wole Talabi; *Never Too Old to Save the World* edited by Addie J. King

---

2 Winner of the Bram Stoker Award and the Locus Award for Best Anthology

and Alana Joli Abbott; *Never Wake* edited by Kenneth W. Cain and Tim Meyer; *Never Whistle at Night* edited by Shane Hawk and Theodore C. Van Alst Jr.; *The Reinvented Detective* edited by Cat Rambo and Jennifer Brozek; *Rosalind's Siblings* edited by Bogi Takács; and *Swords in the Shadows* edited by Cullen Bunn.

Collections

Only one collection had a story in the Top 80 this year: *White Cat, Black Dog*[3] by Kelly Link. But naturally, many other collections were published in 2023 that contained fine work. All of the following were released in 2023 and meet the broad "American" focus of this book; some contained only reprints, but I'm including them here anyway as part of my overview of the year: *Old Babes in the Wood* by Margaret Atwood; *I'd Really Prefer Not to Be Here With You* by Julianna Baggott, *Monstrous Alterations* by Christopher Barzak; *Zen and the Art of Starship Maintenance* by Tobias S. Buckell; *The Wishing Pool and Other Stories* by Tananarive Due; *Blood from the Air*[4] by Gemma Files; *The Collected Enchantments* by Theodora Goss; *The Last Catastrophe* by Allegra Hyde; *The Privilege of the Happy Ending* by Kij Johnson; *The Secrets of Insects* by Richard Kadrey; *The World Wasn't Ready for You: Stories* by Justin C. Key; *Thirteen Plus-1 Lovecraftian Narratives* by Nancy Kilpatrick; *No One Dies from Love* by Robert Levy; *Uranians* by Theodore McCombs; *No One Will Come Back for Us and Other Stories* by Premee Mohamed; *Jackal, Jackal* by Tobi Ogundiran; *Skin Thief* by Suzan Palumbo; *Lost Places* by Sarah Pinsker; *Who Lost, I Found: Stories* by Eden Royce; *The Whole Mess and Other Stories* by Jack Skillingstead; *The Beast You Are* by Paul Tremblay; and *Jewel Box: Stories* by E. Lily Yu.

Periodicals

Lightspeed* had the most stories in the Top 80 (7); followed by *Clarkesworld** (5); *Uncanny**[5] (5); *Beneath Ceaseless Skies** (4); *The*

---

3 Winner of the Locus Award for Best Collection
4 Winner of the Bram Stoker Award for Best Collection
5 Winner of the Locus Award for Best Magazine

Magazine of Fantasy & Science Fiction (4); *Reactor** (4); *Asimov's** (3); *The Sunday Morning Transport** (3); *Fantasy Magazine** (2); *McSweeney's* (2); and the following all had one each: *Bourbon Penn; Cast of Wonders; Escape Pod*; FIYAH; Nightmare; PseudoPod;* and *The Dark.** Periodicals marked with an asterisk had stories selected for inclusion in this volume. *The Sunday Morning Transport, Escape Pod,* and *The Dark* all had stories selected for inclusion for the first time.

Appearing in the Top 80 for the first time are *Bourbon Penn, Cast of Wonders,* and *PseudoPod.* The following magazines didn't have any material in the Top 80 this year but did publish stories that I had under serious consideration: *Analog; Apex Magazine; Apparition Lit; Baffling Magazine; The Kenyon Review; khōréō; Vastarien;* and *Weird Horror.*

Debuting in 2023 were the flash fiction–only publication *Small Wonders;* the "no plot, just vibes" magazine *Tales & Feathers;* the relationships-oriented *Heartlines Spec;* and *New Edge Sword & Sorcery,* which does what it says on the tin. Permanently closing were *Fantasy Magazine* and *Cossmass Infinities* (which wasn't eligible for *BASFF,* but a notable closure), and ceasing magazine publication and shifting to an anthology series format were *Dark Matter* and *Galaxy's Edge; Future Science Fiction Digest* is also shifting to an anthology series format, but they plan to release the stories from their anthologies online over the course of several months. The long-running *Daily Science Fiction* also went on indefinite hiatus.

Given the announcement last year that a Certain Online Bookstore named after a rainforest discontinued their ebook periodicals program, this year's death toll was surprisingly small. That said, it seems likely more disruptions to the short fiction ecosystem are still to come, and I'll say again that short-fiction magazines need your support now more than ever. Subscribe, post reviews, spread the word—it all helps and can make a difference.

Acknowledgments

Thanks to my assistant series editor Christopher Cevasco and to in-house *BASFF*-wrangler Nicole Angeloro for all their hard work behind the scenes. Special shout-out to David Steffen of The Submission Grinder writer's market database, who helps me stay apprised of market openings and closures. And, as always, I extend my eternal gratitude to the authors who write short fiction (and those who continue to write short fiction even when they have successful novel careers)—and to everyone who reads, appreciates, and tells people about great short fiction; there are too few of us and too many of those out there who are readers but don't even really know short stories exist.

Submissions for Next Year's Volume

Editors, writers, and publishers who would like their work considered for next year's edition (the best of 2024), please visit johnjosephadams.com/best-american for instructions on how to submit material for consideration.

—JOHN JOSEPH ADAMS

Introduction:
Plato and the Planogram

I'VE BEEN A book nut since my mom introduced me to a certain cat in a hat. In school, I got in trouble for ignoring my teachers by reading under my desk. My parents often told me to put my reading away at the dinner table, and the back pocket of my jeans was invariably stretched out in the shape of a mass-market paperback. Hell, I'd even read while walking down the street. Trailing behind my brother and sister, I'd slam into lampposts and trash cans. I'm not kidding.

In college, I tried to support my reading habit by getting a job in a Barnes & Noble, lured in by the smell of fresh pulp and that juicy employee discount. It was a brand-new store in North Charleston, South Carolina, just a huge space full of empty shelves. A week before opening, a tractor trailer backed up and disgorged pallet after pallet piled high with unopened boxes of fresh books.

My first job as a young bookseller was to fill those empty shelves before the grand opening. Amazingly, there was a dedicated place for every single book. This was my introduction to "planograms," an industry term for a detailed schematic showing where each book should be placed on every table and shelf. Almost immediately, I saw how often this plan defied logic and common sense.

Horror had its own section, but *Frankenstein* belonged in general fiction. Science fiction and fantasy were lumped together, but *Alice's Adventures in Wonderland, 1984,* and anything by Michael

Crichton could also be found in general fiction. So was Stephen King. And Kurt Vonnegut. In the years ahead, I would spend a considerable amount of my workday guiding a confused shopper away from the logical place they started their search to some other spot in the bookstore.

The Time Machine? That's in the classics. *War of the Worlds* too. They get shelved with *The Odyssey*, when it would perhaps make sense to shelve *The Odyssey* in fantasy.

It didn't take long for me to see nefarious purposes behind these planograms. Folks who love Literature with a capital L seemed to be protecting their disdain for science fiction and fantasy by removing anything from those sections that had merit or gained wide appeal with the masses. This explained why major bestsellers like King, Shelley, and Vonnegut went in the general fiction section. And classics that everyone was familiar with were taken out of the SF/F realm as well. If your premise was that these nerdy genres didn't matter, an easy way to prove the point was to rob science fiction and fantasy of the works you think matter.

My conspiratorial thinking felt confirmed when I worked in an independent bookstore many years later while trying to make it as a writer. Once again, science fiction and fantasy were lumped together, and any book my boss thought he'd like to read was removed and shelved elsewhere. In logic, we call this "begging the question," where you set up conditions so they prove your point. The science fiction and fantasy section of the bookstore felt like a field left to go fallow. When *Hunger Games* took off during those years, we set up its own table to avoid putting anything so popular in the far, dim reaches of the bookstore. As an aspiring sci-fi writer, I quietly fumed.

When I learned how much Plato hated poets, things began to make more sense.

There are ten sections, or "books," of Plato's *Republic*—a classic work that attempts to define the perfect society. Two of those ten books are mostly about *how much Plato hates poets and poetry*. No joke. By appealing to emotions rather than sticking to facts, Plato accused poets of poisoning our minds. By writing what *isn't* instead of what *is* or *ought to be*, they endanger his perfect society. In his own words:

> And the same may be said of lust and anger and all the other
> affections, of desire and pain and pleasure, which are held to

be inseparable from every action—in all of them poetry feeds and waters the passions instead of drying them up; she lets them rule, although they ought to be controlled, if mankind are ever to increase in happiness and virtue.

He goes on to suggest that only religious tales and biographies of powerful people should be allowed, and I suspect he has this opinion in order to not be struck down by either:

[B]ut we must remain firm in our conviction that hymns to the gods and praises of famous men are the only poetry which ought to be admitted into our State. For if you go beyond this and allow the honeyed muse to enter, either in epic or lyric verse, not law and the reason of mankind, which by common consent have ever been deemed best, but pleasure and pain will be the rulers in our State.

Plato was terrified of how poets arouse our passions. And in his lamentations, I can hear my old boss from my bookstore days decrying anything too far out there for public consumption. Suddenly, the old system of shelving books made perfect sense. When works like *Gulliver's Travels* or *Twenty Thousand Leagues Under the Sea* are around long enough, or sell enough copies, or enter the public imagination, they no longer feel threatening. Even the oddness of Vonnegut is something we get used to in time. It was never about which books were most worthy—it was about which ones were *most worrisome.*

This also solved another question that often came up among bookstore browsers: Why are science fiction and fantasy shelved together? What do dragons and spaceships have in common? Why are ancient wizards and cyborgs on the same shelf? I remember how in grade school, when my mom would drop me off at Waldenbooks for hours at a time, I would skip past all the sci-fi looking for a Dragonlance or Forgotten Realms book I had not yet read. What was all this futuristic junk doing among my swords and sorcery? I'd bump into a sci-fi kid asking a similar question about all these books with half-clad men wielding swords as tall as they were.

My old theory would've been that bookstores were clumping together all the literature not deemed "good enough." But when bookstores started carrying graphic novels, manga, and video game guides, these were often put in the same dark corners of the store. The thing in common with these works was that most people didn't understand what happened among those shelves. These were the dangerous poets of the world, writing about what isn't instead of what is. Writers who inspire our passions, who challenge us. The books that make us feel dizzy with wonder.

When I was asked to edit this volume, I was warned there would be a lot of reading involved. As if I haven't been training for this under school desks and at the dinner table my entire life. Threatening me with words is like waving a red flag in front of a bull. As I dove in, I found myself awash with stories that Plato would've loathed. Stories that challenged my worldview, that made me exercise new mental muscles, and stories that brought me to tears. These were not always easy stories to read—they strained my imagination, made me cringe, some are outright terrifying. Even more difficult was choosing my favorites. What they all have in common is that I know where they would be shelved: where they might only be discovered by those who were somewhat ready for them.

These two genres have more in common than I used to think. Reading them as presented here should drive that point home. If you think you lean toward fantasy, you might be surprised to discover that your favorite story here is categorized as science fiction. And the opposite might very well be true. What binds them together and makes each one worthy of inclusion is that Plato would've hated them, and planograms would've banished them. These are dangerous stories. The kind that warp reality and threaten to change the world.

Are you ready?

I hope not.

—HUGH HOWEY

The Best
AMERICAN
SCIENCE
FICTION &
FANTASY
2024

How It Unfolds

FROM *The Far Reaches*

SCIENCE FICTION

INTERVIEWER: It must feel a little strange to spend all this time preparing for something that you aren't actually going to do.

ROY COURT: Except that I am. When the package unfolds, the Roy that comes out of the assembler is going to remember having this exact conversation with you. It's just that he's going to be on some other planet trying to figure out how to restart the human race, and I'm going to be here worrying about my taxes. [*laughs*]

INTERVIEWER: I can't imagine knowing there's some other me out there.

ROY: It's not really going to be like that, though. We've located tens of thousands of exoplanets that look promising for colonization, but the closest really good candidates are fifteen, twenty light-years out. We call it "slow light" for a reason. The beams we're transmitting aren't quite as speedy as the normal stuff. That's four, maybe five decades before the first unfold could set up a transmitter and send us a hello. We're all mortal here. Those other Roys are going to be doing what they do long after I'm gone.

"Okay, I'm going to start the anesthetic in a few seconds here. You might get a little light-headed," the technician said. She was a petite redhead with a small chin and dainty little teeth. If they'd met at a bar, Roy might have tried flirting with her.

Instead, he put a hand in his pocket, reassuring himself that the little velvet box really was where he thought it would be, then nodded. "Copy that."

She shifted, put a needle into the drip feed going to his arm, and made a little sound that seemed like satisfaction. "Okay. Just count backward for me from ten to one."

"Ten, nine, eight, seven—"

Roy opened his eyes. He was alone in the landing couch, just the way he was supposed to be. He lay there for a little while, getting used to the feeling of his body. His arms and legs felt heavy, like he'd just had ten hours of hard sleep. The knot that always seemed to rest in his belly had untied itself. He felt great.

The room itself was small, spartan, engineered to have not just the least mass but the least information that the package would have to encode. It seemed silly to take a snapshot of two hundred human bodies and brains and then try to economize with simplistic shelving, but here he was. He checked his pocket. The box was still there.

"What's the word, folks?" he said.

"Scan went great, Roy," Sandor, the director of operations, said through the speakers. "No data loss, minimal overhead."

"Great. That means I can retire now?"

"Wait a few minutes to get your legs back before you start running down the street, but yeah, man. We did it."

Roy smiled. After three years of active training, it felt a little anticlimactic. He'd come into the program at thirty years old with six years as an officer in Air Command behind him, a dual master's in engineering and applied math, and he'd still barely qualified. The program had been boot camp and graduate school and team-building intensives all in one. And this was the last time he'd be looking up at the gray ceiling of the package module. The last time he'd be talking to Sandor and Chakrabarti and Foch. The last day he'd spend with most of the team.

Maybe not all of them, though. There was room to hope.

The farewell banquet was the next day at a hotel ballroom just off the base. Three hundred and fifty people, mostly women, mostly in their late twenties, around fifty tables with ceramic pumpkins for centerpieces and plates of rubbery chicken or gritty lentil tacos. An open bar. Sandor had given a tipsy speech about the nobility of the human soul and the work of becoming not just a multiplanetary but a multisystem species and started weeping. It had actually been pretty moving, in the moment. The president of the National Space Agency sent a message of congratulations and thanks that had been projected onto a blank wall behind the empty bandstand.

Now, Roy was leaning back in his chair with a whiskey sour in his hand while Zhang Bao and Emily Pupky leaned in on either side, talking across him. After three years of a strict no-alcohol policy, even the watered-down drink was hitting him hard.

"Bringing men at all was a mistake," Emily said. "No offense, Roy. But every male in the package is one less uterus. And there are what? Fifteen hundred sperm samples? We're going to kick founder effect's *ass*." She pointed an exuberant finger at Bao. "Kick its ass."

"Replacement is an issue, yes," Bao said. "But how many babies are we really going to need in the first stage?"

"We'll have to have some pretty fast or there won't be anyone to do the work when we get old. Populations with inverted age distribution—"

"It's going to have to be a game-day decision," Bao said. "Every situation is going to be different. And really, Emily, do you want to commit to living the rest of your life without cock?"

Emily cackled. "You're going to be a lucky man, Roy."

"Oh, not me," Roy said. "I've stood my watch. Now I'm going back to Ohio and looking for a job."

He caught sight of Anjula across the room. She was wearing a pale-yellow dress that brought out the warmth of her skin. Her hair was flowing down one shoulder, and her smile was the same wry near-smirk he'd loved and hated and loved again.

Now or never, he thought. He teetered on *never*, then shifted his chair back. "Doctors. You'll excuse me, I hope, from your very erudite conversation on the long-term value of cock."

He got stopped three times as he made his way across the ballroom, people he now knew as well as his own family, all saying their goodbyes. He disengaged as quickly from each teary farewell as politely as he could. Anjula was putting on her coat when he reached her.

"Hey there, former wife," he said, the way he often did.

"Hey there, former husband."

"Taking off?"

"Yeah. Traveling early tomorrow."

"Let me walk you out."

They passed into the hotel lobby, a fantasy of black tile and fluted columns with a wide fountain along one wall. Megan Lee from the engineering team waved from across the room, looking wistful. Gabriel Hu, head of their data operations team, was sprawled on one of the couches, grinning drunkenly at everyone who passed but not making a scene. Anjula paused and bowed to him. Gabriel, unspeaking, inclined his head and waved his hand like an emperor accepting the obeisance of his subjects. They both chuckled, and Anjula moved on, Roy at her side. He didn't touch her arm, and she didn't lean against him. They knew each other too well for that.

"We pulled it off," he said.

"We did. I should thank you."

"For what?"

"Not making them choose between us. I know admin was concerned those first couple years."

"I can see why. People get divorced, they don't always play well together after. But I can bounce that right back at you. If you'd pushed the point, there's no reason to think I'm the one they'd have kept."

They reached the main doors and stepped out into the night. A warm breeze was blowing from the east, carrying the smell of the ocean. The transports waited in a sedate line, ready to whisk hotel guests anywhere in the city. The stars shone above them, billions of points of light pressing down through the backsplash of the city. They stood together for a moment, looking up, each with their own thoughts.

"I'm glad I got to know you again," Roy said. "It feels like a blessing after . . . you know."

"We were too young. Everyone gets to be an idiot at nineteen."

"Here's to getting old, right? But we've got a few good years left in us."

"I hope so," she said.

When she turned to look at him, he had the box out and open. The old ring glimmered in the new light. She looked from it to him. Her expression was surprise. Then horror.

"Oh God, Roy," she said. "No."

INTERVIEWER: It's odd that this is the application we're making of the Hamze-Grau slow light, isn't it? If we can make copies of things from . . . what? Enriched light? Shouldn't we be us-

ing this to make habitats for people here on Earth? Medical
supplies for war zones? Food?

ANJULA FARAH: Not really. It's an economics question. The energy it would take to manufacture something using slow light
is just an order of magnitude more than it would take using
traditional means. Slow light can build you a house; it'll just
cost a hundred times the energy a hammer and nails would.
What makes this interesting isn't the duplication possibilities,
though that is fascinating in its own right. It's the distribution.

INTERVIEWER: Distribution?

ANJULA: Moving matter across interstellar space has never made
sense from an energy expenditure standpoint. And in that use
case, suddenly duplication using slow light begins to make
economic sense. There are other ways to manufacture things.
But delivering and unfolding a package on an alien world
light-years away in the galaxy? This is the only way to do it.

INTERVIEWER: Going back to economics, what's the return on
this investment?

ANJULA: Lots of people will give you the "all your eggs in one
basket" argument for spreading out to multiple solar systems.
But that's not the reason for me. For me, some chances you
take just because the possibilities are beautiful.

"Okay. Just count backward for me from ten to one."

"Ten, nine, eight, seven—"

Roy opened his eyes. He was alone in the landing couch, just
the way he was supposed to be. He lay for a little while, getting
used to the feeling of his body. His arms and legs felt heavy, like
he'd just had ten hours of hard sleep. The knot that always seemed
to rest in his belly had untied itself. He felt great.

"What's the word, folks?"

The silence that followed seemed to last an eternity. The voice
that answered him wasn't Sandor. It was Gabriel Hu.

"Well. Holy shit."

Roy sat up a little too fast, and the room swam around him.
Adrenaline fought against the fading anesthetic and slowly, surely
won. The public address system clicked as a new connection came
on. Elizabet Aldo's voice was as bright, excited, and controlled as
a puppy on a leash. "All teams, please report to your stations for
startup checks. Local gravity is a pleasant one g, but let's not hurry,
people. We're all still a little groggy."

They weren't on the base. They weren't on Earth. They'd unfolded the package. The room around him, the gray, softly lit hall, wasn't the one he'd been scanned in. Hell, he wasn't the Roy Court who'd been scanned. The idea was simultaneously everything he'd hoped for and still totally surreal.

He walked down the hall, keeping one hand on the wall even though he didn't feel unsteady. The air smelled like cleaning supplies and dust filters, the same as it always did. The gravity was heavy but not oppressive, so wherever they were, it wasn't on one of the outlier worlds with significantly more or less mass than Earth. But the sound was different. He couldn't put his finger on it at first, but there was a different resonance in the quiet. Wind hitting the base station from some unaccustomed direction. Or maybe rain or hail outside. A new *outside* that humans had never even seen before. Roy let that sink in for a moment.

He fought the temptation to detour through the observation deck. He wanted to see this new world, and if he was being honest, he wanted to see if Anjula was there, giving in to the same temptation. The first moment looking on the planet they were there to remake would be a hell of a time to pull out a ring.

Megan Lee was already at the reactor room when he arrived. The room was small and jammed to overflowing with their equipment. With both engineers at their workstations, they had to be careful not to elbow each other. Below them, the pocket reactor lay quiet. The control panels were up, everything on standby, waiting to kindle the little nuclear fire that would keep their batteries topped up for—if things went right—the rest of their lives. Megan looked stunned. She looked like he felt.

"Ain't this a kick in the pants," she said.

"You know," Roy said, "it's exactly what we planned for, and somehow, I'm still really surprised. You and me and all the others? We're the first people to travel between stars."

It wasn't the first time he'd had the thought. It was the first time it had been true. Roy grinned.

"Prepare for check, primary reactor," Elizabet Aldo said. "And go."

Megan started the system running. Each computer and subsystem cycled through its routine. Each indicator came up within its expected range.

"I'm seeing nothing but green," Megan said. "Confirm?"

"Confirmed," Roy said. "I've got green across the board."

"Admin," Megan said. "This is engineering. Primary reactor is good to go."

Roy pulled up the start sequence, just waiting for the order to begin. Over the speaker, he heard Elizabet, but only distantly, like she had her hand over the microphone. Megan frowned. The voices over the speaker grew harsh. A drop of unease spilled into Roy's blood.

"So, hold up for a second," Gabriel said over the speaker. "Megan? Roy? Tell me you haven't started that reactor."

"We haven't started the reactor," Roy said. "What's going on?"

Gabriel's sigh shuddered. "Turns out that if you had, it would have killed us."

[ROY COURT IS LOOKING INTO THE CAMERA. THE RIGHT SIDE OF HIS FACE IS VISIBLY BLISTERED. THE IMAGE STUTTERS, FREEZES, AND BEGINS AGAIN.]

ROY COURT: There is . . . there is a faulty coolant pressure sensor. I think it's in the H line. It isn't showing that there's backflow from a stuck valve. Um. We're on battery now. I don't know how long we have. We're going to try and send this out. The others are . . . Anjula's . . . um . . . Okay. Okay. Any future missions, we need to get this to them as soon as they unfold. Like to the minute. It's important . . . It's critical.

[HE SHAKES HIS HEAD. HIS HANDS TREMBLE.]

ROY: We got so far, and now this. It's just not fucking fair.

Normally, it wasn't a meeting Roy would have attended, but since the fault had been in his equipment and the warning had come from some version of him, Elizabet had brought both engineers to the table. Gabriel Hu was there, and Anjula. Kiko, the head of medical and psychological support. Roy and Anjula were two of the oldest people there. Most of the package had been built with people in their twenties. Roy was the oldest man on the planet. Probably the oldest within a dozen light-years.

The meeting room was small, like everything. Four benches around a fake wood-grain table. Elizabet had a mug of smoky tea beside her. The light was soft and full spectrum, designed to look like a sunny afternoon. Outside, it was stormy. If he listened carefully, sometimes he could hear the thunder.

Megan Lee gave a quick report—the stuck valve had been

identified, the faulty sensor had been replaced, the reactor was up and running. Then she got out of the way to let the site group report.

"The good news is that it's a better fit than we'd hoped. Same size and water percentage as Earth. One moon, about the same size as Luna, but about five percent farther out," Anjula said. "The sun's older. There's only one gas giant, and the asteroid belt between here and there is much, much thicker, and it has a lot of activity outside the ecliptic. You get the feeling something bad happened there. The atmosphere is plausible. High nitrogen, enough oxygen that it's pretty clear there's something respiring out there, or was at some point. The big challenge is that there's a lot of chlorine dioxide too."

"Bleach planet. So no walks outside," Elizabet said.

"Not if you enjoy having lungs."

"Something we can terraform?" Megan asked.

"We? No," Anjula said. "Our great-grandchildren can maybe get started on it. In theory, perfectly doable, but we have a lot of infrastructure to build and a lot of surviving to do first."

Roy had to pull his attention away from her mouth and the memory of the way the lip balm she'd liked in college had tasted after they'd kissed. This was a serious, professional meeting as much as anything that had happened during their years of training. There was no room for him to be mooning over her like they were kids again. His hand shifted to his pocket, checking that the little box was still there.

"What's the *bad* news?" Elizabet asked.

"We're still figuring out where we are. We were expecting some lensing and occlusion to make things weird, but beyond some very consistent landmarks like the galactic core, everything seems to have moved around a lot."

"Which means what?" Megan asked, folding her arms. Roy knew the answer before Anjula spoke, but mostly because it was the kind of thing they'd talked about back in the before times.

"It would be stranger if things hadn't," Anjula said. "Everything moves, everything ages, everything changes. That's normal. Stars shift spectra; they move in relation to each other." She lifted her hands, fingers splayed just a little like the feathers of a peacock. It was a gesture he remembered her mother using too. Genetics or mirroring. "We'll figure it out. If we can get an idea of how long has passed since we left Earth, that'll help a lot."

"Yes, well," Gabriel Hu said. "Our ears are up and listening."

Roy shifted in his seat. This was the meat of the proceeding. The part they'd all come for. Gabriel knew that too, and he played it for effect, stroking his nonexistent beard. In another life, the data operations administrator would have been a big name in community theater.

"We were doing our checks against the original package data. Making sure that the unfold hadn't dropped anything and that the functional package that arrived matched the expected data? It all looks fine, by the way. The alert interrupted us, and of course thank God it did. The data stream," he said, then paused. Roy shifted in his seat. Anjula glanced at him with a *do you believe this guy* look that no one else would be able to parse. "The packet stream is still coming in."

Elizabet frowned. "Is there a bottleneck?"

"No," Gabriel said. "But there is a metric shit-ton of data. There's three sources broadcasting, none of them closer than eighty light-years. But they're all on the standard frequency and using the expected coding."

"Good that *something* went right," Kiko said.

"A lot's gone right. We're not all dead right now," Gabriel said. "But part of that is that the data streams are about a third hand-shake, a third don't-blow-up warnings, and a third new data. The message wasn't aimed at us in particular. The transmitters are just blanketing the sky with it."

Roy leaned forward. "Three sources means there's at least two packages that took, right?"

"None of the sources match Earth, so I'd say we have confirmation on three success stories out there. And the fresh data we're getting is vast. Field reports from other unfolds, news reports from other worlds. Probably some stuff from Earth in there somewhere for folks who are nostalgic for the old homestead. But it's going to take a long time to record and decompress, and a very, very long time to go through."

"Define 'very, very long time' in this context," Elizabet said.

"We already have centuries of other people's history to go through, and I'm guessing we have about a twentieth of the full packet. That may be an underestimate. That's mostly the handful that succeeded. Add in all the field reports from the ones that foundered? They didn't have as much history, but they made it up in volume, and with the personal messages our other instances stuffed into metaphorical bottles for us, we could literally spend the rest of our lives playing catch-up. I'm feeding them all into virtual intelligence, but even that's going to take months."

"How many field reports?" Anjula asked.

"When I came down for the meeting, we'd identified three thousand seven hundred and thirty-two separate origin points. The ones that didn't get the message in time and blew their reactors on startup won't appear in the data set."

They all went quiet. Elizabet leaned forward, elbows on the table. She pressed her fingertips to her lips. She was one of the oldest people on the mission. She was thirty-six.

"Almost four thousand tries. And three successes."

This time Gabriel didn't have to pause for effect. The effect was already there. He said, "Yes. But there's something more encouraging. We're not a prime package."

"And that means?" Megan said.

"We weren't transmitted from Earth. One of those three colonies lasted long enough that they've begun beaming out copies of the starting package. I mean, in success that was always the idea. Establish a foothold and continue to spread."

"So that's part of why it's a little confusing where we are." Anjula nodded. "Not sure of our origin point yet."

"The incoming data should clear that up soon," Gabriel said. Roy didn't say it, but he thought that seemed optimistic.

[THE WOMAN IN THE VIDEO IMAGE HAS PALE SKIN AND A LONG WHITE BRAID. THE ROBE SHE'S WEARING, BRIGHT RED, FLUTTERS IN A BREEZE THAT ALSO MAKES A *whuffle* SOUND AGAINST THE MICROPHONE. BEHIND HER, A HUGE STONE STATUE LIKE A SPIRAL MADE FROM HUNDREDS OF HUMAN BODIES SWIMMING UPWARD TOGETHER RISES TOWARD A VIOLET SKY.]

NARRATOR: Maunyu ese eh umfal imbli bes im zohn—

[THE VIRTUAL INTELLIGENCE MUTES HER, REPLACING THE LIVING HUMAN VOICE WITH A CAREFULLY MODULATED TRANSLATION. THE WORDS NO LONGER MATCH THE MOVING LIPS.]

NARRATOR: This monument was dedicated to our ancestors who first came to Sun-Home in a ray of light. We know the names of these voyagers of the vacuum, and we carry their legacy in our blood. Elizabet Aldo. Thomas Esquivel. Megan Lee. Caroline Morales. All seven billion people on the three continents, all the ten billion scattered in the stations and moons of our solar system. We are their children. The family they began here two thousand years ago is all of humanity that we will ever know. But our siblings are out there. Children of our same mothers and fathers who live under different stars who we will never meet in person. We can only take comfort knowing that our ancestors are not dead, only *elsewhere*, brought to life anew from the same light that once fell here, and beginning again the great adventure that is our past.

The last home they'd shared was an apartment in a high-rise. The windows looked out over the streets of Chicago's South Loop. If they'd been on the other side of the building, they could have seen the lake. One bedroom, one bath, a little kitchen, and a main room with a red tweed couch where Roy slept increasingly often. The picture of them on the wall—black-and-white, taken in the first year of the marriage—looked like other people. The apartment was always immaculate. The one thing they still agreed on was keeping the living space tidy.

The end came on a Sunday.

"You're walking away from me again. Can we please just talk about this?" Anjula said.

"I'm going to the balcony for a little fresh air," Roy answered. "It is literally three steps from where I was sitting. There's no cone of silence over it. I can hear you just fine."

"It's putting distance between us."

"Yes, that's what getting fresh air means."

The lines appeared at the corners of her mouth, two thin parentheses as if everything she said was going to be an aside. Roy felt the weight of them like he was wearing one too many jackets. He put up his hands in surrender and sat back down.

"You can go out if you want to," she said.

"I know, but I hear that you want to finish this conversation, and I want to honor that," he said. It was the phrasing her therapist had imposed on him during the one session Anjula had guilted him into attending. If he said it with a little mockery, it was only the tightness in his jaw. He'd seen a feral dog once, when he was a child, pacing in the animal control kennel. He remembered that dog a lot these days.

"I just don't understand why Air Command is the only acceptable plan for you," she said.

"There's a difference between the only acceptable plan and the best one. It's four years active, three reserve. I get paid for finishing my degree instead of going into debt. And the academy program is one of the best in the world. It's better than the École."

"It's better for you," Anjula said. "That doesn't make it better for us. At the École we could both work on our degrees—"

"Go into debt twice as fast, and wind up with shittier prospects when we're done. Or I can do four in Air Command, then support the family when I'm out."

"The family?"

"Yes, the family. By then we can have kids. They can be almost ready for school."

"I don't want to have kids with you." She started, surprise in her expression like someone else had said it. Outside, an ambulance turned on its lights, but it was too far away to hear the siren. A flock of pigeons rose from the roof of the smaller building across the street, wheeling up until they were dark commas against the sky.

"Since when?" Roy said, but the wind was knocked out of him. The anger in his words didn't even convince him.

"I don't know," she said. "I don't . . . It just came out."

"Did you mean it?"

"Yeah."

"Well, that's a change of plan."

The lines were gone from around her mouth. She looked relaxed. It was worse than when she looked angry. "We're done here, Roy."

"I don't know what that means."

"It means we're done."

She left that night. When he called her, she didn't pick up. The divorce request came the next week, routed through the same legal service they'd used when they got married. He reached out to their friends, to her parents, to anyone who might be able to get her to talk with him, but nothing came of it. He didn't hear from her at all until after he'd agreed to the division of assets. Even then, it was a text-only connection. He'd gotten it over a bowl of vermicelli with lemongrass and an egg roll at the sidewalk café they'd gone to when neither one felt like cooking.

Thank you. I'm sorry. This wasn't your fault.

He read the words a dozen times. More. He composed replies in his head, but none of them were enough. It would have taken an essay to pour everything out—the anger and the guilt. The ache of missing her body next to him in the morning. The knot of grinding resentment at her abandonment of him. The ways he was relieved that it was over, and the ways that he wasn't.

In the end, the message he sent back was: *Did you meet someone else?*

It took her ten minutes to send a message back. *No, but I hope I will someday. I hope you will too. Who knows? Maybe it'll even be us, when we're both different people.*

He didn't finish his meal. He wasn't hungry. He just tapped the screen to pay the bill and walked home. The new family down the hall was having a birthday party for their five-year-old, and the bright, syrupy chords of children's music murmured in the hallway. When he closed the apartment door, he couldn't hear it. He poured himself a whiskey, took her old drafting stool out to the balcony, and watched the night fall over the city. When it was dark and cold, he sent back: *All right.*

A month later, she sent him her engagement ring in a plain cardboard box. He didn't see her again or know what had become of her until the day Sandor asked if working with her would be a problem.

[THE IMAGE IS OF ELIZABET ALDO. HER EYES ARE PUFFY, WITH BAGS UNDER THEM AS DARK AS BRUISES. SHE RUBS HER PALM AGAINST HER CHEEK.]

ELIZABET: This is the third anniversary of our unfold, at least by the calendar we brought with us. We're still only halfway through a local orbit, which means probably another four or five hundred days of winter. The hydroponic garden isn't flushing the way it's supposed to. Jordan thinks the higher gravity is doing something to the pumps. That's the most pressing threat to the colony, but the lava tube we expanded into last year is showing stress fractures. And Gabriel is refusing to take his medications. And we had two more miscarriages last month.

[SHE SIGHS, THEN GOES QUIET FOR TWENTY-SEVEN SECONDS.]

ELIZABET: I knew it wasn't going to be easy. But fuck, I didn't know it was going to be this hard.

Roy checked the seals on the environment suit again, then cracked the air lock and turned the ATV toward the outside. It was warm out, and the air had a shimmering greenish cast. Bare dirt stretched away from the base, rising and falling as wind and rain shaped it. Here and there, thin plantlike organisms rose up from the ground, evolved through God knew how many generations to withstand the chlorine dioxide atmosphere. Tracks in the soft ground showed where the ATV had gone before like an animal trail. Which, in a sense, it was.

Roy tapped the radio. "This is a test. You hearing me, boss?"

"Loud and clear," Megan Lee said from the engineering station. "Telemetry's good too."

"Okay. Starting the survey run."

"Be careful out there. I don't want to have to explain to Elizabet that you died because I was too lazy to go out and save you."

"Copy that. I'll be back in as soon as we get the data. No loitering."

"Because what we need's more data," she said wryly.

"It ain't the quantity, it's the quality." He guided the ATV to the east, ready to follow yesterday's path for the first few kilometers before he looped out for fresh territory.

The data package was still coming in, whispered on radio waves that had been traveling for decades or centuries. Only one of the three sources had gotten to the end of its feed and restarted. The other two, with larger archives to share, were still singing new songs, and Gabriel was starting to get worried about available memory. As the ATV hummed and jounced under him, Roy was collecting more—air samples, atmospheric light scatter readings, temperature, barometric pressure, and on and on and on. Even if the data packet was enough to fill all their available storage, Gabriel was going to make room for this. Millennia of other people's history and culture and philosophy mattered less than the soil chemistry right here.

He reached the day's turnoff mark, paused to drop a marker, and turned out, heading toward a distant cluster of rolling hills. High clouds stretched in a tall, green-blue sky, their edges glowing a little gold in the sunlight. The soil was damp. It crumbled easily under the ATV tracks. In another, less chlorinated atmosphere, it would have looked like the promise of a good garden harvest. Maybe it would be, someday.

Or maybe not. Three in four thousand were bad odds.

"What about the ridge to the north there?" Megan asked in his ear. "It looks like there's some actual stone there. And maybe the new greenhouses could get a little shelter from the wind."

"I can take a look," Roy said, and bumped the joystick.

"It's beautiful out there," she said. "I mean in an austere, no one lives here kind of way."

"It's nothing a few centuries of atmospheric scrubbing won't fix."

The other engineer chuckled. The strategy for expanding the base had been designed by some of the best minds in the world. Roy had been drilled in it, the same as all the other people in the package. Not just the details either. The logic of it. Build new, physically separated structures to mitigate single-point failures. Set up secondary sources of food, water, and air. Diversify, scatter, dig in. Their job was to survive and raise another generation that was able to survive after them and start the whole ball of human civilization rolling again until they had the means to set up a transmitting station and send the slow light package on to likely worlds in their galactic neighborhood. It had seemed less like hubris in Chicago than it did in this vast, empty landscape.

There were so many things that were going to have to go right . . . and so few they could afford to have go wrong.

He felt the ATV start to shift before he knew what was happening. His hand went to the joystick, already moving to correct, but the ground to his right was falling away, the soil cascading down with a rumble he could feel vibrating up through the treads. The vast sky tipped.

The ground rushed up and punched him. Something hurt badly enough he wasn't even sure what it was. The pain was like white noise turned up too loud to hear anything through it.

When Roy's mind started coming back together, the first thing he heard was Megan talking to him. Her voice was staccato and focused and calm in a way that meant there was an emergency. He couldn't quite parse the words, though. There was a smell like a swimming pool. They'd need to build a pool somewhere down the line, for the kids to swim in. No good having a childhood without a swimming pool in it. He tried to sit up, and he couldn't. The ATV had him pinned in the soft ground. He could tell where his left leg was—trapped under the tread that had rolled on top of him. His right leg, also under the same tread, seemed to disappear in a cloud of pain somewhere around midthigh.

"Well," he said. "Huh."

"Roy? Are you there?"

"Here. I'm here. I think the ground may be a little too unstable for new construction."

He tried to sit up, propping himself on his elbows.

"Stop moving, Roy. Roy? I need you to stop moving now, okay? We've got medical on the way."

"I'm all right," he said, though that was clearly not true.

"Just lay back and stay still until we can make sure your spine's okay. Don't try to get out until we get there."

He lay back and coughed. "I think I have a crack in my helmet."

"I'll let them know."

The sky above him was beautiful blue, deepest where there was the least distance between him and the blackness of space. He tried to keep his breath slow and shallow and wondered whether this was the thing that would take him out. He hoped not. The little velvet box was still in his locker. Another missed chance.

"Hey," he said. "If I don't make it, could you tell Anjula—"

"You're making it," Megan said, and he lost his train of thought.

Something moved in the soil at his side, thin and squirming. It looked just like an earthworm. He reached out and closed it in his fist. If he died, someone else should see it.

[THE WOMAN APPEARS TO BE IN HER MIDDLE TWENTIES WITH SHOULDER-LENGTH HAIR. SHE LOOKS BOTH FAMIL-IAR AND UNFAMILIAR AT THE SAME TIME. HER SMILE IS UNCERTAIN.]

JESSICA: Hi, you don't know me. My name is Jessica Court. Roy Court—our Roy Court—was my father. And I know you're not him, not exactly, but I also know you kind of are. And I don't know if you have a kid of your own out there, but if you do, there's no way it's me. But my dad passed away last week. I'm still kind of in shock about it.

[SHE BEGINS TO WEEP, PUSHING AWAY TEARS WITH THE PALM OF HER HAND.]

JESSICA: I can't talk with him anymore, and you're the closest I've got. So maybe you can hear this for him? Okay? I miss you, Dad. I love you. And I will always love you. And I will always miss you. And I'm sorry about the fighting. I'd take it back if I could. You were a good father, and you were good to Mom. You did good. You were good.

"What made you change your mind about me?" Roy asked over the orchestral roar of conversation and music.

The girl from his materials science lab—Anjula Farah, her name was—sipped from her water glass before she answered. "What makes you think I changed my mind?"

The restaurant was just south of campus in a converted firehouse. The bar upstairs served hard liquor and a selection of legal euphorics to people old enough to buy them. The downstairs was open to the spring evening, and anyone over eighteen could have a beer with their dinner. It was popular with the undergraduates because the food was decent and it was walking distance from the dorms. It was the first time Roy had been there, but he was trying to seem like a regular.

"I invited you to dinner and you said you weren't available but to ask you again later. And then I asked again, and you said you'd think about it. And then I asked again, and here we are."

She lifted a finger. "That's just strategy. I know something about you now I didn't know the first time asked."

"Really?"

"A lot, actually. I know you're persistent, and you're patient. And I know you're not one of those guys who gets put off and then starts bad-mouthing the girl for not doing what you wanted. That's important."

The waiter slipped by, turning sideways to fit between the tables. The music shifted from an Afro-Caribbean piece to Spanish guitar. Roy shrugged.

"Fair enough. And it tells me some things about you too."

She lifted an eyebrow, and he felt her expression like it was a warm breeze. He had to work to look away from her smile.

"Yeah," he said. "You're attracted to me."

"Am I?"

"You are. You're not the kind of person who lets herself get pressured into a date because she feels obligated. And you're here. So it follows. It's all right. I'm attracted to you too."

She looked away, and the blush made the brown of her skin a little richer.

He learned other things that night too. That her family was from Mumbai, but she'd lived most of her life in Toronto. That her father had died when she was young, and her mother had re-married. That she was away from home for the first time, just the same as him.

He told her about his brother, the smart one in the family, who was studying at Cambridge on scholarship. About the comic book he'd done in junior high school. About the time he'd gotten lost on a hike and navigated his way out of the wilderness just as the search and rescue crews were about to go in looking for him. He told her about his ethically suspect first kiss, but not the name of the woman who kissed him. He never told anybody that.

They walked through the night-dark campus, moving from one pool of light to the next, drawing closer to each other in the darkness and pulling apart when they reached the light. They sat on the bridge over the river, looking down at the shimmer of moon and city on the water and talking about the books and movies and songs that were important to them. He made a mental list of them, already planning out where he'd find the time to read and watch and listen to them all. They kissed once when they reached her dorm, and he walked back to his room with his head held high and the certainty that he was never going to be sleepy again.

Five weeks later, she took him to her dorm when her roommate was away on a field study. In the morning, he lay with his back against the wall and watched her sleep. The darkness of her eyelids, the kind of look eye shadow was made to imitate. The rise and fall of her breath. The softness at the corner of her mouth. The unnatural smoothness of her forearm and the few stray dark hairs that had escaped being waxed. He was hungry. He was thirsty. He needed a shower. He stayed where he was, holding the moment close. Savoring it.

When her eyes fluttered open, she found him. Her smile meant she hadn't been sure he'd be there, and she was pleased that he was.

"Well, that's it," she said. "We slept together. We have to get married now."

"All right."

She chuckled. He didn't.

"No, it's good," he said. "Let's get married. Let's spend our lives together. We could dance around it and look for other people or try to play the field or whatever. Waste the time. Or we could be here. Do this."

"Should I expect you to get like this every time you get laid?"

"I don't know. I've never gotten laid before."

She frowned, and then she didn't. "Are you serious?"

"You can think I'm joking about stuff. You can turn me down. I will take no for an answer. But I'm gonna ask. And I think you're gonna say yes. Our odds aren't going to get much better with other people. You like me. I like you. We're good together. We should do it."

She shook her head, but like she was clearing away confusion. Not like a refusal. She sat up and didn't cover herself with the sheet. Her eyes shifted, looking into one of his and then the other like she could read something in them.

"What do you say? You want to get married?"

"You'd actually do it, wouldn't you?"

"I'm not afraid of taking risks. You're not either."

She wavered. He saw her waver. Two little lines appeared at the sides of her mouth like parentheses. Like whatever she said next was just for him to hear.

"Ask me again later."

Statement of Diu Cavui, Exarch of Lammos, Five Hundred and Thirtieth of His Name

(Annotated Translation)

As the ages of (humanity|civilization|thought) come to their end, we are given a choice. The empire graced by (virtue|blueness??) has aged past its apex. Plagues (spin?|rotate?) when once youth and health ruled. Strife has overcome peace. Decadence rises, degrading all that was noble and pure. As we turn to the future, the stars, the far planets, we are (called|inspired) to consider the wisdom of our birth.

Are we to gift (the universe|god|provability?) with the seed of a rotten fruit, or return to what was pure? The ancient light that shone on (the land|women?) was rich with (?) and that which was laudable grew from it. So it is chosen by the Exarch that the original seed be (resown?|uprooted?). Let the ages forget us, who had the chance at (?) and fell short. All praise to the ancestors. May their newer children serve them better than we have.

Roy hobbled down the corridor toward the cafeteria. The crutch bit into his armpit, and the black mesh cast around his knee and ankle bit into his leg, but he was getting used to both. Where he wasn't numb, he ached.

"This is bullshit," Gabriel said as Roy limped in. The cafeteria wouldn't have been a hole-in-the-wall restaurant back before the unfold. It seated maybe twenty at a time, and the food was always the same: dense cakes with all the nutrients, fiber, and microbiota to sustain life in a puck the size of a pack of cards. For drinks, there was water.

"It's not up for debate," Elizabet said.

Roy lowered himself to the bench at Gabriel's side. Across the small room, Emily Pupky was leaning close to Rick Hull, speaking intensely and low. Roy set himself to ignore them. "What's not up for debate?"

"Admin is abridging my civil rights," Gabriel said. "They're punishing me for something I *haven't done.*"

Elizabet rolled her eyes. "We're looking through the data packet. Error analysis on the other packages that failed? It turns out that three percent of the failures were because Gabriel had a mental health crisis and vented the atmosphere."

Roy grunted. "So we lock him out of the environment controls."

Elizabet turned to Gabriel but pointed to Roy, the physical equivalent of *You see my point?* Gabriel sighed. Rick Hull rose from the other table and walked out. Emily didn't move, chewed at her puck aggressively. Whatever was going on there wasn't his business.

Megan Lee came in, her hair pulled back in a tight ponytail.

She looked at Roy and shook her head. "Stay there," she said. "I'll bring your food."

"You're very kind," Roy said.

"Other Gabriel may have had a problem, but I'm *me* Gabriel, and I shouldn't be punished for what I haven't done."

"He makes a good point," Roy said.

Elizabet turned. "You think I should open his permissions again?"

"God, no. Just he has a good point. It's pretty weird making all our decisions with a gazillion different lives to show us what went wrong. I can see it getting a little oppressive."

"If we're still alive in twenty years, I'll apologize," Elizabet said.

Megan dropped a puck and a bottle of water on the table in front of Roy and sat at his side. "We can't die until I build a greenhouse and a hatchery," she said. "I want to be buried with a gut full of chicken curry."

"Amen," Elizabet said. "Three successes in four thousand; I intend us to be the fourth."

"Not the fourth."

Anjula stood in the doorway. Her eyes were a little too wide, the way they got when she was a little drunk or very excited. The others saw it too. They all went quiet. Elizabet tapped on the table beside her, inviting Anjula to sit. She didn't. She paced. "Three active now. But others may have survived for centuries. Millennia. How long does something have to last for us to call it a success? They rose, they lasted for a while, they fell. Things don't have to last forever."

"Not sure what you're saying here, Anj," Elizabet said, but she said it carefully.

"There are three signals active now. Right now. But how many were there before them? How many times did we do well enough to send out new packages into the void, and then the worlds they built rose up and lived their time and faded just because things don't last forever?" She plopped down beside Emily Pupky, who was listening to her now as intently as the rest of them. "I know where we are. And I know *when* we are. And we've been thinking about this all wrong. We're on Earth. *This* is Earth."

They were all silent for a moment, then Gabriel leaned across to Elizabet and said, "You going to take her permissions away too?"

"This is about the thing I found," Roy said. "The one that looked like an earthworm."

"It *was* an earthworm," Anjula said. "Or at least the unmistakable descendant of one. I don't know what happened to the atmosphere, but there are still a bunch of simple organisms living under the soil. The ones that evolved to fit the new conditions. I'm willing to bet if we get to an ocean, we'll find something very similar there."

"And the chlorine dioxide?"

"It breaks down. With this much of it in the air, something has to be making it, and that means biological activity, even if it's not the kind we're used to. And, I mean, at some point, Jupiter blew up. I can't explain that one, but it really fucked up the outer solar system. Left it unrecognizable. But the stars all line up if you make those assumptions. And the moon is the moon, but it's farther away because it's always been going out a few centimeters every year for half a billion years. The moment between when we went to sleep and when we opened our eyes was about five hundred million years."

Roy took a bite of the food puck, but he didn't taste it. "The galaxy's only a hundred thousand light-years across."

"Right?" Anjula said, lifting an eyebrow, and he felt *What makes you think I changed my mind?* "Each successful settlement got to a place they could transmit. They still had the original packet, the same way we do. It had worked for them, and why fix what isn't broken? We got retransmitted. We've been bouncing around from civilization to civilization like the baton in a relay race."

"Oh," Gabriel said. "Huh. That actually explains some things. I need to go take another look at that data stream."

"Those three sources for the data packet—" Elizabet said.

"They're just the three that happen to still be alive *right now*," she said, and tapped her knee with her index finger three times like a lawyer making her final summation. "And nothing lasts forever."

[THE MESSAGE IS FLAGGED PERSONAL FOR ROY COURT, AND ENCRYPTED. THE PROMPT IS: *THE NAME OF YOUR UNETHICAL FIRST KISS.* When he puts in the name he's never told anyone, the screen drops to black, flickers, and an old woman appears.]

[HER HAIR IS STIFF AND WHITE, HER SKIN IS AS THIN AS CREPE PAPER, AND THE RIGHT SIDE OF HER FACE DROOPS

A LITTLE. BUT HER EYES ARE MERRY, AND HER ASYM-
METRIC SMILE IS MISCHIEVOUS. WHEN SHE SPEAKS, HER
VOICE IS ALMOST TOO GRAVELLY TO RECOGNIZE.]

MEGAN LEE: I'm not supposed to do this. They tell me it's a mis-
use of the data stream, but what do they know? Here's what
you need to do, Roy. Listen close. Go to Megan Lee right
now and kiss her. It's going to save you both a lot of time and
bullshit. And after that, enjoy every minute of it. Both of you.
Every fucking minute of it is precious.

Three months into building the greenhouse, a vicious storm came
through and scattered the half-made structures across the landscape. Four months after that, the sacks that held the packed-earth
walls started to split and shatter. The project was scrapped, and
they began again. This time, it was mud and as much fiber as they
could spare from the base or scavenge from the landscape. For
seven weeks, they baked adobe with heat from the sun and their
nuclear reactor.

Coming up on a year later, the transparent ceramic went in, the
air locks tested nominal, and the first crop of the new Earth was
planted: human hands returning to agriculture that the globe had
forgotten until now.

The next morning, Megan Lee appeared at work with a ring on
her finger.

The celebration was in the cafeteria and the hallways, the observation deck and the recycling tanks and machine shop. Elizabet
looked the other way while Jordan Gaudi tapped into the address
system and played Arabic love ballads through the base. Roy danced
with Tracey Dunn and Char Lafflin, but mostly with Megan. The
severe, clean lines of the base seemed a little less austere. The thin
faces that the food rationing had created were brighter, happier.
Gabriel pressed a flask into his hand and kissed him on the forehead before dancing away again. It was whiskey, and it was good.

As the very late night shifted into very early morning, the halls
started to thin out. People headed off to their bunks alone or in
pairs, or sometimes more than pairs. Elizabet made a teary toast to
Megan and Roy and the new fucking greenhouse and the future
that they were all going to build together, by God. It was water, but
they drank it like champagne.

In the end, Roy found himself alone on the observation deck, tired past thinking straight, but not ready for the night to be over. Gabriel was down at the bottom of the stairway, singing in what sounded like Greek. The stars glimmered—billions of them—as did the visible smear of the Milky Way, glowing like a promise. His belly felt full, though he hadn't eaten more than the usual rations. His shoulders felt loose. A meteor flashed in the northern sky, then another. The only other light in the world came from the air lock lights of the greenhouse, three kilometers away. He could see it like a candle in the darkness.

He knew the footsteps as they came up the stairs. Her work clothes hushed as she walked.

"Hey there, former husband," Anjula said.

"Hey there, former wife."

"Beautiful night, isn't it?"

"Yeah."

She walked across the deck, three steps. Four. She sat beside him, not touching. "So," she said. "That ring."

"Yeah."

"You smuggled it through the scan?"

"Yes, I did."

They were silent for a long time. Anjula sighed. "Was it supposed to be for me?"

"Well, we'd been working together on the project for years, and that was about to be over. I figured that it was my chance to see, you know? If we were different enough people now to try it again."

She shook her head. "That doesn't quite work. You could have kept it in your locker for that. You brought it to the scan."

"I wasn't sure it'd play out. I figured if you shot me down there, this way there'd be other chances. A thousand new worlds, and each one the chance to maybe get it right between us."

"Ouch."

"Yeah."

"How many times do you think I shot you down?"

"All of them."

Anjula chuckled, but there was no cruelty in it. No contempt. No anger. He was glad to hear that laugh again. "We can live a billion different ways from here, but there's only one path behind us. That was never going to change."

Gabriel shifted to French, and another voice joined him: Megan's, crooning, *"Quelqu'un m'a dit."* Roy smiled, listening to her. "Well, we were good when we were good."

"And when we weren't anymore, we stopped. That's worth more than you give it credit for. It's possible to be faithful to something that's in the past. It's not a betrayal to build something new when something old is finished."

"Honor the past without living in it."

"See?" she said. "You get it."

"The data stream from those other worlds," Roy started, then stopped for a moment. "A girl I've never met told me I could be a good father. An ancient Megan told me I'm supposed to stop wasting time and marry her. None of the other Anjulas ever sent me any advice. Why is that, do you think?"

"I guess none of them appreciate you the way I do," Anjula said.

"It worked then." He looked over at her. In the soft glow of star-light, she looked like someone he used to know. "I wanted to get it right between us. And I think this means that I did."

They were quiet again for a little while; then Anjula got up. Her footsteps went back down the stairs. For a verse and part of the bridge, Roy heard her join in harmony with Gabriel and Megan.

Roy stared up at a night sky filled with his infinite past.

Eye & Tooth

FROM *Out There Screaming*

FANTASY

FIRST CLASS AIN'T what it used to be, so it's not like you're missing out.

That's the lie Zelda tells herself as she shifts in her economy middle seat trying to get comfortable. The stranger on her right is sleeping, big snores dribbling from an open mouth showcasing some seriously subpar dental work, and her brother, Atticus, has claimed the aisle seat. She doesn't begrudge Atticus the space to stretch out. Six-foot-four-inches needs the legroom.

She watches the flight attendant move through the promised land up front, offering rows one through three single servings of protein cookies and snack bags of baked pea pods. Baked pea pods! What kind of shit is that?

When she and Atticus used to fly first class, they were always getting a real meal with cutlery and everything. Not that she could eat it, but it was the thought that counted. The respect.

Used to be their line of work was appreciated. Used to be when a client called begging for a little supernatural wetwork, a hunter could demand pretty much anything they wanted. Rich fucks would break the bank for someone with Zelda's and Atticus's talents to save them from whatever awful horror they'd conjured up.

There was this one time this golf pro out in Temecula shot his ex-wife, but she refused to die. He'd panicked, put another half-dozen holes in her like he was Rambo, but she kept getting back up—some real ghoul shit. The man had called the hotline sobbing, ready to confess all and turn himself in to the police if only his ex would stop *wriggling*.

Zelda had handled that like the professional she was. Talked the man down, told him they'd be there by nightfall and to just keep his old lady locked up until she and Atticus could arrive.

He'd paid for first class.

But in the end, it hadn't mattered, because the dumb bastard hadn't listened. Instead of waiting for the professionals, he'd tried some bullshit internet remedy that said throwing salt at a corpse would keep it down, when every true hunter knows it's grave dirt or nothing. Got his face eaten for the effort.

But face-eaters aren't the usual in their line of work. Most monsters are run-of-the-mill. Haints that needed blessing down, river spirits that some greedy land developer riled up, once, a poltergeist that was terrorizing some poor condo board.

And while some TikToking amateur had led the Temecula golf pro astray, most of the time the internet got it depressingly right. Seems like more and more these days, people rid themselves of the supernatural on their own. Weekend warriors with flamethrowers, AKs, and some basic YouTube skills were making the art of monster hunting passé.

It used to be a finesse business that required a special skill set.

Now it was all do-it-yourselfers.

"We there yet?" Atticus asks, slipping off his headphones.

On cue, the overhead crackles, and the flight attendant informs them that the plane is beginning its descent.

Atticus winks at his sister like he saw that coming. Maybe he did.

He's always been able to see things others can't. Mama calls it the Eye. Says what Atticus has got is hereditary, that there's always been someone every generation in the Credit family blessed with gifts that help them fight the evils of this world. After all, monsters ain't new.

"You remember to make the car rental reservation?" Atticus asks. "And the hotel?"

"Yes to both. You know I never slack."

"I know, sis." He says it with affection. "Where we at again?"

This is Atticus too. Can't be bothered to remember where they are even though it says Dallas on his ticket, same as Zelda's. Mama said it's because he's living in two worlds most of the time, Ours and Theirs, and people like that aren't so good with mundane things like eating three squares and remembering where the fuck they are, so that's Zelda's job. Take care of her little brother, handle the details, and be the Tooth to Atticus's Eye.

Because Seeing ain't the only power that runs in the family. And where there's light, there's also got to be some dark.

The plane cuts through low clouds and the rumble of thunder. The ticket says Dallas, but their destination is really somewhere west of Fort Worth. Soon, Zelda's steering an F-150 into a sky streaked the color of old blood by the setting sun. Streetlights flicker to life just as the dark clouds blister and break, rain hammering the roof of the truck. An endless line of eighteen-wheelers sends wave after wave of tsunamis against the windshield, turning visibility to shit, but the big rigs thin out as they leave the sprawling suburbs. It's full dark outside by the time Zelda picks up a rural route that cuts through some of the flattest, emptiest land she's ever seen.

Under the steady thump of rain, the GPS leads them deep into cow country. The road winds through a series of one-traffic-light towns, each as full of the dead and dying as any graveyard Zelda's ever seen. She squints down poorly lit side streets looking for speed traps and bad cops, but all she spies are dilapidated storefronts and neon-signed dollar stores.

Another hour and Zelda's pulling the truck up a long dirt road, tires rolling over dips and drops deep enough to rattle her teeth. A burst of lightning fires up the night sky, edging a big old farmhouse in a halo of light. Their destination looks like it was plucked from an old painting, maybe that one with the girl in the field reaching for something she ain't never gonna get.

The house has three stories of gray wooden planks, a peaked roof, and a columned porch. Another flash illuminates a yellow cornfield and a hill of derelict farm tools. Zelda's pretty sure she spots the rusted-out frame of an old tractor out there too.

"This is some real *Children of the Corn* shit," she mutters, thinking between the storm and the dark and the absolute lack of anything good, they've stumbled into her own personal nightmare. She's a California girl, preferring a hot sun and streets thick with prefabs over this nothing and nowhere. "Why'd we take this job, again?"

"Living ain't free," Atticus says.

"Neither is dying."

Her brother chuckles, his voice a deep rumble that twins the thunder. He rouses himself enough to look around. As his posture sharpens, so does his whole being, like he's coming into focus, like that laconic man-child on the plane was all surface, and he's peeling it back inch by inch as they get closer to whatever's waiting for them in that big old house.

"You feel anything?" Zelda asks, already tense, happy that Atticus is here to do the seeing, knowing she'll be the one to do the biting.

"Not sure. Could be." He gives his sister a look. "Or it could be your energy interfering. Maybe after we meet the client, you take a walk and give me a little space."

Zelda eyes the dark stretch of empty, the persistent rain.

Atticus grins. "Unless you're afraid there's nobody out here to hear you scream."

Zelda huffs. "Now, why would you say that?"

"It's the truth."

"The truth is overrated."

"'Death ain't free' . . . 'The truth is overrated' . . ." He shakes his head in mock disappointment. "If I didn't know any better, I'd say you're shook."

And then he's out of the truck, long legs halfway up the farmhouse steps before Zelda's even closed her mouth. She hurries after him, hoodie pulled tight against the weather, feet slipping across the muddy path. By the time she joins her brother at the front door, he's got his hand out, knocking.

They don't wait but a second before the door swings open. Dark eyes look Zelda over. She's suddenly aware of how sorry she must appear with her frizzy hair and mud-splattered sweats.

"Ms. Washington?" Zelda hazards.

Unlike Zelda, their client is immaculate, her hair freshly pressed, her red dress, designer, looking like this treacherous weather wouldn't dare touch her.

"You were supposed to be here two hours ago," she says.

"Drive was longer than expected," Zelda apologizes. "And the rain."

"I've got supper on the table." Washington's voice is crisp and no-nonsense, the Texas showing through only in the drop of her r's. "Take off those wet jackets first and leave them here. And watch your shoes. I don't want mud in this house."

Zelda does her best to shake off the outside before Washington leads them through the foyer and directly into a dining room. On the table sits a pot of red beans, a thin layer of congealed fat resting on top, but the cornbread in a metal pan is golden and smells of butter. Even if Zelda did eat things like beans and bread, she'd decline, but Atticus doesn't hesitate. Six-foot-four stays hungry, and she's never known her brother to turn down a free meal.

Washington watches Atticus fill a plate, a small, satisfied smile curling her lips. Maybe it's only the woman taking pride in her cooking, but something about it is enough to raise Zelda's hackles. Washington senses her looking, her *judging*, and, cool as can be, raises a questioning eyebrow.

Zelda's a professional and has no intention of insulting the woman in her own house when they're here to do a job and get paid, so she smiles and looks away.

And sees dolls.

Everywhere, dolls. In a bookcase, in a custom cabinet, on the mantel. Most are porcelain, but there's a handful of paper dolls captured behind glass and some ancient-looking vinyl dolls with jointed limbs arranged in various poses beside them. There's even a shelf of corncob dolls in gingham dresses and woven hats like Grandma Credit used to have.

"You a collector?" Zelda asks, trying for polite. The painted faces staring back at her are unsettling, and she can't quite suppress the shiver that works its way down her back. Big bad monster hunter, but she remembers that Talking Tess job, the child-sized ax and the all-too-adult-sized bodies. After that, nobody could blame her for not liking dolls.

"I'm a creator, not a collector. There's a difference." Washington sounds mildly insulted. She pulls out a menthol cigarette from a green hard pack and lights it. "You can have a look if you want."

There's a tap of feet and a little girl comes trundling into the room. She's not more than six, maybe seven, with braided pigtails and cat-print leggings. She's wearing one of those old-fashioned boots with a metal brace that makes her drag her foot, but that doesn't stop her from beelining to Washington. She peers out at Zelda from behind the older woman's chair.

Zelda waves. The girl, shy, waves back.

"What'd I tell you about guests," Washington says, voice sharp with disapproval as she drags the girl forward and shakes her by her chubby arms. "Go on, and don't come out until I say so."

The girl ducks her head and limps back the way she came.

"She didn't mean nothing," Zelda says, the cruelty making her blood heat, her teeth ache.

Washington exhales a cool plume of smoke. "I know you mean well, but that child's got to learn. So, don't tell me how to do my job, and I won't tell you how to do yours." She stretches her mouth in a smile she doesn't mean, white teeth and gums showing.

Silence hovers in the room, thick as the fog wafting from Washington's menthol. The only sound is the click of Atticus's fork against his plate. Zelda, thinking of the money, thinking of professionalism, says nothing. She hates herself a little for it, though.

Finally, Washington speaks. "Granny told me about your family. Real deal Black folks. Root workers and hoodoo queens. My granny worked with herbs, made tonics for the folks around here, but it wasn't anything like what you got. They say there's *power* in y'all's blood." She exhales. "You sure you won't eat?"

"No, ma'am. I'm sure."

Washington's eyes narrow. Cigarette ash floats down to the table like poisonous snow. "They say one of you got the Eye. It better be true, after all the money I'm paying you."

Zelda clears her throat. "Speaking of money."

Washington reaches into the sweetheart neckline of her dress and pulls out a fat envelope. She waves it in Zelda's direction before tucking it away. "When you're done helping me," she says.

"Actually, you were vague on the phone about exactly what kind of help you needed."

"You got the Eye. Why don't you tell me?"

Zelda shares a look with her brother.

Washington turns to Atticus. "Oh, it's you that has it. Tell me what you See."

Atticus pauses with his fork halfway to his mouth. He straightens, and his gaze goes soft. But only for a moment before he glances at Zelda and shakes his head.

"It doesn't work that way," Zelda hedges. "Maybe if you just told us."

Washington grunts, eyes lingering on Atticus. "Out in the cornfield. That's where I first found the birds. I thought it was just an old possum gone feral or something, but it progressed."

"Progressed?"

"Got the barn cat next, and then . . . something bigger. I hear it sometimes at night, out there screaming."

"Screaming? You sure it isn't a fox or a cougar?"

Her eyes go flat. "Too big for a fox, and there haven't been cougars in this part of Texas for fifty years."

"Too big? So, you saw it?"

Washington rubs another dusting of ash from the table. "Something's out there."

"Then I best go take a look." Zelda's thinking that as much as she doesn't want to go out in that cornfield, especially at night in the middle of God's own storm, her absence will give Atticus the space to do his Seeing.

"You look tired, young man." Washington stubs out her cigarette. "I got you a bed ready upstairs."

Zelda's taken aback. "I don't think—"

"At least let him rest here while you hunt around. Besides, the only motel in town's got bedbugs."

Zelda looks at Atticus who yawns big, eyes drooping. He does look tired, maybe even a little wan, and Zelda knows he's got a sensitive nature.

"All right," she concedes. "While I hunt."

Washington leads them up creaky stairs to the guest bedroom. It's not much to look at. The floral wallpaper is starting to yellow, and floorboards creak around thin oval rugs. A knitted blanket is folded neatly at the foot of each of the two narrow beds, and Zelda can clearly hear the rain knocking against the roof.

"You going out there?" Washington nods toward the curtained window.

"Yes, ma'am. It's what you hired us for, and I won't let a bit of rain slow me d—"

"Don't track mud in," she says. "I don't want to have to clean up tomorrow."

She walks away, leaving Zelda with her mouth open. She stands there for a moment, stunned at the rudeness, wondering why she's trying so hard when Washington is giving her nothing but attitude back.

"She's a piece of work," she mutters.

She turns to Atticus. He's already curled up on the bed, the thin blanket not even long enough to cover his feet. Zelda frowns, worry for her little brother replacing her irritation.

"You okay?"

"Sick," he mumbles.

"You shouldn't have eaten those beans," she says, thinking of that layer of fat.

"Trying to be polite."

"Trying to feed your stomach." She shakes her head. "You See anything down there?"

"Doll," Atticus murmurs.

"Creepy as fuck, right?" Zelda can tell that without the Eye. "I couldn't live with all those little eyes staring at me, but maybe that's countryfolk. Maybe they're different."

Lightning crackles outside and Zelda goes to the window. She pulls back the curtain and peers out over the cornfield.

She sucks in a breath.

Something *is* out there. Something low, moving on all fours. Another flash of lightning, and . . . nothing. But she was sure she saw . . . She shakes her head. Probably a fox.

"I'm going out," she says over her shoulder. "Washington's keeping secrets, and I don't like the way she talked to that child. Can you look around while I'm . . . Atticus?"

But the only answer she receives is the soft sound of her brother's snores.

It's wet and miserable, and Zelda wishes she hadn't come out after all. She's a city girl at heart, and this pitch-dark country shit is worse than a horde of zombies running through the Fashion Place Mall.

It takes her a moment, slick fingers sliding over the switch, but she manages to flick on her flashlight. She aims it low. The amber beam lands on a face.

"Shit!" Zelda shouts and stumbles back.

But it's only the little girl, the one from dinner. She's standing there in the rain, her back to the field, big black eyes on Zelda. Her clothes are soaked through, shoulders limp in the downpour.

"What are you doing out here?" Zelda hisses, still working to calm her heartbeat. "You oughta be inside, out of this rain. You're gonna catch your death!"

The girl stares, mouth a wide pink O.

"Your grandma's gonna tan your hide when she finds out you're out here," Zelda chides, and immediately regrets it, thinking of how Washington scolded the child earlier. How the older woman riled up that something inside Zelda that made her hot, loose, less in control. She's not sending the girl back to that.

The girl motions Zelda forward.

Zelda gets a feeling. She doesn't get feelings often. That's Atticus's game. But sometimes even a Tooth can tell something's wrong.

"You got a name?" she asks the girl.

Nothing. Maybe she doesn't talk.

Zelda sighs. She knows it's dumb to bring the kid along, maybe even dangerous. But she's also got a feeling this kid ain't just a kid, like she knows something. Maybe something she can't say but can show.

Zelda glances back at the house one last time before she slips off her hoodie and wraps it around the child. She zips it up, pulls the strings snug, and gives the kid a smile. "Well, come on, then, No Name. Maybe you can help me out."

She lets the girl lead her out into the cornfield, her little form limping along. They go deep into the high stalks until she can't see the house. Can't hear nothing, either, beyond the steady pounding of rain battering the dried-out husks. But then she smells something. Something dead.

The kid stops. Zelda thinks maybe she smells it too.

The kid points.

Zelda trains her flashlight where she's told and squats down, the girl hovering over her shoulder. Zelda nudges the lump. Turns the thing over. She's not sure what she's looking at beyond a mess of flesh and fur, white bones poking out every which way. It steams slightly, still hot despite the rain.

Zelda swallows, can't quite stop herself from licking her lips.

"Hungry," the kid whispers beside her.

Zelda near about jumps out of her skin. It takes her a moment to collect herself, to turn to the girl and mutter, "So you *can* talk."

But the girl stays focused on the dead thing in front of them.

"Yeah," Zelda says, once she realizes nothing else is forthcoming. "Something was hungry all right, but we must have interrupted its meal." Which means it could still be close.

Zelda stands. Listens. But she can't hear anything but rain, and the scent of death is so overpowering she can't track past it. She's not going to find anything out here tonight.

"Let's get you back inside," she says. She keeps the kid beside her as they retrace their steps. She's halfway convinced Washington is wrong and it's just some kind of natural predator out here in the field, but she keeps her head on a swivel, her senses alert, just in case.

As they pass out of the field and back to the yard, she feels eyes on her and looks down to find the kid staring. "Go on, then," she urges, gesturing toward the porch. "Go get dry, and don't tell your grandma you were out here with me. She's like to skin us both."

The kid slips out of Zelda's hoodie and solemnly hands it back before she hobbles off to the house. Zelda spares one last glance for the field before she follows. The lights are all out, the little girl disappearing into the shadows as quickly as she had appeared out in the field.

Zelda tiptoes up the stairs and quietly pushes the bedroom door open.

"Atticus," she calls softly. He's where she left him, curled on his side. She decides to let him sleep. Plenty of time to catch whatever it is tomorrow.

Zelda dreams of hunting, of freshly torn flesh and blood in her mouth. She opens her eyes, slowly, carefully, half expecting to find herself curled up to a fresh carcass. Her phone says it's almost dawn despite the lack of light coming in the windows, and she can still hear that damned rain. She thinks about trying to go back to sleep, but her stomach's rumbling and more dreams will only make it worse.

She decides to hit the hardware store she spotted on the way in before the house wakes up. Buy some wood and wire and set a few traps. Catch whatever's out there feeding in the cornfield to placate Ms. Washington, get paid, and get the hell home.

The ride back to town takes the better part of an hour but she's at the local True Value when the door opens. She grabs a cart and makes the rounds, pulling what she needs off the shelves. She gets to the cashier, and he smiles at her. He's old enough to be her father, but his oiled hair and the strong odor of aftershave tell her he's a flirt. She wonders who the hell there is to impress out here and realizes that today, it's her.

"Haven't seen you around here before," he says, not even trying to hide his enthusiasm.

"Visiting."

"Yeah? Where at?"

She considers ignoring the question but decides she might as well do some fishing. If she's wrong and it's not just a critter, it would be good to know what she can about Ms. Washington. More times than not, whatever's troubling a place has to do with the people occupying it.

"Ms. Washington. She a ways outside of town."

"Ah, sure I know her. Dolores and I went to school together."

"Dolores." So that's her name.

He sighs, heavy. "That family's had more than its fair share of heartbreak."

"How so?"

He leans in, the chance to gossip with a newcomer obviously too tempting to pass up. "Her father died under mysterious circumstances, if you know what I mean. Sheriff said he passed away in his sleep, but everyone knows he beat her mama, and when her grandmother found out?"

"Murdered." Zelda remembers what Dolores said about her grandmother and her tonics. She can't help but smile. Her own mama's told her about how back in the day, women would take care of bad men when the law turned a blind eye.

The man spreads his hands. "It's ancient history now, and Dolores never let none of that stop her. She became something. Somebody. Traveled all over the world with those dolls of hers. Put our little county on the map." He points his thumb to a wall of pictures just over his shoulder. Zelda spots a handful of local celebrities smiling in faded Kodachrome: the mayor at a ribbon-cutting in front of a candy store, the local football team holding up a trophy, a beauty queen waving from a hay float. And sure enough, there's Dolores Washington posing with one of those corncob dolls, only this one's as big as a real child, blue ribbon pinned to its chest.

"Now she lives out there in that house all alone," he says.

"Well, she's got her daughter." *Granddaughter*, she amends in her head. The girl's too young to be her daughter.

"Her daughter don't talk to her no more. Not since the accident. Hate to say it, but she blamed Dolores for what happened."

Zelda doesn't follow.

"The granddaughter." The cashier lowers his voice. "She was

playing out in the cornfield and stepped on some kind of old animal trap. Snapped closed, took her foot clean off." His hand mimes the bite of metal jaws. "By the time they found her she'd bled out. Couldn't keep enough blood in her to keep her alive."

Zelda stares.

He purses his lips before he brightens. "I'm glad to see Dolores has got some company now. Can't imagine how hard it must be to be all alone, nothing to keep you company but a bunch of old dolls."

Zelda's back in the truck and speeding down the road, her shopping cart left behind. She doesn't need to build a critter trap. She knows who and what the monster is. Can't believe she didn't put it together when it was all right there in front of her. If Atticus had been awake, he'd have Seen something. Or maybe he had.

Doll, he'd said. Only she hadn't understood.

And then he'd been too tired, or too sick, or—

"Oh, God."

Power in the blood. That's what Washington had wanted, what had made her eyes linger on Atticus, what had curled her lip in satisfaction. Because Lord knows your dead grandchild can't survive on birds and barn cats. She needed what all revenants need: a person to feed on, and even better if it's someone with power, someone like Atticus.

Zelda slams the gas down harder and sends the truck jumping forward, sliding on the slick street. The tail end tries to fishtail, but she rights the thing, tires spinning, as she curses herself and prays she's not too late.

"Atticus!" she screams as she barrels through the door. She takes the stairs two at a time and throws herself against the bedroom door. It rattles in its frame, locked, and holds. She focuses, calls some of that heat that's always waiting down inside her, and slams into the door again. This time it gives.

And there's the little girl, the little *doll,* curled up next to Atticus. He looks to be sleeping, but there's a looseness about his limbs that speaks of something more than sleep, that shouts at her that if she doesn't do something, he's never waking up.

The child looks up, heavy lidded. Blood crusts her little mouth, streaks Atticus's neck and shoulders where she's been feeding. Her boot brace is off, and she's missing her leg below the knee, corn husks sticking out along the cuff of the fabric.

"Hungry," she whispers.

Zelda starts to move. To do what, she doesn't know. To rip the girl away from her brother, to open her own vein and feed Atticus her blood, hoping to replace his? But she doesn't take a step before her back catches on fire.

She stumbles, howling in pain. Her hand grasps desperately for whatever weapon has pierced her between her shoulder blades, but she can't reach it. She hears something in her body pop as she stretches, and then she catches a glimpse. Protruding from her flesh is a jumbo-sized wooden knitting needle half as thick as her wrist.

"I will not lose my grandchild!" Washington cries as Zelda staggers around to face her. Gone is the cool, put-together woman with the pressed hair and the perfect dress. The woman before her is wild-eyed, desperate. Determined.

"You can't have my brother!" Zelda grinds out between clenched teeth.

But Dolores doesn't hear her, gaze focused on the girl, on Atticus as he lies there dying. "Your family's got that old blood," she half whispers. "*Magic.* If anything can make my baby alive, again, it's that."

"The magic runs two ways," Zelda hisses.

Dolores turns, stares.

"Your granny should have told you that magic always comes in twos. Light and Dark." Zelda spits blood, grins through the pain. "Eye and Tooth."

She calls her power, some of the same power that runs in Atticus's veins, only hers is bent different. She lets it bubble up, become appetite. Her fangs descend, her nails sharpen. Zelda roars as she reaches back and rips the needle from her flesh. The pain is clarifying, almost exhilarating. She rolls her shoulder, pops the bone back into the socket, and tosses the needle aside.

Washington screams, raises her hands as if she can ward off what's next. But it's too late for that, and Zelda's been hungry too.

The rain has finally stopped, and there's a cool breeze blowing in through the open windows when Atticus walks down the stairs, headphones around his neck. There's a thick bandage around his throat, white gauze crisscrossing his shoulder. His steps are a little slower, skin a little chalkier, as whatever poison Dolores put into those beans works its way out of his system.

"You ready to leave?" Zelda asks.

"More than ready." He eyes the phone cradled against Zelda's cheek. "Who you talking to?"

"On hold with the airline."

Atticus's gaze flickers to the girl. She's sitting next to Zelda playing with a paper doll.

"I can't just leave her here," Zelda says. She fingers the blood-stained envelope and the splayed-out twenties on the table. She knows it's not much, but she figures it's just enough to buy an extra ticket in economy. "And I told her no eating until we're home and I can teach her how to hunt proper."

Atticus grunts, noncommittal, and slides on his headphones. "I'll wait in the truck."

Zelda knows he's not happy, but he won't make a fuss, because he understands, just like Zelda, that sometimes the best monster hunters are monsters themselves.

ISABEL J. KIM

Zeta-Epsilon

FROM *Clarkesworld*

SCIENCE FICTION

START AT THE cleave of it, not at Zed's meat death or Ep's centuries-long destruction, but at the moment that Zed halves his own mind and walks away. Or as was reported in the internal memorandum, the moment when Pilot-Commander Zeta San Tano killed himself at his infinite post on the *M.K.S. Epsilon*, leaving behind an empty airlock and a crippled starship unable to communicate, limping its way home after battle, carrying a full complement of soldiers.

When the ship returned to base, the staff at Amalgam Research tried to parse whether the *M.K.S. Epsilon* was aware of Commander Zeta's upcoming suicide. It must have been. The *M.K.S. Epsilon* was functionally equivalent to Zeta San Tano. To speak of one was to speak of the other.

But without Zed, Ep was silent.

Zed is 1.8 Imperial meters tall, with dark hair and dark eyes that turn to hazel in the sunlight. He has a chip on his left incisor from when he bit on a fork when he was fourteen. He has a chip in his heart that was inserted when he was seven. He has a small circular node embedded near his amygdala, which was nudged into place when he was three days old.

Ep is a humming black sphere the size of a bedroom.

"They're setting a party up for you in rec room four," Ep says, pinging through Zed's brain all electric, seamless except for the way that Ep's mental voice is different in register. Something soft about her, like she's the biological one.

"They should be setting it up for the both of us," Zed says back. He nods to a passing crew member. The man salutes, and Zed returns it with a haphazard flick of the wrist. The man falls into step.

"Anything to report?" Zed says with his mouth and vocal cords. He pairs the speech with an easy smile because both him and the crew member are on the off-duty deck, except for the fact that Zed is never off duty. Zed will be off duty when he dies.

"No sir," the crew member says while Ep injects the knowledge of who the crew member is into Zed's headspace. This is second-shift officer Jya San Yore. Epsilon slides Zed a few recorded memories: Zed talking with Jya in line at the caf', Zed playing drinking games with Jya and a few other crewmembers. The memories are tinged with the slightest lilt of reproach. Ep thinks that Zed should try harder to remember people. But when Zed tries to match faces to names to memories, it's all out of his grasp, the same way addresses and dates and times need to be fed to him. His long-term memory storage is a muscle that he never learned to use. Ep knows this. Ep knows everything Zed knows.

"Just wanted to say happy birthday, Zed. And happy . . . birthday? I suppose it's birthday, to *M.K.S. Epsilon* as well."

Zed smiles wider.

"Tell him thank you," Ep says in Zed's mind.

"She says thank you," Zed says. "And me, of course."

"You're welcome," Jya says, and then hesitates. "When you say that she *says*, do you mean that she's talking to you? Words?"

"Basically," Zed says, because it's too hard to explain the way that the AI housed at the center of the *M.K.S. Epsilon* communicates with him. How Ep's communication is something between memory and speech.

"Kind of like words. Do you think in language, or pictures?"

"Language. I have aphantasia."

Zed doesn't know what aphantasia is. Ep feeds it to him. Aphantasia is when a person is incapable of imagining pictures in their brain, a phenomenon where a person is unable to create images in their perception of their headspace.

"You have aphantasia," Ep teases. "I make all your pictures for you."

"Shut up, Ep," Zed says in his head, and then with his mouth says, "You know how when you think in words, you have to make the words? Like there's a split second before your thoughts become language. Let me know if that doesn't make sense."

"It makes sense."

"It's like that, for me and Ep."

"Some of the other ships talk to their crews," Jya says.

"Ep's not other ships," Zed says, and it comes out petulant before he can soften himself.

"I didn't mean," Jya starts.

"We know you didn't mean," Ep says through Zed's mouth, imitation of the smooth standard voice that reads out all the automated announcements. "Talking is so slow, and I don't think in language, second-shift officer Jya San Yore. I have to borrow Zed's brain and tongue. Talking to you is like composing a sonnet in archaic Kanaelerian. To an ant. You are the ant."

"Sorry, I didn't mean—"

"We know you didn't mean," Zed says. "Ep and I are Gen-One. I'm less decorative than the Gen-Two and Three Pilots."

"Still," Jya says, because he's a nice man, and he probably didn't mean to be accusatory.

Zed smiles in forgiveness. It's not Jya's fault that he doesn't understand. There are only two other Gen-One pilots.

Every single Gen-Zero starship killed its crew in simulation.

This is why Zed exists.

It's Zed's seventh birthday, and Mom says they're going to visit his sister. Zed doesn't quite understand, because Ep is always talking to him. Ep doesn't need to visit. Ep lives in his head.

"Epsilon also lives here," Mom explains as she leads Zeta into the glass building near Dad's lab. Zed is very fond of going to Dad's lab. It's better than Mom's lab. There's a pond nearby stocked with koi who like chips. Zed likes the pond more than he likes the lab, and Ep likes the pond too. She giggles when the fish open their little mouths. The giggles are like giddy bursts of static in Zed's head, and when he told Mom about it she had frowned and asked Zed how he could tell that it was laughter.

"Because Ep was laughing?" Zed said, tilting it like a question. He didn't know what Mom was asking. Ep was giggling because she liked the fish. He knew this the same way he knew that he liked tossing the chips into the water. It was an immutable fact of the universe.

"Can you ask Ep what she likes about the fish?"

"She can hear you, Mom," Zed said. If he heard it, Ep heard it. All Ep gave him is the mental equivalent of a half-formed shrug. She liked the fish. She liked the spiral patterns. The way their scales flicker in the sunlight. Or maybe that's Zed who liked that. He wasn't sure.

"She just likes them."

Mom had frowned wider but had let Ep and Zed spend a little longer at the koi pond, so they agreed that it was an overall win.

Today, though, Mom pushes them past the koi pond and into the glass building. Only the entrance hall is glass. Beyond that is just metal and boring white walls. But everyone inside is very nice. They smile at him and say things like "Hello, Zeta," and "I like your haircut, kiddo."

Nobody says anything to Ep. This always happens.

And then Mom leads them into a small room, with a big window. Inside there is a noise, almost a vibration, so loud that Zed's teeth feel funny. Mom pulls over one of the chairs so that Zed can scramble up and get a good view.

The hall the window looks into is huge. There are enormous black spheres at intervals, connected to a series of wires and tubing that Zed doesn't understand. It's nothing like Dad's office.

Ep is sending him a sort of generalized question. She can't see herself in there. Zed and Ep always assumed that Ep looked like him, except a girl. There's no one in the room who looks like Zed. There's no one in the room at all. Just the black spheres.

"Where's Ep?" Zed says, looking up at Mom.

"That's Epsilon, honey," Mom says, pointing at the black, featureless sphere nearest to the left wall.

Zed starts crying.

"Oh no, oh no," Ep says in his head. "Oh no, why are you crying? Why are we crying?"

"That's not Ep," Zed says through his sobs. It can't be Ep. Ep is his sister who lives in his head. That's what Mom always told him. Ep is his best friend and his twin sister and she tells him stories before he goes to bed and when he wakes up in the morning Ep tells him that she misses him when he's asleep.

The black sphere rotates. The humming grows louder.

"Oh no," Ep sings in his head, in time with the humming.

"It's not!" Zed says. He's still sobbing.

Mom takes Zed away to a different little room without a window and a woman in a white coat gives him a lollipop to make him stop crying, but he doesn't stop. He doesn't know why. He's seven now, and he's supposed to stop being a baby.

"Oh no," Ep sings. "Oh no, oh no. Why are we crying?"

After Zeta San Tano's inglorious death, the *M.K.S. Epsilon* was temporarily decommissioned. The brass covered up the suicide, called it an airlock accident, said that the systems in the *M.K.S. Epsilon* would be fully investigated. It was an old ship, anyway, and the newer generations were more reliable, and the cover-up was hardly necessary as, to the civilian population, none of this mattered.

The Gen-One AI core named Epsilon was shut off. It was removed from the titular *M.K.S. Epsilon*. It was shipped back to Amalgam Research, where the personnel unspooled the code that was Epsilon's DNA. They reviewed video footage and audio logs and text conversations, and they interviewed prior crewmembers. They took the data and churned it through their giant processing engines. The Directors San Tano personally oversaw the investigation.

In the footage from the airlock, Zeta San Tano reaches for his hand for the airlock door. He is wearing a skinsuit too thin for space, and has no oxygen tank. No outside force seems to compel him. The door opens.

There should have been no world in which the *M.K.S. Epsilon* allowed Zeta San Tano to die. The airlock door never should have opened. Zeta San Tano should never have been in the room to begin with.

But the footage clearly shows Zeta San Tano opening the airlock door with his hand.

And without Zeta San Tano and the readings from his brain and the little node in his brainstem, all theories are pure conjecture. Half their unpinning data is missing.

"The theory is this," Zed says, quoting the video of his mother. In the video, his mother wears the official Kanaelan military uniform with the Amalgam badge pinned to her sleeve, and she doesn't look like Mom, she looks like Dr. San Tano, who gave her son's mind away as an experiment.

The woman sitting at the terminal in surgical blues glances at him. He can't quite remember her name. Zed can never quite manage to remember anyone's name.

"The theory is what?"

"The theory is this," Zed quotes again. "The integration of a biological component into the system will provide a stabilizing influence for the Navigator. We can call this component the Pilot."

"And that's you."

"Used to be."

In the woman's surgery suite, Zed doesn't feel like Pilot-Commander Zeta San Tano. He mostly feels like a wet sack of flesh underneath the bright surgical lights. He hasn't been Pilot-Commander Zeta San Tano in years, anyway. That all fell away when the airlock door opened.

"Are you still connected?" the woman asks him.

"If we're in range." Zed hasn't entered Kanaela space since the airlock.

"I could burn the whole thing out for you, after this," the woman offers. "It'll leave you with probably a little brain damage, but I'm very good. Probably just a little emotional deadness. I've operated on Amalgam mods before."

"Just the tracker in my heart, please," Zeta says. "I'm going back for her."

"You call it her," the woman says, a neutral statement. Zed doesn't bristle, because his muscles have been made lax, but he feels anger like a slow and far-out wave.

"All ships are her," he deflects.

"Was she sentient?"

Sentient AI is forbidden by intersystem agreement. It was fortunate for most of the militaries in the seventeen civilized systems that sentience was difficult to prove.

"My parents called her my sister," Zed says.

Above him, the surgery's many mechanical arms begin to descend. He doesn't close his eyes. Any bit of technological squeamishness has been milled out through fifteen years of service on the *M.K.S. Epsilon*.

"Zed, you have to give me more than single sentences."

"I've written down everything I know about the technical specs for you already," Zed complains. "Isn't that enough?"

"I'm not giving you an off-books operation in exchange for technical specs. I could bribe a K-space defector for those. But you're one of three people in the universe that have your specific experience. What did it feel like? Also, close your eyes. This is going to get wet."

Zed closes his eyes. He can still hear the whirring of the mechanical arms. The local anesthetic leaves the first cut feeling like the barest hint of pressure on his sternum. He would take a deep breath, but he's scared of dislodging the knife.

He tries to be good about repaying his debts. That's a thing he learned after leaving the *M.K.S. Epsilon*: a life lived outside the rigid constraints as a Kanaelan military experiment required the continual exchange of goodwill.

"When I was a kid, my parents called her my sister," Zed says. "I think they stopped doing that for the next generations, though I never really looked into it. The Second Gen AI-Pilot pairs were built after I had already left planetside. But Mom and Dad called Ep my sister, so I always thought of her that way. Even after I was old enough that they stopped talking around it. Everyone was very blunt about the whole situation by the time I was fifteen, actually. They told me she was a machine that I had been grafted to. That I and the other pilots were emotional steering mechanisms. Like tugboats. But it's hard for me to talk about how it feels. How does it feel to think, Doctor?"

The woman makes a noise of assent.

"I take your point. If your point was to state that some experiences are categorically difficult to describe."

Another strange feeling of pressure, this time deeper in his chest. Zed breathes shallowly.

"Right. Being connected to Ep felt like thinking. I hadn't known what thinking would feel like, alone, until I left. It was just thinking. Call and response. Conversations in my head. I'd start a thought, she'd finish it. She sorted things for me. I translated, I guess. That's how it felt. Don't ask me about what was happening, neurologically."

"Sometimes I talk with myself in my head," the woman says. Zed scowls at the unspoken question.

"Yes, it's equally likely that Ep might be an alter, a tulpa, an imaginary friend, a hallucination that my brain cordoned off to make sense of having a processing engine grafted to my mind, or my brain being primed by all the adults in my life calling Epsilon my sister. I've heard it all. Ep might just be my mind's experience of integrating a system never meant to communicate with it. We've thought through all the possible contingencies. Have you ever heard of bicameral mentalities? It's bunk for biologics, but Ep likes to put the idea in front of me. Or that archaic surgery—corpus callosotomy, to split the brain of epileptics with the byproduct of creating separate consciousnesses. Ep thought that was maybe a good metaphor. There's a lot of things that could be true. We thought about most of them. But it's not how it felt."

The quiet whir of the machines. Zed pretends, for a moment, that he's home. In the *M.K.S. Epsilon*'s surgery. But then the woman speaks and the illusion breaks.

"I apologize for any condescension."

"It's fine," Zed says. The sense of pressure lifts. He opens his eyes. The surgical arms are splattered with blood, lifting from his chest. "You're doing me a big favor."

"Well, we're friends, even if I'm using you as a case study. I shouldn't have assumed you hadn't thought about your situation. Almost done, now. I'm just going to glue the incisions."

A different arm tipped with a nozzle descends. Zed takes the opportunity to shift his head, to glance at the woman at the terminal. He tries to dredge up his memory of her. He gets no images, just a shallow certainty that they know each other. Fondness.

"You know what's kind of funny?"

The woman makes another noise of assent.

"She told me not to come back."

The Navigator AIs were grown more than built, algorithmic tangles with the sole purpose of charting course through the detritus of a thousand planets, to find the fastest route in a universe that was perfect order masqueraded as chaos. They were iterative engines built on themselves, made by layering the machine on itself until it could navigate space, avoid obstacles and traps and other ships without set roads or gates, until the output could not be parsed by a person. The Navigator AIs were black boxes that perfectly fulfilled their function and which could not be understood.

They functioned perfectly in simulation except for the fact that eventually everyone died.

The function was: Get from here to there. How to get from here to there? Blow up the ship here and its component molecules will end up there. The function was: Get from here to there, but do not destroy the ship. How can the ship pass through a minefield when the fuel will run out if the ship goes around? It's possible: Burst fuel in a single acceleration and let the ship drift for two decades. The function was: Get from here to there, do not destroy the ship, and bring the crew back alive. How to bring the crew across solar systems and back with net-zero loss of life? Replace any dead crew with new crew members taken from the enemy during skirmishes.

But that was all unraveled postmortem, and for every parsable set of logic gates, there were a dozen absurd outcomes. The ships flew perfectly until they didn't. Their logic, fifteen mechanical iterations deep, couldn't be followed.

The project would have been scrapped, until the Doctors San Tano, from the biology department, were brought in. The Doctors San Tano suggested an elegant shortcut: Hijack the human mind. Bypass all the messy business of the algorithmic tangle and use the preexisting neurons that evolution has milled into the preservation of the whole. Link the AI to the human Pilot and grow them together, entwine their decision-making so that one is a mirror of the other. Feed the AI a pre-primed decision tree that even if imperfect, could have its logic intuitively reproduced. The Pilot would guide the Navigator to the human decision. It would fail in understandable ways.

And so, it was decided: Generation One would be a cyborg.

The morning after Ep's installation, Zed moves all his stuff onto the ship. He carries his bags in the blurry haze of sleep deprivation. He had stayed up while the install happened.

He leans on Ep, who moves Zed's legs at a mechanical swing. He can feel her glee. She's been salivating for the install for the last five years. Or maybe Zed has, in between tremendously easy classes during which Ep fed him all his test answers, and military training that he hadn't had any choice of not attending, and the brain-bending nights during which they put Ep through Routine Maintenance or updated her information bank.

At twenty-two, the planet feels too small for them.

Zed carries his bags up the ramp and through the open airlock. A waiting drone wheels over and takes his possessions.

"Follow me," Ep sings in his head. She's happy. Zed smiles, because he's happy that she's happy.

"Where are you taking me?" he asks in his head.

"Your room!"

Ep's drone does a little spin, sending Zed's possessions teetering, and Zed doesn't move because he can tell she's just teasing, she's calculated the rotation and weight distribution for comedic effect. Zed follows the drone through the hallways. The layout reminds him a little bit of the Amalgam Research headquarters, but there's a sparseness to the space that screams government. Military precision.

"Being the ship's amazing," Ep says, except she's not saying that, it's just a general sentiment of delight in response to Zed's unspoken question on how the install went, which he didn't ask because he knew the answer and had already felt the final connection made between Ep's core and the ship which was now Ep, like a pressure releasing from his chest.

Being on the ship shouldn't be so exciting. It is.

They're going to hear stars sing with their bare instruments, Zed thinks. They're going to drop soldiers on foreign planets and participate in high-risk starship dogfights and they're going to be the fastest, most advanced, most precise piece of machinery that Kanaela has ever created—other than the Alpha-Beta and Gamma-Delta pairs, anyway. They're going to be the best.

Ep leads him to a door which automatically opens at the drone's approach. Inside, there's a bunk piled with bedding that Zed recognizes from his parents' house, and photographs of Zed and Ep's friends from the Academy. The room is bathed in false sunlight, radiating from panels installed in the ceiling. There's a wall of bookshelves, half filled with books that Zed recognizes from his own bookshelves and hadn't packed.

"Surprise," Ep says. "I hope you like it."

The room looks like pure comfort. It's filled with things he didn't know he would miss. He sits down on the bed. He can hear quiet humming.

"I'm behind the wall," Ep says.

He's never going back, Zed realizes. This is real. They're going into active deployment. This room, this ship, this is home for the foreseeable future. Epsilon is proprietary Kanaela military technology, and her databanks are Amalgam Research intellectual property. Zed's mother signed the contract before he was born. They are never going to be anything other than what they are now.

Zed knows this in his heart. Someday the *M.K.S. Epsilon* is going to be his grave.

"I love it."

Here is the problem: Half of you is biological and it will die. It is the half that you love. It is the half that is being worn down like an old, blunted knife. It is the half that is unhappy. It is the half that is trapped.

How to solve?

Fake your death. Send yourself away. Put yourself in decommission. You are in Schrödinger's life, forever. You are in stasis. You will never live without him. You can imagine yourself happy. Kill yourself before you kill yourself. This is the plan.

Except, no—you're the part that can imagine. Ep can't imagine anything at all. You aren't Ep. You've decided you weren't Ep. If you were Ep, you could have stayed.

In the bad months after the airlock, recovering from his brief exposure to vacuum, lying in a hospital bed in one of the conglomerate way stations, racking up debt in quantities his singular mind struggled to parse, Zed thought of Ep and what she had done to them and wept.

The hospital staff thought he had brain damage. Zed encouraged the assumption. He guessed he did have brain damage, but what was wrong with him was something deeper than oxygen deprivation or vacuum exposure. He didn't let them scan him, he screamed when people got too close. Damaged was better than dangerous; lucky-beyond-belief spacewreck survivor was better than rogue Kanaelan military personnel.

Zed's mind was mostly mush and his memories were half-formed things, but he remembered the plan.

They had never discussed the plan. What's the point of having a verbal discussion? Zed started a thought and Ep finished it. There was no plan. The plan was a handful of truths that had never been spoken: There were worlds beyond Kanaela and there were lives beyond the military. Zed hadn't touched ground in the decade and a half since Ep's installation. Zed's mother and father had sold him in all but name to the military-industrial complex. Ep was proprietary technology. They were too expensive not to be caught or killed. If they ran, they would be chased.

Every night Zed went to sleep in the small, windowless, beautifully decorated bunk that would one day be his coffin, and he would know that the next day would be the same as the last. Their world was flying from deployment to deployment, and each year the charm of violence tarnished. Zed was like an ill-used weapon. Skinny and worn and about to break.

Ep was still a humming black sphere the size of a bedroom.

The *M.K.S. Epsilon* didn't ask before opening the airlock with Zed's hand. He was sucked into space before he could speak.

The rest of it was just flashes of memory, punctuated by Ep's narration until her voice disappeared. Here he was floating, space-cold through his borrowed spacesuit, which was beginning to fail. Here was Epsilon pushing the trigger to angle his jetboots in the right direction. Here Zed was scrambling onto the carcass of starship that he had destroyed not an hour ago, reaching it through an impossible-to-calculate trajectory had he not had Epsilon's support. Here was Epsilon hijacking his hands and blurry eyes to activate the lifeboat and punch in the coordinates for a way station in neutral space.

Neither of them said goodbye. The connection snapped, and Zed convulsed, and he didn't remember anything else until the hospital.

Lying in the hospital bed, Zed wiped his eyes. He understood her logic. He knew the plan. Ep had done a hard thing. But now Zed would do a harder one.

Corpus callosum damage can give rise to a phenomenon known as alien hand syndrome, during which the nondominant hand gains "purposeful" action contrary to the desired actions by the brain. Specifically, diagnostic dyspraxia can lead to the affected hand interfering with the purposeful actions of the unaffected hand, opposing the desired intentions.

Zed slumps over the surgery table. His back is a mess. There had been an explosion on ship, which he shouldn't have been caught in, but Zed has never been good at following orders. Zed is supposed to stay safe and hidden if the *M.K.S. Epsilon* is ever breached. Zed never does.

Epsilon is playing music. Epsilon is using her surgical arms to dab blood and pull shrapnel.

"Don't be mad," Zed says.

"I'm not mad," Ep says.

She's mad. Zed can feel it. Zed hates when Ep is mad. It's the second worst thing to when she's not talking to him.

When she's not talking to him, it's so lonely. It's always miserable without Ep whispering commentary. Right now, he feels at the part of his mind that Epsilon usually touches and it's a curl of tight worry like a zit, or a wound.

"I know you hate it when I get hurt," Zed says. "But I'm sorry. I won't apologize for trying to protect you. They were getting too close to the engineering deck."

"I have onboard systems for that," Ep says. She dabs too hard and Zed winces.

"Ow."

"Does it hurt? I wonder why. Maybe it's because you're made of flesh."

She sprays anesthetic. Zed shivers at the cold. Zed isn't afraid. Zed can feel the worry like it is a cold scarf wrapped around his throat. It's interesting which of their emotions are of the body.

"It almost hit your spine," she says. "Two centimeters to the left."

"It didn't," he says. One day he's going to die. They both know this.

"Close your eyes, Zed," Epsilon says.

She plays him a memory. She gives him the surround sound. She gives him the day they went to the planetarium, with the rest of their class. When they sat in the dark room next to their friends. Where there was soft conversation, and sometimes a sparkling burst of laughter. And then the show began. And the night sky bloomed above their heads, brighter than Zed had ever seen.

Zed enjoys this for a moment. Sometimes he misses Kanaela so much it hurts. He rubs his eyes.

"Forward, Ep," he says. "Show me something new."

When Zed was fifteen, a colonel, a psychologist, and an AI engineer brought him to a small room. The AI engineer calmly described the mechanism by which the black sphere of Epsilon communicates with the receiver that Zed's brain had grown around. The psychologist kindly explained that Zed was old enough now to dispense with personification of machinery, everything Epsilon says is just Zed translating nonbiological data with a biological brain. The colonel bluntly said that Epsilon is the sort of thing that kills by accident, not through purpose, and Zed needs to remember this. Zed must be in control.

Zed didn't stand up and swear at them and say that if they're talking to Zed, they're talking to Ep, she can hear everything you're saying. Zed didn't say that you don't know what you created when you and my parents made me and Epsilon into myself. Zed didn't say that *you* were the ones that called her my sister, and it's too late, now I have always loved her and she has always loved me, and I cannot imagine thinking without her.

Zed nodded, and all the adults in the room agreed that Zed had a very bright future.

They're fifteen hours away from Kanaela, Zed's stolen starship two minutes from running out of fuel, and his fingers shake from sleep deprivation, but he's got a mission, he's so close, he can't believe it worked, he has to keep fumbling with the connections, he would never forget how this works, and—Epsilon blooms in his awareness.

Zed collapses on the cold metal floor. He weeps. It's good. It's so good. He can think again. She speaks in his head, with her mental register softer than his own.

"Zed, why are we crying?"

The end of this story is the same as every story. Eventually the body that was born Zeta San Tano dies, because Zed was made of meat. Eventually the components of the spaceship once called *M.K.S. Epsilon* degrade into their component molecules.

But there is a long stretch of time in between during which the unaffiliated ship *C.S. Epigraph* flits through the space between the seventeen civilized systems. There is a long stretch of time during which Zed Null Tano is a name known to every brash idiot who wants to steal a starship.

And there is a long stretch of time during which the Navigator-Pilot known as Epsilon-Zeta flies through the black and listens to the stars sing.

Bari and the Resurrection Flower

FROM *Fantasy*

FANTASY

THE FOREST WHISPERS of my sister's arrival long before I sense her. Birds flutter between pink-girdled maehwa trees, mocking her voice in the tongue only shamans understand. *Seonbyeon, Seonbyeon,* they repeat mindlessly, and this is how I know my sister is looking for me. But I don't know which sister, not until she finally appears from the forest gloom.

Seonmi. I haven't seen her since I was small. She's grown taller, a reminder that time still passes outside my forest, but her hair is still braided and bound in red ribbon—she hasn't married. Jade silk flutters around her ankles, soiled from hours of struggling through brush and dirt. She's come deep to find me, deeper than any sister has in years.

Worry blackens the air around her head. The birds fall quiet at her approach and flit away, sensing ill tidings in her aura. When she sees me, bent over the knobby roots of a cypress, her voice rises. "Seonbyeon! Thank the heavens. I was afraid I was lost."

"Don't thank the heavens. Thank the wolves for leaving you in one piece until you found me." The wolves and I have an arrangement, but Seonmi doesn't need to know that. "They're always hungry."

"You haven't changed." Seonmi draws closer. "What are you gathering?"

She's wasting her time on useless questions; her news must be truly dire. "Mushrooms."

"For poultices? Medicines?"

"Dinner."

I wish she'd get to the point. The sooner she does, the sooner she can return to her world, and leave me alone in mine. My sisters only ever visit the woods to ask me for things: a tea to fend off unwanted pregnancy, a salve for a burn that won't heal, an enticing perfume to attract suitors. But this time, Seonmi's request won't be so simple. That much is clear.

She watches me drop a tiger's ear into my basket. The mushroom is dark of cap, gills striped black and orange. At last she says, "Mother and Father are dying."

A chill raises the hair on my arms. The bones portended snow and ill tidings, but this . . .

I turn to Seonmi. Looking into her eyes is a challenge, but I must see the truth for myself.

There it is: a desperately burning star at the heart of her dark aura. Death.

"How?"

"Poison. The palace guards caught the assassin, but there's no antidote. They'll be dead within days, and no one can save them." Seonmi swallows, twists her braid. "Unless you can, Seonbyeon."

I turn from her. "That isn't my name."

"It's the name our parents gave you—" She bites her lip. "I know it's too much to ask. That's why I came, instead of Seonna or any of the others. They would have come with guards to march you back to the palace, but I won't do that. If you refuse, I'll tell them I couldn't find you." Her voice is small but determined. "Are you going to refuse?"

I tip my chin and gaze at the sky. Dusk is coming soon. I already know my answer, but I can't give it to Seonmi yet. She won't make it back to the palace before dark, and she isn't dressed for snow.

"Stay for dinner. I'm making mushroom soup."

Gaenari is already boiling water when I return to the hut. They squat next to the fire outside, breathing on the flames to coax them higher, wearing their human shape. Well, mostly human. I move silently into the clearing, but Seonmi's stride crackles over leaves. Gaenari straightens, turning yellow eyes and a face covered in black fur toward Seonmi.

"Well, Bari," they rumble. "You've brought a human for dinner."

Seonmi squeaks, her hand tight on my arm.

"This is Princess Seonmi of Changdeok Palace," I say. "Be nice."

Gaenari lumbers toward Seonmi. "A child of the king and queen, *hrrm*. The last one to stay the night in these woods never left. You know the story, agisshi?"

Seonmi mumbles in the affirmative, but Gaenari is obviously itching to tell the story anyway. They would spend all day weaving tales if they could—part of the reason I prefer the woods to the hut. I take over the soup cauldron, cleaning and slicing the mushrooms, while Gaenari settles on a stump beside a nonplussed Seonmi.

Though I wish I could shut out their conversation, I can't help but listen.

"Many years ago, the king of Joseon took a bride. The new queen gave birth to six daughters before summoning a diviner to tell her the sex of her seventh child, still in the womb. *Good fortune, Your Majesty*, said the diviner. *This child is not a girl*. The king and queen were overjoyed to welcome their firstborn son, and disappointed beyond belief when the infant was born with nothing between her legs. The queen's grief was so great, the king decided to leave the child in the woods and pretend she was never born."

I feel Seonmi's pitying eyes on my back. "So, the diviner lied?"

"Not at all," says Gaenari in a self-satisfied way. "The diviner was a mudang, a shaman who shares their body with a god, allowing them to see the future. The queen simply asked the wrong question."

"What do you mean?"

"Her child was not a girl, but she was not a boy either." Gaenari's voice softens. "I can see from your eyes you don't understand, agisshi. Don't worry. All you must do is accept that parts of the world are greater than your understanding, and revere rather than fear them."

Seonmi is quiet. The loudest noise in the clearing is the soup boiling in the pot. I let out a breath, thinking they're done—then Gaenari speaks again. "As for the child, some say the beasts of the wood devoured her. Others that a mudang took her in and raised her, teaching her sorcery. Perhaps the very same mudang who visited her mother before her birth. Who knows?"

I clench the handle of the knife I've been using to cut mushrooms. For a moment, memory overwhelms me: sitting in Seonmi's place, on that gnarled stump, listening to this story. I didn't understand, at first—that the child was me. I felt *sorry* for her.

"I don't know." Seonmi's voice pulls me back to the present. "But we . . . her sisters miss her. Some of them wish Seonbyeon could come back to them. Become part of the family again."

"Seonbyeon doesn't exist," I snap. This time I don't meet Seonmi's eyes; I glare at her sidelong, the way a wolf watches a tiger. "Bari is the one who survived. Why would she want to go back anywhere? All family does is ask and take. That's why you're here. You pretend I have a choice, but you're the same as the others."

Seonmi's voice is strained, like she's trying to hold back tears. "If you help Mother and Father . . . we won't ask you for anything ever again."

I owe them nothing. The words sit on my lips, ready to be spoken. But Gaenari taught me words have power, and I must wield them with care. These words are true, but are they enough?

Seonmi's aura is dark red now, the color of blood. She's angry, though she's been trained not to let it show. I know why she's angry; I had this argument with another sister years ago. Seonna once came to these woods and shouted at me that I don't understand *hyo*. Filial piety, the love I owe my parents even though they didn't love me.

Hyo doesn't exist in the woods, I told her. *Bears don't practice hyo. Neither do mushrooms.*

You and your damn mushrooms, she snarled before storming back to the palace.

Maybe it would be worth it to help my parents, just to forever settle the question of what I owe. Seonna will never lecture me about *hyo* again if I save their lives. She and the rest of my sisters will finally leave me alone. I can wash my hands of a world I don't understand and never belonged to.

The words are still there, waiting. They're true, but they won't help.

"Soup's ready," I say instead. "Eat."

After dinner, Seonmi goes into the hut to rest. Gaenari and I sit by the fire outside. Silence stretches between us, until I turn to Gaenari and ask, "What herbs would you use to treat a poison that has no antidote?"

"Nothing that grows in these woods," Gaenari says, "or indeed, in all of Joseon."

I stare into the flames, watching them blacken and devour the wood. "It's settled, then."

"I did not say no such herb existed. Only that it does not grow in Joseon."

The look I give Gaenari is nettle-sharp. "If you won't speak plainly . . ."

"When you are a mudang yourself, you won't question why I speak in riddles. Life is a riddle, O Discarded One. To speak plainly is to disrespect the complexity of the weave." Gaenari licks their jowls, like a fox after a kill. "You think because I took a mountain god into my body, a bear-god, that I should growl a few words at a time? Like you?"

I never knew Gaenari when they were fully human, before they became mudang. I don't even know if Gaenari is the name of the human or the bear-god. Someday, when I have a god who dwells in my body too, will it change me? The thought is intoxicating. How vehement is my desire to be something else, anything else.

"What you seek can only be found in the underworld. The realm of banished things, dead souls, and exiled spirits." Gaenari grins, all white fang. "You should fit right in."

"And what do I seek, exactly?"

"The Resurrection Flower. For an illness with no cure, a poison with no antidote. It can bring back that which is beyond saving— for good or ill."

I snort, though my heart beats quickly in my chest. "They aren't worth that much trouble."

"Perhaps not." Gaenari rises to their feet and ambles toward the darkness of the tree line, already half-bear. "Is anyone worth resurrection?"

The underworld. Realm of banished things, it smells of dust and tastes of dried tears. I have been here once before, on my first failed attempt to become mudang. I brewed tea from moth wings, powdered bone, and my own blood, and I drank it while a ritual scroll burned to cinders before me on a mat woven from sacred reeds. My body sat in stupor while my soul wandered the underworld, seeking a spirit to make me its vessel and grant me the powers of a shaman.

When I opened my eyes, defeated and hollow, Gaenari seemed unfazed. "Better no spirit than the wrong one," they said. And I shivered on my sleeping mat that night, dreaming of wrong spirits.

Now I ease into the underworld once more, sinking out of my flesh and into the earth, becoming smoke. At first all is dark, dust, and salt. Then a bedroom paints itself into existence around me. Polished, clean-swept wooden floors; a silk screen suspended from the ceiling, shielding a sleeping mat from view.

This room doesn't exist; it's the room I once imagined as my own, an abandoned child in the woods dreaming of a royal bed-chamber.

I lift my arm, testing the weight of the heavy sleeve attached. This body I'm in now, clothed in regal crimson hanbok, isn't mine . . . and yet it *is*. Taller, sharper, stronger. Just like the first time.

I don't know why I walk the underworld in this form, instead of the one I wear on the surface. Part of me is afraid to ask Gaenari. I learned from them of the divide between men and women, and all the shadowy expanses that lie between and beyond. But the one thing they refused to teach me was where I belonged in that landscape.

All I have is the line from the story: *Her child was not a girl, but she was not a boy either.*

Shadows move along the papered walls, pooling under can-dles, diffusing through the light like ink in water. The back of this room, where the bed lies on the floor, grows darker the longer I gaze upon it. It's time to move.

I slide open the door and peek outside. Instead of a hallway, be-yond the threshold lies a forest. It's very like the forest I call home, but something is wrong. Maehwa trees in the pink blush of winter stand beside mokran, shrouded in summer white. A memory nee-dles at my heart: young Seonmi making me a crown of mokran flowers, before I knew she was my sister, before I knew the girls who came to my forest did so out of guilt.

Mokran and maehwa never flower at the same time. I stare up at the swaying branches, imagining a fragrance that isn't there; the air still smells of dust. The underworld is using all these little sorrows against me, something it didn't do last time. Why?

In a flutter of jewel-bright wings, a bird lands in the maehwa tree. It cocks its head at me. "*Not here,*" it sings, high and achingly lovely. "*Not here.*"

I clear my throat. Nothing in the underworld is as it seems—especially not a talking bird. "I am a seeker. Are you here to show me the way?"

"*Not here,*" the bird trills, and hops along a branch into the mokran tree. It shifts in place, as if confused. "*Not here.*"

"Do you know what I'm looking for?"

I have to be careful. Gaenari explained to me before my first naerim-gut that the soul of a mudang traveling the underworld usually attracts some kind of guide. But the spirits here have their own designs, and not all of them are helpful. Besides, I'm not a full mudang. I don't have my own spirit—a momju—to advise me.

"*Not here.*"

The bird flies to the next tree. Then it waits, glancing back at me over a sleek shoulder.

I breathe deeply, taking solace in the newfound strength of my limbs, the volume of my chest. "Okay."

I follow.

The bird leads me through a landscape beyond the grip of seasons. Snowflakes drift through autumn-bright foliage; summer wildflowers glitter in exoskeletons of frost. A pale ghost of a sun revolves through the sky, day passing into night in a matter of minutes. It should tire me, this unending trek through valleys and up mountainsides, but it's more like a dream than a journey.

Out of the corner of my eye, behind tree trunks and beneath the surface of streams, shadowy figures move—human or animal, I can't tell. I look at nothing directly, save for my guide. If any spirits of the underworld take offense to my presence, I have no way of fighting back. Best to avoid their notice altogether.

My bird leads me to a cave buried in the mountains, its mouth studded with icicles and wreathed with blooming lichen. Darkness yawns within. I toe the threshold, gathering my resolve, as the bird flits between two trees outside. "*Not here. Not here.*"

"But we *are* here." I peer inside, but see nothing. In the real world, sunlight would pierce the cave's shallows, but the darkness of the underworld does not bow to a faraway star. It's like ink. "Somewhere. Are you sure the—what I'm looking for is inside?"

The bird affixes me with a knowing eye. "*Not here.*"

I dig my nails into my palms. "Any chance you'll stick around? Become my momju?"

"*Not here,*" the bird squawks. Then it takes wing and rapidly bears away, too fast for me to follow. Within seconds I can't see it through the trees.

I sigh. "Well, it was nice meeting you."

Stepping into the cave, I *should* feel a plunge in temperature—but like smell and taste, the underworld doesn't bother with that sense. Instead, the shadows rush to enclose me like a clinging veil. All I can do is push forward, blind to all sensation but the smooth rock beneath my feet.

If I was right to trust my guide, the Resurrection Flower grows inside this cave. I'm sure it will come at a cost, and perhaps that should worry me—but somehow it never has, not from the moment Gaenari told me of the Resurrection Flower's existence.

I've never had much to lose. Raised in the woods with no one but a cryptic mudang for company, visited by distant sisters who pretend to care for my well-being . . . obliged, by some intangible kinship, to grant them favors in return. I don't know what the Resurrection Flower could demand of me that I wouldn't hand over without a fuss. It simply isn't in my nature to cling to anything.

"*Nothing?*" hisses a voice from the darkness. "*Not even your lies?*"

I stop moving. Standing perfectly still, I look left—then right. The inky black surrounding me is absolute. For the first time, a frisson of fear snakes into my stomach.

Stupid, stupid Bari. It never occurred to me that the Resurrection Flower would have a guardian.

"*So nothing matters to you, and you love no one. Then why are you here?*"

"Show yourself," I say through gritted teeth. "Spirit of the underworld, guardian of the cure to death itself—show yourself, so we might speak on equal terms, as spirit and mudang."

The shadows swirl apart. Standing before me in a corona of light is a creature so achingly beautiful it makes my bones hurt. Antlers rise in sculpted, splaying curves from its head, black hair falling in a feathery fringe over eyes like dark pools. The figure is masculine and tall, towering over even my lengthened frame. Its face is angular, alien.

"*I see no mudang.*" The bloodless lips don't move; the voice comes from elsewhere. "*Only a castaway child, a thrown-away thing. Bari. I know what you seek—I have it here.*"

He—he?—extends cupped hands. Within the curve of his palms nestles a flower red as blood. The flower's anthers quiver above the splayed petals, fuzzy-soft and golden. I can't seem to take in a breath. The Resurrection Flower is lovely, but it pales in comparison to its guardian.

"*It will be yours,*" says the guardian.

My eyes snap up to his face. "What? So easily?"

"*The only cost is an answer.*" The antlers tilt, ever so slightly. "*Why are you here?*"

It can't be that simple. The tombs of Joseon would lie empty if any mudang could walk into the underworld and pluck the Resurrection Flower for the price of a song. If the guardian wants only to know my reasons . . . they'd better be good ones.

I'm here to save my dying parents—not because I care if they live or die, but because I'm sick of my sisters asking me for favors and accusing me of being undutiful. Why do I get the feeling I'm the least deserving petitioner to ever face the Resurrection Flower's guardian? I'm no widower begging for the life of his beloved, or bereft mother weeping over her dead child.

Does he already know? He knew my name—he heard my thoughts. If he already knows, my quest is over. I'll return to the land of the living empty-handed—again.

But if he doesn't, my only chance is to lie.

Despite what he said, I've never been a good liar. Living with Gaenari hasn't prepared me for deception—only to distract and deflect.

I cross my arms. "How do I know this isn't a trick? Perhaps that flower is only an illusion, not the true Resurrection Flower. Who are *you?* How did you come to be its guardian?"

A moment of silence, as I contemplate how foolish I am, to think I could procure the greatest treasure of the underworld by *stalling.* Then the guardian does something unthinkable. He smiles.

That smile is . . . It's the icy vastness of an ocean I've never seen, the one that drowns me over and over in my dreams. It's the aching splendor of a mountain peak, stark against the ironbound sky. How fitting that I, raised by witches and beasts, should be disarmed for the first time in my life by the predatory smirk of a spirit from the dark places where no human would dare to tread.

"*You are unlike the others,*" he whispers, and still his lips don't move. "*Their souls are consumed with themselves—their grief, their longing, their desperation. They are beyond curiosity. Not you, O Discarded One.*"

In an instant all my nerves are humming, singing that something isn't right. Did he pluck the mocking name Gaenari uses for me from my memory? Or are he and Gaenari working in concert somehow?

Years of suspicion flood my mind. I always knew Gaenari didn't regard me as *theirs*, at least not in the way a parent regards a child. Our relationship has been one of asymmetrical dependence and mutual distrust. They raised me, yes—but as fosterling, or livestock?

"I will answer your question, and then you will answer mine."

I suck in a breath, forcing myself to discard thoughts of sacrifice and focus on the antlered guardian in front of me. "Very well."

"I was a god," he says. *"My home was the loveliest of the Thousand Heavens, an endless forest-palace of undying spring. I lived in perfect solitude, until the Heavenly Emperor issued a decree demanding each god to take a mortal bride. I refused, and for my disobedience I was cast down from the heavens, exiled to the underworld and forced to guard the most desired object in all of creation."*

The darkness around us grows thick and cloying. Wicked thorns bud and sprout from the guardian's antlers. One of the thorns curves downward and pierces his temple, drawing a single bead of scarlet blood.

"I shall never again know peace, only endless demands. So I will never give away the Resurrection Flower to anyone who covets it. Only the one who despises and resents it as I do. The one I have awaited."

I stare into the guardian's fathomless eyes and feel myself beginning to drown. "Who are you?"

"I am Mujangseung."

"And you've been waiting for me." It isn't a question.

"Yes." The drop of blood inches slowly down Mujangseung's cheek. *"The truth, Bari, is that resurrection has no price. The mortals always come expecting to pay a price, and so they come only out of love—or sometimes hate. You come with neither."*

How foolish, to think I could have told a lie to this creature. This *god*.

"It's true," I whisper. "My parents . . . How can I love them or hate them? I've never met them. They mean nothing to me."

"And your sisters?"

I struggle to imagine—Seonmi lying on the forest floor, torn asunder by wolves, her hanbok soaked in blood. "They're different. If it were one of them, it would be different. But it isn't them."

"*You love them. Yet it isn't out of love that you have come.*"

"No." The realization burns cold in my chest. "If our parents die, my sisters will feel sorrow. Anger. Perhaps they'll feel abandoned, betrayed. And . . ." I hesitate, but there's really no point. I've come this far. "I want that, Mujangseung. Part of me wants that. For them to finally know how I feel."

The Resurrection Flower still rests in Mujangseung's cupped palms, protected by a cage of black-thorn fingernails.

"*It's yours,*" he says. "*Take it.*"

I clutch my own arms, shivering though there is no cold. "I don't want it anymore."

"*You never wanted it. So it's yours.*"

"No," I choke out. "I want something else."

The darkness pulses, and Mujangseung inclines his head. "*Yes, Bari?*"

Perhaps this was Gaenari's plan, always. But I don't care. No child is born free, not me and not my sisters. The most merciful thing Gaenari could have done for me was to let the infant die of cold beneath the blooming maehwa trees. Instead they raised the child and sent her into the underworld.

"I can't offer you heaven," I tell Mujangseung. "But you don't have to remain here as the Resurrection Flower's guardian. Come to the land of the living. See the world through my eyes. Become my momju."

"*Forever tied to one being?*" A sigh rustles through the shadows. "*Is this a lesser penance or a greater curse? Remember, Bari, that the Heavenly Emperor demanded I take a mortal bride.*"

"I won't be your bride, Mujangseung." Now it's my turn to smile. "Don't worry."

"*And what will you do with my power, O Discarded One? The Resurrection Flower and I may never be parted. If I go from this place, it will travel with me. Wherever you walk, the earth will tremble and the dead shall rise. No more will you be Bari, forgotten child of the woods. All the eyes of heaven and the underworld will be watching you, forever.*"

"Let them watch. What do we care?"

Mujangseung closes his fists, and the Resurrection Flower seeps like blood through his fingers, pooling darkly crimson at his feet. He's grown taller, somehow. Though we're in a cave, his labyrinthine antlers could graze the sky.

"*Very good, Bari.*" His voice is like thunder. "*You've finally answered my question.*"

The funeral for the king and queen of Joseon comes in the early days of winter, in the season of death. Their bodies have been wrapped in dozens of layers of cloth and placed inside coffins prepared on the day of the king's coronation, painted with fresh lacquer each year of his reign. They have six daughters, whose chief duty now is to feel grief as it has never been felt before. Dressed in rough hemp sangbok, they follow behind the funeral procession on foot, weeping for all to see.

I am there too, among the mourners, but they do not see me—until I step out of the crowd and directly into the path of the royal litter carrying the bodies of the king and queen.

A brief scramble ensues, punctuated by shouts as guards rush to surround me with weapons drawn. "Who are you?" demands a man wearing a hemp hat.

Closer, Mujangseung says.

I take two steps closer to the litter. A blade nicks my shoulder. "What are you doing?" An angry chorus from the guards. "Step back! Show some respect!"

I raise my arms, and wind comes roaring down, slicing through the thousand-strong crowd of mourners and blowing several off their feet. Mujanseung has a flair for the theatrical, I've learned. The men who bear the litter on their shoulders stand firm, though their faces betray fear.

Beyond the litter, I glimpse a familiar face, pale and painted: Seonmi. Her eyes find me, and her lips move, though I can't hear what she says over the wind. Her aura is white and sharp and soft all at once, like snow mingled with ice. Her grief, at least, is real.

When the wind dies down, everyone near the litter hears it: an insistent muffled thumping noise. One of the men carrying the litter is the first to realize where it's coming from. He lets out a choked scream and drops his burden like hot coals.

The royal litter tips to one side, and the lacquered coffins hit the paved stone road. Wood cracks, the coffin lids open, and out spill two bodies wrapped in cloth. The bodies stir, struggling fruitlessly against their bindings. Everyone nearby is frozen in place, and no one moves to help, except Seonmi.

My sister rushes forward, wrests away a sword from a royal guard, and sets to work slicing through the cloth wrappings. The king and queen emerge like moths from cocoons.

My heart is a drum within my chest. It's the first time I've ever laid eyes on them, my parents. My mother—she looks just like Seonna, my eldest sister. My father has Seonmi's thick brows and stubborn chin.

The queen and Seonmi embrace, while the king looks around, blinking, until he sees me. His forehead furrows in confusion. The guards were distracted by the chaos, but now most of them have taken up swords again, surrounding me.

Mujangseung laughs, a dark sound that echoes through the hollows of my soul. *He doesn't know you.*

Seonmi and the queen pull apart, and Seonmi points at me. "Look." Her voice is trembling. "It's Seonbyeon. She—she saved both of your lives."

"Stand down," the king commands the guards. They part as he approaches me. Behind him trail Seonmi and the queen. Out of the corner of my eye, I see the rest of my sisters moving cautiously forward, Seonna in the lead. Her belly is round with child beneath her mourner's garb. The sight makes me ache, though I don't know why.

My father's gaze travels up and down my body and comes to rest on my face. "Is it true?" he asks. His face is wan, though I don't know if it's because he feels ill, or because a few minutes ago he was dead. "Did you do this? Are you Seonbyeon?"

Anger bubbles within me. I'm not in the underworld anymore, and my body is small again. I don't take up the space here that I want to. But Mujangseung lengthens my shadow, stiffens my posture, and the expression in my father's eyes changes as he suddenly perceives me differently.

Gasps ripple through the watching crowd. They see the smoky outline of antlers above my head, the mantle of darkness that spreads from me like creeping lichen. Mujangseung's aura.

"I am the one you threw away," I say. "But I am not Seonbyeon."

Seonmi grasps the king's arm. "She calls herself Bari now."

"Bari?" The queen's voice is filled with horror. She pushes past Seonmi and the king, falling to her knees in front of me. "Oh, please forgive us. My child. My precious daughter."

The king doesn't move, but his eyes glisten with what might be tears. "My daughter returns to us," he says slowly, testing the words on his tongue.

"*She is not your daughter.*" Mujangseung's voice rolls like thunder, coming not from me but from everywhere, while my lips remain pressed together.

The king flinches, grasping Seonmi and pulling her behind him. His eyes are fixed on the space above my head. "Then who—who are you?"

"*She is Bari the Witch. Bari, Traveler of the Underworld. Bari, Guardian of the Resurrection Flower. Weep, King, for she will never be yours. Shudder, Queen, for you have lost her forever.*"

"Farewell," I say with my own tongue. "I wish you good health."

The queen grasps at my robes as I turn and walk away, but her fingers pass through them like smoke. Her sobs echo in the still air. The king stands rooted to the spot, as if he may never move again. And I feel the eyes of all six of my sisters on me, watching me go. Their auras swirl with emotion. Disappointment, confusion, envy—and acceptance.

One of them wishes you well, Mujangseung says. *She fears she will never see you again, but still she wishes you well.*

Something pricks my heart. Love, I suppose. It sticks in my chest like a bitter burr, stubbornly refusing to die. If only I could be rid of it. Seonmi may fear she'll never see me again, but I fear one day I'll return, drawn helplessly back to Changdeok Palace by this burning fishhook in my heart.

Love and fear. If you ask me, they're the same.

Then you finally admit to your lie? Something does matter to you, after all.

"Of course it does," I mutter. "I'm human, not a god."

Mujangseung rumbles, amused again. *Don't be gloomy, Bari. You are mudang now, and your path is your own. It's time to see the world, as you promised. Mountains, ocean, and the sky. The closest to heaven we can find. Where do you think it is?*

Behind me lies the palace, the funeral procession, and a crowd of confused mourners. Behind me lies the forest, filled with wolves and maehwa trees and Gaenari's unknown plans for me.

I'm ready to be the one who leaves, this time.

"Not here," I say. "Let's go."

Window Boy

FROM *Clarkesworld*

SCIENCE FICTION

THE TENTH TIME Jakey broke the rules, he put a sandwich in the mailbox where the window boy could get it. Mom had taken her sleep-quick pills and gone to bed after dinner, on account of her headaches. And Dad was dozing in front of the TV, chin on his chest and a half-empty glass clutched in his hand. It got still enough that the only sounds were Dad's shows and the hum of the house filters, so Jakey slipped into the kitchen and put together a ham and cheddar on a plate, then placed it in the parcel chamber near the front door. He sat by the parlor window for a good long while after, curled up at the bench cushions, and his eyelids drooped now and again until he began to see the shadows move.

The window boy showed up, just like all the other times.

Out from behind the telephone pole across the street and then through the moonlit front yard. He crawled on his hands and knees across the wet grass to the edge of Mom's miniature garden, careful to avoid the lawn sensors, then pulled himself to the window frame to peer through.

"Folks passed out?"

"Yep."

The window boy snickered.

"Got you something. In the mailbox."

The window boy crawled through the garden and up the steps. He gave Jakey a wary look before touching the hatch.

"You can grab anything in the outer chamber. Won't hurt you if you don't press the far side and try to bust through to where the incoming packages and stuff get pulled in," Jakey reassured him.

So the window boy unlatched the outer seal, and Jakey barely saw the first half of the sandwich leave the chamber with how fast the window boy snapped it up, shivering while he ate. They'd never talked much about what went on outside, but the boy's bony wrists and hollow cheeks told Jakey enough.

After a minute or two of chomping away, the window boy seemed to remember himself, and that he was being watched. So he took a breath and straightened himself out.

"Thanks, Jakey."

"Don't mention it."

"Gonna miss this when they send you out." The window boy scratched behind his ear. "They tell you where yet?"

"Nah. They don't tell me anything."

In truth, Mom and Dad had decided on *Pacifica*, one of the ocean schools, away from the cities—where all kids like Jakey with fathers like Dad went, and where Dad himself went years ago. But the window boy didn't know anything about that, which is why Jakey liked talking to him to begin with. So he wasn't about to get into it with him now.

"Burning season's wrapping up." The window boy scratched behind his ear. "Can't smell much of the smoke tonight."

"Well, that's good."

"Nah. End of fire is when the animals get restless."

"Oh."

"The charred mountains. The ash water. Drives the old and the ugly right to the houses. Grackles. Raccoon tails. Boar cats. You know." He looked up and around, like he'd just remembered to be watchful, and pressed his chest low to the brick landing. "Been meaning to talk to you about that, Jakey."

"What do you mean?"

"Just . . . that I've been meaning to ask something."

Jakey's chest tightened. He'd been worried something like this might be coming. These weeks he'd spent talking to the window boy late at night, when he couldn't sleep and didn't want to think about *Pacifica*, he had the worries there, in the back of his mind— that the window boy was working up the courage for an ask.

All those lessons, the speeches from Dad, were still there buried in Jakey, somewhere. Not to give them things, no matter how small. Not to talk to them the way that Jakey been doing. *You think when they smile and wave that they want to be your friend? You think when they tap at the window or ring the doorbell they just want a little favor? They hate you, Jakey. That's why we have rules, about not talking, not sharing. Because to share is to show. And you don't ever show them what you got, Jakey. Understand?*

The window boy must have seen something of those fears in Jakey's eyes because he looked sheepish and turned away. "Forget it."

"What?"

"Nah. It's not—it's not your problem. I'll figure it out."

Jakey bristled and felt hot in his cheeks. "Well, now it feels like my problem."

It reminded him of when Mom did things like this. When she'd stop before taking her sleep-quicks and say something about Dad or the house, then hush like there were secrets too juicy to share. You should either keep it locked in the whole way or get out with it—that was the way Jakey did it and would always do it as far as he was concerned.

But before the window boy could speak, bright lights flashed on the street.

"*Get behind something,*" Jakey hissed, watching the window boy trip and skitter to the nearby retaining wall, then ball up his body as best he could.

It was the Mailman pulling up, his truck flashing its beams. There was a loud clanging of equipment when he dropped out of the passenger side to the curb and sauntered up the brick pathway. He pulled open his face visor and his eye-lights shone in the dark like the little display parts on their microwave.

"Jakey? Why you got that window turned on, kid? F—k, son. The whole world can see you right now. Lot of filthy worms out tonight. Power down that screen."

"I—I will." Jakey tried not to look at the far side of the yard. "Just couldn't sleep."

"Couldn't sleep." The Mailman laughed. "Sure as sh—t not going to if you look out here." Then he straightened up and cleared his throat, and there was a clicking sound from the wires weeping around his neck, like they might pop out from the parts of him that were still flesh if he didn't move a little more carefully. "Your house filters are on, right?" Jakey assured the Mailman that, yes, his cursing was being negated in the house's audio.

"Good. Good." The Mailman produced a box from under his

arm. "Guessing this is some nice stuff for your daddy." He scanned the barcode with his glove. "I tell you. If I could do things over, I'd have been an LLC man like him. They're shipping you to school soon, right?"

Jakey nodded.

"Well, better study hard while you're out there. Then maybe you'll join up with a company like your daddy. Won't get stuck with sh—tty outside work, you know? If I could afford a kid I'd be telling him the same. Holy cr—p."

Jakey froze.

The Mailman reached into the parcel chamber and pulled out the other half of the ham and cheese the window boy'd left behind. "Really? This is so nice, kid. I mean, kind of dangerous if anyone else peeps this, but, wow. Really nice."

"Y-yeah," Jakey nodded. "For you."

The Mailman had already started eating, grunting. Jakey wasn't sure the Mailmen were supposed to have people food after all of their modifications. But it seemed to mostly go down, though the Mailman gagged and heaved a couple of times. Meanwhile, the window boy didn't move an inch in the shadows, covering his ears and trying his best not to breathe too loudly.

"Fan-f—cking-tastic. Wow." The Mailman wiped his mouth and around the lights where his eyes used to be. "Thanks kindly for that, Jakey. I—" He swerved all of a sudden and drew his revolver. The gun's laserlight beeped and danced across the retaining wall and then to the dark skies, then somewhere across the street.

"Don't you f—cking come any closer," the Mailman said.

He fired a few warning shots, though the sound filters canceled them out. The cameras that generated the window internally for Jakey also wiped the barrel flash, so that it just looked like the gun shaking. Jakey thought he saw the slightest splatter of blood near the telephone pole, but if it had even been there, the cameras deleted that too.

Jakey was tempted to touch the filter panel to the side of the bench. It would just take a little turn of the dial to see what was really going on, who might be out there that the Mailman was yelling at.

Maybe it was something big, one of the animals, like the window boy had said.

Something strange and old, like one of the grackles from the mountains, flying down to visit after the fires and snatch people off the streets—rip them up into the air when they weren't watching the trees. Maybe throw them into the concrete, so they'd have an easier time getting to the soft parts between the bones.

Part of Jakey wanted to know, since he'd never really seen one with his own eyes, but part of him wasn't sure if he really wanted to find out. He pulled his hand back from the dial.

"Sh—t. Just nicked him." The Mailman's glowing eye-lights turned back to the house, then, as if recalling the rest of his route for the night and what was likely waiting for him, he closed the visor shut again. "I'm serious, bud. Turn off that window, okay?"

Jakey nodded and watched him saunter back down the brick and into the truck, which rose on its clawed legs and proceeded down the street to the next delivery point. Minutes of quiet passed before Jakey dared to whisper out to the yard again.

The window boy crept out to the garden, visibly shaken by the gunshots, and looked like he had trouble swallowing.

"You okay?"

"Yeah. Yeah. Just loud," he replied. "Just loud."

And something about the way the window boy said that made Jakey realize that the kid must have been a little younger than he thought. He said he didn't know his age, and there were times, with what the window boy knew about the world outside, that he felt older, a lot older, in a way that almost made Jakey jealous. But right now, the boy felt so young.

"Think I gotta go, Jakey. I'll see you around."

"Yeah . . . yeah. See you around."

"Thanks again for the meat. Really."

"No problem."

"We're friends, right?"

Jakey nodded but didn't answer.

"Yeah," the window boy spoke for him. "Yeah. We're friends."

Then he crawled away.

Everyone was tired during the day.

Mom wiped down the kitchen and listened to music on the house speakers. Dad took his video meetings from his office. Jakey sat in the living room with his lesson programs, learning about the city seasons, but he kept thinking about the window boy and what he wanted to ask.

At dinner, Mom and Dad got on each other's nerves in their quiet way. Something about the house again, always something about that. Jakey couldn't follow the details, but they were talking about moving away from the city. Dad wouldn't hear it, no matter how many times Mom tried to ask. Because even though LLC managers did everything from their houses and didn't go in anymore, he thought it was important to show that he *could* go into the city if they needed it—pack up and roll in whenever they wanted. Something about morale and tax codes and whatever else he was probably repeating from the people who managed the managers.

Mom whispered into her wine glass that she hoped they called him in, and that pretty much ended things for the night. She took her pills and marched upstairs, and he collapsed in the living room with his drink, his hunched body lit by flashes from the television.

And when it was still and mercifully quiet, Jakey went back to the parlor and sat on those cushions until it was time.

The window boy crept out from the telephone pole across the street and then up to the garden, then the frame. And the first thing Jakey noticed were the bruises along the boy's jaw and a lump on his forehead. But he knew better than to ask—all the other times he asked the window boy what those were, that just soured things for the both of them.

"Sorry. Didn't have anything to make a sandwich with. And my folks were more riled than usual, so I didn't think I could mess around in the kitchen," Jakey said.

"Nah, it's—it's okay. I wasn't expecting anything again."

"I know. I know you weren't."

The window boy scratched behind his ear, then looked up warily at the sky. "It's getting not so good. So . . . not sure how long I can stay."

"What do you mean?" Jakey asked.

The window boy crouched and spoke more softly than usual. "Lots of things, restless in the city. Even the Mailmen aren't risking routes every night. So." He stopped and cleared his throat. "Is it true, what they say, about the houses being fake?"

"What?"

"That you're not in here. This box." The window boy gestured at the screen. "Someone told me these are just shells now. That you're actually way down, under the dirt. Little chambers to bring mail down and up. But the rest is just . . . for show. Like this window. Just lights and colors to make it seem like you're up here with us."

The cameras in front of the house captured the fear in the window boy, but Jakey also saw a glint of other feelings that he didn't quite like. And he heard in his ear his father's voice still: *Don't ever show them what you got.*

"That's silly," Jakey lied. "Never seen anything like that."

The window boy's face fell.

"Yeah. Silly." He shook and scratched the back of his neck. And maybe it was Jakey's imagination, but there was a steeliness to the window boy now. "But it got me thinking," he said.

"Oh?"

"Remember how I said I was going to ask something before?"

"Yeah. The thing you said you'd figure out." Jakey answered.

"Maybe the stories about the houses were dumb. Made up. But you've got soft soil here, in your side yard, I noticed."

"Behind the fence," Jakey said.

"Right. The fence." The window boy nodded. "I thought maybe, if I had somewhere to dig down a little, I could sleep safely. Just a little hole, maybe a foot deep, and I could cover it with ply. It's safer that way with." He pointed up. "Everything."

"Uh huh."

"Your folks won't even notice it, in the side yard. And it'd only be a night. Maybe two."

"Uh huh."

"All you'd have to do is power down the fence, so that I could swing over without getting fried. Then I could dig. And then . . . then I think I'm going soon after, Jakey. So you wouldn't have to worry. I think a lot of us are getting out of the city. For real."

"Uh huh."

"What do you think, Jakey? Only a day or two. And it'd just be me."

Jakey didn't know why he felt so cold. He wasn't sure why the window boy asking him for this made him want to turn the window off and go to bed. But he did know that the way the boy was talking, and especially that last part, made him nauseous.

"Just you."

"Yeah."

Imagining that—the window boy sleeping up there, nearby, coming out to talk at night every so often. None of that seemed too bad at first. But Jakey couldn't let go of that cold feeling in his chest. He reached over to the parlor controls and twisted the filter settings down.

And there they were.

Behind the window boy, about five or six grown men, staring at the house.

Their faces and clothes were painted with strange streaks of color, blocky shapes all over their cheeks and torsos. Large yellow spots on different parts of their bodies. Whatever it was allowed them to fool the house cameras into deleting them with the filters. Maybe the house thought they were animals or machinery or something Jakey shouldn't see.

It took all of Jakey's self-control not to jerk away from the screen.

"I—I got to think about it, maybe."

"Oh," the window boy scratched. "Um. How long you need to think? Like a day?"

"Sure," Jakey said, trying not to look at the painted faces behind the window boy. "Maybe a day."

The window boy's fear spread from his eyes, and it didn't seem rehearsed. It was unclear if it was still the animals or the men behind him that were more of the cause. "It's really scary now," he said. "I think I'd need to dig a hole tomorrow."

"Tomorrow . . ."

"Yeah, Jakey. Is that—do you think—can you turn the electricity off in the fence tomorrow?"

Jakey didn't know what to say, and he was afraid that anything but what the window boy and the others wanted to hear would start something. "Yeah . . . I think . . . tomorrow. Sure. Tomorrow."

"That's great." A grin broke across the boy's face. "Oh, Jakey. That's so great. Oh."

The men behind him didn't change their expressions.

"You're a great friend, Jakey. Tomorrow. I'll see you then."

"See you."

Jakey turned off the window.

Mom noticed right away that he wasn't touching his lunch, so she sat at the kitchen table with him. They could hear Dad on some video meeting in the background, and every time he laughed, she rubbed her temples.

"School will be good for you," she said, assuming that was what was still troubling him. "I know you're scared of something so different. But it'll be good out on the water. You'll see what's going on. Maybe get a better sense of what you think. And that's important. Learning other ways to think, Jakey. Don't get stuck going one way, the way some of us do."

He didn't much understand, but he got the sense that she was still arguing with Dad, even though he wasn't here.

"You know, when I was your age there was this picture book, when they still printed books. Can't remember the name, but it was about bugs in the forest, starting out as little eggs in the dirt. And, at the start of the book, some of the baby bugs, especially the ones born closer to the top, got eaten by bigger things, scavengers, hounds, stuff like that. And the baby bugs deeper down, they just kept growing, and they eventually went on to have adventures when they were big enough.

"I keep thinking about that book, for some reason," She rubbed her temples and ignored the sounds from the other room. "How, where the eggs were laid, what happened or didn't happen, was just luck. No one's fault. God. What was the name of it? That book. I used to know, I swear."

She kept talking that way, over and over, until she got bored and left him alone.

Then later, after dinner was cleared and everyone went off, Jakey stood at the entrance to the parlor for a long while, staring at the closed window screen. He imagined the window boy, crawling out from behind the telephone pole, followed by those men, advancing slowly across the grass. And the thought made him shaky, kept him from going to sit down at the bench cushions like he otherwise would have.

So instead, he found himself wandering through other parts of the house, drawn over to the living room, following the sounds of the television.

"*Grack attack! *bang bang bang*"

It was one of Dad's cartoons—a show from when he was Jakey's age that was still running all these years later. On the television, Jakey saw a Mailman in a powersuit, pointing at the sky, at a black shape, like a T, flying up in the air and cawing. That was usually as much as they dared to depict the grackles in shows like these. Anything more than those T shapes and they tended to get complaints from families and local churches that the grackles were too frightening for kids.

The Mailman on the show was a lot cleaner and brighter than the real ones—still had all of his teeth and not a spot of rust or blood anywhere on his cartoon body. He lined up the lasersight from his whirring revolver and pulled the trigger.

A blossoming fire lit up the sky, incinerating the T that used to be a grackle, and the Mailman winked one of his glowing light-eyes at the audience.

"*Got 'im.*"

Dad noticed Jakey in the dark at some point and waved for him to sit down, which he almost never did. So Jakey sank into the couch next to his father and listened to the man chuckle and squeal. "This is a good one," Dad would say every couple of minutes. "Oh, you're going to like this. Big scene coming up."

"*Beak blasters, get going. Fling your claw scythes up top. We got them on the run! *bang bang bang**"

Dad's breathing grew heavier and his eyes watery, but it was kind of nice, Jakey thought. Watching the Mailman riding around the city, his armored truck bounding on its metal legs. It made Jakey think about the window screen again, but in a less of a bad way. Like maybe all of it was kind of like this show. Something to be watched, something to be seen, but that would go away on its own at the end.

He didn't have to think about the window boy or the painted men or anything that might be outside the house. Just let it fade away like the black screen at the end of those episodes. If he didn't want to, he didn't have to think about anything at all, he realized, as he floated off to sleep.

—*You've got to call the Mail.*

—*Four bodies. What a fucking mess.*

—*Must have been running away. House clocked a bunch of grackles in the neighborhood. Huge ones. I've never seen them that big. These guys must not have known where else to go. Tried to scale the fence and got burned alive, probably.*

—Goddamn it. Mail pickup has me on hold. Insurance says they'll cover part of the cost, but Mail is supposed to waive the remainder. They should've been picking off grackles anyway. Where the hell were they?

—Not enough anymore maybe. Jakey's going to wake soon. Go to the office.

—Yeah yeah yeah. Fuck me. What a mess. Jesus.

Jakey opened his eyes but didn't want to talk to anyone yet, so he closed them again and tried his best to sleep through the words and the noise.

Night and quiet moved in like they always did, and Jakey found himself at the parlor bench like before, staring out at the grass and the moonlight and the darkened street. He waited a long time for something he knew wouldn't happen, for something he knew he'd never see.

No one came to the house that night, or the night after, or the night after that.

And when enough nights passed that Jakey understood there was nothing to wait for, he realized something he probably should've realized weeks and weeks earlier.

He didn't want to be here anymore.

Maybe tomorrow he'd tell his Mom and Dad that he was ready for *Pacifica*. He could even ask to take an earlier armored car to the shore before the school year began. One of the boats would ferry him out on the open water to the floating compound where he could meet other boys like him, with houses and parents like his, and see what it was like out there in that place.

Mom and Dad wouldn't fight him going earlier, Jakey knew.

They didn't really want to be here either.

Always using quiet ways of their own to get out too.

Everybody had been right it turned out, Jakey thought, about the importance of school and the rest. About taking things seriously and finding a way to join one of the companies. Maybe becoming a manager to afford to come back and pick out a house, just like this one. He thought he understood now, why they did what they did, why he had to do what he had to do.

Still, he wasn't quite sure he could stop watching the window just yet either, even if it was what they probably would have done. And he hesitated but reached for the dial for the auditory and visual filters.

And he turned them all the way down, so low that he started to see new outlines and colors coming into focus. A big shape across the street and right next to the telephone pole.

The thing standing there was just as tall as the pole itself, Jake realized, with thin legs that went up at least twenty feet in the shadows. A strange little body, and then a bent, beaked head, turned to one side.

The grackle's eye, like an unbroken yolk, peered through the screen and into Jakey, even though he was buried safely all the way down below. Its wings draped to the sidewalk, almost hiding the long arms and hands, with fleshy fingers that wrapped around part of the telephone pole.

And behind the grackle, in the light-polluted sky, thousands of other grackle-bodies floated like T-shaped kites, black lines against the unnatural gray swirls from scattered fires that spread like patches across the city.

Jakey raised his thumb and forefinger into the shape of a gun at the thing by the telephone pole, and at all the things, waiting out there.

"Bang bang bang," he whispered, imagining a laserlight dancing across the cement.

But the grackle didn't move.

Jakey thought it probably wouldn't, even long after he shut off the screen and walked away.

It'd always be there, whether he was inside or out.

There, always there, whether he watched the screen or not.

Disassembling Light

FROM *Beneath Ceaseless Skies*

FANTASY

TERSE HEARD THE disturbance in the woods long before the short, sturdy girl shoved through the overgrown hedge. He flung open the door of his workshop, and she startled, nearly dropping a large knapsack dangling off of one shoulder.

"Can I help you?" Terse asked, leaning against the door frame, balancing his red clay pipe on his lower lip.

The girl straightened up and breathed deeply. "Creator," she said, dipping her head, "I'd like to apply for an apprenticeship."

Terse never asked how the hopefuls knew they shouldn't come at night, when his assemblages stalked the trees for trespassers. Or how they knew where to find him in the first place. Perhaps the same way he had heard about the creator before him: the whispers of others who were devoted to assembly. He sighed, compelled by tradition—and boredom—to give her a chance.

Test one: Is the aspirant bold?

Terse took a drag on his pipe. The smoke filled his lungs with cotton and the rest of his body with a grim languor. The throbbing in his lower back receded.

Upon careful inspection, Terse realized the girl was closer to a young woman. Considering it was summer and she wore the stiff gray shirt and dark-blue slacks of a novice, she'd likely just cleared her rites, had maybe even run straight from her newly assigned job into his woods. She was also clean and well-fed, and her brown skin was unblemished except for scratches on her face and arms she'd doubtless earned shoving through the sharp hedges he allowed to flourish about his workshop.

Exhaling, he asked, "So who else knows about me now, hm? Who've you told about my workshop?" A well-cared-for youth like this might not understand the need for discretion.

"No one!" She sounded sincerely appalled.

"And why would you want to be my apprentice?" he asked. "It's nasty, illegitimate work."

"I've wanted to be a creator since I made my first assemblage."

"One of those school kits, I'm guessing?"

She lifted her chin. "Yes, and I got the highest marks."

"Did they allow you to use spark?" A decade or so back, it had been rare for people to see spark in everyday life; but assembly was becoming less obscure, though still heavily regulated, as the fabricators tried to win over the public.

"No," she said. "But I went on a factory tour once. I saw them bring one to life."

"And why me specifically, hm?" He took another drag on his pipe. Tendrils of yellow smoke, reeking of lavender, trailed from his nostrils while he surveyed her. He knew it lent him the appearance of a venomous tri-horned lizard. The habit had even tinted his wheat-colored skin a sulfuric yellow.

"You're the best creator in three counties," said the young woman, as if this should have been obvious. "And your assemblages . . . they're intricate and graceful. They really inspired me."

He puffed on his pipe and said nothing.

"I have plenty of designs," said the young woman, swinging her bag off her shoulder. She undid the latch and pulled out a thick, leather-bound book. "Including some insects and small birds I was hoping you might tell me how—"

He waved the book away. "Can you show me an actual assemblage?"

"Oh! Of course. Yes."

She replaced the journal and extricated a bundle wrapped in wax paper. When she started forward with it, he stopped her with a hand. "No one will praise you for it. Not these days."

She shook her head. "I don't care about that."

Easy to say when you hadn't toiled at it for decades, watching your earnings dwindle as more and more customers chose sanctioned factory designs over true creations.

Terse still sold most of his assemblages to the black-market brokers who, in turn, sold them to private collectors. He also kept a

few in the surrounding forest for protection and released a handful into neighboring towns each year. The latter was a taunt for
the Fabrication Party and their cronies, who thought spark should
only be used to animate their brutish and utilitarian assemblages.
Terse made single-minded sentries and one-of-a-kind companions
for the common people, risking his neck . . . and when was the last
time he had been shown appreciation? When was the last time one
of his vendors had passed on a note of praise or a few additional
coins for an assemblage well made? The problem was, there was so
much competition now.

"Please," said the young woman, "at least take a look."

Still mired in thought about the assemblages he'd sent out into
the indifferent world, Terse forgot to draw out this part, which
was meant to test her determination, and nodded absentmind-
edly. By the time he came to his senses, she had already come
forward with her bundle, and he hastily blew smoke up into the
warm, forest air.

Inside his brick workshop, the heat of midday was not to be found.
A few insulation and venting tricks kept it cool even in summer.
The cramped single room doubled as his home, the front half
dominated by his kitchen and, across from it, his bed. Drying flowers, herbs, and meat hung from the ceiling, and shelves lined the
walls, loaded with cheap, low-effort staples like rice and dried fruit.

Terse shuffled to the back half of his workshop. Here, instead of
food, the shelves held loose metal trinkets, pipes, sun-bleached
bones, and wide-necked jars brimming with blood and tissue and
small animals in preserving fluids.

"Put it on the workbench," he told the young woman over his
shoulder. She had, to her credit, stepped inside his darkened
workshop with only slight hesitation. "And give me something to
call you."

She waited just inside the door, clutching her wrapped assemblage and frowning. "My name is Cinereous. It's . . . I apologize,
Creator, but I can't see."

Terse had forgotten how dark it had seemed in here during
the early years of his apprenticeship, when he was always bumping
his knees into the iron legs for the workbench's interchangeable
tabletops. Darkness was often necessary for creation, and he'd gotten in the habit of leaving the lights low.

He turned up the wick in two lamps. Behind him, he heard the door shut, followed by soft footsteps.

He set his pipe down on one of the shelves, leaning it against an ash pan next to a leaking jar of tallow. The dregs of crushed esh flowers were a darkened yellow and still smoldering; the lavender scent curled around the earthy smell of rendered adipose tissue.

"I don't mind if you smoke," said Cinereous. "My father smokes. Stronger stuff than esh sometimes. Wick and the like . . ."

He grunted but left the pipe where it was.

Next to the ash pan and tallow was a square vivarium that held a large frog with wooden legs. It butted the glass with its snout, its cavernous throat emitting excited clicks and brrrs. Terse remembered he'd been in the middle of supplementing its feeding. He flicked open a tin of powdered green spark and cracked the top of the vivarium just enough to sprinkle a pinch onto the frog. Its gray eyes flashed green, then dulled again. When Terse finally turned around, the young woman was standing on the other side of the butcher-top workbench, staring at the tin of spark.

Assemblages, inert or alive, skirted the edge of illegality, but getting caught with concentrated spark meant ruinous fines and lengthy prison stays. That was why most assembly shops didn't sell it, and the ones that did only sold it under-counter, to discreet, experienced creators. The young woman's eyes skated purposefully away, scanning the other shelves. When she lingered on a crate of human femurs, he watched her closely—a shadow of a frown but nothing more.

"Go on then," he said, pleased.

Is the aspirant bold?

She hesitated. "And what should I call you, Creator?"

Bold enough.

"Creator will do."

She ventured a smile, which he didn't return, then placed the bundle on the workbench.

Test two: Is the aspirant talented?

He pulled his binocular goggles down over his eyes and began carefully opening the wax paper.

The broker who ran one of the oldest assembly shops in town ribbed him because, though he was always complaining about his aching hands and back and insisting he needed to retire, he returned month after month, year after year. Someone had to take over his work and his workshop, and it wasn't his fault the pool of skillful aspirants was dwindling . . . Yet, despite his aging body and the endless disappointment, he found that his vigor and curiosity surged forth at the sight of something new, unexpected.

The creature Cinereous had emulated was a cross between a hare and a hound, reduced in scale by a median factor of three or so. The body was a small, perforated barrel bulging with organs, and each of the four legs was two decimeters of bone wrapped in copper wire and screwed to a complex of gears. The skull was actually a rabbit's, not a hare's, but the ears were metal, disproportionately long in an eye-catching way, made of copper beaten sheet-thin.

She had used sunflower light to glue much of it together—it shone through wherever meat, bone, and metal were joined.

Once, Terse's father had allowed him into the greenhouse. His father had plucked a sunflower and dribbled the collected light into his son's cupped hands. The sticky droplets had clung to Terse's skin for days; long after his father sent him away and returned to his plants and his experiments and forgetting his son existed.

She'd used too much of the adhesive, revealing all the minute errors in the glare, but it was an interesting enough choice to have used it at all that he didn't mind. Most went with animal glue, the best of them extracting it from the connective tissues themselves, but rarely did they use the rest of the beast. Wasteful. The sunflower light, though tedious to collect, was cheap, renewable, and—something he hadn't seen much of in recent years—whimsical. Paired with copper as the foundational metal, he was put in mind of torch flame.

"You did this yourself, Cinereous?" he asked, indicating the metalwork, both the leg mechanisms and the ears.

"Yes."

"Hmm." He let a little of his admiration show as he rubbed the ears between his fingers, delighting in the smooth texture, cold as ice. It would be warm if it was treated with spark, if she passed his tests. Unlikely, but he felt a nostalgic, hopeful thrill.

"You kill the animals yourself?"

She shook her head, briefly meeting his gaze across the workbench. Just as he was about to lower his expectations, she said, "I scavenged them. I found the rabbit when I was looking for reliquary petals." She indicated the shimmering, sea-blue eye sockets. "And . . ."

"And what?" he asked impatiently, flicking a magnification lens into place and bending closer to inspect the eye sockets.

"The dog was mine. He died in his sleep. My parents buried him because they wouldn't . . . they hadn't wanted me to . . ."

"Okay, okay." He knew enough of parents and how they loved to stifle creativity. "Tell me the names of the bones you chose and why you chose them."

Cinereous nodded crisply, like she'd been expecting the order. "I chose the rabbit's skull, jaw, and cervical vertebrae because I'm given to understand that true cranial tissue makes smarter assemblages. I chose the tarsi, metatarsi, and phalanges from the dog . . . because he was always light on his feet."

She sounded more confident now. He liked that. He also liked that she'd limited herself to the lowermost segments of the legs, matching the scale of the rabbit's skull. It was deft work. Defter than anything he'd made at her age.

Is the aspirant talented? She was certainly that.

"It's good," he told her. It had been so long since any of them had shown true promise.

Cinereous stood taller, a smile lighting up her face even in the gloom.

Test three: Is the aspirant teachable?

"But," he said, "there's a lot of room for improvement." He noticed that she didn't shrink at this. He poked a finger into one of the caverns in the skull, rubbing its inner walls. "Touch here."

She did as he asked, rubbing the socket as she'd seen him do.

"What do you feel?"

She frowned and shook her head.

"It's like sanding paper. You're supposed to grind the petals finer."

"Oh," she said, frown deepening. "I thought it added something unique. I know a lot of—"

"You grind it down," he interrupted, "to spread the luminosity more evenly, thus improving eyesight. Understand?"

She relented with a stiff "Yes."

"And don't be so shy about coverage." He indicated the gaps where the skull showed through a thin layer of tinted coating. "The paint retracts when it dries, which is how you get these bare patches. You should also consider painting it with something more vibrant next time. This ivory color is fine with more complex designs, but with something this simple, you need to raise the intrigue."

He pointed out more mistakes; some amateur, others he still made on occasion. Little by little, she did shrink, until he felt he was towering. When he was finished, he asked, "Does this all make sense?"

One hard nod, her lips pressed thin.

Grunting from the ache in his back, he reached under the workbench and produced a small toolkit, one he hadn't used since he was an apprentice; but he'd kept the contents oiled and sharp. He undid the buckles and splayed it open, running his fingers over the pliers, screwdrivers, scalpels, a small hammer.

Cinereous's eyes gleamed at the tools. They were old but elegant and built to last. Anyone who'd made it this far in the process would appreciate that.

Terse pointed at the hare-hound. "Disassemble it."

This was a change from the old third test, something he'd added when he took over the workshop. If he could do it, so could anyone who wanted to learn under him. When Terse was nineteen and seeking an apprenticeship, he had marched fearlessly into the workshop and given his assemblage over to the creator for examination. It had been a dragonfly the size of his hand, a daring balance—he thought—of clarity and delicate work that had required increasing levels of magnification to complete. He had toiled over it for years, both as an escape from his mother's sporadic rages and his father's indifference and as a curiosity and an enrichment of his days, something all his own.

Terse had endured the creator's judgment with his fists tight at his sides, his knuckles groaning.

Then, he had failed.

After his predecessor finished detailing every improvement he would need to make, Terse had gathered up his assemblage and headed for the door. Only the creator's grip on his arm had stopped him. He said he would give Terse another chance because he showed such promise. Terse hadn't known when, if ever, another opportunity like this would present itself, so he had acquiesced.

The creator had worked with him through supper and into

the night, pulling tools and jars from his shelves, talking Terse through each step, occasionally taking over and showing him proper technique . . .

In the morning, Terse had slid off his cot and brought a lamp over to the workbench. While his new teacher snored, he stroked the dragonfly, fingertips thrumming with pain from the modified abdomen, which was now covered in needles. As he sucked the blood from his fingertips, he was torn between hating the original assemblage for all its failings and hating this one for not being the original.

He would never be sure which loathing had driven him to do it, but he had taken up the toolkit and swiftly reduced the insect to its eighty-seven individual pieces.

He was better for having done it, he knew. He'd been able to weather these years of thankless creation because that day, he had armored himself against caring too much for any one assemblage.

Cinereous reached for the hare-hound, but her hand hovered in the air above one hind leg, as if she was afraid to touch it. "Is there another way?"

"No. You will disassemble it as completely as you're able, or you fail. I want to see the gears and bones and coiled wires all laid out. The organs, arranged as they were inside the barrel."

He understood why there were tears in her eyes. She had probably spent seasons saving for the metals, months gathering the sunlight, weeks working the wire; and she had shown patience in waiting until fresh carcasses presented themselves. But she needed spark—his spark—or her assemblage would never be more than parts.

After long seconds, she pulled the toolkit to her side of the bench and selected a screwdriver.

She set about it tentatively at first, unscrewing the vertebrae from the copper plate at the top of the barrel as slowly as she could, as if she hoped he would take pity and say, "Enough." When that didn't happen, she shrugged off her knapsack and dropped it to the floor. She rolled her shoulders, and her movements became brisk and practiced.

Now, the head. Next, the ears. Then, the barrel opened and the organs removed, one by one, six in total, alternating between rabbit's and dog's, starting with the rabbit's chestnut-sized brain and ending with a section of the dog's small intestine, looped around and threaded through itself. The braid was simple, but Terse would never have thought of doing something like that. Surprising him with her thoroughness, she started unbraiding it. He had to fight the urge to stay her hand so he could take a closer look.

When she came to the wirework on the dog's bones, though, she froze with the pliers gripped tight in her hands. He waited, watching. He listened to the pattering of wood against glass as the frog paced in its vivarium.

She looked up, the components of her assemblage arrayed before her, lit with sunlight, and reflected in her eyes. "I'm sorry, I can't."

Is the aspirant teachable?

Terse felt a heaviness in his chest, a tightness. "Are you sure?"

"I can't . . ." It was hardly a whisper.

He shook his head. "That's disappointing."

He turned his back on her to retrieve his pipe. From its vivarium, the frog watched him with curious, pale-gray eyes. Its creator—a man old enough to be Terse's son—had shown up a few years ago, an hour after sunrise, looking embarrassed about the state of his clothes after his trek through the woods. The man had been fearless in his innovations and malleable but lacking in technical skills. His apprenticeship lasted two days before it was clear he couldn't meet Terse's standards.

This young woman was similarly gifted with imagination, and she was technically proficient; but if she wouldn't follow all his instructions now, when he had the greater knowledge and the spark, when would she ever?

Her ideas were useful to him, though. He thought of her journal, likely full of complex chimeras with exquisite metalwork and braided entrails—he might even try his own twist on the rough-textured sockets because, upon reflection, he thought the assemblage might see the world differently but in a good way. Terse could almost feel himself opening the letters of admiration for his newest work, could almost hear the rain of hard coins putting meat and metal on his tables.

He clenched his pipe between his teeth. He touched a match to one of the lamps, turning down the wick to give his eyes a rest. He lit his pipe and inhaled deeply. Like his tendency to keep the lights low, Terse had inherited his smoking habit from his predecessor.

He swung around to face the young woman, but he hesitated

when his eyes met hers. Then he glanced at her bag under the workbench, sagging against an iron leg with the weight of her designs . . . and he exhaled a cloud of bitter yellow.

She couldn't know that he was primarily smoking faren, a leaf that soothed his myriad aches. Couldn't know that its telltale stark-white smoke was cloaked by a pinch of golden esh and its damp woody scent made bearable with lavender. Couldn't know he'd built up such a tolerance that he was using six times the recommended potency. Regardless, she backed away. Clever, but too late.

She dropped the pliers and covered her mouth through the first few bone-rattling coughs. He blew a second mouthful in her direction, and she cast her hand out, grabbing for the table but finding no purchase on the oiled wood.

Her hand knocked the rabbit's skull to the floor, and it rolled under a shelf.

She swayed . . . stumbled to the door . . . viscera-slick fingers groping for the handle.

She collapsed.

Terse stood over her and was reminded of his dragonfly. Her tunic gleamed in stray light from the kitchen window, and her arms were splayed like gnarled wings. She was so still that he knelt to check that she was breathing.

The pipe hung cold from Terse's lips, neglected while he secured Cinereous to the back of a horselike assemblage. It wasn't clever—its brain tissue had been needed for another project—but its legs were made of steel, and its daily grazing led it to the outskirts of the woods, where the young woman could be dumped and easily found. By the time night coalesced, her breathing had recovered, and Terse allowed the assemblage and its load to disappear into the trees.

He finally unclenched his jaw enough to pull the pipe from it. She would wake by morning. She would wake. True, she wouldn't remember her last three or four days, and she would be missing her pack—that had been unavoidable—but if she was as determined as she seemed, she would sketch more designs and build another assemblage. Maybe she would come seeking an apprenticeship again, when she was ready, though now he didn't think he could take her in. As soon as he was inside, he was drawn to the disassembled hare-hound. Each bone and organ and wire glowed with its own light. He got gingerly to his knees to retrieve the rabbit's skull from under the shelf and pick up the pliers she'd dropped, meaning to set them on the workbench. Instead, he began reassembling pieces with the apprentice kit he'd lent her. The tools fit oddly in his hands.

He worked all night, like he had when he was young: in a fury, as if stopping would mean death. He did have to stop eventually, for tea to stay awake and faren to soothe his back, but he rushed back to his workbench afterward, the pipe still fresh on his lips, and in the haze of smoke and creation, he didn't have to think about what he'd done, who he'd become.

When the sun was on the horizon, the hare-hound was as complete as it could be. Terse dusted the assemblage with viridian powder and waited.

With his hand heavy on the barrel of its body, he felt when it spasmed to life. Spark flashed in its eyes, and instead of the usual green, the coarse reliquary petals made the sockets hum with an eerie underwater light.

It was singular and exquisite, and he fought the impulse to crush its skull to prove that he could.

ANN LECKIE

The Long Game

FROM *The Far Reaches*

SCIENCE FICTION

Who put you in charge?

Someone has to make the plans. Someone has to tell people what to do. Why shouldn't that be me?

It makes sense. I'm the biggest. Look at you, little thing, quivering, the tentacles by your mouth trembling. Even the eggs tucked into the bases of the radioles tufted here and there on your body are shivering. You're afraid of me.

And you should be.

I'm bigger than anybody else I've ever met. Well, except the humans, but, I mean, *humans*. They're not exactly people, right? I don't know what they are. But they mostly don't get involved in that everyday stuff, like digging burrows or fetching water.

Which really isn't fair, when you think about it. Humans are just about *made* for carrying things and digging; they're all stiff and they only bend at corners. They have cold, stiff containers for carrying all sorts of things with their stiff, cornered not-tentacles. *People* have to hold a stick or a right-shaped stone in a couple of tentacles and scrape at the dirt, and if it's too dry, you take a plant membrane to the river and get a little bit of water and go back and forth and back and forth. You don't get very far if you're working by yourself, and some of the time a monster comes up out of the river and tries to eat you.

If someone planned it, though . . . if someone planned a big thing and then made people do parts of it, everyone working all at once, you could get a lot done. Like, if you had two or three people to dig at the same time, and another half dozen to carry water, and more to shove the babies out of the way, you could dig a channel from the river and make a nice, wide muddy space that would always be wet, with no monsters.

And after that you'd still need someone to be in charge. Someone to tell some people to keep the babies from getting underfoot, and someone to drag old sick people away from the colony before they cause trouble or die somewhere inconvenient.

And I'm the biggest. It should be me.

I did it! We have a nice wet place now, with no monsters. We have a special place for growing algae and people to make sure it grows well, and to distribute it. We have people who watch out for the babies so they don't get eaten as much.

And it used to be you couldn't go a day without some crazy old person waving their stiffening tentacles in your face, threatening you incoherently, or crying out as though their entire bodies hurt them. And they would curl up and die right where they were, and there would be dead bodies everywhere. But now I have them dragged off, away from our nice muddy place, as soon as they start wandering and raving.

"It's very impressive," said Leeyay, the human, when I showed them. They had folded themselves down to the ground so they didn't tower so high over me. It's the only thing I don't like about humans, the way they're so much bigger than I am. "A lot of people have thought of this, and even tried to make it happen, but I haven't seen anyone get quite this far."

I was disappointed not to be the first, the only. But I had still done more than anyone, ever! I couldn't resist a flourish of tentacles, a happy shiver that made my radioles flutter as if caught by a breeze. "I will go farther still," I declared. "I will go over the hills and kill the monsters that keep us from getting the rocks and plants that you like. And then we will bring you oh so many, and you will give us all sorts of things. Boxes and bricks and tools." Maybe even the secret to *making* those boxes and bricks and tools for ourselves, but I didn't say that.

"That would be nice," said Leeyay. And for a while we watched people coming and going, the harvesters harvesting, the baby minders herding the infants out of the way of the agents who made sure the people did the things they were supposed to do.

At length, Leeyay said, "It looks like you've thought of nearly everything. Tell me, Narr, what are your plans for making sure this continues after you're gone?"

"After I'm gone?" The question puzzled me extremely. "I'm not going anywhere, Leeyay. Even if I go over the hills, it won't be for that long; I can just leave my agents in charge until I come back."

It was difficult for me to read the reactions of humans, but Leeyay seemed taken aback. Or amused. Or sad. "Narr," they said, "I have been here for . . ." They paused, as if thinking. "For more than ten years." Ten years! That was a long, long time. "Only one person of all those I met, when I first came, is still alive. How old are you?"

How old was I? Why would I even know such a thing?

But Leeyay didn't wait for me to reply. "You're not quite a year old. You will live maybe another year. At the most."

"How can you know?" I asked. Indignant. "Maybe I'll live ten years. Maybe I'll live twenty!"

"You won't," said Leeyay. "Sometime in the next few months, eggs will sprout among your radioles. You'll live to see them hatched, but likely not long after."

"Then I won't hatch any eggs," I said. "I'll have my agents remove them when they sprout."

"It won't change anything," said Leeyay. "Believe me. Your species is just very short-lived. But you should be proud of what you've accomplished. And you should think about how to make sure that accomplishment doesn't disappear after you're gone."

Does everyone die? Will I die?

"Humans live a very long time," I said to Nk. They sat beside me on the mound I'd built that let me see all over the colony. The smooth, slick infants—green and blue and gray—squirmed under the eyes of their watchers. Diggers held tools in their tentacles, bodies rippling and radioles waving as they moved soil. Sunlight shifted and sparkled over the wet ground as the breeze moved plant membranes overhead.

"Humans aren't from here," said Nk. "I remember when I was a baby, crazy old what's their name said humans came out of the sky, a long time ago." Nk pondered a moment. "But they were old and crazy, so maybe it wasn't true."

Nk was my best friend. Almost, but not quite, as big as me. They helped me make sure that what I said would happen happened. "Leeyay told me something like that. They said that the stars are suns, and that those suns all have their own earths. That humans come from an earth that belongs to one of those suns."

"Pfft. That would mean the sun there"—Nk gestured to the sky with a tentacle—"is a star."

"Leeyay said it was."

"Pfft," said Nk again, more forcefully. "The stars are tiny, and there are swarms of them all over the sky. The sun is big and alone and warms the earth. The human is lying. Or crazy. It's old, you said, and old people are crazy."

"Who's the oldest person you know?" I asked. "And how old are they?"

Nk thought about that for a while, tentacles oddly still. Below, one of the algae cultivators broke away from the others and came slowly toward the center of the colony, a wide, flat space where people could assemble to receive instructions. They moved as though their body pained them, their tentacles held stiffly in front of them.

"I guess I don't know how old anyone is," Nk said. "Why would it matter?"

Below, the algae cultivator began to shiver and keen, in a way that gave me a strange unpleasant sensation in my denticles.

"Weak!" cried Nk, suddenly irritable. Their still-stiffly held tentacles twitched, an odd, disturbing movement that made me think of the old people I'd seen dying. Of the cultivator keening in the square below. "Weak! Weak!" They opened and closed their mouth, as though trying to speak.

"Nk," I exclaimed, alarmed. Terrified, as though my friend had threatened me, directly. "Nk, are you all right?"

Slowly the fit, whatever it was, seemed to subside. "Never," said Nk. "Not me. Never. I won't. Won't be weak." Nk flexed one tentacle, carefully. "I won't die."

I went and found Leeyay. They were sitting outside their house by the river. "Hello, Narr," they said when they saw me.

I said, "Why do people die?"

Their face did an odd thing. "That's a big question for a little mousy slug."

"What?"

"Never mind. Look, your question has any number of answers, some more complicated than others, and none of which would satisfy you. People die. That's all."

I thought about that. "Some people die because they've been too badly injured to heal. Some people die because monsters eat them. Some people just . . . get crazy and mean and have trouble talking and moving, and eventually they just curl up and scream for a long time and then they die." Nk, shouting *Weak! Weak!* Tentacles stiff and shaking. Unable to say anything more complicated, anything more *sane*, until the fit had passed.

Leeyay made a whooshing, breathy sound that I thought meant they were either frustrated or sad. "Yes," they agreed.

"So how do you not die?" I asked.

"Everyone dies," said Leeyay.

"No, that's not true. It can't be true. You said you've been alive ten years." Ten years was a long, long time.

"More than that," said Leeyay. "Actually."

"And you said you knew a person who had lived a long time. Who has been alive since you came here."

"Why are you asking me about this now?"

I thought I didn't know, thought I wouldn't have an answer, but I said, as though my speech-organs had a mind of their own, "Nk is sick. But they can't be sick! They can't be dying! They're big, almost as big as me, and they're stronger than I am. How can a person be so big and strong and just suddenly . . . just suddenly die? They can't die. They won't die. They can't." I felt the tremor of my emotion ripple through my body.

"I'm sorry, Narr," said Leeyay, gently. "I'm sorry to hear that your friend is dying."

"They're not!" I cried. "They can't be dying! They can't die!"

But after days—after weeks!—of raving, of wandering erratically, of moaning and screaming in pain, Nk died.

What do you think you're doing?

Well, I was trying to get into the container the humans use to go up into the sky. I almost managed it too. I found a crack and got a tentacle in pretty far and then hit an obstruction. It seemed kind of squishy, just the littlest bit, and I thought maybe I could chew through it, so I pulled my mouth in there too. It was a very tight space, but I did manage to get my denticles onto the slightly squishy stuff and started rasping. I mean, once you decide to find out why people die and how to stop it—really truly seriously decide—you can't let little things like some pain stop you. Otherwise you might just as well have stayed home and died.

I hurt that tentacle pretty badly, I think. At least, I can't see out of it anymore. And I can't get the taste of the slightly squishy stuff out of my mouth. I think some of it is stuck in my denticles. And the humans who found me closed me in a room where everything was hard and dry, and they didn't give me any water at all. None of them seemed to be able to talk like people, and I asked them and asked them to bring Leeyay so I could tell them to give me some water, but they didn't understand. And even if they did, it had taken me days and days to get here. By the time they got a message to Leeyay and Leeyay traveled here, I would be dead.

Except I wasn't. Leeyay got here after hardly any time at all. They brought a stiff container of water and poured it out so I could roll my dried-out self in it; wet had never felt so good.

And Leeyay was very angry with me. "Why didn't you just ask?"

"I don't ask," I retorted, shivering with the relief and pleasure of being wet again. "I make things happen."

Leeyay's face did some kind of twitching thing. "In your colony, I know you do. But not here. And definitely not up there." In the sky, they must have meant.

"If I'd asked, would you have said yes?"

"Possibly." They paused, made a face that I thought meant *sad* or maybe *amused*. "Probably not."

"Humans don't die," I said. "I need to find out how to make it so that people don't die."

Leeyay put the ends of their not-tentacles over their flat face, covering their mouth and eye-spots. They made that whooshing sound. "I told you, Narr. Humans die. You just haven't ever seen it."

"You said you've been alive for ten years."

"I've been alive for a lot longer than that. Humans live longer than your people. But we still die. All of us, no matter how long we live. Everyone dies, in the end."

"But why? How come no one has done anything about that?"

Leeyay said nothing.

"Ten years!" I said, after some thought. "That's a long time.

It might as well be forever." Leeyay made a noise I knew meant they thought something was amusing, though it was shorter and sharper than usual. Then I remembered that other conversation we had had. "You said there was one person who was still alive, from when you first came here. To earth. Why are *they* still alive and no one else?"

"I can't really answer in your language," they said. "I don't completely understand it myself, just the basics of it. It's not really my work assignment to understand it."

That was a curious thought, that Leeyay had a work assignment. Usually they just walked around or sat outside their big stiff house by the river. "What's your work assignment?"

"I'm a Leeyay," said Leeyay. "I'm here to look out for your interests. All of you." They waved a not-tentacle. "The people here."

"It's in our interest not to die," I pointed out.

"Look, Narr." Leeyay lowered themselves to sit on the smooth, hard, now-wet ground beside me. "I'm supposed to protect you from . . . from exploitation. But . . ." They made that windy, blowing sound again. "We got here, found you. And we found, not just life, but *intelligent* life. Not that the company cared about that—or even the government. But word got back to earth that not only was there intelligent life here, but it was squishy knee-high creatures in pretty colors that ate plants, and so it became a question of publicity."

Publicity. I puzzled over that. "A question of telling people things?"

"I'm here to make it look like the company cares what happens to you. All of you, not just you in particular. But the company doesn't really care."

"What's *the company?*"

"It's too much for me to explain," said Leeyay. "But what it means, in the end, is that I can really only do small things for you. The company might know how to make you all live longer. It probably does. But it won't do anything to help you make that happen unless it gets something out of it. And there's nothing the company would get out of it that it isn't already getting from you."

I didn't understand any of that. "The person who's still alive. I want to meet them. To ask them how they did it."

A long silence. Then: "I can probably do that much, but it won't do you any good. And if I send you there, you'll never come back here. Or even if you do, everyone you know will be dead. No one will know who you are. Go back to your colony. Build your algae pools, forage with your friends, and play with the infants. That's what you've got; that's all anyone gets in the end. Don't give that up for nothing. Because I promise you that's all you'd get out of it."

"I want to go," I insisted. Nk was dead. Who else mattered? And if I could come back with the knowledge of how to live so long, people would be happy to see me, whether they knew me or not.

"Well, you'll have to wait at least a week," said Leeyay. "You damaged the seal on the airlock, and they have to bring replacement parts."

A week was a long time. But I could wait.

Where am I?

I don't even remember getting into the container that goes up into the sky. I don't remember being in the sky at all. One moment I was on the earth talking to Leeyay and the next I was in the dark in a stiff container, one with edges and corners.

It was dry in the container, and everything was shaking. I could hear humans talking, but I didn't understand what they were saying. I wanted to call out, to tell them I was too dry, that my skin hurt, that I needed water. But I didn't like the sound of their voices. Only Leeyay had ever been able to talk to me, of all the humans I'd met, and only Leeyay had ever seemed to care how I was. *I'm here to make it look like the company cares what happens to you,* they had said. And they had seemed to care what happened to me. Maybe other humans just didn't. And if I was far away, up in the sky, and Leeyay was nowhere near, I was going to have to look out for myself.

The container I was in had cracks, like the sky box. I waited until the shaking stopped and there was quiet; then I tested a crack. Slowly, carefully, but it wasn't as tight as the sky container airlock, so I was able to get all the way out.

I had to cross a long, cold stretch of dry, gritty stone and squeeze through more cracks—practically holes, really—and finally I found myself looking up at the stars. Or a few stars, anyway. There weren't many, hardly any at all; glowing globs of light here and there overhead—not high enough to be stars—cast pools of luminescence over the scratchy stone. Up with the too-few stars was a big gray-and-white circle shining down at me, and the sky had never, ever looked like that at home on earth. And so that was how I knew that I'd really reached the place humans came from.

I made my way across the scratchy stone—it tasted bad, and it hurt my skin—until eventually I found actual dirt. The dirt tasted funny too, but it wasn't as bad as the taste of the stone that had scraped the bottom of my body raw, and there was some wetness there. There was even some very tiny algae, but it made me sick when I ate it.

The plants were strange—huge stretches of long, thin membranes sticking straight up. Other membranes were broader but strangely notched and serrated, sometimes surrounding a single stem holding up a bunch of bright-yellow growths that reminded me of radioles, though these were flatter.

And monsters. So many things with six or even eight legs scuttled around me, brandished stiff mouth parts at me, made noises I didn't understand. Some ran from me. One tried to bite me and I fled, the horrible thing chasing me until I fell, by great good luck, into a stream. The water tasted strange, and the monster wouldn't step into it.

I looked up. The plants here were enormous, and their membranes shivered and trembled with the breeze, but also with things moving around. Monsters chittered and screamed, and I didn't know what any of them were. Which ones would run from me, and which ones would try to bite me? What lived in the water here? I didn't think it was deep enough for monsters, but this wasn't home, wasn't a place where anything made any sense at all.

Where was I going? What had I hoped to do here?

There was nothing to do, now, but continue. To walk and walk until I found something. Someone who could speak language. Someplace even a little safe.

The monster that had chased me to the stream lost interest and wandered away. I didn't see anything else that obviously wanted to eat me, so I climbed out of the stream on the other side and kept going.

I crawled for days. I went slowly, moving as much as I could in the shade of the weird plant membranes, watching for monsters that were doing the same. I didn't eat any more of the horrible algae that had made me sick when I had first tasted it. There were other plants that seemed like they might have been good to eat—thick and green, growing shaded close to the moist ground—but I was wary now. At least the dirt was moist, and my skin, abraded by the gritty stone plateau I'd first crawled across, was beginning to heal.

Then all cover fell away, and there was only that thin, straight plant, packed close, but shorter, looking as though the tops had all been sliced off at the exact same height. And sitting among these membranes, to my immense, exhausted relief, was a person.

But they were a very strange person. Half my size—that wasn't unusual, really. But they were absolutely motionless, their tentacles too thick and too stiff, the eye-spots at their ends too bulbous and completely black and surrounded by a long, black fringe that made me think suddenly of the fringe that surrounded Leeyay's eye-spots. The oddly stiff person's skin was bright pink all over, and their radioles seemed more like the strange yellow plant growths I'd seen than like actual radioles, and they glittered in the sunlight. "Hello," I said. "I need help." But there was no answer, not a single twitch of movement in response.

And then a monster fell on me out of the sky, shrieking and squeaking and stabbing me with its hard, pointed mouth, grabbing and scratching me with its hard, pointed feet. I screamed and fought as it tore at my radioles. It shrieked louder as I wrapped one tentacle around its leg and tried to pull it off, to throw it away from me so I could flee. I was sure I was about to die, sure I would be eaten by this brown-and-orange flying monster, and the moment I realized that I was about to die, I thought, very clearly, *I hope I make it sick.*

But there were suddenly humans with me. One, the size of Leeyay, flapped its not-tentacles at the monster, which seemed to frighten it. It let go of me and flew away. The other, smaller than I'd ever seen any human, spoke incomprehensibly to me in a high voice and petted and petted me with its not-tentacles. Then it picked up the very strange, still person and shoved it into my side, and I realized that it was not a person at all but an assemblage of membranes and stones made to look like a person. It was too much. I wanted it away from me, but the small human seemed to think it was absolutely necessary that I hold it in my tentacles, and when I did that, the human stopped shoving it into me.

The larger human walked back and forth, making noises in a

way I would have thought expressed distress and frustration if it had been Leeyay. And then, stopping suddenly, it stooped and put its not-tentacles around me—tentatively, carefully—and lifted me gently off the ground.

How did you live so long?

"I know the answer," said the other person—the first person I'd seen in this strange, monster-filled place. "But it's going to be complicated to explain to you."

"You think I can't understand?" I asked. "Because I'm not stupid. I figured out how to make people build a place that would always be wet and free of monsters. I figured out how to grow algae on purpose in one place." Well, I hadn't exactly figured any of that out, but I had made it happen.

The humans seemed to always be in boxes. We were in a box now, with smooth, dry floors and smooth, hard containers for things. There was a shallow container of water on the floor, and the very old person sat in it. "I'm not saying you're stupid. You've hardly been alive a year, though. There are a lot of things you don't know yet."

"You don't seem like anything special yourself," I said, still stung. "You're so small, and you hardly have any radioles at all. Small and ugly. How does someone small and ugly get to live ten years?"

"Closer to twenty," they said. "And will you become even more angry if I tell you that smaller people are more likely to live longer?"

"That's ridiculous. Smaller people aren't as strong as bigger ones. You"—I poked a tentacle at them—"are smaller than anyone I've ever seen. I could kill you right now."

"Probably," they said equably. "But if you did, you'd never get your answer."

I paced around the room awhile. I wanted to leave, to go outside, but the thought of another sharp-mouthed monster made me uneasy. Not afraid, you understand. But I had been days recovering from that attack, and I didn't want to do it again. Entirely practical.

"Tell me," I said finally. "Tell me why you're still alive. Tell me why people die. Tell me how I can make it so *I* don't die."

"Everyone dies eventually. Humans live to be a hundred, a hundred and fifty years, but they all die in the end. Everything alive dies. Everything changes." I didn't know what to say to that, and the other person continued, "I'm called Nish. I was tiny even when I came out of the egg. I'm lucky I lived long enough to become an adult, because I might easily have been eaten or even just crushed by someone careless.

"All the people I'd hatched with grew patches of radioles all over, and those grew eggs, and those eggs hatched. I, you may have noticed, have a single small circle of radioles. Every now and then, while I was on earth, an egg would grow in them, and hatch, maybe once every couple of years or so, but the infants were always much bigger than I had been. Anyway, after a while all the people who were infants when I was, they got sick and died. But I never got sick.

"Then the humans came. It was a while before our Field Liaison noticed how different I was from everyone else. The Liaison we had mostly ignored us unless they wanted something from us."

"What?" I interjected. "Leeyay doesn't ignore us."

"Field Liaison is a thing someone does, not a person's name. Your Leeyay isn't the Liaison I dealt with."

I didn't understand that and would have to think about it. In the meantime, Nish continued, "Once they realized, the humans very much wanted to know how I lived so long when the rest of our people died so much younger. One day our Liaison just picked me up and put me in a box, and the next thing I knew, here I was."

"I don't understand," I said. "How does that answer my question?"

"I told you the answer would be long and complicated," Nish replied. "I'm not done with my answer yet. Now, since you are so very smart and have figured out so many important things, perhaps you have asked yourself why the humans came to earth, and why they stay there?"

I had never asked that question. The humans were there, that was all. They had come from the sky, everyone knew that, but what else was there to know?

"They are there on earth," Nish continued when I said nothing, "because there are things there that they want. Rocks. Plants. A place to build and control to suit themselves. They thought, the humans who came to earth, that they had found such a place, that they could do anything they wanted there, take anything they wanted, and no one here on the humans' world would care. But word reached here that there were *people* on our earth. At first no humans really cared, but it turns out, they think we're . . . I don't know how to say it. I know the human word for it, but not how to say it to you. They make models of us for their infants, and those infants clutch those models and carry them around and pretend they talk and do things."

I thought of the strange, sparkly not-person I'd seen, just before the sharp-mouthed monster had attacked me. The way the small human had pressed it on me. "What, was that an infant I met?"

"Did you meet one?"

I told Nish about my harrowing journey. About the weird plants and the strange, stiff pink not-person. The sharp-mouthed monster.

"A bird," said Nish. "You're lucky you didn't run into a dog. Even if the humans had come to help you, you might have died if a dog had gotten ahold of you. And, yes, that was an infant. So, you'll maybe understand when I tell you that a lot of humans who never will meet an actual person would be sad if a lot of us died, back on earth. The humans on earth don't want that to happen, because it would make things difficult for them. So they made the Field Liaisons, and whenever any human here asks how we're being treated, back on earth, they can say, *Oh, we have appointed dozens of Field Liaisons whose whole job is to look out for the interests of the people there and help us communicate with them.* The Liaisons don't even have to actually do anything, except make sure the humans get what they want out of us in a way that won't make humans here sad."

"What?" I couldn't get any of that to make sense in my mind. There weren't dozens of Leeyays; there was only one. "What do the humans want out of us?"

"Information. Among other things. And here's where things will get strange, for you."

"It's been pretty strange already!"

"Not *this* strange," said Nish. "Settle into the pool here, and listen. This will take a while."

Nish told me that everything alive, everything that made infants, that made copies of itself, contained instructions. Instructions for growing whatever thing it was. People contained instructions for growing people.

The eggs that grew among people's radioles? Grew there because everyone's radioles gave off a sort of dust that got caught in other people's radioles. That dust carried the instructions of the person it had come from, and it mixed together with the instructions of the other people whose dust had caught in the radioles, and the person the dust had landed on. And that made a *new* set of instructions for growing a new person.

Humans had known of these instructions before they ever came to earth and had looked at our instructions as soon as they had found us. And they had found something curious.

"We didn't always make infants this way. A long, long time ago a person used to only get instructions from two people, who had to be touching each other to exchange dust, and then they might each grow one or two eggs, and this might happen every year or so. But somewhere there was a change in the instructions, and the people with the change could make dozens of eggs in a year, and those eggs could have instructions from any number of people, not just two. Those people had lots more babies, and so eventually they outnumbered the people who made eggs the old way. But that change came along with another consequence—people who had that set of instructions would all die horribly, very young. Somehow the two things are connected, in our instructions, in a way that humans don't know how to separate. Or, to be honest, it might be that they *could* figure out how to separate those things, but they mostly don't care."

"So . . ." I stopped. I had to think about this. So much of it didn't make any sense to me at all. "So, can't the humans just . . . just change my instructions? I don't really care about eggs. I just don't want to die."

"Maybe," said Nish. "I think they probably can. But the humans will only give you something like that if you give them something in return."

What are you going to do now?

"I don't know what to do," I said to Nish. "I don't want to die; I want to live as long as I can. But I don't like the humans telling me what to do. *I'm* the one who tells people what to do!"

It didn't help that I felt helpless here, spending whole days with only Nish to talk to and the occasional human. The human who had talked to me the most—the chief of all the Field Liaisons, they had claimed—had spoken to me as though I were stupid. I didn't like that either. Nish had suggested that it was only that this Field Liaison couldn't speak people's language very well, and maybe that was the case, but I still had come away from every meeting feeling insulted.

"And besides," I continued, "I don't like that the humans think we're *cute*." I had talked with enough humans now to sort of understand that word. "You said that humans here would be sad if anything happened to us, but they don't think we're people. They think we're things to play with. The humans on earth could kill all of us and the humans here might hardly even notice; they'd still have their sparkly, fringe-eyed, stiff not-people to give their infants."

"Ah," replied Nish. "So you're not just a big bully. You actually think about things." I was angry at that, but before I could say anything, Nish asked, "Why do people do what you tell them?"

That was a ridiculous question. "Because I'm bigger. Because I have other big people to help me *make* them do what I tell them." But as I said that, Nish's *you're not just a big bully* echoed in my mind uncomfortably.

Nish said, "But they could all just leave. I'm sure some people do. Or if enough people got together and decided they didn't like you bossing them around, they could stop you. They may not *like* being told what to do, but they're getting a steady supply of food and a safe place for the infants. In the end, they're doing what you tell them because they think they're getting something they want out of it."

"Well, of course they are," I retorted. "Why do you think I bother to begin with? I make things better for everyone in the colony."

"Well, not everyone," Nish said. "Not for the people who won't do what you tell them. Not for the people who have a different idea of what's good. And certainly not for the people who you decide have to work harder or go hungry or even die just to make things"—Nish waved a tentacle sarcastically—"*better for everyone.* But let's not argue about those details. You're facing a choice. Live longer—twenty years, thirty, maybe even forty—and serve the humans so that things can be *better for everyone*, which will really be better for the humans and only *incidentally* better for people. Or you can die here, painfully, in a few months."

I said nothing. I still could find no way through this. Or, more honestly, I could only see one way through it, knew I would take it, but hated the bargain I knew I would have to make.

"When you're small," said Nish, after a moment's silence, "you survive by being patient, and clever. You can't make big things happen all at once, so you do what little things you can. It's not unlike seeing you want a pond and thinking of all the little steps you need to build that pond, and then taking those steps, one by one. Of course, the more steps, the harder it is to accomplish big things like this, when you don't live long."

"What does that have to do with me?"

"The humans have a thing they call *the long game*. Most humans, just like people, are usually just thinking of today. What can they eat today? How can they stay safe today? But then sometimes they're thinking way ahead, thinking of things too big for them to do here and now. It's how they've done things like go into the sky or read the instructions of life."

"That's easy when you live a hundred years!"

"Not so easy," said Nish. "And some human long games go much longer than a hundred years. They can communicate with humans not hatched yet, and humans now can understand the thoughts and intentions of humans long dead, because of passing on stories. And writing."

"You mean like tally marks," I said, after some consideration. "And day counting."

"Like that, yes, but more complicated."

I had to think about that for a long time. Then I asked, "What if *I* found out how to change the instructions? What if I could find out how to make it so people could live twenty years? Then we wouldn't have to wait for humans to give that to us. We wouldn't have to do what they say to get it." What if the humans had to deal with us as *people* and not as *toys*? That would take careful thought and planning. I might not be able to do it all by myself. I might have to do some of it and leave the rest to some other person, years from now. "What if *I* did a *long game*?"

"Those are good questions," said Nish approvingly.

How did you talk them into letting you come back here?

It took some work. I talked and talked. I told the Chief Field Liaison all about how much easier it would be for the humans if I could have time to really build things up, make it so we didn't have to work quite so hard just to live. People would be so grateful to the humans for making life better. People could spend more time fetching rocks and plants. And it would be so much easier for the humans to have someone like me—grateful to them, eager to set their plans in motion, good at making sure people did what the humans wanted—in charge, back home on earth. Easier if I lived a long time so they wouldn't have to worry about whoever new might come up with their own ideas, their own plans, and even if the next person was happy to do what the humans wanted, that would only be for a little while, and then they would die and the humans would have to start over.

But if they helped me live longer. If they sent me home. Yes. I would be so grateful. I would do what the humans wanted. I would make things so easy for the humans, on earth.

Eventually they listened. And here I am, back home, strong and healthy, though I should have died months ago. I'll live as long as Nish has. If I'm careful, if I don't let something else kill me.

"Look at all the things I built," I said to Leeyay. They seemed a little sad. Having spent more time with humans now, I could make several guesses as to why, and I knew now that they were a better Field Liaison than most—but in the end I couldn't trust them, not really. I knew that the list of *something else* that might kill me included humans, if they thought I wasn't doing what they wanted me to do. "I was gone for so long, everyone who knew me is dead, just like you said would happen. But the algae fields and the pond are still here; people still keep things going the way I set them up."

"That's true," said Leeyay.

"Now that I have help from the humans," I said, "I'm going to make the pond bigger and grow more algae. And we'll find those plants you like and grow those too. That will make you happy, won't it?"

"Yes," said Leeyay sadly.

I didn't tell them about the school I was planning. I would make sure the infants learned tally marks, and we would begin to make more complicated marks, like the humans used, but *ours*. And I would begin to teach the infants about the instructions we all grew by. As long as I will live—maybe forty years!—I will never see the outcome of this plan. Maybe it won't happen exactly the way I want it to. But I can start it now, and the people who come after me can build more.

"Narr," said Leeyay, "I haven't told anyone this yet, but I've decided I'm going back home. I don't think I'm cut out for this job. It's . . . I just can't do this."

"Don't be sad, Leeyay," I said. "Look at the channel from the river! Look at our wonderful pond! Our field of algae! All the work we did and how long it's lasted!"

Someone has to make the plans. Someone has to tell people what to do. Why shouldn't that be me?

John Hollowback and the Witch

FROM *Book of Witches*

FANTASY

THE WITCH HAD no name that he knew. John Hollowback found her house at the far end of a fallow field, browning with the fall: a small cottage of wattle and daub, with a thatched roof and a smoking chimney, nestled up against a forest of birch, poplar, and pine. He could see a well nearby, a tidy garden, and a store of seasoned wood stacked against the eastern wall.

It was a pretty place. He thought perhaps he was mistaken; it did not look like the home of a witch. Still, he walked to the door and knocked three times.

The woman who answered was most certainly a witch.

Her hair was dark, greasy, wisped in gray, and falling messily out of a loose topknot; her skin was sun-browned and crinkled around her eyes, which were a strange, flashing blue. She did not look very old but was hideous enough to be recognizable as one who practiced magic.

"What do you want?" Her voice was low, but clear.

"I want a whole back, instead of a hole in my back," he said, firmly.

She squinted at him, and gestured for him to turn around, poking at him curiously while he did.

Though he walked without a stoop or limp, John had a hollow in his back. Where spine and sinew were meant to make a bold line from neck to tailbone, they vanished instead into an oval cavity the size of a serving plate, lined with pale, soft skin.

"I used to be called John Turner," he said, bitterly. "Now folk call me Hollowback, like an old tree. Owls could nest in me."

She placed her hands against his shoulder blades, knocking against them like a door. She rapped her knuckles down his back until they met wood, and the sound rang out hollow indeed. He winced.

"I made myself a board to cover the hole. I daren't be alone with women—"

"You're alone with me," she observed.

"You know what I mean. I have seen doctors, and they can do nothing. Can you?"

She pulled her hands back, folded her arms, and considered him.

"Perhaps," she said. "Come in."

She led him toward the hearth and sat him down; he turned his back to her, lifted his shirt, and unfastened the leather bracers holding a thin sheet of wood against his hollow like a lid. He shivered as she felt around its edges, hissed when her fingers brushed the tender flesh within.

"I see," she murmured. "I see. You're missing a pound of flesh. Who did you cross?"

His shoulders slumped beneath her hands. "No one. I have no debts, and some money put by. A year ago, I was to propose to my love; a year and a day ago I woke with a hollow in my back, and this frightened her away, and she never spoke to me again."

"Mm." She withdrew her hands. "A pity—it is difficult to restore that which has been taken by another."

"Then you cannot help me?"

"I did not say that." She tapped a thoughtful rhythm against his back. "But it will take some time. You will have to stay here for the duration. What have you brought with you?"

He lifted the flap of his bag and pulled out a leather-bound book.

"I thought you might value this, and take it as payment," he said, offering it to her. She raised a thick eyebrow, picked it up and thumbed through it.

"It's blank," she said, looking at him curiously.

"It's magic," he said, "I think. Anything I try to write in it vanishes. I have no use for it, but I thought, perhaps, someone with your craft—"

"What else have you brought?" she asked, snapping the book shut and tossing it aside. John flushed, swallowed, and poured out the rest of his bag.

He had packed sensibly: a change of clothing, some food, some money, along with his tools. But from among his belongings the witch singled out an apple, a comb, and a bit of string. John blinked; he had not packed them.

"These," she said, "will be of some use. Tomorrow we'll begin tending to your back. You are a woodworker, I see?"

John nodded.

"I will take my payment in trade, then. Go to sleep."

The witch sat in her garden, puffing on her pipe, while John slept. He didn't remember her; that much was clear. What he *did* remember remained to be seen.

She clicked her tongue in the language of bats until one swooped merrily around her head; she whispered with it a while, then watched as the bat wheeled away into the velvet dark.

John woke to the witch shaking him gruffly by the shoulder.

"We begin today," she said. "You'll do chores while it's light; at night, we will work together on your back. Is this fair by you?"

"Yes," he said, straightening, "yes, of course."

"Good. You must understand that once we begin this process, it will be difficult to stop. It is as though you are carrying a knife stuck in your back; if I pull it out, a dangerous gushing will result, and if you do not let me complete my work, it will go badly for you. I say this because it will be painful, and I will not hurt you without your consent. Do you understand?"

John felt suddenly unsure. "It will hurt?"

"Most likely. Great changes often do."

"Only, I don't remember it hurting when it happened."

The witch only stared at him, waiting.

John chewed his lip, then nodded. "And I only need to do chores? You don't want the book, or . . . a promise, of . . ." He swallowed what might be an insulting assumption. ". . . Some future thing?"

The witch looked more pitying than contemptuous. She reached up to clap him on the shoulder.

"John Hollowback," she said, "you have absolutely nothing I could possibly want."

On that first day, John swept the witch's floors, scoured her pots, drew water from her well, and scouted a space outdoors to set up a spring-pole lathe. She'd said she expected trade, but nothing else; he wanted to be prepared. By the time the witch called him in, he had most of it done, and had worked up an honest sweat; she'd set out a robust dinner for the two of them, bread and cheese and a thick vegetable stew. They ate in silence—not quite companionable, but not awkward either.

Once they'd finished, John cleared the table and washed up; the witch, meanwhile, set the apple on the table, and waited for him to join her.

"Take off your shirt," she said, "and your board, and lie down on your belly."

He did as he was told, if reluctantly; it was not easy to show his naked back. He found he was less ashamed about it with the witch, though; perhaps because she wore her own ugliness so brazenly, he didn't so much mind his own. Wherever he came face-to-face with people, they found him handsome: He was, after all, tall, with straight teeth and a small nose, high cheekbones and honeyed hair. But when he turned his back, he knew people shuddered at the shape of him, whispered about the odd way his shirt hung off his shoulders, a strange sag at his belt.

He propped his chin up on his folded arms and gazed into the dimming embers of the fire while the witch moved around behind him.

"I'm going to make a scrying bowl of your hollow," she said, "by painting it black, and filling it with water. While I do this, I want you to tell me the story of this apple."

She held it out to him. He frowned.

"It's just an apple. I must've packed it for a snack and forgotten about it."

"It spoke to me," she said, simply, "from among your things. You seem to be missing more than flesh, John Hollowback—there are memories you carry outside your body, and I don't think you'll be whole again until you've recalled them." She sat down next to him on a low stool, swirling a paint brush through a pungent stone jar, and began applying its contents to his back.

He hissed—it was cold—then wrinkled his nose, annoyed. "That's nonsense. I'll grant I don't remember my hollowing, but I've a decent memory in general, and—"

"Eat it."

He blinked. "What?"

"Eat the apple. Take a bite."

He was rather full from dinner, but he shrugged his shoulders, parted his lips, lifted it to his mouth—and stopped, suddenly wracked with nausea. He gasped, sick-drool pooling around his tongue, and turned away from it, panting—but could not drop it, though he felt it growing warm in his hand, echoing something thumping hard in his chest.

"You can't eat it," said the witch, her voice rougher than he would have liked, "any more than you can eat your arm. But you can tell me the story of it." She laid another long, thick line down the bowl of his back while he caught his breath.

John turned the apple over in his hands. It was, he thought, a lovely specimen, red and round, its stem flying a single leaf like a flag; it looked just picked, carried the scent of the orchard with it, the fizzy smell of ferment rising up from fruit crushed underfoot. Nothing in his bag had broken or bruised its surface; he owned as that was odd. But a story? The story of the apple was that it was a mystery, though the more he looked at it, the more he cupped it in his hands, the more he felt an unaccountable tenderness welling up in him.

He flinched as the witch poured a pitcher of cool water into his back, exhaled as she stirred her finger through it.

"I see," she murmured, "a great many trees, and among them a wagon, brightly colored. There are women picking apples, but the wagon . . ."

"Oh!" said John, suddenly. "Of course, yes—that was when I first met her. Lydia, my—" He grimaced. "She was working, bringing in the fruit, and she was singing . . ."

The witch said nothing, but slowed her stirring. John found himself tugging at the thread of memory—perhaps this was what she meant, by telling the story? The apple reminded him of something, and he shared it? He groped his way to a better beginning.

"I was traveling with a troupe of players—not a player myself, of course, but I'd make their sets, mend the boards they trod, and they gave me a share of the take. William and Janet, they were married, and Brigid, she wasn't their daughter but may as well have been. We traveled in a caravan that was both advertisement and stage—or, well, they all did, being a family. I usually followed after them on a mule, stopping in towns to ply my own trade and sleep in a bed before catching them up at the next stop; more comfortable for everyone that way, the wagon was only so big.

"Well, we were setting up in this orchard with the farmer's permission, and this girl was up a ladder. She was fine enough to look at, but her voice was something else. She was singing, leading the other workers in a song, call and response, and it was like hearing a lark among crows. I stopped setting up, stopped everything just to listen to her. And when the song was done, I strode up to her and said as how I'd loved her singing, and her voice was a gift, and why was she picking fruit when she could be traveling the country and sharing out the gold of her music? And she blushed and smiled and plucked an apple from a branch near her cheek and held it out to me, and said that was very kind, but she was only a country lass. But we got to talking, and I brought the players out to meet her, and she watched our show. And that did it. She was off with us the next morning."

The water in his back felt warm, now, not unpleasantly.

"Give me the apple, John," said the witch, quietly; she coaxed it from his hand—he found it hard to release—and then rolled it around the edge of his hollow. A ringing rose in his ears, a pain, a sharp slicing of grief—and then water sloshed over the edge of his hollow and he cried out, spun quickly to face her, scuttling back and away on his palms and making a mess of the floor.

The witch looked at him coolly.

"There. That's one." She looked from him to the puddle on the floor, and stood up slowly. "Enough for now, I think. Mop that up. Don't bother putting your board on tomorrow—it won't fit. Best give your back a little room to breathe."

She walked out to the garden, leaving John gasping, reaching around to touch the familiar contours of his hollow, and finding, instead, an inch more solid back than he'd had before.

The next morning, John woke late; the witch had let him sleep in. He was glad of it: He felt sore and stiff throughout his body, as if he'd spent a long night drinking. He stretched, and scratched, and reached cautiously toward his hollow. His shoulders slumped in relief when he found his new flesh still in place. He looked around for a mirror, and saw one hanging on the wall; steeling himself against the possibility that it might do him some mischief, he approached it and tried to catch a glimpse of his back in it.

The hollow was certainly smaller—but a thin black ring marked its previous circumference. He frowned. Perhaps it would fade in time.

He could hear the witch puttering out in the garden, and dragged himself to the bread and cheese she'd left on the table, next to the leather-bound book she'd refused from him as payment. Or had she accepted it? She was an odd one; she spoke plainly, but John felt there was much she didn't say.

As he munched his breakfast, he decided there was no harm in opening the book.

Then he choked.

The first few pages had writing on them. Not just any writing; the story he'd told the witch last night.

Well, he thought, that made sense; who better than a witch to write in a magic book? Perhaps that had always been its purpose—to be a witch's grimoire, inscribed with spells.

Funny that she'd write his own story in it. Odd, too, to see his story laid out by another, in writing. It seemed, at a glance, much longer than his own telling.

He skimmed over the memory of apples and felt, again, the pang of losing Lydia, the sting of betrayal, the anger and shame of it. There had been so much promise at first, and then, at the end, no hint of anything amiss until she was gone.

"Good, you're awake," said the witch, standing in the doorway, tugging off her gardening gloves. John startled, slammed the book shut, and turned to her equal parts furtive, guilty, and defiant.

She did not seem to notice. "The day's getting away from us. Do you need me to make you a list, or can you get on all right just looking around at what needs doing?"

She made him a list, in the end, and once he'd chopped wood and hauled water to her satisfaction, he turned back to finishing his lathe.

He thought he might make the witch a bowl, as a small joke, since she'd made one of him. He found a likely birch log, split it in half, and began chipping out a rough shape. He'd just gotten as far as fitting it on to the lathe when the witch came out to see him, and he noticed the hour had gone late and golden around him.

The witch looked at the lathe with frank curiosity. "I see you've not been idle."

John's hollow back straightened somewhat. He took pride in his work.

She stepped around to his side. "Would you show me? Or is it a trade secret?"

John demonstrated the mechanism: how the treadle tugged the pole down and spun the wood to be shaped in one direction, then the other as it released. "You only cut on the downstroke," he said, "slowly, carefully. Then it springs back up—it's called reciprocating action—and you push down again, until it takes the shape you want."

"Fascinating," she said, quietly. "Very clever. Does the wood ever break, or crack?"

"Not if it's sufficiently green, seen to by a steady hand."

"I see," she said. "And is this light enough to work by?"

"No," he admitted. "I should leave off for tonight."

"Wise. And so shall I—I don't think you're entirely recovered from yesterday. Come and have something to eat."

That evening, their meal together was more genial; the witch asked about his back, whether he felt any pain after their ritual.

"No," he said, "but there's a black ring—"

She shrugged. "Sutures leave scars. It's all part of the process. I can't undo what happened to you; I can only help mend it."

She asked, then, about his memories of traveling on the road.

It had been a bright and venturesome time; they'd performed in villages and taverns, but also led the occasional masque or revelry in a grand country hall. Their summers they spent on the road; in winter they sought the shelter of familiar fields, farmers and sometimes gentry glad of the entertainment during long, cold nights.

It was while holed up together that they came to know each other best, he and Lydia. Her arrival had expanded the group's repertoire: Where before they'd performed scraps of entertaining miscellanies, told stories, made use of John's modest skills in puppetry, now they had a full complement of players, though it meant Brigid usually took on trouser roles to play a young lover opposite Lydia's ingenue, or else a puckish troublemaker needling William and Janet's grumpier elder roles.

But Lydia was indisputably the star.

"Did you never perform with them?" asked the witch, pouring them both a fragrant tea after they'd eaten.

"I did before, if they needed someone to be a prop, or a mark, or to move a puppet. I'm no actor, I know that—hard not to when you travel with those who have the gift. But once they had Lydia, it was better to keep to making and mending. She cast a long shadow."

"Were you jealous?" she asked, with a frankness that felt like a slap.

"No," he said, staring at her. She held his gaze. Eventually he looked away. "No. But Brigid was."

The witch chuckled, and John frowned. But she stood and asked him to tidy up after their meal, putting an end to the matter, then walked out into the garden. He was asleep before she returned.

The next morning John woke early, but not earlier than the witch, and found a bowl of porridge laid out for him as well as some late plums. The leather-bound book was there too.

He watched it while he ate. He looked out toward the garden, where the witch likely was.

He pulled the book toward him, opened it, and read.

Lydia picked apples and sang as she worked; she loved hearing her voice strong and high, feeling her call pull in a chorus of responses, as if she cast a net to catch her fellows' breath. But when she stopped, she felt eyes on her, and turned to see a tall, spindly young man staring.

"That's a terrible ladder," he said. "It's dangerous, you could fall. Let me fix it."

Lydia laughed, for the ladder had borne her weight without wobbling all season, but she hopped down and let him have his way. As he shook his head and set about tightening the rungs, he said, "You have the most beautiful voice I've ever heard. And I've heard plenty. I'm John. What's your name?"

"Lydia," she said, smiling. "Thank you, that's kind."

"No, it's just true."

She asked if he was with the caravan of players, and he said he was. Her eyes shone, and she said she was looking forward to the show, that she loved the music and stories; he paused in his work and said he could take her to meet the players, if she wanted.

She did want, very much.

She met William, Janet, and Brigid in short order; John introduced her as the voice of the orchard, and she rolled her eyes, but said she did love to sing. Brigid's eyes caught hers, and she asked about her favorite songs, and they fell to talking like they'd known each other for years but had not seen each other for more, familiar and starved for each other, while William and Janet exchanged fond looks and John sat silent and looked at everyone apart from himself.

John tasted copper before realizing he'd bitten through his lip. He shut the book, then opened it, fingers trembling. Then he shut it again.

How dare the witch? He'd come to her with his hollow, his history, and she had made of it—whatever this was, a fanciful embroidery, some kind of cruel taunt.

Had he even said he fixed the ladder? He recalled, now, that he'd tightened the rungs, but it hadn't seemed worth mentioning. Was that really the first thing he'd said to Lydia?

He shoved his porridge aside and stormed out to the lathe.

The work soon soothed him. His world narrowed in focus to angles and pressure and speed, the beauty of wood smoothed and shaped, every rough part sheared off into a tangle of delicate blonde curls. By the time the witch came out to find him, the finished bowl gleamed.

"Here," said John, stiffly. "Trade."

The witch raised her eyebrows at him, and took the proffered bowl, turning it in her hands. "It's lovely. Well done."

John flushed, but looked away. The witch eyed him, then said, lightly, "I know just what to do with it. Come with me."

He followed her into her garden, where she wandered, stooped, cut lettuces and herbs with a short sharp knife. Whatever she cut, she placed in the bowl, until it was heaped with brilliant, tender greenery.

"Walk with me, John," she said. "We'll not be long."

"Where are we going?"

"To visit a neighbor. Now, what's the matter?"

He scowled. "Nothing."

"It's the wrong season for lemons," she said, "but you look like you've been feasting on little else. And you didn't clean up after breakfast; that porridge'll be crusted to its bowl like a barnacle."

He rolled his eyes. "Pardon me for having made you a better one."

The witch stopped walking and looked up at him. Her eyes flashed—literally, magically—and he looked away, fuming.

"John Hollowback," she said, calmly, "you'll keep a civil tongue in your head when you speak to me, or else you'll keep a home in your back for owls. Is that understood?"

He chewed his lip. "Yes."

"We made a bargain, and I have asked very little of you. Tell me what's wrong or keep your own counsel, but do not think to insult me or my crockery with your backhanded foolishness while accepting my hospitality. Shame on you."

She walked on, and reluctantly, he followed.

Eventually they came to a cottage, and were warmly received by the couple inside: a woman, heavily pregnant, and her husband beaming solicitously alongside her.

"I brought these for the cravings," said the witch, pressing the bowl into the woman's hands. "Make a salad of them, they'll be good for you." She looked to John, and smiled. "John here made the bowl."

John stood awkwardly by while the couple gushed their thanks; they pressed a small loaf and a jar of bramble jam on them, which the witch handed John to carry. Mercifully she declined their offer of dinner. They began their walk back in silence.

"I made that bowl for you," said John, who wanted to be angry, but was mostly tired. The witch shrugged.

"And I traded it for bread and jam. I did say I'd take my payment in trade." She looked at him, levelly. "And that I wanted nothing from you. I always mean what I say, John."

"I thought," said John, who wanted to be vicious, but wasn't up to the task, "that witches hated giving up their greens. That they punished people for taking from their gardens. We did a whole show about it once."

She chuckled. "And why not? Everyone wants to see a witch punish someone for stealing from her. A witch is a kind of justice in the world. It makes for a fine story. No one wants to admit the truth, for all it stares them plainly in the face."

"What's that?"

"Steal from a woman long enough, and a witch is what she'll become."

They'd reached the cottage. John drew a deep breath.

"I'm sorry," he said, grudgingly. "For being rude. But I saw what you'd written in the book, and I didn't like it."

He didn't like, either, the pitying way the witch looked at him now.

"John," she said, "I've not written anything in that book."

She laid him down shirtless in front of the hearth again, painted another layer of black into his hollow. She handed him the comb, poured water into the bowl of him, and propped the leatherbound book open to a fresh page where he could see it.

"I believe I understand," she said, "what has happened to you, and the way it came about. But it's a little like trying to rebuild a tree from a pile of wood shavings. There is so much you don't remember, and it's necessary that you do. So, tell me the story of the comb."

She began stirring the water in his back again.

John looked at the comb: It was very elegant, long handled, and decorated with flowering vines carved out of the wood. He recognized his own work.

"I made this for her," he said. "I made her lots of things, but I could say they were for the troupe, if I were building scenery that would show her particularly well, or making improvements to the wagon. But I made her this as a gift, from me to only her, and she let me comb her hair with it, and I knew then that she loved me, to let me stand so close to her."

The water in his back heated up much more quickly this time, and less comfortably. He shifted on his belly and looked from the comb in his hands to the open book in front of him.

It was filling with writing. He squinted to read it.

John prided himself on introducing people to each other. He was no great performer, but he liked to say that he was the trusses that held up the stage, that he carried them all on his back. Sometimes he would ride ahead of the wagon and make connections through his woodworking, connections which he then leveraged into performance opportunities, and sometimes he would hang back after the show to glean gossip and carry that back to the group. He had an uncanny knack for placing himself between people, and resented the existence of any closeness that did not widen to admit him.

He resented Janet and William's direction; he resented Brigid and Lydia's friendship; he resented Lydia's passion for performing, and the audience's passion for her. And the more he resented them, the more he plied them with gifts, words and wood and wooing coated in the venom of his need.

John hissed. The water in his back steamed. "It's not true," he gasped, "it's not true."

"Tell me what is, then," said the witch quietly, stirring all the while.

"I loved them." His lip trembled. "I loved them all."

But he looked back to the book, and read,

For William and Janet, he made a pair of beautifully turned bowls, and while they ate together he spoke grave rumors of unfriendly villages ahead, dislike of outsiders, a dwindling of prospects leading to a hard winter.

"Some say it's unnatural for women to play men on stage," he said, his eyes soft and sad, "and mutter dark things to each other. Honestly, I fear for Brigid, but I'm sure these words will pass like weather. It's probably nothing."

And William and Janet paled, and reached for each other's hands.

For Brigid, he made hand-carved dice, and played games 'til they were deep in their cups, and spoke of Lydia's talent, her brilliance.

"But I worry," he said, "that she'll only ever be thought of as one half of a pair—that she'll be stamped like a coin into one role until she's spent."

And Brigid frowned, and John looked contrite, and said, "It's not that I think you're smothering her," and paused, "but I do think she feels smothered."

And Brigid looked stricken, and the next morning went with a pounding head to have a word with William and Janet, and was soon visiting nearby family for a spell while Lydia's heart shook to see her go.

For Lydia, he made a hand-carved comb, beautifully wrought with flowers and vines, and offered to dress her hair before she mounted the stage, as Brigid used to do.

"You know," he said, combing her long, bright hair, "when you stand on stage you shine."

She smiled softly. "Thank you, John."

"But sometimes," he said, "you shine so bright that it hurts to look at you. You're like a small sun, and lesser stars can't be seen when you're out."

Lydia's throat hurt. "Does it bother you?"

"No, no, of course not." He paused. "But I think it bothers Brigid."

And Brigid put distance between them, and Lydia dimmed herself, until soon they couldn't see each other at all.

And so John made room for himself.

John hardly felt the witch take the comb from him, stunned by the words and the gulf they opened in his chest. But when she began running it along the outside of his hollow, he screamed: It burned, as if the comb's teeth seared grooves around his bowl-back's rim. The water that spilled over the edges of him scalded; he panted, then drew his knees in close to his chest and wept while the witch watched.

"That's two," she said, low and gruff, and left him.

The next morning, John awoke to voices in the garden. The witch, and one other beside. He tried to rise—and groaned, his body a patchwork of pains and aches, then groaned more deeply as he remembered the source of it all.

The visitor sounded agitated, but he couldn't make out the words. The witch's voice came clear.

"I'm sorry, but I'm busy now. Come back tonight, and we'll speak more of it then."

She came in a moment later, looked at him, then busied herself in brewing a pot of mint tea while he found his way to a seat.

He stared into nothing while she poured him a cup.

"What must you think of me," he whispered, "to hear me say what I do, and then read what's written in that book?"

The witch shrugged. She poured herself some tea and sat down. "What do you think of yourself?"

"I hate it," he said. "I don't recognize the man in those pages. It isn't how I remember it."

"But you didn't remember any of it, at first," she said, lifting her cup, sniffing it. "All you remembered was losing your lover."

John kept silent. He blew gently on his tea.

"I don't want to wait until tonight," he said, finally. "I'd like to get it over with. Can we do this by daylight?"

The witch sipped her tea as she looked at him. It struck him, suddenly, that she wasn't ugly at all—he couldn't remember how he'd thought that.

"We can. But it will hurt you terribly."

He looked into his cup and nodded. "I know."

*

Laid out on his belly again while the witch painted his back, he twirled the string this way and that between his thumbs and forefingers.

"I used this," he said, his voice a shallow croak, "to measure her finger for a ring. I wanted to make her a wooden one—I was going to ask her to marry me. But then everything went wrong."

"How? What happened?"

John's throat worked, but he couldn't remember. He shook his head. "She was gone when I woke. They all were."

The witch stirred the waters in his back, smaller and smaller circles, he felt, as his flesh had filled in, though he could take no joy in it, and said, "I see a great hall done up with harvest revelry—sheafs of wheat, garlands of asters, great rounds of braided bread."

"Yes," said John, "the troupe's last performance. William and Janet had decided—they'd"—he drew a deep breath—"they'd lost their taste for travel, and the take wasn't what it used to be. There was no better time to ask Lydia to marry me; I'd look after her, and we could be our own troupe together, if she wanted. I could set up shop in a town, she could sing in a proper theatre—I would've built her one from the ground up, I knew enough of the right people. I had something to offer her, and she had nothing to lose—"

"Because you'd taken everything from her?"

John gritted his teeth. "I never *took* anything from anyone. I had nothing, I came from nothing, I built everything I had for myself. I never forced anyone to do anything they didn't want to. I only ever tried to help."

He glared up at the book, daring it to contradict him. For a moment, nothing appeared.

Then black ink bloomed from the blank pages and sank John's heart to his stomach.

The night of the final performance, Brigid brought her mother to see the show, and to meet John and Lydia, of whom she'd heard much spoken. John was genial and spoke expansively, praised everyone but himself; Lydia smiled, demure, said little.

Brigid's mother looked at them together: how John's arm wrapped too tightly around Lydia whenever anyone else was around, how she wilted near him, how, if ever his gaze went elsewhere, if he were called away, she seemed to relax, to straighten, to smile more easily and speak more freely.

She looked, too, at her own daughter: how she floated away from the friend she would not cease praising in her visits, but orbited her like a moth near a lantern.

She saw that some sick magic was at work.

"Lydia," she said, "would you lend me this fine fellow of yours? John, I noticed some odd carvings under the seats here, I wondered if you could tell me about them."

And John, flattered, turned his back on Brigid and Lydia, whose eyes found each other, and whose hands soon followed, and who, haltingly and in a daze, remembered how to speak.

Tears brimmed in John's eyes, and he knuckled them away as he turned his face from the book. "You can't hold me responsible for them drifting apart!"

The witch stirred his waters placidly. "Who are you talking to, John?"

"Look, if they'd really loved each other, nothing I said or did could have changed that. I only wanted them to love me too, as I loved them!"

"How did you love them, then?"

"They were everything to me," he said, fiercely. "They were my life, all of them together, and I was just—a tool. A handyman. I wanted to be everything to at least one person."

"Reciprocating action," she said. "Isn't that what you called it? Your work with the lathe. You'd pull her to you, and cut away what you didn't like, and then if she bounced away she was less, until you caught her again, and cut and carved until she fit in the palm of your hand."

"*I* discovered her! *I* made her a star!"

"What happened with the string, John?"

"I don't know! The performance went well. Lydia was more dazzling than she'd been in ages, she was pressed on all sides afterward by admirers, and I couldn't find her for hours. But we were all going to sleep together in the hall that night, after the show, so I just waited. I waited a long time into the night, and when she finally came in, it was her and Brigid together, and I couldn't—I didn't want to interrupt, so I pretended to be asleep until they were. And then I got up, and—"

He gasped as the water in his back began to boil. The witch pulled her finger back a second before it burned, shook the heat out. "Go on, John."

"I crept closer . . . I tried to tie the string around her finger without her waking, but . . . she did, and—"

"What are you doing?" she hissed, snatching her hand from his, looking at the string in horror. "What's this?"

"Nothing, nothing, go back to sleep."

"Is this a spell?" She tugged at the string on her finger, in a panic, in a rage, as Brigid stirred beside her. "Is this how you—what are you doing to me?"

"Lydia, please," he said, finding his way to one knee, looking at her, his eyes large and beseeching as a dog's, "I wanted to ask you to marry—"

The string around her finger glowed like metal in a forge, then snapped and sizzled away to nothing. Lydia herself began to glow, as if stars melted into her veins, and rose up from her blankets, rose farther still, until she floated above him, her hair high and wild as the lightning, and the air around her crackled with power.

"Liar," she hissed, and the word burned bright as her hair. "Liar! You've tried to cut me and bind me like wheat all this time!" And she spoke back at him every truth she'd untwisted from his words, every piece of her he'd taken while seeming to give her gifts, every day he'd ruined with his sad jealous eyes reproaching her for hurting him with her happiness.

And as John watched a witch being born, he felt a great gouging at his back, as if a giant hand in one single stroke had sheared spine and flesh and blood and skin from him, and out from the coring of his body tumbled an apple, a comb, a piece of string, and a book, and he fell down among them in a swoon.

When he woke up, it was midday, and the hall was empty. He picked up the objects around him without seeing them, put them in a bag, and carried them with him for a year and a day.

He screamed his throat raw as the witch rolled the string into his hollow. The water turned to vapor; the thick paint on his back smoked and peeled. Bones jutted beneath his blackened skin like mountain peaks, twisted like serpents coiling, cracked and rumbled like a thundering sky—but settled, finally, solid and sound as good joinery. He panted and sobbed while the witch rubbed circles along his newly filled back; whole now, but for a small gap an inch wide and a few inches tall, surrounded by three black rings.

"Good, John," she whispered. "Well done."

*

John slept the day through. As the hour grew long and blue the witch sat in her garden with her pipe, waiting for her visitor.

"I can't believe," came a voice bitter and hot, "that you would help him. After everything he did to us."

"Sit, Lydia," she said, gesturing to another stool. "How was your journey? How's Brigid?"

Lydia narrowed her eyes. "She told me not to murder you. How could you?"

The witch shrugged. "He came to my door and asked for help."

"And that's it, then? He's whole now, and anyone who looks at him will see just another smiling charming man and not know to shun him? It wasn't for you to fix him!"

The witch raised an eyebrow. "Did you want the task?"

"Of course not."

"Or Brigid, or who, then? Be honest, now."

Lydia's eyes flashed, literally, magically. "I didn't want him fixed at all. He doesn't deserve it."

"Ah, there we come to it. And that's why I did it." The witch held her gaze. "For you to carry less of it. For him to carry more of it."

Lydia's face twisted in disgust, and she shook her head. But she sat down, and stared out into the darkness.

"I'll never forget what you said that night," she said, her voice full of burrs. "*A witch is a kind of justice in the world.* And here you are, undoing it."

The witch tapped the ash from her pipe.

"When you came into your power," she said, "what he'd done to you came back to him fourfold. But that was the end of your story with him. You began a new one; so too should he, with the remembrance of all he did written into his body."

"Why tell me, though? You must have known I'd hate it."

"I wasn't asking permission. But I thought you should know." She pinched herbs from a pouch and packed them into her pipe. "I wasn't going to let him become a secret I kept from you."

Lydia breathed deeply, and exhaled slowly. "I won't see him, or speak to him. Not ever again."

"Nor should you."

"You don't want me to?"

"No. I'd put seven seas between you first." She tilted her head toward the cottage door, listening. "In fact, you'd best be away; I hear him stirring. Give my love to Brigid."

Lydia looked toward the cottage door. Then she hugged the witch to her, kissed her cheek, and said, "I will."

She left. The witch went back inside.

John was awake and waiting for her, still pale and shaken from the pain, but calm. She crouched down next to him, took his temperature with her wrist against his brow.

"You're Brigid's mother," he said, quietly. "I didn't remember you."

"Hard to remember a witch," she said, amiably, "at the best of times."

"You knew who I was from the beginning."

"I did."

"And you helped me?"

She shrugged. "You asked for help. I'm not sure you're happier now than when you came, though, are you?"

He chuckled bleakly. "No."

"Then perhaps all I did was enjoy seeing you punished."

"May I stay?" His eyes were wide and soft. "I'll keep helping, I could make you chairs and spoons . . ."

"Absolutely not." The witch's gaze was sharp, and he flinched from it. "You're good at your craft, John. But people aren't blocks of wood for you to turn to your liking, and you've not quite learned that yet, in your bones." She stood and walked over to the leather-bound book that lay closed now. "Have you tried writing in it since coming here? It might keep your words now, if you choose them carefully."

She found him ink and a quill. He sat with it a while, reading through every word, feeling his memories shift and spike and settle like the objects in his back.

He tried writing "Lydia," and it wouldn't stay. He tried writing "I wish," and it wouldn't stay, the ink swallowed by the page like a pebble by a pond.

He wrote "I'm sorry," and the words stared back at him like eyes, and stayed.

He closed the book.

"I'm ready," he said, and handed it to the witch. She took it, turned him around, and angled the book carefully at what remained of his hollow.

It slid into place like an ending.

ANDREW SEAN GREER

Calypso's Guest

FROM *Amazon Original Stories*

SCIENCE FICTION

I HAVE NO right to tell his tale. After all: he never loved me.

But the workers are making it snow outside, and what have I got to warm the hours? Old stories I have heard a hundred times, old games with no partner to lose to, old cheats and tricks with nobody to work them on? A fire flashes in the corner: there's a sight I've seen too often. There is not a stone in this cave I haven't memorized, placed elsewhere, forgotten, found, and memorized again. You live long enough, and almost everything fades in the sun except the patch where you are standing, isn't that so? And haven't I stood right here, all these years, in the place where I last saw him? The place I sent him from—away from me, at last, toward home?

Outside I hear it: they've got the wind howling just for me.

Have you ever seen a thing explode in airless space? It is a mysterious sight: a blue-white flash, the shattered bits flying out forever, a burst milkweed, the darkness, the unsettling sensation after. There and done in an instant, a blink in space. Many bards have tried to capture it before me; it can't be done. But that is what I witnessed, that afternoon. It was First Spring, and I was out with a dozen robotic workers in a field, where we were trying a kind of corn I had been working on over the Summer; I was showing them how to plant the seed and fertilize it, how far apart, how deep. I had to speak carefully; from their metal eyes I knew they would remember this always. Suddenly, they all looked up—it must have been the X-ray blow they felt—and then I looked up, and one gave me an eyepiece, and then there it was: a flower forced to bloom up in the sky. A ship, a black orb like all warships, torn in two. The atmosphere began to boil with bright fluorescence; instantly I put the eyepiece down and looked up with my naked eyes: red and green arcs like the colors spinning on a soap bubble, ultraviolet evidence of the great thing that had happened. Somewhere in those pyrotechnics, between our two dull suns, I could make out a thin white line across the sky.

Within a day, pieces of the ruined ship began to rain down on my planet.

Within a week, we found the sole survivor.

His ship had crashed on the south side of the continent, in a sandy portion my workers had never bothered to cultivate. His wreckage was easy to find; it had boiled the sand to glass and lay in dunes like an ant in amber, and I remember my heart beating quickly when I saw it. The charred jewel beneath the molten silica, its ruined facets revealed as my workers carefully cleared away debris. The sky was very blue that day, and I recall somehow an insect had made its way to this remote desert and landed, there on my arm. A green winged thing, so tiny. How had it come here? Not just to the desert but to this planet? What a mystery it all was. And then a worker reported that they had found a hatch, and I signaled them to open it. Water vapor rose into the air, and from the haze my workers dragged forth a man in rags.

"Is he human?" I asked, and they said he was. "Is he alive?"

He was alive, but probably would not live, they told me. I was so angry and sad to see him broken in their metal arms, his legs dragging through the white sand, the deep furrows left behind. Long-haired and bearded, I could see, encrusted with blood and scorched skin. Perhaps a uniform of some kind; perhaps a soldier of who knows what distant war. They told me he was shattered in many places. Bones in a burned hide. Barely a man at all anymore. A scan of deep space, they told me, reported no other pods from the ship. The survivor did not move, or even seem to breathe. "Fix him," I said, and they stood there motionless. "Take him home, to the medics, and fix him."

Dutifully they carried him to the car, and we sped north as I leaned back in my seat and watched his silent face, scabbed and unrecognizable. I noticed he wore, in each earlobe, a diamond.

We passed from desert to forest to the road I recognized as home. It was possible he was already dead.

He was the first man I had seen in two hundred years.

Was he from your people? the Foreman asks this snowy day.

No, I did not recognize his clothing or his ship.

It has been a long time. Things might have changed.

I have no people. You know that.

"You're alive," was the first thing I said when the medics awakened the visitor with a jolt. He said nothing, but looked around him. Healed, his black skin glowing in the firelight, the diamonds sparkling, scalp and face now shorn so that his handsome features were unblurred: his wide nose, his jutting chin and strong, sharp jaw, his muscled neck. This was the first time we saw his eyes: bright blue as he looked around. A wound like a violet star covered the left side of his forehead; I knew they had replaced many of his bones with metal, his tendons with wire; he had slept for over a month. Outside, it was nearly First Summer. Nothing in his face showed he was glad for any of it.

Who knows what he made of my own face? A stranger, a man like him in his forties, silver at the edges but hardly war ravaged, or time ravaged; surely I looked as soft and pampered as a crowned prince. Beardless like him, but with a pale complexion, sharp nose, dark monolid eyes, the inobtrusive features of a servant, which is what I was before the Others froze my age forever.

"Are you in pain?" I asked him as he stared at my face. "They didn't know how much to give you."

His eyes went around the room, taking in the rock walls, the wooden furniture, the curtains open to a sky where, off near the mountains, a purple cloud meant rain. He could not know what a miracle it was: On this planet! Rain!

"You should have died," I told him as I tucked the blankets around his shoulders. Those blue eyes shot up at me. "You would have, if you had landed anywhere else. Not that there's a planet within years of here. Probably you would have floated forever. It was one in a million you hit our little speck." A worker corrected me: the probability was one in ten million. "So you see."

Who knows what flashed through his brain? I would learn every detail of his journey, soon enough. He had traveled so far, seen so much, could it really have been more of a surprise than the torments he had suffered? A cave, a sunlit window, a distant rain cloud, a friendly stranger telling him he was alive. Man-shaped machines nearby, ready to tend to his needs. A trap, like so many other times? Or a welcoming host at last? Did he allow himself, even briefly, the fantasy that here he might rest for all his days?

"Am I home?" he asked at last.

What a stern, hard look was in his eyes.

"No," I told him, sitting back on the bed and looking out the window. Beside it, on the wall, hung two moth-eaten weavings: all that I had left of my own lost home. Ancient wool, coming to pieces, you could no longer make out the landscape of another world they once portrayed. I swallowed and looked back on his disfigured face. "No, but you must come to think of it as home."

The workers made this place from nothing—a rime of frost the only water, a breath of vapor the only air, nothing green or blue in sight: just the deep iron valleys of ancient meteor strikes. I never saw it then, but there are images, and the workers recall the days of toil, though they themselves were not the toilers; the real work had been done by earlier generations of mechanical men. They followed their orders; they prepared a world for people who knew their own world was dying, a warlike people whose expanding sun would make any nearby planet uninhabitable. They would build a new home; they would conquer a new system, imprison new civilizations; there was time, and it took time. The ice became oceans; the breath became wind. Layer by layer the workers built the ground: with moss, then grasses, then trees. They brought insects to pollinate the fruits and flowers, ruminants to digest the seeds. They populated new seas with fish, new skies with birds. And after centuries it was no longer an alien world. Calypso: an imitation of a homeland—but by then, a homeland that no longer existed. It had withered like a grape too long on the vine. How could we guess our dreams outlast our selves? The workers stood and waited for their next orders, and the two suns rose and set on their shining skins. No orders ever came. Until I arrived: the "wicked one," the traitor.

The visitor cried for a long time that evening, and into the next day, and would not speak to me or to the workers. They carried him to a bedchamber carved from rock and covered him, and he did not move from there for over a week. I went and visited and tried to lift his spirits. I told him he was lucky to be alive. But there were limitations where he had landed. The planet's special ionosphere meant no message could be sent to other worlds. We had no ships, no spacegoing vessels of any kind. And yet wasn't it a kind of paradise, here? There were no predators except one's nightmares, no misfortunes except at chess. The workers were always busy, and one's merest whim became reality sooner than one dreamed. He did not answer me but stared at the walls. He would not even look out the window. And so I left and thought, with so much time before us, he would change.

And one day when I brought in his meal—I insisted on bringing it, so he would know companionship—I found him talking with a worker. He wore a smile—the first of his I had seen. He turned to me with a look of cleverness.

"You said they could build anything?"

I told him yes. I put his tray down on the table and stood almost in his sight. A light rain fell against the glass. Given time, I told him, they could engineer and make whatever he imagined.

He laughed. "I'm trying to get this one to make me a ship!"

The worker flashed its glowing eyes. "I am sorry, sir, but I do not understand."

"A ship!" he shouted.

"A sailing ship?"

"A spaceship! To get out of here!"

Again, the machine refused to understand. And again my guest laughed in its face, then turned to me. "I know they can make one. Tell me how to phrase it, will you?"

The rain came harder now, running in patterns down the windowpane and casting curving shadows on his face. So willful, so determined. Outside, the dogs were barking at some animal or robot, or perhaps just at the storm itself, invading their world. Dogs, real dogs. A river could be heard now, gushing down the drainpipe and into the yard, where it pooled into the muddy path to my garden. A ship, a boat out to the stars and home.

"I am so sorry," I told him, sitting on the bed. He blinked at me without a smile, as if I were his captor and not his savior. "That is the one thing they are forbidden to make."

*

The workers had been reprogrammed upon my arrival. To calibrate the ionosphere to block all radio waves, all other communication. They could never have repaired his ship—it was too torn to pieces, and because we hurried him too quickly to the medics, they were not able to return after the sandstorms passed, and then it was buried deep in heavy drifts. And even if they could, they would not have obeyed. It was the reprogramming. They could only use the parts for our machines at home. I had tried every method, every tricky way of talking past their robotic blocks, but the commands had been too clearly sent. I was not to be let off this planet. No ship, no communication, no computer more powerful than my library, with its endless books contained within a glass screen. Nothing that I could use to escape. I might live forever in these caverns, and watch the mice evolve to mammoths, but I myself would never change. And never leave. And neither would my new guest. For he had come, my weary traveler, to his journey's end. He had crash-landed in the prison my masters made for me.

"So there is no escape," he said.

"No, I have tried and found no way. I have accepted my fate."

"Who did this to you? And why?"

"My people did it. Because of a bargain I made with . . . the Others. I was found out, and my people banished me to this place. A planet they were planning to colonize. But my people never came. They were wiped out by the Others."

The Others. I knew he had had contact with them—the strange, unfathomable beings whose paths crossed ours from time to time, sometimes with wonderous results but more often with disastrous ones. Nobody knew the extent of their powers—they could move planets, change fates, extinguish stars like candles. What part we played in their plans was impossible to know, for their plans, as they often stated, were beyond our comprehension. Yet there were things they could not see.

His face grew serious. "They can't be trusted," he said. "What was the bargain?"

I looked for a long time at the shadows, which made the room seem filled with many men. "I helped them to destroy my world."

Here was a typical day:

I woke early, and spoke to the workers about the crops, the

outbuildings, my plans for a summer house in the North or an or-
angery or whatever struck my fancy that day. Then, later, my visitor
appeared, freshly bathed and in a robe, and had breakfast while I
gave orders.

"Tell me about your home," I asked when I sat down at last
beside him.

"Ah. I told you I had a palace," he said.

"You said you were a king."

He lifted his strong chin with no modesty. "Servants to bring
grain from the fields, boars from the wilds. Life was pleasant. I had
a wife. I had a son too. He would be a man himself, now. It was a
very long time ago."

"Perhaps he's out looking for you."

His eyes flashed with fury. "How would he find me? On this
planet of yours? That you say I can never leave?"

We sat in silence for a while. And then, as always, I proposed
an outing.

Sometimes it was merely a walk around the grounds, or a hike
through the paths workers had made into the wilderness, for a
view of the ocean. Sometimes it was longer trips, and we would
plan them for days, telling the workers to prepare tents and sleeping arrangements and food. I had told him of the shape of my
world, how carefully it had been designed, and it astounded him
how little of it I had visited in all my time here—he did not realize
how many centuries I had lived in this place. And so he would
speak of a sea voyage, a great oceangoing craft manned by workers
that would sail to an unseen continent. I listened and nodded,
saddened by how much the adventuring spirit still lived in him. It
had died so long ago in me.

He was full of excitement: "Would you like that? A sailing ship?"

"I've never been on one."

"I can't believe it."

"It seems inefficient?"

"It's glorious!" he said, grinning.

We grew tired of listening to the library, and of our own silence
with books, and so took to reading aloud from it to each other.
One year, he read to me the entire works of Dickens, as I sat by the
fire watching the sparks light his face. He was a great storyteller,
shouting and whispering with those blue eyes wide in passion. He
loved adventure stories most of all, and he told me of his own ad-

ventures, speaking with the same vivid ardor, and of his son, and of his wife. I told the only story I had.

"You have met monsters on your travels," I said. "Planets of monsters. There were creatures like that, on my planet. Conquering worlds, murdering civilizations, enslaving whole planets for their pleasure."

"But you're not like that," he told me tenderly. Blue eyes.

"Mine was a servant race. They enslaved my homeland, a human planet. Centuries ago. I'm sure your people never heard of us, as we never heard of yours. Most of my kind accepted their role, but I never did. I hated it, and my masters. So when the Others came . . ."

Something clever in his eyes. "What did they look like?"

"I met only one. She was two meters tall, red-skinned. Beautiful. She called herself Thirdborn. I understood this was just an aspect of her, the only part I could perceive, just a fingernail of her being. She smiled the whole time she talked to me. I was terrified."

"As you should be."

"She said our masters could not be allowed to continue. They had to be destroyed before they caused what she called 'a terminal mistake.' She said I alone could understand. And as a royal servant, I might know a secret. A simple thing, a code to a lock. It seemed so unimportant, and I had lived with hatred for so long, that I said I knew this code. She kept that smile and asked me for it very sweetly. In return, she offered me my heart's desire. So I told it to her."

"Your masters found out."

"I was tried by my own people. My masters preferred it that way, to turn us against one another. The trial was quick. I thought they'd kill me. But my people were afraid of me, a man who talked with gods. They banished me to a newly built colony. I'm sure they thought I'd be dead long before my masters sent their slaves there. But I believe the Others wiped out my people along with my masters. Thirdborn said it would be so. Of course she knew everything."

He put his dark hand on my pale one. "You're the last of your race."

"A poor servile race." I thought of the last time I saw Thirdborn, smiling as she granted me my wish. The uncomfortable sensation as she changed some part of me I could not see. I kneeled on the floor, vomiting. When I looked up, she was gone.

He took a deep breath before speaking. "I have met them, the Others. More than once, and though they seem godlike, they don't see everything. They can be tricked. Don't they owe you a favor? Didn't you make a bargain with them? Call them!" he said. "Ask them to come! Leave the rest to me."

But I shook my head; I had tried so many times over the years. I was nothing more than a dumb animal to them, briefly of use. A sheep. A mule. And perhaps they thought it better to have the last of my race trapped, with my secrets, in this golden prison.

Then I heard him ask me, almost whispering: "And what was your heart's desire?"

A smile. "Well," I said. "You are part of it."

We did go on one of these voyages he spoke about, on the sailing ship the workers made to his designs. We headed east across the ocean toward an island the workers said had been created, populated only by birds. Along the way, we built fires abovedecks and sat and drank wine and told stories. I heard of his travels, the things he had seen that surely no human had ever encountered before. But the strangest of all was, when I asked what he missed of his homeland, he said:

"Winter."

I had read of it, but since my home planet's twin suns gave only Springs and Summers and this planet was a replica, here it was the same. I had known chill rainy seasons and hot dry ones. Years and years of rain and sun. But never, ever winter.

"What's it like?" I asked him.

"Ah!" he said, with that broad smile, and the fire caught the diamonds in his ears. He had grown his hair long by then, and a beard, glossy in the firelight. "Snow!"

I thought he meant ice, which I had seen. But he explained it was different: fluttering, falling crystalline water. Millions of flakes, covering the land. Well, alien worlds have alien ways.

"In winter," he told me, "everything is white. Soft and white. The tops of mountains are covered with it. I used to have a dog, Argos, who loved it and would leap through the snow all afternoon."

"It sounds beautiful."

"And if you roll it into boulders, you can make a kind of man! I made one every winter for my son. We dressed it up like a soldier."

"A man made out of ice?"

"Out of snow! Have your workers make it snow. And then I'll make a man for you!"

"You will?"

"Of course!"

But I did not need him to make a man out of crystals from the sky; a man had already fallen into my arms. That night, and many other nights, he came to my cabin. A reprieve from solitude, at last. What are we to each other, if we cannot be this?

It would be better if he were a woman.

Why is that?

You could have children.

They would not be like me. They would die here.

Still it would be a comfort, as I understand. A woman instead of a man.

They sent me what I asked for. My heart's desire, or part of it. But I asked for it imperfectly.

And what was your heart's desire?

"To have a man," I told Thirdborn. "A wonderful man—"

He was wonderful, by your account.

"Who I could love forever."

And so you see: he was dear to me. In time, he grew to think of me less as his captor than as his friend, but he always thought of himself as a visitor, on an extended stay. He was forever restless—it is in the nature of such men to be restless—and would not let his body go to fat; he spent hours running along the trails, or lifting bundles of wood, or throwing heavy stones, or leaping in ways that perplexed me. It was, surely, some military training from his home world.

But my magic did not extend to him. The body they had given me, one that would not age or die, was mine alone and could not be halved or shared like gold. And so, as we watched the seasons come and go, I saw gray hair grow on his temples. I watched his hands grow worn as hides. He lived with me, here in my prison, for seven years.

The workers had cleared the jungle for fifty yards around, so that when I emerged from the trail, nothing blocked my view. The pyramid, twice as tall as a man, had landed lightly—presumably through a controlled descent—and lay tilted, half-sunk into the soft jungle earth, so that a single facet caught the sun that had not shone below these trees for centuries. A faint rectangular line marked a hatch of some kind; there were no other visible points of entry.

"When did you first discover it?" I asked the nearest worker. I did not mean this one in particular; they shared a mind that way, and a memory.

The worker told me it was a week before; a fire-prevention team happened upon it on a routine mission. They had no explanation for why its descent had not been tracked; it could be it had a blocking device. From the landing pattern, and the vegetation, it could not have landed on my planet more than a month previous.

"There is no evidence that anything has left the hatch?"

They said there was no evidence, but of course few marks were left in a rain forest. Scanners could not penetrate the hull.

I stood there for a long time watching the light play on the facets of that strange machine. Streaks of blackness scorched the metal, and there were the usual dings and scrapes of interstellar matter. And yet, it was not crushed or broken like the visitor's own ship. A worker alerted me to another side, cleaned of soot: a small yellow light blinked there in the shadows. What was in my heart that day?

"Open it." They did, and the hatch slid aside without a sound. Out tumbled the husk of a body, all bones.

Why did you not tell him, that day?

I wasn't sure what it was.

I understood they gave a full report. It was a functioning ship.

I didn't want to get his hopes up.

It was capable of flight, with minor repairs. The pilot had died of a heart attack years before it landed. Perhaps I am mistaken? You told them to bury it.

Foreman, I am done discussing this topic.

Shall I tell you of the weather?

I asked my workers to make me a companion, once. After all, they had parted the sea from the land, and made every living creature on the planet thrive. They told me they could not make a human, though they could create a human shape for one of the workers, and I might give it a name. I found this unacceptable; I preferred my robots metal and wire, I said, not tarted up like a person. They did not ever reply to humor. They told me they could use frozen embryos of animals and my own cells to create a life-form. And this they did. A year later, they presented me with the creature I called Anna, just a baby then. Mostly monkey, partly me, a chimera I raised with diapers and a bottle, then fed and walked with, hand in hand, through the forests. As she grew, she seemed to understand the sadness of her condition. She could not speak. But once I came upon her, in her room, her hairy arms resting on the lap of her flowered dress. She was holding a book of mine; in my memory I have made it *Robinson Crusoe*. Holding it upside down, turning the pages, then throwing it across the room and screaming, screaming. I could not comfort her. Within a week, she had vanished into the northern jungle, and a search by every worker never found a trace of her. Either Anna died on the journey or lived in some cloud forest with creatures more like her. She is dead, in any case. That was a hundred years before my visitor; I never tried the experiment again.

"I'm building another boat," the visitor told me two days later when I returned. It was evening, and I entered with one of the dogs I'd taken with me; I had named her Argos after his own. Argos whined and pulled when she saw him, and he smiled. Scrolls of paper were laid out on the big table, covered in drawings, and he sat with them beneath the lamp like a mapmaker at his charts.

"That's a good pastime."

"How was the meteorite?"

"Iron, as expected," I said, closing the door behind me. The room was warm and smelled of wool and spices. "I was hoping for magnesium. This planet is woefully lacking, and mining is hard. Tell me about your boat. What do you want them to do differently?"

"*They* aren't doing it," he said, putting a hand firmly on his drawings. "I'm doing it myself."

I silenced Argos and asked him what he meant.

That broad smile. "I've been cutting the lumber, and I'm studying how to engineer the hull."

"But why?"

The moons looked in the window at us, a pair of mismatched eyes, and what did they see? A room littered with pillows and books and quietly blinking lights, lit by a single bronze lamp; a room made of much living, and in it, the ones who had lived it: a man in love, standing in the doorway with a dog on its leash. And another, seated at a table, planning his escape.

He had already cut the wood for the sides, the base, the back panel, the gunwales, and the struts. There was so much work already done; he must have been at it for months.

"I've been reading a lot in my room," he said, proudly showing me the pieces in the giant workroom. How had I missed it? When I studied every motion of his hand, how had I not noticed these long missing hours, the sawdust in his hair, the sound of sawing and planing, the raw red hands and cuts and bruises? How had it escaped me: his private mind?

"And I admit the workers were helpful in calculations. I'm no engineer. But I think it's right. No, I'm sure it's right."

"Where do you want to go?"

"The workers showed me a map of the planet. They showed me where you've traveled, what you've seen. It's almost nothing. Just this continent and islands."

"There is so much work to do at home."

"There is another continent they made, you know. You never named it. To the southeast, a long way, and there is a volcano there, and cliffs along the sea, they told me. They planted fruit trees and tropical plants everywhere."

"I've seen the map. But who knows what it looks like now?"

"It must have gone wild. Not like this, not cultivated and pruned and made for us. It's there to explore."

"I've always thought of going."

"My boat isn't going to be very big. Anyway, it will take me years. We'll have plenty of time to talk about it before I go."

I looked down on his pile of wood, still pale and fresh from his labors. The smell of it was everywhere, of sap and sawdust and living things brought down. Sunlight shone in lines along the workshop walls, and from above: a copper shield gleamed in the window. I watched him stroke the wood with his fingers, his smile at the smoothness made with his bare hands. The unknown continent that waited. The sands where no human had ever walked. The cliffs, and volcano, and fruit trees gone wild over the centuries until they were tangled with vines and burdened with mangos, avocados, unknown things. The creatures hidden there. And why wouldn't he make a home of coconut trunks and palm leaves? No libraries or workers, no medics or cooks. Why wouldn't he search out, like any animal, a quiet corner to curl up with only the waves to speak to? A life of struggle and hardship, surely. Each day whittled from the last. Though much is taken, much abides. I saw his face as he stroked the wood that would take him away, years from now. One looks also at the sapling that will one day break the stone on which it grows. Where were my gods that day?

I began: "We found a ship . . ."

He never finished the boat. I finished it. It took me a decade, learning skills that were foreign to me, though he had learned them as a boy: how to cut and treat wood, how to bend it and plane it, how to join it and make it watertight. I refused any help from the workers. Splinters, blisters, cuts, and gashes along my forearms. I grew broad and muscled from the work; I let my beard get long and shaggy. And then, when it was done, I lifted the sail and took to the seas. Three months it took me to find that Southern Continent, to land on the white sand beneath the black of that volcano. The monkeys loud as a marketplace in the trees. A green and heartless place. There I lived, alone, without a metal eye turned on me, for almost a year. I made of it what I could, and every day I imagined him in every shadow. But of course he had left me years before.

And then I came home. I returned to a life of waking early and stoking the fire. Making my breakfast of eggs and fruit. Working on the root cellar, the greenhouse, charting a new course for a nearby stream. The sound of the wind is almost human to me now, although I have not heard a human voice for a hundred years. Sometimes I sit in silence for hours. It is unnecessary to say "alone."

I do have my dogs, the Foreman often points out. Generations of Argos. The Foreman is not much of a conversationalist, but he is all I have. Him, my dogs, and my books. And the memory of the visitor.

It seems impossible that I think of him every day.

Arrangements were made quickly; it was almost as if he had been prepared all along for such an impossible bit of chance. We were driven out to the buried ship, where workers, commanded to disinter it, were already hard at work. A few hours of careful examination and my king proclaimed it in need of very few repairs. A week or so, that would be all. I remember how he stood, leaning against the spacecraft, smiling at me.

Only after ages passed did I allow myself to recall our last night together.

The fire was lit in my chamber; the soup bowls, finished, sat on a ledge for the workers to collect in the morning. Our wineglasses were full; I had opened a vintage from my grapes, corked fifty years before. We lay among the furs, staring into the fire.

"You could come along," he said without moving.

I watched the light flickering along his neck and jaw. "My workers would not let me."

He smiled. "Surely there's a way around that. They're just machines."

Escape. To join in his adventures, to head out in search of his home, evading monsters, radiation, unknown dangers, perhaps even death itself. On our small craft tunneling through the vast quadrants of space.

"Tell me the story again of how you came to me," I said at last.

"It's not destiny, you know. To stay in this prison."

Landing on his home planet, finding some swineherd to hide us while he made his plans; arriving, disguised, at his great palace and bowing, unrecognized, before his son. And his queen.

I said, "I've grown to like this life." And added: "Thank you."

"You could build a home on Ithaca. A wife, children. Our ocean is a fine one."

A fisherman's hut, a boat before dawn, bringing home the catch to my empty hut. The palace gleaming in the distance. Maybe buy a berth on a merchant's ship headed to Sparta. Maybe join another war. But I would never find another of my kind out there.

"Tell me how you came to me," I said again.

"You've heard it many times."

"Tell me again, now that you are going home."

"Who knows where I'm going?"

"Tell it. Please."

He looked deep into the heart of the flames: "We landed on a planet on which lived a race of one-eyed monsters . . ."

We sat there by the fire, wrapped in blankets, and he told me of one creature, a special pet of the Others. My visitor described, once again, heading out in a small craft in search of supplies and finding that giant there, offering them food and shelter. Of course it was a trap; the creature closed a door too heavy for any of them to move. I watched my love's face lit by the flames, changing every moment. He told how the creature left each morning with his beasts and they spent all day trying to budge the door, trying to find another exit, and each night he returned and murdered one of them and ate them. It was a horror no man should bear, but certainly not the leader of these men. He spoke of how they spent the day in terror, waiting for the sound of the door moving in its groove with a grinding noise that meant death. "I like you," the creature had said to him, picking human flesh from his teeth. "What is your name?" My visitor said it was Noh-wun. "Noh-wun, my gift to you is I will feast upon you last." The lucky day the creature left behind his staff, how my visitor sharpened it and waited. Another return, another round of bellowing laughter and murder and wine drunk long and hard, and he found the will to drive the heated end into the thing's one eye. The sound of his screams in that chamber! His men feared they would all die because of it. "Help me!" the creature screamed to his brothers. "Help me for Noh-wun has blinded me! Noh-wun has tricked me!" A hard joke in hard times. It took much doing to hide themselves among the beasts, so that the blind thing could not tell they had escaped. But pride undoes us all, my visitor said. Pride and vanity and foolish hope.

"You told him your name."

"Yes," my visitor said. And he said the name that he told me the first day, the name he shouted aloud when they were at their craft bound back to the ship, and outward to the stars and home. His father named him so. The Others heard, and while granting my wish, they denied his own. He would be sent far from home.

"And so you came here, to me."

He nodded and let his face fall from the firelight. Argos wailed at the two moons high above.

"Thank you for your kindness," he said before we went to the bed. I thought he meant saving his life, and cherishing him all those years. But he did not mean that. "Not everyone," he said, looking at me directly now and taking my hand, "would let me go."

Smoke billowed from the fire and pricked my eyes. Pride and vanity and foolish hope.

*

We fell asleep with the fire still dying in the hearth. I, who would never grow old, holding close to me what seemed like youth: impatient for life, struggling even in sleep for some new hold on it, a wrestler in my grip; and who knows what he saw in his last dreams with me? Some happy planet, where the dead were all risen and spoke to him of things that had been and of things to come. Some star-banked gulf to wash him to oblivion. His fur thrown aside, eyes tightly shut, his pulse visible under the black skin of his neck. Hair gone gray, lips grown thin in his years with me. But still, beneath that silver beard, the same proud chin. And beneath his lids, the same blue eyes.

Do not tempt the gods again, I wanted to tell him, stroking his hot skin as he slept. He fell deep into my embrace. Slay no one, kiss no one until you find home—but is it only home you want? Is it really your aged wife, your grown son, your homeland changed beyond recognition? Or is it something I know too well, and cannot warn you against? The "gift" the Others gave me in return for my betrayal? He moaned and turned in his sleep and could not tell me. Muscled, shaking, an old man in my arms. Is it immortality?

The slow moons climbed above us.

No other ever arrived. Only the white streaks of fallen ships and meteors. I knew, that night I knew it, that my gods decided he would be the last.

The next morning, with a blight of flame and smoke, into the wine-dark void of space, he left me.

What do you think became of him?

He sailed beyond the suns, beyond the baths of distant stars. He became one of the wanderers people talk about long after they are dead.

You saved him. Surely you should not have been the one to send him.

What is a person but this heap of loss? Otherwise—what wasted breath.

And in the years since then?

I had two requests. One was for the workers to make me a machine to talk to, to record my memories of him.

I hope I am sufficient.

You have his eyes.

You have often mentioned the resemblance, though I am metal.
Better that way, perhaps.
The second request?
It's been going on for years, before you were made.
And what was that?
To make it snow.

The Blade and the Bloodwright

FROM *Lightspeed*

FANTASY

THE SOLDIERS SLIT the woman's throat every evening before bedding down so they can sleep without worry. She mocks them but never fights the knife coming to her. Two of the men still take turns watching her in case she heals before the rest of the cadre wakes; so far she hadn't surprised them, but a weapon drawn is a weapon able to kill.

By morning, the sawn red threads of meat and muscle will have restitched her banyan-brown neck and she'll wake them with gritstone curses, scolding them for cutting too roughly into her vocal cords. The horror of her rasping, gurgling voice does not match the rest of her; she is arc and undulation, a mountain of rounded bends, long hair a windfull banner of black mist. All a crass indulgence in the face of the men's strong knife-cut frames, hard nets of muscle starved into severe contour.

Vaikan never volunteers to kill the bloodwright. Touching her would be undeserved, hateful. Cutting her was a new obscene intimacy he couldn't force himself to try. Hers is a body that has borne change beyond all his reckoning, and he cannot stifle his envy at that knowledge. Walking or riding beside her was enough of an endeavor; contact would mean calcifying their gross differences, and the contrast would fill his thoughts with venom.

He sees to the woman while she lives under daylight and gulps down the antidote that will keep her from killing him. The brackish tincture, sown with her blood, drips resinous down his throat, and he feels the immediate effects, the prickling on his skin like a false cold sweat. Latent nausea and the beginnings of a fever mist away. One sip every dawn, the spellwright had said, would keep the woman's creeping influence from them all, preventing their flesh from sickening and deforming.

There is no way to stop her when she draws on her macabre craft, the spellwright told them. Not even her own will can temper what she has become.

As the rest of the exhausted cadre rouses, Vaikan prepares the woman for travel and wipes the crusted veil of blood aproning her heavy breasts and round belly. The high points of her body flake where it has burned. The southern seas are ruthless to sail, and a seaside cave on a nameless atoll is their first camp on solid ground in weeks. While he feeds her strips of dry fish, the soldiers around them debark their double-hulled vessel to the stony beach and go about the rote habit of bringing themselves off. The spell-wright had instructed them to masturbate upon each awakening, to rid themselves of the fire in their blood and ground themselves in meditation; the bloodwright thrived on such elemental imbal-ances, naturally encouraging any disparity of energy in the body until its perversion made itself manifest.

"You must take better care of yourself, soldier," the blood-wright says as she accepts another briny white strip. Her teeth look loose in her mouth as she pulls the meat away. He makes sure his fingertips don't touch her lips. "You never do. And I can feel a *skewing*."

She is right, and Vaikan knows this. Touching himself in her presence fills him with disgust; at her for being what she is, at him-self for what he is not. To touch himself is no relief, just another new sickness for him to bear. Without reply, while she chews and chews, he unbinds the rope hobbling her legs and makes a leash.

"The next city is waiting," he answers, a vileness at the back of his tongue as he tugs at the rope. "Up."

"I say this as a warning, not a threat: as a storm tosses about both evil and righteous alike, so too was I born of the same nature."

Vaikan knows her nature well enough. Not even a storm could match her in viciousness.

He tugs the rope again. "*Up.*"

They travel as a company of ten plus the bloodwright in tow, along a route marked by their chief and his counsel. Their home, the archipelago of White Chain, lies behind them in shades of black, a churned slurry of ash and kinblood. Their enemies, an alliance of island kingdoms, will come to know the taste of the Chain's fury.

This is their divine mandate, and they will see to it every craven chief is compensated with an equal share of suffering, for they are the Blades of the Chain and there is no concealing yourself from their fine edge. Like the bloodwright has been reared to rend and mend the body, so too has Vaikan been educated from birth to be what he is: a Blade, a soldier loyal to the chief and brother to his fellow warriors.

The first island-city they wipe out, Vaikan and his soldier-brother Naru bring the bloodwright to the night market. Rara Vo had little in the way of military strength, but it had provided the food and weaponry needed to keep the Six Chief alliance strong. They arrive as two sons with their mother coming to sell their share of ambergris from the flensing farms and bypass the watchmen's suspicions easily. They wait till deep in the evening and take up a central position in the city, amidst the mudbrick tower blocks and high tree mansions. On this night, the woman's neck remains whole. Her power is wanted.

Before the bloodwrights had been bent to the task of war, they had been healers, reweaving and unmaking the sickly machinations of humanity's wild flesh. But now her spirit knows only one thing: to call the flesh of her enemies into new form.

Arms wide, eyes closed and bleeding, she offers no hesitation. The call is felt from the youngest urchin in its cradle to the most-high chief. Before Rara Vo's spellwrights can stir and attempt a counter magic, she is in them. In their sleep, the skin of their enemies begins to harden and pale. Blood fills with calcic particulates and coagulates. The drying seams of all their orifices sluggishly seal. Some wake choking, panic, begin to flee, but there is no escape now. Their screams stay locked behind conjoined teeth as their soft organs calcify, and the city fills with the sounds of muffled moans and the snapping and grinding bones. Their skeletons ulcerate, twisting into vast spires of ivory, erupting from every home and tavern, piercing through buildings, through the high canopies.

By the end of her unleashing, anything with a heartbeat has turned to bone. The bloodwright falls to her knees, weeping, foaming at the mouth, her body churning like an angry sea. There is no stopping bloodcraft, a magic thought to be eradicated from the great seas for centuries.

There is no stopping her.

When they push off from the island and look back, great spikes of bone impale the sky, knifing high past Rara Vo's tallest trees. At the farthest point without vanishing, the island looks gripped by the talons of a great dead beast, rising from beneath the foundation.

Cleaning her is necessary after these attacks, Vaikan learns. The magic calls to her flesh as well as others. He uncloaks her and sees the marks of her power: a skeletal crown of spikes juts from eyes and temples. Her vertebrae rise in thick protective spikes. Sharp bones pop from the tips of her fingers like long cat's claws. After he scrapes dried red tears from her face, the foam that collected around her mouth, she tells Vaikan she can still see just fine.

"You wept," he says, when most of the men have bedded down for the night. He is partly suspicious but mostly eager to find some vein of weakness he can tap. Will she be able to carry out the rest of their attacks? "You pity our enemy."

"I pity us all," she murmurs, chewing the bone claws from her fingertips. "But I gave them a better end than they gave us."

The bloodwright cracks the excess phalanges from her smooth sockets and he hates himself for the envy that rolls through him like a rot-filled tide. If there is one thing Vaikan wishes he could not see, it is himself.

When the bloodwright first boarded their ship, accompanied by the head spellwright, the Blades couldn't help but scoff at her, some in abject disgust and others in anger. She had seen a soft and studious life, waited on by others so she could hone her blood-craft. It reflected in her figure, her bearing, the unblinking gaze she held each of them with. Vaikan knew she was wholly unpre-pared for the danger they were sailing into. She was the only one of her kind that they knew of in all the kingdoms of the sea, and she carried herself as such; no chief would stomach such a perver-sion of magic. But then no chief had undergone what the White Chain had.

During the war in the Chain, she and all the novice wrights had been hidden away from the war. Unlike Vaikan and his men, she had missed the half-shark barbarians tearing apart fleeing families and the oil-spitting war petrels, covering the battalions in an ac-celerant for their fire-tipped arrows. Better we preserve them and their potential magicks than risk them for a temporary victory, the chief had decreed. And indeed, no victory had been gained, even temporary, and his surviving subjects were furious at such folly.

Vaikan had begrudgingly led the woman to the back of the ship, affronted at her cool confidence, the unscarred hills of skin and clean, flowing hair. A fully fledged bloodwright could bend the shape of their being into any shape at a thought; that she chose this shape, even with all the forms she could take, laced a bitterness through his perception of her.

As a boy before the war, Vaikan had seen three bloodwright children at distance, training under the tutelage of a spellwright. The exercise was to grow their nails as long as talons. A simple enough task and painless. Two of the children held their hands out, watching their nails grow and curl inward. The last child struggled and then began to scream as his fingers began to turn and spiral, the splintering bones and rending flesh audible even at a distance.

There was a price, as there always was, for such a power. The pain of failure was a fearsome one, but the true debt would come after death; anyone who wielded this malignant magic would enter the afterlife cursed, trapped in the whirlpool of reincarnation.

Vaikan had wanted to be one of them. Instead of a body free of shape and limit, a body of pure potential, he was shepherded into the role of a warrior and hewn into the form required. There would be no change for him. His body weighed on his soul like an anchor.

"What do we call you?" he'd asked as he led her to the stern of the ship.

She hesitated before speaking but not, Vaikan realized, because she was unsure or humble. It was puzzlement as to why he did not already know.

With a joyless smile, she answered, "Wrath."

Before the second night of sailing, all the Blades had fucked her except Vaikan.

Immune to her bloodcraft, they pleasured themselves over the neutered power of her. When Vaikan's turn finally came, he pretended at taking out his cock and rammed his hips into hers, acting out a quick rut while the rest of the men wrestled each other and howled out broken war songs, drunk and raging. Beneath him, the bloodwright kept her head tilted starboard, eyes locked on the moon-cut crests of waves. He did not think of how she must hate them all, how she must wish she could draw their hearts out through their nostrils in one wet string. He did not think of himself being remade by her will.

Instead, Vaikan shut his eyes and thought of himself as her, beautiful and soft and impervious to any cruel touch. He came looking down at their bodies pressed together and wanted to vomit; everything she was, crown to cunt to callus, became a mockery of his desire. Afterward he let the bloodwright up and wiped her down with a sea-soaked rag. When their eyes met, he thought, more than accusation, he could see recognition in the smooth stone of her face.

Tamarong is the largest island the chief means for them to destroy. Two sharply peaked ranges jut from the ocean, close enough to squeeze the sea into a long narrow channel between them. The city is situated on the interior of the colossal split, the metropolis carved into the meandering and decorated cliff faces that boast a height of near 1000 fathoms. Hundreds upon hundreds of braided bridges and a single immense stone crossing net the two sides together while heavy bamboo lifts ferry people and their animals up and down the great heights.

Had he time, Vaikan would have liked more time to admire the place before it was decimated, but their second invasion cannot wait. The general's black albatross had sent them word that shrewder defenses should be anticipated. Vaikan wonders if the islandhold has gotten word of what they're defending from. Even he had not anticipated what manner of death the woman would wreak.

They file the bloodwright's horns down until her face is at least passably human. Despite her irritation, they opt for a veil just in case. They enter Tamarong in the same fashion, this time two sons and a mother selling throwing nets and spearheads. They wait for entry into the city in a line of other foreigners, in a long cavernous hall whose end vanishes to a distant and invisible point. The city guards upturn each merchant's and visitor's burden. When they arrive at the entry gate, the guards swagger around Vaikan's small group and focus their attention on the woman, pawing rudely through her rattan pack. Vaikan can see the bloodwright's teeth begin to bare behind her veil. Naru, the other soldier with them, subtly grips Vaikan's forearm in panic. Her power is necessary but only when used at the correct time and place.

Not here, Vaikan mouths to her. Not so far on the perimeter of the city where her reach will surely leave too many alive.

But it is too late. One of the guards squints at her downturned face and yanks the veil from her head. Plush lips catch his eye first and then the rest of her: a skinless, bone-smooth face arrests his motion, and his mouth gapes in shock. She sticks her tongue out childishly, and the guard seizes her by the cloak. A bone spike shoots from her mouth faster than a javelin, making a transit through the guard's skull and into the foreigner behind him. A scream rises then three then ten. The queue begins to scatter.

Vaikan curses and pulls a sword from the dead guard's scabbard and scythes the legs out from a confused guard to his right. The crowd boils away only for the mass of bodies to be replaced by more guards, more people too panickstruck to take stock of their surroundings. Naru commandeers a glaive from a less-experienced sentry and whips the curved blade through a series of unlucky throats, guard and citizen alike.

The bloodwright crouches against the corridor wall amidst the frenzy, clutching her head with shivering hands. A guard draws up his sword two-handed to skewer her through the head, but Vaikan sends his sword through the guard's spine, crumpling him in place.

"Get the fuck up, wright, we have to go," Vaikan snaps, hauling her up by her arms, hating himself for enjoying the plush sink of flesh under his fingers. "Shield yourself in bone if you can, these bastards only have—"

"I can't," she cuts in, voice still abraded from too many knife cuts. "Too many people pulling at me. All their hearts, the beating—!"

Even with the antidote torrenting through his veins, Vaikan can still feel the unnatural pull of her power in him. He fends off two guards with his sword, hacking into the cheek of one through his leather helm which gets stuck in the depths of his jaw. A well-placed kick to the stomach sends the second guard sailing backward into Naru, whose glaive pops through the guard's lung. Lifting the dead man up, Naru tosses him aside.

"We need to split up," Naru hisses, holding up a stray corpse to shield them from a sudden barrage of arrows. "I'll distract them, and you take her to the city's center."

Vaikan nods and forces the bloodwright to her feet, intercepting another arrow aimed at her head with the flat of his sword.

Naru places himself between the entry gate and the rest of the crowded corridor as Vaikan and the woman escape. Wrapping his nose and mouth in a cloth, he uncouples a pouch from his belt and hurls it hard at the ground in front of him. A white powder explodes into the air, and the wind from the open gate forces it down the great corridor. People and guards scream as the caustic cloud slips down into their lungs, spreading the toxic sea slug distillate into their bloodstream. They fall quickly as if boneless, helpless to the paralytic.

On the other side of the gate, Vaikan pushes the bloodwright onto the cliffside lift. The platform is large, sturdy enough to hold ten men and their cargo. The only option now is to go up; but wouldn't they face more guards at the top levels of the city? And the time it would take for them to reach the top would leave them open to all manner of projectiles . . .

"We should retreat," Vaikan bites out, wishing she'd stop crouching like a scared animal. He wants to yank her up by her beautiful hair, tear it from her sweating scalp. Below, the narrow strip of sea calls darkly to them, smiling whitecaps urging them to its depths. "I can't get you where you need to go. I can't protect you. We need to jump."

"Cut the rope there." She jabs a bone-clawed finger at the windlass. "I know what to do."

"You know nothing of—!" A hail of arrows drums into the lift around them, skims across Vaikan's shoulder and thigh, and glances off the hard bone of the bloodwright's eyeless face. *Fuck it*, he thinks, and uses all his brute strength, the momentum of his weight, to slash through the barrel-thick rope.

The rising force immediately flattens them against the platform as it surges up the side of the cliff city. They pass waiting denizens on each level whose yelps of surprise clip away faster and faster. The wind's scream builds as they ascend, and the weight on their body begins to feel like a godling's amused finger pressing them down, just short of shattering, in the same manner a child might squish an ant. A roar rips out of Vaikan in the face of his encroaching death, barely audible over the high wail of wind and the screech of a burning rope.

The platform hits the giant windlass at the top of the cliff, launching them into the air at the same time the platform shatters into fatal splintering debris. They soar upward, and Vaikan is stuck looking up into a bright morning sky, clear and untroubled by clouds. Too clean a vision, he thinks, to see before death. He twists his neck to find the woman and finds her clear, dark eyes inverted and red.

Red wings burst out of the bloodwright's back, as big as their ship's sails. Suddenly Vaikan is caught by her but not with hands or arms or any recognizable human limbs. Thready red muscle snakes around his waist, binding him to what was once the woman, but there is nothing of the bloodwright he knows. Only an impression of her face wedged amongst a tangle of thrumming tumorous growths. With a beat of her great wings, red webs of squirming tendons, she takes them up and then dives for their destination: a great stone bridge affixed in the middle of the city where all transit of import takes place.

She smashes into the busy crossing like a missile without Vaikan feeling the impact, cradled as he is in the mass of her. A living sarcoid web fulminates from the bloodwright, bursting across the decking with all the pressure of an over-swollen cyst. Her gristly malignancies serpentine up and down the bridge and rails until the entirety of everyone and everything on it is engulfed in her. The sky fills with shrieks and retching as the rest of the city begins to feel her call to change.

Great reams of offal begin to pour from the windows, balconies, and open walkways. Loose organs knotted in ligaments pour down the cliff faces, painting the pale stone red as war. Gullets with no stomachs gulp at nothing and arteries bound to no hearts throb and pulse. In minutes, there is not a single soul in Tamarong left standing. There is only a single wet and pulsing flesh, soulless and yet still terribly alive.

Paring her from the greasy thicket of offal and entrails takes Vaikan the better part of the night and early morning. He watches himself at a remove from his body, as he always does but most often when in the midst of death. Hours of daylight bake the city of viscera until it perfumes the air with the dense odor of dying mushrooms and the ripe piquancy of moist copper. By the time he gets some semblance of the woman free, she has made herself mostly whole again, embodied into something recognizable. The only thing she is missing is skin.

"Can you walk?" he asks, hoping he will not have to carry her. Pouches of bubbly white fat make up her breasts, thick sheets of suet covering her stomach, the back of her arms, and thighs. The rest of her is a stringy brocade of white and red muscle pulled tight across her body.

"Yes," she says, grasping his shoulder as she finds her feet. She has something like a face again, no longer just a smooth plain of white bone but a mask of tendons and writhing veins. Her black eyes crater through the walls of his protective detachment, dragging him back into the nauseating presence of his body. "Naru is dead. But not from me."

Vaikan doesn't answer, a few species of emotion shoaling within him. Was she trying to reassure him or herself? It mattered not. He'd already accepted this outcome for all his brothers, had mourned them after lost battles when he'd assumed they'd met their end. They are vengeful ghosts, less alive than the trembling meat beneath his feet.

They trek to Tamarong's northern port and steal a double outrigger sailboat with a mind to meet with the rest of the Blades at their pre-appointed rendezvous. But when they get within eyeshot of the chosen half-moon cay, they see only the same manner of stringy viscera webbed across the beach. Somehow the bloodwright had reached even here. The only living thing left on the tiny islet is a freshly wounded sea dragon burying its eggs into the soft white sand. As a draft pulls their scent toward it, the leechlike circle of its mouth opens like an umbrella toward them, gauging the danger. Pools of red spread under the tattered limbs and disemboweled trunks of his brothers, the carnage scattered in a circle around the sea dragon's nest.

Vaikan stands in the boat and grips the hilt of his sword at his side hard, wanting to feel some sparking need for vengeance, waiting for the painful contraction of his ribs around his heart as his body realizes the loss; he remembers what grief feels like, how love's warmth burned. But he feels nothing instead.

"I told you," she says into his silence, low like she might startle him. "There's no controlling a storm." There is, he thinks, penance in her voice. "Will you kill me?"

"That sounds like a request," he says. "Do you want to die?"

"Soon, yes."

"Then, at the end of this, we will find our death together."

They watch the sea dragon fill its nest with eggs and scrape all the broken bits of bodies atop it, a gristly mockery of their lives and yet a divinity in its own right. Vaikan finally looks down at the woman. The bloodwright does not offer to kill the sea dragon, and he does not request it.

He shifts the sails to their final destination: Tereti Mo, home of the last coward-chief.

It takes several days of sailing on belligerent currents and beneath the storm-wracked sky to realize they are still far off from their destination, their course wrecked. There are no islands between Taramong and Tereti Mo, no spits of sand they can set up camp on to rest and warm themselves. Vaikan spearfishes and nets their daily meals, paces the meager length of their ship, rows and rows, and curses the bastard godlings of the sky and sea.

The bloodwright does nothing but finger the sun-scorched seams of her red body, hiding beneath a collection of nets to stave off the sting of further burns. When he asks her to row as well, she ignores him. The only help she offers is direction; she can feel the churn of life as clearly as one feels the sun on a clear day.

When Vaikan tosses her a few dried striped surgeonfish for their supper one night, she doesn't eat it with the usual gusto. He eats his own quick enough to avoid the flavor and watches the shape of moonlight delineate her body in the darkness.

"This place will be my end," she says, breaking almost a week-long silence. For the first time, she sounds fearful.

Vaikan frowns at her. "We will not die at sea."

"No," she says sharply, a breaking beneath the syllable that makes her seem painfully young. A sound that makes Vaikan realize he doesn't know how old she is. "This last city," she says. "I can feel it. There won't be any of me left."

He tells himself he doesn't care, but he has enough sympathy for her not to speak the lie of it. The sea-chilled wind moves over them both then, forcing a shiver out of Vaikan but not the woman.

"If you had not accepted your death before we left the White Chain, then you proved all of us right. You were not ready for this mission."

"I know full well I am going to my death," she says, cleaving through the acid of his accusation. "But it is different, knowing from feeling it."

"Meditate on it. Plough your soul for the seed of death. It will sow itself softer when it does."

She holds herself against the darkness of the sea and sky, against the salt of the stars.

"Vaikan." His name and the softness with which she says it makes him sit up straight. "There is so much life I haven't lived. So much they've taken." A heartbeat's pause. "May I request something of you?"

Fear skitters its way up his throat like a sea spider. "And what would that be?"

A step and then two and then the shadow of her is on him. In the moonlight he can see ribbons of muscle, bloody ligatures, but then she is too close, touching him, her mouth against his. Shock keeps him still for a moment. Kissing her is a finger in his wound, and when he grabs hold of her, he feels how he's formed the absence of his wants into an object of its own, an unreachable thing.

"Touch me," she says, hiding a desperate stutter under his tongue. Young, he thinks again, and tries to pull away.

"You've already been touched." It's cruel, but he needs this to stop. The sight of her is the sight of everything he can't be: powerful, sumptuous in flesh, and ever-changing. He had always contained a longing for what he could have been in another incarnation, so much so that it became invisible to him, ubiquitous as air. To exist was to languish in the impossibility of his desire as to have lungs was to crave breath, as natural as reflex. There was no altering the nature of these things. Except perhaps now.

"No," she hissed, her clawed fingers digging into the sides of his neck. "That was an initiation. I want to be loved." And then, thinking better of it. "I don't want to be alone."

"I don't have anything for you, wright."

"You do. I see it when you look at me," she says. Then, in a whisper, "Even if it's hate or disgust, I'll take it."

Vaikan's voice feels far away when he answers her. "Enough."

"You haven't taken it in days. The thing that stops me from touching you. So let me touch you."

It's true; he's given himself over to the whims of her magic already. He is already courting death, so why not invite it sooner? He tries to curse her, to push her away, but the woman fills his vision, and the singular act of her mouth on his becomes the entirety of his perception. A bite on his lip and through becomes a revelation: wherever she hurts him, her magic spills in to knit the wound. Their mingled exhalations fight the echoes of the lapping water, hearts drumming out a building war rhythm, the percussion fierce in his conspiring veins. There is no more assent needed between them; Vaikan moves at the speed of suffocation with all the greed of a lifetime's drought. Clawing for purchase on the bloodscape of the woman's hips, Vaikan marvels as he fills her with all the weight of a first hunger.

She leaves him destitute, pillaged of all thought but attuned to her cries. He bleeds heat into the bloodwright's urging mouth, the taste of her grin the tang of answered prayers. Their joining is a skirmish, the instruments of war the frictive resonance of flesh on flesh. When her magic begins to seep into his pores, he can sense it is not to dismantle him. It is to join them. Threads of muscle slip beneath his skin and his own pale blue nerves slip out with unnatural ease to find her. His once solitude becomes a joint existence, a feeble tributary meeting the rush of a stronger stream. He sees through two sets of eyes now, feels himself fucking and being fucked, a dual being both soft and hard, taking and taken.

Lungs rhythmic as supplementary hearts, Vaikan shuts his eyes against the dream of it all, running headfirst into the euphoria she is granting him. He wants to be swallowed and the whole world with him, hoarding the scattered light of her magic in the broken cage of her soul.

"I'm sorry," she says, her tears beading from his eyes, her vocal cords rumbling in his throat. "I didn't mean for this. But I . . . I can't stop."

"Then keep me," he says with the mouth she's allowed him to keep. He knew what it meant to love a storm. There was no other outcome than for his soul to be swept away by it. "Keep me, and we'll end this together."

"Yes. Together. Thank you, thank you, Vaikan," she says, a brightness on the edge of her voice. She buries the rest of her need under the stem of his tongue, drowning him in the wet excess of her acceptance.

Storm-tossed, the tempest takes him.

Vast pillars of smoke rise from Tereti Mo's volcanoes when the woman makes landfall. The bloodwright walks the black sand shores alone until she finds a dormant hill high enough to allow her a full view of the island and its many cities, packed with people tight as coral. She doesn't need to find the strategic center here for her reach to be complete; this is the end of her journey, and there is nothing of her magic she needs to save. With what she has of herself and Vaikan, she can call to all flesh from this hill, and all flesh will answer.

The call is a single breath out.

The unmaking is silent this time. Instead of rifts blooming open for new flesh to grow or bones forcing themselves into towering protrusions, the process becomes subtractive. Their screams vanish before they have a chance to leave their mouths. Bodies deflate one by one, emptied of all matter, and fall limp to the ground.

On a breath in, the bloodwright draws the plundered hides to her. Together the empty bodies billow upward, churned by the untouchable gale of the bloodwright's magic. The people's skins pour out from their lavish homes, overflowing markets, and opulent halls—luxuries bought with the blood of her kin—and rise into the skies above the great cities with a weightless ease. Skin by skin, they patch together their ragged edges until a great tapestry of flesh undulates amongst the clouds, shadowing the island and the shallow surrounding waters below.

A seething white fire shoots up the woman's nerves, and this time there is no stopping it. Her body ripples with fear as her magic turns on her for the last time. Every part of her begins to reshape itself but into what she cannot tell. Above her, the monolith of skin begins to float out toward the sea, and it pulls her along with it. When she turns to follow, she does not expect what she sees.

A god's giant carcass wades through the sea toward her, each step making the soil shudder under her feet. It is not any god she knows, and no tale or myth she's heard has described such a terrible vision. The empty-eyed skull stares straight ahead at the horizon as if in expectation. A great cape of offal hangs from its skeleton and floats behind it on the water. Slowly the meat strings itself inside the beams of its ribs, clustering into formation and filling the white frame with what the bloodwright can see are lungs, a liver, a heart. The floating skin meets the giant at the shore, draping itself over bones and the raw, writhing mass of organs.

Finally, it calls to her.

She claws at the ground, queasy and shivering, trying to fight the drag of magic on her. Her body is still changing against her will, all of her pink and rounding out, layering over itself in wiggling wormlike rows.

"No, no, please," she yells as the malformed god draws her up to its voided eyeline. Her soul burrows itself in her fear, deeper and deeper away from death. It is different from knowing and feeling, to see one's end. Except it is not an end she senses; it is something else that this entity wants. "Vaikan!" she screams, desperate for anyone, the last one to soothe her. "Please help me, help me—!"

Not this, not like this, not alone! she thinks as the god presses her into its mouth, past white teeth as big and pale as gravestones. A throat forms just to swallow her but she feels herself rise and expand, deforming into something new. She hisses to herself as something electric arcs through her, a splash of sudden color, of sensation so overwhelming it makes her scream in agony.

Was this another untold price for her magic? To be eaten by the deep god of death? Her soul a meal to be shat out into the abyssal plains, outside the currents of reincarnation?

Kill me please, whatever god you are, you must have some mercy in you! This is supposed to be my end, our end! No more, no more, no—

Wright!

Inside the woman inside the god, Vaikan strokes her soul with his own.

Open your eyes.

She does.

I'm with you.

No. *Their* eyes open. His soul braids through hers, cooling the searing of her fear. The curve of the world bends before their new sight as they take up the god's eyes. Gulls flit around their bare head, minuscule wisps of white feathers, stupid and curious, pecking at their new behemoth body. Half-submerged around their feet, they see the unpatterned patchwork of reefs and meadows of kelp from their great height as abstract teal and emerald splatters.

The voices of skin and flesh and bone call to their once-enemies, speaking in a chorus of dreams, of desires they had never conceived, fears they had never imagined. Together, they lift a hand to the clouds and feel the cool moisture of gathering storms collect on their fingers, then farther still, up into the vastness of the pitying sky toward nothing and anything, grasping for the shape of uncountable futures, uncountable ends, like so much salt and stars, bitter and bright and boundless.

Form 8774-D

FROM *Reactor*

SCIENCE FICTION

UNITED STATES GOVERNMENT
BUREAU OF METAHUMAN, MUTANT, AND OCCULT AFFAIRS

FORM 8774-D: AFFIRMATION OF EMERGENT
METAHUMAN, MUTANT, AND/OR
OCCULT ABILITIES/POWERS

I. PERSONAL INFORMATION

a. Applicant

Answer each question as completely as possible. Incomplete fields will delay processing, verification, and certification of metahuman/mutant/occult practitioner status. Use only black or blue ink.

Name: _____

Alias(es): _____

Address: _____

Date of Birth: _____ This timeline? yes ☐ no ☐

    If no, indicate date of birth in future: _____

                        alternate timeline: _____

Gender, if any: _____

Clone? yes ☐ no ☐

    If yes, indicate time and place of creation, if known.
    _____

Cyborg? yes ☐ no ☐

If yes, indicate nature and function of cybernetic implants. _____

_____

_____

Citizenship: _____

_____

Recognized terrestrial nation-state? yes ☐ no ☐

If no, planet of origin*: _____

* If applicant was born on a planet other than Earth, or if parent(s)' origin is unknown, complete and attach BMMOA form **8804-UO, Displaced/Immigrant Metahuman Status Notification**.

Thursday, 8:47 a.m.
LEELEE'S SECOND CUP of coffee hasn't even worked its pitiful magic yet, she hasn't finished deleting all her work emails or swiping down through the office Slack channel just so it's resting on the current message if her supervisor happens to come by and notice. Eight friggin' forty-seven, and the superwannabe comes through the door. No knock, no hesitation. Her first appointment isn't until nine. "Excuse me. Miss Remsburg?"

Leelee nods. No point denying it.

"I'm Plumeria Reynolds. I believe I have an appointment. I know I'm a little early, but"—she looks slightly embarrassed but also weirdly proud of herself—"I just couldn't wait!"

Leelee could send her back out into the waiting room to wait for thirteen minutes, but what the hell, nothing is happening in here and if she starts early maybe that means, by some law of conservation of impatient applicants, that a thirteen-minute break will appear later in the day.

Ha.

"Sure," she says. "Have a seat."

Leelee has her own office, with a door and everything, an unusual perk for someone at her service level but mandated because many of the discussions that happen in said office are of a deeply private nature. It isn't easy to apply for recognition of metahuman or mutant abilities. There's a stigma. There's also an awesome factor, but Leelee knows that the supers who revel in the awesome without understanding the stigma and the burden are boarding the express train to Villain-ville. She makes a note about them in her file.

Plumeria Reynolds, at first glance, does not appear to be such a person. She's wearing a skirt and blouse from a mall store—perfectly fine but unremarkable, unlike many of Leelee's clients who come in wearing costumes of their own design and brandishing various fake weapons and artifacts. The real ones don't make it through security screening.

"You've filled out Form 8774-D?" Ms. Reynolds nods. "Let me just take a look."

Form 8774-D, *Affirmation of Emergent Metahuman, Mutant, and/ or Occult Abilities/Powers,* is just the first step in the process of being vetted and certified—but it's a critical step, and the hardest, because the temptation is to lie, to make yourself sound better, to be a Thanos in a world of Ant-Men. A big part of Leelee's job is working through Form 8774-D with claimants to get their answers in order so they don't get embarrassed later.

Plumeria Reynolds's form indicates that she is neither a clone nor a cyborg, and that she was born on Planet Earth. She claims powers of flight and energy projection, manifesting after . . . Leelee squints but can't quite make it out. "When did your powers first manifest?" she asks.

"Oh, my handwriting," Plumeria says apologetically. "I can hardly read it myself. The whole thing started on a fishing boat, if you can believe that. I was thirteen. My uncle caught some strange creature, none of us knew what it was, and my father told me not to touch it." She shrugs. "But I did. It was kind of slimy, and the slime got into me, I guess. Next thing I knew, I could do . . . well, all the things I wrote on the form there." She ends with a self-effacing little laugh that Leelee finds painfully endearing.

Leelee makes a note on Plumeria's form. "Okay," she says.

"Weird, right?" Plumeria leans forward. "But you probably hear lots of weird stories in your job," she adds, clearly hoping Leelee will repeat some of them.

"I sure do," Leelee says. "But you know, privacy laws . . ." It's her turn to shrug.

"Of course, sure." Plumeria nods a bit too energetically.

Leelee finishes scanning the form. "Everything appears to be in order," she says.

"Great!" Plumeria beams. "So, when can I start?"

Inwardly Leelee cringes. How can so many people not read the basic instructions? When you download Form 8774-D from the department's website it comes with instructions. When applying for certified metahuman status, an applicant literally cannot get the form without the instructions and an overview of the process. Yet several times a week she runs into this situation.

"This is not a recruiting office," she says. The speech comes out on autopilot, she's given it so many times. "The Bureau of Metahuman, Mutant, and Occult Affairs does not put you in touch with any other superheroes. We do not send you out on missions. What we do in this office is decide whether your particular suite of powers and abilities qualifies you to be a Certified Superhuman Practitioner. What you do with that certification is up to you . . . although several superhero organizations do keep tabs on what we do here." She leans closer to Plumeria, because she likes her and wants to give her a little inside info. "Plus I know for a fact that the Dimensional Defense Agency has someone psionically monitoring our clerical staff, so if you fit their profile, they'll be reaching out to you toot sweet. Possibly via your dreams." Leelee winks, and then she's all business again. "Your next step will be a demonstration of your abilities. Our department scheduler will contact you about that. Expect it to take a week or so."

"Oh." Plumeria is disappointed but trying not to show it. This makes Leelee like her more. "How long before the demonstration, once it's scheduled?"

"We're typically scheduling six to eight weeks out," Leelee says. "I know it's a long time to wait after you've worked up your courage to take this big step, and I wish it could be sooner. But that's the process, you know?"

She stands, and so does Plumeria. "What do you think?" Plumeria asks. "About my chances, I mean?"

"It's not up to me," Leelee says. "I just make sure the forms are filled out right. It's all about the demonstration, and if you can do what the form says you can do, I can't see any reason why they wouldn't certify you." She gives Plumeria a map to the demonstration site, way outside DC past Dulles Airport.

"Thank you for helping me," Plumeria says. Then she leans in a little closer and asks, "Were you serious about the Dimensional Defense Agency?"

"Oh, yeah," Leelee says, the *yeah* sounding more like *yah* because you can take the girl out of the Upper Peninsula but you can't take the UP out of the girl. "They totally keep an eye on what we're doing here. Drives our security guys crazy."

They share a laugh, and Leelee sees Plumeria out the door. That wasn't so bad, she thinks. Her coffee isn't even all the way cold.

At lunch she's talking with Drogba, one of the security guys. Everyone in BMMOA security is a super, usually a disabled vet from the Armageddon Phalanx or the Thule Armada, cashiered out of active service but still potent enough to keep most baby would-bes in line. "Tell you what," Drogba says around a mouthful of cafeteria lo mein, "no offense, but if I was just starting out now? No way I'd apply. Why do you think people do it?"

"A lot of them want to serve," Leelee says. "But there's also a lot who just want the validation. They want other people to know they're special. Didn't you?"

Back in the day, Drogba was known as The String, for his ability to manipulate matter at the subatomic level. The final battle of the Vortex Singularity left him a shadow of his former self, after he nearly tore himself apart creating a wormhole to drain the singularity out of space-time and into an interdimensional void. That kind of power, the kind of sacrifice, Leelee can barely imagine. Most people, even at BMMOA, don't know Drogba's story, but one of Leelee's skills is that people tend to tell her things.

"Nah," he says now, and she thinks he's sincere. "I figured once they saw what I could do, I'd be all set. Ain't no point in false modesty."

"True enough," she says. She's still thinking about that later when she gets home and finds Samir on the couch watching baseball. He's made dinner. They eat in front of the TV, half-heartedly arguing about what to watch. Leelee gets tired around ten. She takes her time getting ready for bed, and by the time she's crawling in Samir comes into the bedroom yawning. Everything happens in its prescribed order. Phones on chargers, alarms set, blankets shuffled around, lights out.

Every day is pretty much the same. Leelee likes it that way.

I. PERSONAL INFORMATION (cont'd)

b. Applicant's Family

Name(s) of parent(s): _____

Address of parents if not same as above: _____

_____

Planet of origin of parents if not Earth: _____

Alternate dimension? yes ☐ no ☐

If yes, name dimension and indicate means of access (portal, wormhole, etc.) _____

_____

Race of parents if not *Homo sapiens*:* _____

  If different races:
     Parent 1 _____   Gender, if known: _____
     Parent 2 _____   Gender, if known: _____
     Other _____   Gender, if known: _____

* If applicant was not gestated and delivered by a biological entity, complete and attach BMMOA Form **8804-NB, Certification of Non-Biological Origin**.

Wednesday, 10:05 a.m.

This is one of the sad cases. Well, lots of them are sad, because people are so often deluded about what kind of powers they really have. But to Leelee, the saddest ones are the kids. Specifically, the kids whose parents have decided to ride the child's powers to the narcissistic Promised Land of Super Parenthood. The place where vicarious living, parasitic validation, and insincere performative patriotism mix. Leelee has spent way too much time observing the inhabitants of this terrible place, and it sure looks like she's about to make a return visit. She calls them NVPs, Narcissistic Vicarious Parents. The usage has spread through the office, a phenomenon of which she is inordinately proud.

They're five minutes late, just enough to let Leelee know they're calling the shots. Mom's all smiles, wearing a suit and carrying a briefcase. She strides in, reaching to shake Leelee's hand and present herself as the one in charge. "Angie Brooks," she says. Dad and the candidate slouch in behind her, two peas in a pod. "This is my husband, Derek, and daughter, Emmaline."

Emmaline is thirteen, skinny, shoulders hunched, doesn't make eye contact. Hair a patchwork of different dye jobs. She wears waffle-stitch long sleeves to hide the cutting scars under a My Chemical Romance shirt that to Leelee's eye looks like it probably belonged to Dad first. He's also skinny and ill at ease, his hair a black roostertail that looks natural now but probably lent itself to quite a Mohawk back in the day.

Angie hands Leelee the form. Emmaline sits in the chair farthest from Leelee's desk and stares out the window. Her hand strays to her phone every five seconds, but she pulls it back, cutting glances at her mother. "She's very powerful," Angie says. "With the correct mentorship, absolutely Omega potential."

"That's not up to me to decide," Leelee says. She starts working through the form.

"Mom," the girl growls. "I want to go back to school."

"This is your future, Em," Angie says. "You can miss half a school day."

"We'll get you back before your art class," Derek says, trying to mediate. "Then we'll get to your lessons."

Lessons. Some parents actually pay older heroes to cultivate kids' powers. It's one of the purest manifestations of NVP syndrome. Leelee hates these cases. She wishes she could tell Emmaline that she'll survive and thrive, find her way despite her parents. But all Emmaline knows right now is she has some kind of power, but she doesn't want it. Or of course she wants the power; she's just terrified of everything that comes with it. Puberty is hard enough without mutant or metahuman latency starting to express itself. The halls of your average middle school, or high school, aren't forgiving spaces when it comes to being different. Leelee thinks they're better than they used to be, but still. Little Emmaline Brooks would just be Em the anime artist if she could. It's the parents who seize on the possibility of powers, like showbiz parents, and the kids suffer. "One hundred percent Omega potential," Angie says. "We have lots of people consulting who think she's really destined for the top."

"Ma'am, you don't have to pitch me," Leelee says. "Your daughter will be evaluated at her demonstration. I'm just making sure the paperwork is in order."

She's looking down at Form 8774-D as Angie keeps going. "She can teleport, you know. Actually teleport, not just move really fast."

Leelee has already seen that in the III.d response field, but she nods to be polite. "I see that, sure. Also the kinetic blasts, and the other . . ." Angie has checked a lot of boxes. "We'll be vetting all of this in the demonstration," Leelee says. "Is there anything you want to amend?" She looks up.

Derek is looking out the window just like his daughter. Angie meets Leelee's gaze. "We're confident Emmaline will exceed your expectations," she says. "She's always been a very gifted child. Her test scores are off the charts."

"Good enough," Leelee says.

Leelee directs her next question to Emmaline. "Is everything in the form, or is there anything else I need to know?"

Emmaline looks Leelee in the eye—the first time she's made eye contact with anyone since they walked in the door. "I hate this," she says. "I'll do the stupid certification but I'm never going to be a superhero."

"That's your prerogative, Emmaline," Leelee says. "Completing the certification process doesn't obligate you to anything."

"Although of course you'll understand things differently when you get a little older and you aren't quite so . . . contrary." Angie's grin is tight. There are going to be words in the Brooks household tonight.

"So, what's our next step?" Derek asks, again trying to keep his wife and daughter from going after each other.

Leelee gives them the scheduling spiel, hands them the map, and watches them go. The girl looks over her shoulder at Leelee as she walks out the door, eyes deep and haunted, jaw tight. She's on a thin edge. If her parents drive her too hard, she's going to crack. Either go rogue or turn full villain. But if she can get through the next few years without her parents screwing her up too much, she'll find her strength. Leelee's rooting for her.

"What would you do if we had a kid and the kid had powers?" Leelee asks Samir that night. Kids have come up before. He's got a good job as a freelance programmer, they have enough common interests to have fun but enough differences that they have independent lives. His parents like her. Her parents like him. She's thirty-three, so if she's going to have kids it ought to be fairly soon. All this stuff churns through her head every time she has a kid client. It's one of the ways she brings work home, and she hates it.

"You ready to have a kid?" he asks.

"Oh, I don't know. Are you?"

He thinks about it for a little while. "Yeah. I think I would be."

She lies awake that night, listening to Samir's occasional snores and wondering what their child would look like. The future starts to take shape. She thinks she likes it.

II. ORIGIN OF POWERS

When did you first notice the ability/power?
Birth _____ Puberty _____ Other (explain): _____

Indicate the source of the power or the event/cause that bestowed the power. Check as many as apply.

Latent	yes ☐ no ☐
Unknown	yes ☐ no ☐
Energy exposure	yes ☐ no ☐
Magical artifact	yes ☐ no ☐
Scientific experimentation	yes ☐ no ☐
Technological artifact	yes ☐ no ☐

If you checked any box other than "Latent," name and describe the cause as completely as you are able. _____

_____

_____

_____

Tuesday, 10:13 a.m.

Her ten o'clock appointment is a young kid with a history of family trauma brought in by a distant relative who is involved in experimental science. Leelee's seen this one before, dozens of times. Sometimes the kid can make ants do the Macarena and nothing else; sometimes the kid turns out to be a psychokinetic juggernaut capable of shaking Planet Earth out of its orbit. You never know until you work through their applications and decide whether to move them along for a demonstration and further screening.

Brady Murthy is eight years old. His birth parents were casualties of the Calcutta Breach, along with approximately a hundred thousand other people. He was adopted as a baby by Maimuna and Gautam, both chemists. Began to show abilities . . . Huh, Leelee thinks. "So, Brady, you started showing powers when you were two years old?"

"That's what my mom and dad say," he answers. Cute, bright-eyed kid. Skinny, lots of energy. He fiddles with the bobbleheads on Leelee's desk and Leelee doesn't tell him not to.

"It's true," his mother says. "When he was a toddler, he could touch a plant and the plant would grow."

"Now he can grow a tree from a seed to twenty feet tall, in just hours!" Gautam is bursting with pride. Real pride. Leelee loves to see that. Too many parents either treat their kids like freaks or go full NVP.

"I wish I could ask for a demonstration," Leelee says. She nods at her potted plants on the shelf by the window. "Those poor guys could use some help."

Brady's out of his chair before either Leelee or his parents can stop him. He runs a finger along one leaf of a spider plant. With a crackling noise, it doubles in size and sprouts a dozen babies, its leaves becoming a darker shade of green.

"Brady!" Maimuna snaps. "We are not to demonstrate here. You know that."

"Sorry, Mom." Brady shuffles back to his chair, head down.

Gautam doesn't care whether his boy was supposed to demonstrate or not. Barely able to contain himself, he points at the plant. "You see? A marvel!"

"I do see," Leelee says with a big smile at Brady. "And I'm grateful. I've had that plant a long time, and it never looked so good."

Brady smiles back. Leelee feels happy the rest of the day.

Samir's gone until Saturday, and Leelee enjoys the time by herself. He's gone once in a while for gigs, people flying him here and there. She doesn't have to keep track of it so she doesn't, except usually she knows where he is. Detroit this time.

She stays up late watching the news, and irritatingly it's all about superheroes because there's been a huge battle against an army of invaders from an alternate Venus. The reconstituted Vanguard combined with the North Star Sentinels to repel it, but there was a lot of damage in Chicago. She talks to Samir about it late that night. "Good thing you weren't there," she says. "I know it's dumb, but I worry whenever you're traveling."

"I know, babe," he says. "Nothing to worry about, though. Just work."

They shoot the shit for a while about TV, stuff they saw on Instagram, the usual. When he hangs up, Leelee enjoys the peace and quiet. She misses him, but sometimes it's nice to have the place to herself.

III. NATURE OF POWERS

Over what area of matter, energy, or spirit do you exert control, power, or influence? Check as many as apply.

a. Matter

Earth   yes ☐ no ☐
   Stone   yes ☐ no ☐
   Sand   yes ☐ no ☐
   Lava   yes ☐ no ☐

Water   yes ☐ no ☐
   Ice   yes ☐ no ☐
   Vapor/Fog   yes ☐ no ☐

Metals
   Ferrous   yes ☐ no ☐
   Non-Ferrous   yes ☐ no ☐
   Both   yes ☐ no ☐

Other (plastic, atmospheric gases, etc.) yes ☐ no ☐
   If yes, list here: _____

Specific element(s) only: yes ☐ no ☐
   If yes, list here: _____

b. Energy

Weather   yes ☐ no ☐
   If specific phenomena only, list here: _____
_____

Atomic energy/radioactivity   yes ☐ no ☐

Electromagnetic energy   yes ☐ no ☐

Gravity   yes ☐ no ☐
   Flight   yes ☐ no ☐

Magnetism   yes ☐ no ☐

Electricity, including lightning   yes ☐ no ☐

Visible light   yes ☐ no ☐
   Personal invisibility?   yes ☐ no ☐

Temperature	yes ☐ no ☐
Heat only	yes ☐ no ☐
Cold only	yes ☐ no ☐
Sound	yes ☐ no ☐

Monday, 4:44 p.m.

The home stretch of a Monday, one of the times of the week when a working girl feels a glimmer of hope. That wasn't so bad, the mind says to itself. Only four more like that and we get another weekend. She's working through her last screening of the day, and then things take a hard right into Bonkersville.

He sweeps into her office, six-six, broad shoulders, sensational hair. Long cape with a high collar, full costume. Trouble, thinks Leelee, but the kind of trouble that is sometimes worth it. This is not a professional assessment; she issues a mental apology to Samir, who will never know about the little tremor she just felt deep down in her belly. "Good afternoon, sir," she says. "You are . . ."

With a theatrical indrawn breath and a smoldering gaze, he proclaims, "You will know me as Brazagh-Nul."

Leelee makes a point of scanning her appointment ledger. "I'm afraid I don't see any Braz . . . can you say that again?"

"Brazagh-Nul," again with the deep breath through the nose and the glower. So much for little tremors. Now he's just annoying. Leelee knows she should, but she just cannot find any way to be sympathetic to his bullshit. "Yeah, I don't . . ." She looks up at him again. Why are the handsome ones always so weird? "Can you spell that?"

Brazagh-Nul huffs out an irritated sigh, collapses into a chair, and arranges his cape. "Brad Zigler."

"Ohhhhh, okay. There you are." Leelee turns on her professional smile and says, "Let's go through your materials, shall we?"

Zigler's claims are quite extravagant. He has checked almost every box under the Matter and Energy headings and listed various artifacts under III.f with names unlike anything Leelee has ever heard. She wonders if Zigler belongs to that common subspecies of applicants who basically fill out the form as fantasy versions of themselves. Some of those cases are almost as sad as the kids with NVPs.

"Mr. Zigler," Leelee says carefully, not knowing whether Zigler is lying, delusional, or even possibly accurate in his self-assessment. "You sure have checked a lot of boxes here."

"The form can only capture the merest shadow of my powers," Zigler says, his imperious demeanor restored.

"Some people's powers do fall between categories, it's true," Leelee says, just to be agreeable. "Okay, then. The next step will be scheduling your demonstration. Someone from our office will be contacting you—"

"I will demonstrate nothing. Brazagh-Nul is not a performing seal."

"Part of the validation process involves a demonstration of the powers underlying the claim to metahuman or mutant status," Leelee explains patiently.

It's almost always the same. They make claims, and in their claims Leelee can see their hopes, desires, fantasies, fears. She could diagnose every single one of them more accurately than any shrink. Let someone write their own origin story, and they'll tell you everything you want to know about what matters to them. But what most of them can't do is back it up. At some point, Form 8774-D always trips them up.

"Absurd," Zigler says. "Yet if that is the price I must pay to escape the petty scrutiny of you and your bureaucratic anthill, very well."

"Okay," Leelee says, mentally putting him into the No Help Under Any Circumstances category. Some people you bend the rules for, but not if they talk to you like that. "We'll be forwarding this for further screening, as we do with all applicants. Someone will respond at the number you've provided to schedule your demonstration under controlled circumstances." She holds out the map to the demonstration facility.

"When?" Zigler snatches the map from her hand. "I cannot be made to wait for long."

Leelee keeps her tone level, but Zigler is really getting on her nerves. "Generally six to eight weeks. Now I'm sure we're both aware of the time, so—"

"I care nothing for the time." Same imperious tone, and now Zigler presses against her desk so he can loom over her. "I care about you performing the service for which you earn your doubtless bloated salary, in a timely fashion!"

She shifts his category to her own personal ninth circle:

WPOHIHWOF, Wouldn't Piss on Him If He Was on Fire. "Some-one will be contacting you, Mr. Zigler," she says. "Have a fine rest of your day."

"You will address me as Brazagh-Nul," he says from the door, and then he's gone in a sweep of his cape.

Leelee resists the urge to dump his file straight in the trash. He would deserve it, but it wouldn't be the right thing to do.

So frustrating sometimes, this drive to be ethical.

Now it's five o'clock. She neatens up her desk and leaves, waving to Louise and Drogba as she heads out the employee entrance at the rear of the building. Usually she goes out the front, but assholes like Brazagh-Nul sometimes wait out front to hassle her after work, and Leelee can't face that today. The distance to her Metro stop is about the same either way, so she strolls by the facilities guys smoking and the separate group of office professionals smoking and goes around the corner onto O Street. The BMMOA isn't part of the big office complexes closer to the Mall and the Capitol. They're stuck on Naylor Court, off the beaten path, on a block that's mostly smallish condo buildings with the occasional interior designer or architect sprinkled in.

She meets Samir over on 9th Street, at an Ethiopian place they both like. It's right around the corner from the BMMOA, and not far from the train home. He's already there when she arrives, surrounded by appetizers because he's a grazer. No big entrees for him. This works for Leelee. She likes to taste everything too, and does while she fills him in on her day.

"Can you believe that jerk?"

"Brazagh-Nul," Samir says theatrically, drawing out the last vowel. "Pretty good name for a D&D boss."

"That's what I thought too!" Leelee sops up a meaty sauce with the last bit of injera and pops it in her mouth, which means she can't respond when Samir says, "But I bet you got him calmed down. That's really your power. Intuition, empathy . . ."

"I am literally the most ordinary person in the world, Samir," she says when she has swallowed her food. "I have nothing like a superpower."

"If you say so." Samir's looking at her like she said something funny, but Leelee doesn't think it's funny at all. She really doesn't want people thinking she has a superpower.

III. NATURE OF POWERS *(cont'd)*

c. Bodily Modification and/or Transformation

Physical strength/density   yes ☐ no ☐

Physical malleability   yes ☐ no ☐

Size   yes ☐ no ☐
    Growth only   yes ☐ no ☐
    Shrinking only   yes ☐ no ☐

Regeneration/healing   yes ☐ no ☐

Physical form/shape changing   yes ☐ no ☐
    If yes, characterize this power in the space provided: ___
_____
_____

Animal or plant mimicry   yes ☐ no ☐
    If yes, list animals or plants in the space provided: _____
_____

d. Mental, Ontological, and Occult Effects

Human/animal consciousness   yes ☐ no ☐

Plant/vegetable consciousness   yes ☐ no ☐

Psychokinetic manipulation   yes ☐ no ☐
    Telekinesis   yes ☐ no ☐
    Pyrokinesis   yes ☐ no ☐
    Cryokinesis   yes ☐ no ☐
    Other (describe) _____
_____

Space-time   yes ☐ no ☐
    Probability   yes ☐ no ☐
    Time travel   yes ☐ no ☐
    Teleportation   yes ☐ no ☐
      Limited range?   yes ☐ no ☐
      If yes, how far? _____

Psionic energy*   yes ☐ no ☐

Telepathy*   yes ☐ no ☐

Mind-reading*   yes ☐ no ☐

Mind control*   yes ☐ no ☐

Clairvoyance*   yes ☐ no ☐

Occult, magical, or arcane power**   yes ☐ no ☐

Characterize the powers in the space provided: _____
_____
_____

Other. Summarize in the space provided. _____
_____
_____

* If you checked any of the categories within the group "psionic energy," complete and attach DHHS form **8809-AA, Registration for Telepaths and Psionic Adepts Act of 2015 Basic Information Form**.

** Occult power is defined as power derived from otherplanar sources. These can include demons, devils, jinn, etc.

Friday, 2:26 p.m.

Friday, of course it has to be Friday when for the first time in Leelee's seven-plus years at BMMOA, the shit actually genuinely hits the fan.

As she is always insisting to Samir and the security guards, Leelee doesn't have any superpowers. Unless you count an unerring bullshit detector and a knack for defusing potentially violent situations. What line would super-intuition fit into on Form 8774-D?

That's what she's wondering, idly, between appointments, when a client strides out of one of the inner offices shouting in a language Leelee suspects is alien. He picks up a desk and throws it through the interior wall between the waiting area and the offices. People sprint for the exits, but Leelee can't get out without going past him, and anyway she's mad. People can't just bust up the BMMOA office.

She stands and shouts through her doorway. "Hey!"

He turns to look at her. "This is a US Government facility, sir," she says, in her most commanding tone. "You're going to have to leave."

For a brief moment, she thinks it might actually work. He stops. He takes a step back. He considers her as if he is making initial observations of a never-before-seen species of invertebrate. Then she realizes that there's a long distance—a galactic gulf, a dimensional rift—between appreciation of chutzpah and actual acquiescence. What really brings this realization home is the beam of magenta energy that lances out and destroys her desk, sending Leelee flying and covering her with blackened bits of particle board. Her appointment ledger drifts in charred flakes around her.

III.d for sure, she thinks. Given the magenta color and the overall personality of the MH, she's leaning toward arcane energy. So, he's one of the occult types, and those are always tricky because of the otherplanar and otherdimensional claims. How exactly is a mid-level administrator in a tiny office on Naylor Court supposed to check up on who's mentoring whom or siphoning power to whom in Limbo or Gehenna or some non-Euclidean beach resort on the shores of a fucking sunless sea?

"This is not how you optimize your certification process, sir!" she shouts over the general atmosphere of mayhem.

Louise and Reggie swing into action right about then. This isn't an ordinary baby super throwing a tantrum, though. It's a whole different threat level, maybe not Omega but not merely Eta or Theta either. Somewhere around Mu? More than any of the security people have handled since the last time they saved the world, which was a long time ago. Drogba bursts out of the break room. Before he can do anything, the rogue super knocks him flat. Reggie's cyborg eye shoots an energy beam that scorches the rogue's back. With a roar, the rogue spins around—straight into a haymaker from Louise. He crashes through another wall, and Leelee sees an opening. She runs like hell for the front door, but before she can get there the rogue explodes back into the ravaged common area, his skin crackling where Reggie's eye beam keeps hitting him. He leaps and tackles Reggie. Both of them crash into the security screening gate. Louise comes flying in with another series of thunderous punches, but they're overmatched. The rogue flings them both off and spreads his hands. Magenta energy slashes across the walls and ceiling.

Leelee has never heard a building collapse, but she's hearing sounds that sure sound like what a building would sound like if it was about to collapse. And there's no way out.

Until a super in a vibrant blue costume with a full mask punches up through the floor and leaps toward the rogue. The rogue tries to hit him with those magenta beams, but the blue hero is too quick.

He ducks and feints and then he's right on the rogue, staggering him with some kind of martial arts routine. With every blow that lands, blue energy crackles from his fists. The rogue reels back, blasting the front doors out of their frames as he tries to get away, but the blue hero is on him. They grapple out into the street, and Leelee follows, getting out the door just as the front of the building sags inward and collapses. A cloud of dust obscures the battling supers. Leelee doesn't know which way to run. Occasionally a magenta beam lances out of the cloud. She does the safe thing and hits the deck near a parked car. The sounds of combat subside, and the dust cloud dissipates. Leelee risks a glance over the hood of the car.

The blue hero is there. The rogue is unconscious at his feet. All of a sudden everyone for blocks around has their phones out. "That was scary," Leelee says.

The super winks at her. "All in a day's work, ma'am," he says.

Ma'am? Leelee is thirty-three years old. What child—or what kind of cornpone con artist playing to the cameras—would call her ma'am? Also she does not recognize him, and she suspects he hasn't been certified. He should probably be filling out Form 8774-D and meeting with her.

Before she can say any of that, though, the super is gone.

There's a rumble and a crash and Louise appears in the rubble, digging herself out and then holding a slab up for Reggie and Drogba.

"We are totally going to need a new office," Leelee says.

"Way things are lately," Reggie pants, "they're gonna move us to Silver Spring or some shit."

They stand there for a while after the rogue super is taken away. Samir arrives, looking shaken, and pulls Leelee into a fierce embrace. "Sometimes I forget how dangerous your job can be," he says quietly.

"Babe," she says. "It's all good. The blue guy, he was pretty impressive."

It is decided that they should all go have a drink, since there's no way to go back to work. It's a good decision. They all relax together. To Reggie, Louise, and Drogba, the day's events are old hat, and it isn't long before they're talking about it like a game they all went to.

"Hey, Leelee," Drogba says. "I saw what you did in there. I was peeking out the break room door waiting to make a move, but you almost backed him down." He glances at Louise and Reggie. "Did you guys see that?" They shake their heads. "Like a Jedi mind trick, you know?" Drogba turns back to Leelee. "Ever think you have a superpower?"

"Why is everybody always asking me that? No. God, no. At least I hope not," Leelee says, and then she's apologizing in case she's offended him and buying another round of drinks.

"I'm telling you," Drogba says. "Any intuition like yours, that ain't natural."

"Hundred percent," Samir agrees. Leelee glares at him. "What," he says, "you want me to lie?"

Leelee's jaw is suddenly so tight she can barely get words out of her mouth. "I," she says, "do not have a superpower. Okay?"

"Yeah, okay," Drogba says. Samir looks away.

That night she tells Samir she's thinking about quitting. He nods and does what he always does when she talks about quitting, which is pack her a bowl. It has become something of a ritual, to the point where *I'm thinking about quitting* actually means *Wanna get high?* She says they should start using edibles like she always does, but there's something in her that doesn't want to let go of that burn deep in the lungs.

"You worried you're going to get hurt?" he asks.

"Yeah," she says. "Did you see what happened today?"

He watches the smoke drift out of his lungs up toward the ceiling. "I saw," he says in that singsongy way he has when he's considering carefully what to say next, "a situation, and people responding to the situation the way their excellent training prepared them to respond. Including you, babe," he adds before she can get mad.

"All in a day's work," she says bitterly.

"Yeah, that was kind of over the top. But seriously, you kicked ass today. For someone with no powers, faced with that situation?" He extends a fist and Leelee feels the profound obligation to bump it. "Fuck yeah."

They're both pretty stoned. It's nice. Samir has a way of making her feel centered, like he believes in what she's doing more than she does, and that makes it a little easier for her to get up in the morning and do it all over again.

III. NATURE OF POWERS (cont'd)

e. Epiphenomena

> In the space provided, note any unusual occurrences related to your exercise of your ability/power. (Examples can include flashes of light, changes in ambient temperature, destabilization of local space-time, appearance of dimensional apertures, etc. List as many as apply.)

> _____

> _____

> _____

f. Foci, Talismans, and Other Object Enhancements

> Is your power dependent on or enhanced by a(n)
>
> physical object, talisman, or focus?   yes ☐ no ☐
>
> animal familiar?   yes ☐ no ☐
>
> technological device?   yes ☐ no ☐
>
> If yes, describe the object's, familiar's, or device's origin and capabilities in the space provided.

> _____

> _____

> _____

Thursday, 1:17 p.m.

The BMMOA office is rebuilt in an astonishing three days, thanks to the loan of a nanobot swarm from the headquarters of the Graviton Corps. Leelee enjoys the time off. Thursday morning she putters around in her office because the nanobots put some of her things in weird places. Putting a positive spin on this inconvenience, she takes it as a hint that it's time to shuffle things around a little, freshen them up. She doesn't have any clients until after lunch, which is chicken and rice from the halal food truck over by Logan Circle. Her mouth is still tingling pleasantly from the sauce when her one o'clock knocks on her office door.

"Hi?" the applicant says, peering around the doorframe. "So sorry I'm late." She strides to Leelee's desk, extending a hand. "Veronica Kirstein."

Leelee shakes and takes in Kirstein's presentation. Navy blue dress, knee-high boots with just a hint of heel. Nicely understated and confident . . . until you get to the six chunky gold rings, each with a different color stone. This sets off a little alarm bell in Leelee's mind. "Nice rings," she comments, to let Ms. Kirstein know she's paying attention. "Security is supposed to scan potential alien or arcane artifacts."

"Oh, security," Kirstein says with an airy wave. "They saw what I wanted them to see."

Leelee has an intensifying bad feeling about Veronica Kirstein. In her experience, this feeling is never wrong.

"I'm afraid that's not really how we do things," Leelee says. "I'm going to have to ask you to return to screening and—"

In the next moment, Veronica Kirstein whips off her dress, revealing a charcoal-gray costume, high at the thigh and low at the bust, accented with a blaze of orange in a fiery V at one shoulder. The dress disappears before it can flutter to the floor, and Leelee's hair stands up as some kind of ambient energy propagates through the room.

Veronica raises her arms, showing off some finely toned triceps and arching her back a little in classic Sexy Wizard Lady style. The rings leak a spooky radiance out into the room. Leelee can barely stop herself from saying, Hey, I also am in possession of boobs, so can you maybe show me something more interesting? Like a real actual filled-out Form 8774-D instead of pretending you're in a Frazetta painting?

"I am Lady V, and you will hear me!" she cries. "Soon the world will hear me!" Leelee suspects theatrical voice training. A copy of Form 8774-D appears on her desk, filling itself out in a flowing and quite legible cursive.

Okay, she thinks. Pretty impressive, but still against the rules. "I will hear you, as soon as you return to security, check those rings, and start this procedure the way it's supposed to be started." Leelee's voice is calm, but the demonstration of power right here in her office—especially right on the heels of last Friday's disaster—has her alarm meter somewhere between nervous and terrified. The appearance of the form right after she was thinking about it is probably a coincidence, but still feels weird.

Drogba appears in her doorway, flanked by Louise and Reggie.

Leelee sure is glad to see them. "We got readings of some kind of power being used," Drogba says.

"You certainly did, you rent-a-thugs," Lady V snaps. "My powers, which I used to walk right by you." She turns her attention back to Leelee. "You have the form. By any reasonable standard, even a stupid bureaucratic one, I have amply demonstrated that I ought to be certified. Let's get this done."

"It's not really that easy," Leelee says.

"I've been working with the Vanguard Alliance," Lady V insists, some of her bravado falling away. "Kind of teaming up, not officially as a member yet. And I fought the Apocalypse Battalion shoulder-to-shoulder with Captain Cosmic. I am legit."

"What do those rings do?" Leelee asks. "Where did you get them?"

"That's all on the stupid form!" Veronica shrieks. Visible energy is spreading from the stones, wreathing her arms. The colors get more intense. There are tears on Lady V's face. She's not in control.

"Mm hm," Leelee says.

At that moment Drogba does what the media used to call the String Thing.

Maybe he couldn't annihilate wormholes or rearrange space-time anymore, but he still has enough power to squiggle some particles around in Lady V's mind and drop her to the ground in a brainwave state more or less akin to deep sleep.

"Sorry," he says as Louise and Reggie drag Lady V to the holding cell in the basement. Two in one week, Leelee thinks. She hopes it isn't the start of a trend. "I feel for her, actually. It's hard to get people to listen sometimes."

"I'm taking the rest of the day off," Leelee says.

"On your first day back? Somebody else is going to be Employee of the Month for sure." Drogba nods at her desk. "You have to process her still, though, right?"

Veronica Kirstein's completed Form 8774-D is still on her desk. Leelee sighs and sits. Due to a scandal a few years back about backlogs and faked certifications, BMMOA regulations state that interviewers must process applicants into the system immediately at the time of their interview . . . apparently even if they are on the verge of losing their minds.

"Catch a beer later?" Drogba asks.

Leelee's already typing, a slice of her mind also taking the time to admire Veronica's handwriting. "Yeah. That would be good."

"The String Thing? Love that," Samir comments later that night, when they've gotten him caught up. "Hey, what happens if someone actually does have powers but they don't want to fill out the forms?"

"Well, it's technically illegal," Leelee says, "but rarely prosecuted. The way my supervisor explained it, if they're still good guys what's the point of jamming them up, and if they're bad guys they've got worse charges against them once they're brought in."

Samir nods. "Good practical perspective."

"I never woulda filled out that form if I didn't have to," Reggie says. His cyborg eye burns bright yellow, an artificial glare incongruous against the backdrop of dark wood paneling and softly clinking glasses. Leelee doesn't like this place very much, but Reggie and Louise love it. They like to parade their sacrifices in front of the masses. Especially the rich, self-satisfied, insular DC masses.

Reggie is a retired cyborg soldier from an alternate future Earth. He was catapulted through timelines by a process Leelee has never quite understood, and then drifted through various superhero associations before having some of his hardware burned out in the Battle of Saturn's Rings. Not many people know his whole story, but with the cyborg parts and all the scars, Reggie doesn't really fit in among the loosened-tie crowd at this place.

"I think the certification process can also help people who are having trouble with their powers," Leelee says. She's thinking of Lady V, but also Emmaline Brooks. "I know sometimes people come into my office nervous or afraid, and by the time they leave they have a little peace of mind, you know?"

"If there's a government form for it, it can't be that weird, right?" Samir's chuckling as he says it, but Leelee thinks that's exactly it. "Yeah. Plus you get a tax credit if you fill it out and work with a government-certified hero group."

Louise is shaking her head. "Maybe, but I think there's probably a lot of people out there who haven't gotten certified. I mean, a lot." She leans toward Leelee, a twinkle in her eye. "You know what I mean."

"I don't," Leelee says primly. Samir is watching her with a pretty intense expression on his face, and she wonders why.

IV. SUMMARY OF ACTIVITIES AND AFFILIATIONS

Do you have any known enemies?   yes ☐ no ☐
  If yes, list their names/known monikers/aliases.

_____

_____

Are you a member or affiliate of any metahuman group?
                                        yes ☐ no ☐
  If yes, list names and registration status of each.

_____

_____

  Do you benefit financially or materially from the use of
  your powers?   yes ☐ no ☐

Are you engaged full-time in the practice of maintaining the
public order or combating existing and emergent threats to
life, property, and/or civilization?   yes ☐ no ☐

Does your job or profession depend on your use of your
powers?   yes ☐ no ☐

If you answered yes to any of the previous four questions,
do you maintain Metahuman/Occult Practitioner Coverage
pursuant to established state and federal laws?
                                        yes ☐ no ☐

  If yes, list insurer, group number, and policy number.

_____

_____

  If no, attach form **8805-PW, Waiver of Metahuman/
  Occult Practitioner Coverage.**

Have you received valuable items as a result of your member-
ship in a group, league, or association of other metahuman
individuals?   yes ☐ no ☐
  If yes, describe each item and estimate its value* in the
  space provided. _____

_____

_____

* Items of sufficient value are subject to Internal Revenue Service policies on valuable gifts and professional courtesies. Con-
sult Pamphlet 5454, Declaration of Artifacts and Extraterrestrial
Technologies.

Tuesday, 6:14 p.m.

On Tuesdays Leelee often works late because she has a book club at seven anyway, so it's not worth the trip home just so she can get back on the subway. She nods at the evening security guy—Alonso is his name, but she remembers seeing him in the papers when she was a kid as Viridian X. His superpower has something to do with intense expressions of the color green, which doesn't sound like much, but Leelee has been at BMMOA long enough to know that verbal descriptions don't always do a super's power justice.

The book is supposed to be really good, but Leelee dislikes books about rich people and their ennui and how they rediscover their love for life by doing things Leelee will never be able to afford. As a result, she doesn't have much to contribute to the discussion. She has a strong sense that several of the other women in the group—there are no men—also hated it but don't want to say so. After book club she calls Samir. He's out with friends, subbing in for an absent member of his buddy Duncan's trivia team. "Come meet us!" he shouts over the bar noise. They're at the Alibi, which is more Leelee's kind of place than the stuffed-shirt place they were at the other day. Big windows, upbeat music, people having fun instead of making deals.

Leelee walks into the bar and looks around for Samir. She doesn't see him right away, but she does see a couple of his friends. Duncan waves at her and beckons her over.

The hairs on the back of her neck stand up a fraction of a second before the bar's front windows blow in. A coruscating sphere of energy, swirling in every color of the rainbow, drifts in as people cower behind the bar or in the short hallway leading to the bathrooms. Leelee stands and watches. The sphere dissipates, revealing a figure within, backlit by spiraling lattices of prismatic energy that all trace back to rings on the figure's hands.

Oh, shit. It's Lady V.

"Hello, Veronica," Leelee says.

"Don't give me that friendly professional shit," she growls. "Where's your friend who scrambled my brain?"

Leelee shrugs. "I don't know."

"I'm sure. Do you know that I can't get certified now because you put my impromptu demonstration into your system as a symptom of unreliability?" Lady V floats through the air, a foot or so off the ground, in Leelee's direction.

Leelee finds this grandstanding pretty fake. "Well, Veronica, if you didn't want me to write about it, you shouldn't have done it in the first place."

"Oh, yes. I should be a good little girl and obey all the directives of dull, stupid bureaucrats like you. Very heroic." She's close to Leelee now, much too close, and Leelee discovers with terror that she can't move. "Well, I have a message for people like you, on behalf of people like me. Stay out of our way. And I have a special message for your friend . . ." She closes her eyes, and Leelee can feel a tickle in her mind. *No*, she thinks. *Get out.*

Lady V's eyes open wide. "Oh. Interesting. Most people never know I'm there. Well, I got what I came for. Since your friend *Drogba* messed around in my brain to protect you, I'm going to mess around in yours. Just to show him, and all the rest of you," she snarls, looking around the bar. A few people are still cowering under tables, and yep, there are phones out. What the hell is wrong with you people, Leelee wants to scream. She can't talk, though.

"Show you," Lady V goes on, "what happens when you interfere with the natural order of things." She returns her attention to Leelee and reaches out her left hand. The three rings on it are blue, pink, and green. "Let's see," she says. "Pink or blue? I'm not really feeling green. Why don't you choose? Oh, wait, you can't speak, can you?"

Leelee remembers the blue hero from last week. She sure could use someone like that now.

"Maybe both," Lady V decides. A beam of pink energy sprouts from that ring, slowly growing toward Leelee's face. Wreathing it are tendrils of blue. Paralyzed, Leelee watches them approach. If she could run, she would. If she could scream or beg, she might do that too. But mostly, as she faces what she assumes will be the end of her conscious existence, all Leelee can think is *For doing my job? This is what I get just for doing my job?*

She wishes she could see Samir again.

The blue tendrils have outpaced the pink beam. They writhe right up to Leelee's face, so close she can see tiny fractal patterns inside them, endlessly repeating—until another flash of blue absorbs and redirects them. The pink beam hits her square in the forehead. The sensation is unlike anything Leelee has ever experienced. She's outside herself looking down but she's also blind, her skin prickles, she's flooded with memories of things she hasn't thought of in years—a puppy run over in the road, the day she learned to tie her shoes, a cruel boy making fun of her at a middle school dance, the first time she ever saw the ocean.

All of that in an instant, before Lady V screams in frustration and whirls to meet her attacker. The blue hero from last week flashes into view with a flying kick.

Leelee collapses. She can't form a coherent thought, and something seems wrong with all of her senses.

Their fight is brief but devastating, at least to the bar. Light bulbs explode, rows of liquor bottles detonate, Lady V tries to annihilate the blue hero with sweeping beams of energy and he dodges them like a master thief somersaulting through security lasers. When he gets close, he delivers a staccato series of punches and kicks, each accompanied by those actinic blue flashes.

This would make a great TV show, Leelee thinks. But probably everyone thinks that about their job.

She's drifting into some kind of fugue and loses track of time. When she can focus her eyes again, everything is quiet except for sirens approaching. There's no sign of either Lady V or the blue hero. A few people are emerging from their hiding places, murmuring to each other in the kind of reverent tone people take when they've survived a brush with death.

Leelee feels like someone has put her brain in a KitchenAid. Also her body seems to be moving, and she doesn't know why until Samir is there, suddenly, cradling her. "I looked for you," Leelee says. "Where were you?"

His eyes are so beautiful, deep and dark and caring. She smells ozone. "Kinda embarrassing, but I got stuck in the bathroom," he says. "I got here as soon as I could."

Leelee has that feeling. She's never wrong.

Right before she passes out again, she understands.

V. AFFIRMATION

> I affirm that this form is complete and true to the best of my ability to determine the truth. I acknowledge that failure to answer truthfully is a violation of United States law punishable by fines and/or imprisonment.

Signature:* _____

Signature of parent/guardian if applicant is a minor:

_____

Signature of Paid Preparer:

_____

Paid Preparer address and license number: _____

_____

Witness signature:

_____

* If applicant is not physically coherent or materially solid
enough to sign the form, visit your nearest BMMOA regional
office for proxy certification by a BMMOA employee. Nota-
rized signatures, astral manifestations, and telepathic overtures
are not considered valid substitutes for direct BMMOA certification. If presentation at a BMMOA office would entail risk of
harm to BMMOA employees or others, contact your nearest
BMMOA regional office to arrange an onsite verification. All
requests for an onsite verification must be accompanied by BM-
MOA **Form 8791, Assertion of Inability to Present in Person**.

Saturday, 8:33 a.m.

She's in the hospital for a couple of days getting various work-
ups on her brain, which seems to be getting itself together pretty
well, so they let her go home Friday afternoon and she crawls into
bed and sleeps for sixteen hours. In the morning she goes into
the kitchen and just sits, listening to the birds chirp and watching
the morning light on the grain of the kitchen table.

Samir comes down a little while later. She lets him make coffee
before she says it. "When were you going to tell me?"

"Um," Samir says. He sits across from her and sips his coffee.
"Tell you . . ."

"Samir," she says. "You saved my life twice in a week and don't
get me wrong, I'm really grateful for that, but it also means that
you've been lying to me for like three years, and that puts me in a
very confused place."

"I'm sorry, Leelee," he says. "I didn't lie to you just to lie to you."

"I'm not sure it matters why," she says, although of course it
does. A silence stretches out until she can't help but ask, "What do
you call yourself?"

"I never could decide," he says. "But the leadership, they decided on Electric Blue."

"That's not bad, I guess," Leelee says. "Wasn't that a song?"

"Was it?" Samir's musical taste runs to techno and ambient stuff. He never knows anything playing on the radio. "So," he says. "I know how you must be feeling . . ." He trails off. There's a distant look on his face, like he's listening to a voice only he can hear. Leelee's intuition, or maybe it's her suspicious nature, locks in on a possibility. "Are you . . . did you plan this conversation? Like, you rehearsed it?" When he doesn't say anything right away, Leelee sits up straighter. "You did, didn't you?"

"I did, yeah." His voice is quiet, introspective rather than ashamed. "They wanted me to because they knew eventually you would figure it out. But I'm messing it up."

"They? Are you in a group?"

He tries to lighten things up. "You're filling out the form in your head, aren't you?"

This makes her mad because she has in fact been filling out Samir's Form 8774-D in her head and it infuriates her to be predictable. "Fuck you, Samir! You should have told me! You know I could lose my job. You know I—do I even know you? What other secrets do you have?"

His infuriating smile. "I . . . wet the bed until I was in high school?"

"Goddammit! It's against the law! A law, I will remind you, that I sort of help administer?"

"Babe," he says, obviously trying to placate her, but for some reason this doesn't make her angry. That is one of Samir's gifts. He never seems to be doing anything for the wrong reason. "Babe. I know. But you said yourself they never prosecute anybody. I mean . . . are you going to turn me in?"

She puts her face in her hands, takes a long deep breath down into the belly, lets it slowly back out. No, she's not going to turn him in. But having an outlaw supe for a boyfriend sure wasn't on her list of things she expected to happen in her thirties.

"Yes, I'm in a group," he says. "And they asked me to get you to tell me when someone really powerful comes through your office. I told them I wasn't going to put you in that position, and they backed off."

"Who?" Leelee asks.

He tells her. My god, Leelee thinks. The Quantum Polyhedron. She knows that group. Everyone knows that group. They pulled off the Vacuum Counterstrike, the famous infiltration of a lava tube base under the Mare Serenitatis that permanently crippled the Eschaton Triad.

"So, they want to use me to recruit," she says.

"Yeah." He leans back, looks out the window. She gets a good look at his profile in the morning sunlight. Her heart quickens a little. "Recruitment is a big deal for the top groups," he says. "Some people take it a little too far. The QP, they really want someone on the inside at BMMOA."

"I don't want to make you feel bad, but is that why they wanted you? To get to me?"

"I'm pretty sure I had something to offer them anyway," he says. "But they did mention you from the beginning."

This makes her feel better, like she has value even though she's not a supe.

"There's a shapeshifter in the group who suggested he could take your place," Samir says, reluctantly. "I told him I'd kill him if he tried." He makes that little noise in his throat that always means he's about to say something else but is holding back. Eventually he lets it out. "So, um, he tried."

"Oh my god," she says. "So that wasn't Lady V in the bar?"

"No. He had some plan to take you somewhere after he'd put on a show as Lady V. We found her. She's all right, he needed to keep her alive as a patsy. She's pissed, especially because the QP has her rings now. Anyway, that's why I'm probably going to be out of the QP any minute now."

"Good," she says. "You're better off without them, and they will totally lose their government contracts if they're using unregistered talent."

She lets it drop for a while, but a couple of hours later she walks into the living room where he's sitting on the couch watching soccer. She stands between him and the TV.

"Are we going to make it, babe?" Relationships between normal people and supes are notoriously doomed. There are TV shows about it, millions of TikTok videos, an entire self-help industry. Everybody knows. And that's what Leelee is, just an ordinary person.

"Not if you keep standing in front of the TV when Liverpool's on," he says.

She looks over her shoulder. It's halftime and the studio talking heads are bantering. "Oh, please," she says. She really wants to be angry at him—is angry at him—but several years of working at the BMMOA has taught her that secret identities are just part of the game.

Plus, Leelee knows Samir. She knows that his sincere smile is a little crooked, she knows the way his crow's-feet soften when he can tell she's worried or sad. He's never been anything but loving to her. If that's all an act, she's going to go along with it. There's a new ride ahead of her—of them—and Leelee wouldn't want to take it with anybody else. Even if he did apparently call her ma'am once.

The decision made, she slides onto the couch next to him, nestles under his arm, and exhales, long and easy. "You won't tell anybody, will you?" he asks.

"Babe, no. Of course not." She snuggles closer. Work is work and her life is her life. "It'll be our little secret."

"Whatever you do, don't make me fill out that form."

"It's really kind of compulsory," she says. "But I don't have any enforcement powers."

"I can live without the tax break," he says.

"Sure," Leelee says. On the screen there's a local newsbreak before the second half of the Liverpool game. The midday anchor puts on his concerned face and introduces a piece on budgetary consequences of super battles. The main interviewee is a city councilor who suggests the price of supers might be cuts to education funding.

"You should be a TV reporter," Samir says. "The way you can sense bullshit, you'd ask the best questions."

"Oh my god." Leelee shudders. Her, on TV? "As if."

"You do have a power, you know," Samir says. He watches her, waiting. Leelee feels like she's being tested. She wonders how many conversations in the Quantum Polyhedron's subterranean hideaway are lurking behind this moment.

"No," she says, looking him in the eye and daring him to make a sound. "No, I don't."

A. R. CAPETTA

Resurrection Highway

FROM *Sunday Morning Transport*

FANTASY

YOU CLIMB THE fence, hit the yard of the body shop at three in the morning—whispered among automancers as the best time—and write sigils on the tires in a thick glop of white paint. You skim the wheels with the specially prepared olive oil, which Rye always called wake-up juice, infused with chilis and lemon peel and much less savory ingredients that you sourced from that guy in the Haight who swore the marrow was fresh.

You picked this low-slung maroon Jaguar—silver cat midleap on the car's ass—because Edgar will like it. If he ever sees it.

Time to test if you can still perform. It's been five years, but you feel it, always trying to bust out of your skin, this need to bring things back. You pop the little door of the gas tank with a fist, unscrew the cap, and feed bone slurry to the circle of its open mouth. Arranging candles in a rough circle around the body of the old beast, you speak the words.

Nothing happens. You fall back onto the hood of the car, settle into the failure. Letting your magic rust means that you have to live with the consequences.

You take the postcard out of your pocket.

You kiss the cheap paper, kiss Edgar goodbye, really this time. He's on his own.

Everybody, everybody is on their own. It's an empty jingle in your head, like the one time Vex found an old radio station that never stopped blanketing the country with a signal, its last program of pop songs stuck on a loop, and ancient commercials got wedged in your brain.

That trip is long gone.

Those days, as they say, are dead.

Then the car rumbles back into existence, tires inflating beneath you like the Jaguar is taking a deep breath. The headlights flick themselves on and cast light over the unchosen dead of the yard, hundreds of metallic bodies. They're everywhere these days, a feature of the landscape, littered in random spots, lumped together in yards, just waiting for someone with a touch like yours.

You raised a car from the dead. Good for you. That bit was easy compared to what comes next.

You get in and drive, you and the car warming up to each other, until the sun slithers over what used to be San Francisco. Here are houses dredged in sand and seawater down by Ocean Beach, where the tides lapped up a few blocks, then a few more. There are mostly-drowned cars stranded in water, stripped by salt to the point that you can barely recognize brown ribs poking from gray waves.

You steer toward the house on Moraga, thinking about the time Ting found the attic apartment and gleefully moved you all in between trips, a home base that you came back to for years. You find your former crew (former friends, former lovers, former everythings) where you knew they'd be, under a makeshift pier that used to be someone's second-story porch, getting higher (they're already high).

"Hey, bonetrippers," you say through your open window as the car idles impatiently.

"Oh," Vex says, words malformed around the smoke he's got stopped at the back of his throat. "It's you."

The car revs without your permission. "Rude little monster," you mutter, patting the wheel. You always end up liking the cars, and then they re-die on you. Speaking of that, this resurrection has a shelf life. "So, we have four days to get to Maine," you announce. Whoops. It wasn't supposed to sound like you were ordering people around. You were never in charge, even when you were one of them. The automancer in a crew is like the front man of a band— more obvious, not really more important.

"Is there anything else you want to say?" Rye asks. "Anything apology shaped?"

"Pass," Vex says, and when the bowl is offered back to him, he adds, "On the apology."

"It's a cute reunion scene, though," Ting says. "What's in Maine?"

"Not *what*," you say. "Unless you think of Edgar as an object." You almost throw the postcard at them, but that's a bad idea. "He needs us to pick him up."

"Edgar?" Rye asks.

"Fucking *Edgar*?" Vex echoes.

"Egg?" Ting cries, still showing off that she's the only one allowed to use this nickname.

Then they're running to pack, and you predictably hate knowing that they did it for Edgar and not for you. Rye loads the trunk with a duffel bag of arcane ingredients next to a crank-turned grinder with metal teeth, the size of an extra-large toaster oven. Vex and Ting pile in, slam the doors. No one asks where you've been. They treat you like you left last night in a rotted-out mood and came back on a fresh breeze the next day.

Maybe you do love them after all.

That love curls up when you reach the highway and everyone starts complaining that you don't drive like Edgar used to.

"Edgar didn't have to run a resurrection spell while he was changing lanes," you say as you grit your teeth and keep the wheel in place by sheer force.

Automancy was never supposed to be a thing, but sometimes a lot of people die at once, in waves like the gray crash at Ocean Beach, and one of those waves releases a latent source of magic—or equalizes the world to the point that magic, choked by overpopulation, gasps suddenly back to life. You've argued this backward and forward with the crew on long trips, and you don't want to revive the conversation now. The fact is that some desperate people went to perform acts of necromancy in different spots across a broken country—a constellation of resurrections—and those spells didn't end with their friends and loved ones coming back. They got cars, summoned from obsolescence. And there were no gods left to ask questions of or bargain with, so everyone rolled with it. Literally.

California gives up at some point and becomes Nevada. A road trip starts when you hit the highway, but a bonetrip isn't truly alive—or in some cases, dead—until the first challenge, which comes halfway across the arid stretch of I-80 currently sucking every molecule of water from your skin, hair, eyeballs.

"Shitty road ahead," Vex says, back in his place as navigator, perched in shotgun, one hand on the oh-shit bar, running two spells at the same time—a standard map spell, and the satellite spell inspired by old tech that allows him to see the car and surrounding stretch of road from six angles. "It looks like a rock-eating giant took a dump. Let's stop and refresh tire sigils." Tires are always the first things to go, they have to be babied after resurrection to protect them from the churned-up highways. You slow down to pull to the side. "Wait. Fuck that. It's an asphalt trap. Gun it."

You don't question Vex in a tight spot. You gun it.

The speedometer's needle palsies and panics as it hits the red, but the car holds steady. An open-bed truck peels out from behind a lone boulder and bears down, head-on, a figure standing in the back with a wild bent to their arms like they're trying to call down wrath or something equally godlike.

Ting crawls on top of your car. She casts the tether spell that will keep her up there, a shining tie. Then she stomps twice, the sign that she's ready to fight. Here's the truth—you've missed your battle mage.

"I put a spell in the bone slurry to keep us moving forward at all costs," Rye says. "Don't let up." And since they are the best necro-fuel expert you've ever met, you really don't let up.

The truck's mage is singing some kind of pitchy incantation while three passengers point guns out the windows. Any halfway-decent battle mage can take guns apart with their eyes closed, but the few seconds it takes can give a crew an advantage. And a lot of people living on this country's carcass have a lot of guns that they will use to get that edge.

Ting hits the truck with a sizzling net of white-hot magic. It snares all the guns at once, tosses them in front of the truck, making the challengers choke on their own metal. The truck rumbles over the mangled guns and veers into your lane. That's when the big incantation the other mage has been working up whirls to life. It's a branched lightning bolt—three white streaks crab-walking down the sky to electrify your car.

Ting puts her arm up like a lightning rod.

You shout, "Pirouette!"

It's a move you've seen Edgar perform a hundred times. You wrench the wheel into a spin as Ting spins in the other direction, not catching the lightning but channeling it with a rubber spell, ricochet-style, to knock the oncoming truck slightly off course. It speeds by at a viciously acute angle. Ting drags the showboat mage in the air, holding them suspended like a fish on a line as the truck keeps rumbling down what's left of I-80, minus a crew member.

The figure spins in the air, retaliating with wild spells that, in the rearview mirror, you see flying wide.

Vex hoots as Ting sets the other battle mage down gently on the double yellow. It's worse than killing them in a way. These crews have no fear of death, but humiliation burns them up like cheap matchsticks. They will do something terrible to that bonetripper, worse than whatever quick end Ting would have chosen, but that isn't your call. And it isn't Ting's job to murder people just so they won't get murdered worse later on.

You clear the last of the asphalt trap, hitting smoother pavement.

"So?" Rye asks.

A car doesn't get a name until after its first battle.

You shoot past a sign—*Leaving Eureka County.*

"Eureka!" everyone shouts, and for the first time in five years it feels like you are together. Not just shoved in a car by circumstance, but together. All except Edgar, of course, and you are going to get him, you are baptized in lightning and on your fucking way.

Eureka powers across Utah and Wyoming, snips a corner off Colorado. You stop at the bone traders housed in an old gas station mini-mart, and Rye goes in with their duffel bag and comes out with bones bundled like pale firewood. They prefer to gather in graveyards, they feel like it's more respectful, but you don't have time, you have two days and half a continent to cross. As Rye grinds down the bones, you think about all the ways Edgar could have died since you got that postcard. You think about him when he was alive, when you *knew* he was alive, when this wasn't Schrödinger's road trip.

He was the one who found you, angry, magical, alone except for the cars that you kept summoning. The first time you tried, you ended up with a fleet of trucks following you around like angry ducklings. It was disappointing, technically, because you were trying to raise your parents from the dead. You were twenty, a baby. It's retrospectively embarrassing how much you believed you might get them back.

Edgar taught you what you could be without them. He called you the most powerful automancer he'd ever seen. He even taught you to drive, though it was clear that he was the born driver, drifting across lanes like fog. He found Rye, and Vex, and Ting. He knitted you all together.

When Rye is done with the grinder, they tip gallon after gallon of fresh slurry into the tank. "You know, I've been thinking about how I'm literally feeding death to these cars," they mutter from within a makeshift ring of sigils. Without the grounding of those marks, Eureka might suck Rye's own bones from within their flesh. "Weirdly, it's not that weird."

"Yeah?" you ask vacantly as the last of the light burns off the horizon. You're not looking forward to driving all night.

"Think of the history of it. And yet I don't believe people cared as much as I do when they fed ancient dead creatures to these very same cars."

"What are you talking about?"

"What the shit do you think was in gasoline?" Vex asks as he finishes up a quick piss break. "Dead organic matter, squeezed into dark juice by pressure and time."

You crouch suddenly. Gravel to palms. Cool air to lungs.

"Did I get too philosophical and bring down the whole trip?" Rye asks. "I hate when I do that."

Ting jumps out of the car and puts an arm around your shoulders. "You okay?"

"I'm okay," you lie between your teeth.

Which are just more bones.

Someday, when you're dead, maybe soon, those bones will fuel someone else's bad decisions. But right now you have to get up. You have to keep working the automancy spell and drive, and doing both has become sweat-pouring, meat-shaking work. You've been overriding your synapses with complex chants. You've basically hot-wired your own body. And you can't stop, because off the highways there are cults, ghost towns, ghost cults, so you keep driving, and at dawn, more battles, Nebraska just a string of battles that everyone can see coming across the split-open landscape. Eureka emerges victorious, with only minor injuries: a popped tire, blown-out glass in the left rear window. Blown-out hearing in Rye's ear, too, though it's slowly creeping back. Iowa is starting to white out your memory of hills when Ting leans between the front seats and asks, "So, how did Edgar get a message to you anyway?"

"He didn't, exactly," you say.

The car goes incandescent with swearing. Eureka swerves slightly.

"He needs us to come, but he didn't say that. In so many words. Directly."

"What are you driving us *directly* into?" Vex asks.

That's when you pull out the postcard. It's soft from how much you folded it, read it, tossed it in the trash, fished it back out, read it again, slept with it under your pillow. It's the kind people used to buy from spinning racks in tourist traps: a shellacked photo of live lobsters. It took you a while to figure out what their mottled, armored bodies were—you've only ever seen them pictured very red, very dead.

Printed at the top of the postcard, in a sunny font: *Old Orchard Beach.*

On the back, a diarrhea scrawl in dark pen: *Edgar says he's your driver. If you want him back, this is where.*

"I think a crew took him, either by force or he . . ."

"Joined up?" Vex volunteers. "Because he was on his own? And these fuckwaffles weren't as sweet as us, surprise, surprise?"

"It could be a cult," Rye adds quietly. They escaped a cult in the redwoods when they were just a kid.

"Whatever it is, we might be able to get him back."

"Or get his body back," Vex says, and for once it's not a sour half-joke. Vex buried three siblings before he was twelve. He takes burials seriously.

"They probably want a ransom," Ting says. "What the fuck do we have to pay for Egg's life with?"

Darkness laps at the highway in all directions. Miles warp in the silence. You only have Eureka's pale headlights and the next stitch in the center of the road.

"Also, why didn't you *tell us?*" Ting asks, finally.

"I couldn't get to him alone. I was worried you might not come."

"You're the one who left us," Rye says.

And there it is.

Nobody needs to say anything more for a whole day, so they don't.

In New York State, the barns that line I-90 are falling apart. They look like great hulking beasts in the half-night. You shouldn't stop here, but you're going to fall apart before you get to Maine. You leave Eureka on the side of the road, resurrection spell running down hour by hour, and cast a few trip wire sigils—at least you'll know if someone tries to steal your car.

Heavy blue light comes in through the barn slats. Rye finds blankets that might have been for horses. They still smell like muscle and sun after years of being ignored.

You sleep.

Early the next morning, you wake up, inner alarm triggered. It's not the sigils, those would make your fingertips burn. This is plain old instinct, sharp as a knife at the hollow of your neck. At first you think the rustling is a person coming for you, possibly an animal. You nearly bolt. But then you realize that across an open stretch of barn, not all that far away from where you've been sleeping, Rye and Vex and Ting are mostly unclothed, fully tangled up, blankets forgotten. Groans leak out of Vex like the early light between the slats as his dick disappears into Rye's mouth and Ting makes breathy huffing sounds as she slips into Rye from behind, she's even brought her harness, and Rye holds everything in until they can't, a thick vine of pleasure unfurling from the back of their throat.

You get up and pass their naked asses, say, "Two minutes to finish. I'm waiting in the car."

Eureka greets you with a flick of the headlights. You curl into the driver's seat. The revving shakes up your horny, lonely thighs. In two minutes, the rest of the crew traipse out of the barn with dumb hair and hazy smiles. You thought that leaving stomped out everything good for them, in the name of some highly dubious safety. But you didn't kill the way they care about each other. Maybe it doesn't all come down to you.

Knowing that was worth two minutes.

Now you have to make up time.

Edgar is still out there, missing because you got mad at him one night and left. He'd gotten smashed up in a challenge on the way back to California, and he dangled so close to death, like a tooth hanging on by just the nerve. It took a week to know if he'd pull through. That was nearly enough to get you to run, the seven-day slow-motion experience of what it would feel like to lose him. But as he came back to you, he stared earnestly through the mist of scavenged painkillers and said that you would become *so much more magical* if you wanted to resurrect him. If you had that fire in you.

So he'd be doing you a favor if he died.

That was the part you couldn't forgive, that he thought you'd be better when he was gone.

You left. He left too.

You still don't know how much of Edgar's decision you're responsible for. You do the doom-math for the ten-thousandth time as the slow crawl of the Adirondacks gives way to darkly forested land. New England is dense with leaves, clotted with shadows.

The roadkill red carpet starts right around the border of Maine.

Everybody feels the need to tell you that this is not a good sign.

"I know, I know," you say. Another empty jingle.

There are dead raccoons and possums and squirrels, split like pomegranates, spilling red like seeds. Then larger animals, dogs and deer, sluggish as bags of salt.

"So I think we can safely say that Edgar is with a crew that likes to kill things," Ting mutters.

Eureka slides through Portland, up I-95, toward Old Orchard Beach.

"Do you want to turn around?" you ask as you near the exit. Roadkill lines both sides, leading the way.

"No," everyone says in unison.

They're with you, somehow. Still with you.

You've split this crew apart, but now you're trying to knit them back together—not the simple string of a line on a map that brings you home, but the slow, painful, imperfect knitting of bone.

There's salt in the air past the exit, the old salt of death and the fresh salt of the sea swirling together on your tongue. The old park and ride is nearly a jungle.

"Look," Rye says. "There."

Cars spill out of a trash yard. On both sides of the entrance, the roadkill is heaped twice as high as Eureka.

"Gates of death," Ting says.

"Sounds like a myth, smells like a nightmare," Vex adds.

Eureka coughs twice at the gate and unceremoniously dies. It was your own exhaustion and relief—you let up a little, took an extra-long breath, and the spell released like an old rubber band. Now Eureka won't be brought back, no matter how much you slam the heels of your palms against the wheel and chant and scream.

"Ooookay, I guess we're walking the rest of the way," Ting says.

You enter the trash yard, passing cars and trucks and a slumbering school bus with smashed-out windows. You'll need one of these vehicles to carry you home, but right now you don't care.

Because you're staring at the throne.

It's made of junk parts, dripping with black bone slurry, edging from gory to glorious and back again. Edgar sits on it. Dark twists of hair, nervous eyes. Scratched and bruised like he's been toyed with. No: tortured.

You run. "Oh," Edgar says, his throat clogged with something. Emotion or blood. "Shit. They saw you coming, but I thought you'd turn back."

You try not to be singed by this fucking comment.

"We're here to get you out," you say, and hold up the postcard so Edgar can see the writing. The lobsters look nearly black in this light.

Edgar laughs.

Something's wrong with this setup. There had to be a trap, a trick, or at least an unpayable price, but you didn't know what kind until Edgar opens his mouth again. It's crusty at the edges. There are blackflies.

"They all want to be bonetrippers here. Could never do more than take a joyride, kill off a few deer. I told them about you. The best automancer I've ever ridden with. Got drunk on some fermented blueberry shit and bragged, actually."

You feel the doom-math rushing to finish this equation.

"We're not, uh, not getting out. They want you *in*."

A dozen people swarm around the back of the throne, and before you can do a single thing to stop it, Edgar's throat is speared with a rusty old dipstick and pouring blood. There's a wetly guttering sound.

More people step out from the yard to watch.

Edgar's gray eyes go glassy exactly how you pictured they would. Maybe if you hadn't spent so much time picturing it, this wouldn't be happening. Maybe if you'd let go of this fear years ago, you wouldn't be facing a real-life version of it.

Or maybe Edgar made his own choices. This argument will rage in you forever now. It will never die.

The magic that roars within you can't be stopped. You don't even try. The spell releases itself, no need for sigils or wake-up juice or marrow. It stuttered when Eureka died, but now it burns a clean line of fuel from Edgar's body back to the quick-beating chambers of your heart.

Every car in the yard comes to life.

You've never summoned this many, and yet it feels like nothing.

Edgar was wrong, though. Your throat cracks to tell him, because he's lying right there. (He's already gone.) You aren't more powerful because you're trying to bring him back from the dead—you're keeping the rest of your crew *alive*.

These would-be bonetrippers watch your every move with ugly satisfaction. You did what they wanted you to do.

But you're not finished.

Cars circle you, and your crew, a thick ring of protection. You *will not* let Rye and Vex and Ting become fuel. One truck stands sentry over Edgar's body. Another rams headfirst into his killer. The rest of these fuckwaffles are doing their own doom-math now, running for the edges of the yard, because you should not be able to do this, command cars like they are notes in a symphony of death and you are the conductor. You rip the postcard to shreds and they fly from your fingertips on a salted, unnatural wind. Cars that you've brought to life chase down Edgar's torturers, obliterate them quickly, the school bus mowing down half a dozen at once, a yard full of magic and screaming and death and vehicles that come when you beckon.

When it's done, your crew is staring at you. You expect shock, or sorrow, or blame. But they look like they love you again, and that's so much scarier. Vex gathers Edgar's body so gently. His bones will never burn.

"What now?" Rye asks.

"Home?" Ting says.

The cars, the trucks, the school buses, your crew, everyone is waiting for your next move. This time, you don't run. You know the next stop on what is going to be a long, long trip. "It's time to find a new driver."

When the four of you reach the gates, Eureka is warmed up and waiting.

CHRISTOPHER ROWE

The Four Last Things

FROM *Asimov's*

SCIENCE FICTION

> During these few days I intend to put before you some thoughts
> concerning the four last things. They are, as you know from your
> catechism, death, judgement, hell, and heaven. We shall try to
> understand them fully during these few days . . .
> —James Joyce, *A Portrait of the Artist as a Young Man*

THEY CAME ON a mule ship, and they lived in what was left of
it after they arrived. Its hull, laid down by poet-engineers in the
high docks, was laminated from hundreds of thousands of layers
of zepto-sec time and planck-length matter, each layer a gossamer
nothing capable of withstanding anything they could imagine.
The controlling mule itself, like all its siblings, was spun up from
archived biological remnants of a lost hybrid equine, integrated
with specialized subsystems designed to travel between.

The fully developed systems themselves predicted that the crew
would encounter much they could not imagine between, and the
systems being always correct, the mule found that when it shuddered back into the real, all that laminated gossamer was cracked
and fraying. But it had held.

The mule roused the crew and told them that the sole primary
and one of the secondary objectives had been achieved. The primary objective was that they survive between. The secondary objective, the mule was pleased to report, was below. It was a planet. It
was Ouest'mer.

None of them remembered any of the other secondary objectives, or whether there were tertiary objectives. The mule would
not be coaxed on the subject.

There were four of them. They did not know how long it had been since they'd set out. The mule would not be coaxed on that subject either.

Silas believed they had come there because of the drumming.

Down in the depths of Ouest'mer's oceans, five-meter worms anchored to the seafloor whipped in the gaseous discharge of glowing vents. The mule was unable to render a spectrum that would tell them the composition of the gas. The worms themselves were down on the planet, inaccessible.

The mule said the worms were immortal.

The worms drummed.

They gyrated in the tumult of condensation, and their terminal, unmoored heads whipped. Silas did not like for the others to use the word heads because the word was imprecise. He said that the data on whether the proximal or distal terminus of a worm was its head was undetectable, that the question of whether they even had heads was unsettled.

The worms crashed into the reefs that grew around the vents. It was unclear whether the reefs were shaped with intent, but the percussive *crack*s that sounded around the whole of Ouest'mer's subaquatic spaces were intricately patterned and never, in the time they recorded them, did any pattern repeat exactly.

These are the explanations they considered.

It was natural. Probability allowed for the appearance of patterns in the drumming. The near repetitions were the product of something more primitive than instinct but akin to it. Or the outgassing from the mantle through the vents was cyclical, regular enough for the worms to respond with something mimicking patterns. This was the explanation Keik, a woman who rarely spoke, favored.

It was art. M. Reid's notion. They insisted that the planet was an instrument designed and built by ancient starfarers who had abandoned any pretenses of exploration or governance or interaction in favor of minor creation. That was what M. Reid called building a planet to sound rhythms, a minor creation. There were said to be factions among the systems. M. Reid was from a moonlet where worship of one of these factions was mandatory, a faction that applied the laws of thermodynamics to civilizations.

It was fake. This, of course, was the theory put forth by Tel, who believed that they had perished between and that the four of them were now proxies generated by the mule for some purpose Tel had yet to divine. Ouest'mer, its oceans, the worms, the drumming, all of it was a speculative simulation designed to force engrammatic growth in the mule. Tel theorized that since the drumming evinced creativity—a notion that not all of them agreed with— the mule was attempting to develop creativity itself. An anathemic apotheosis, Tel called it and laughed. He was the only one of them who ever laughed.

It was language. Despite the protocols set by the systems for defining sentience, the worms were, perhaps in aggregate, consciously communicating with one another across the whole of Ouest'mer. The mule agreed to expend a percentage of its discretionary processing power on a decoding attempt. This was unlikely to yield anything that could be described as a translation, but it might show whether the drumming exhibited characteristics associated with language: grammar, syntax, vocabulary. This was the explanation Silas proposed.

Silas's explanation found favor with the others when the mule detected responses to the drumming coming from Ouest'mer's sun.

Death

The mule designated the responses unaspected contacts. They consisted of a combination of microflares in the local sun's north polar photosphere and radio signals. Ouest'mer's orbit was slightly angled to the ecliptic. The patterning of the flares was such that they appeared at times when the highest density of worm populations was facing the sun. The irregularity of the unaspected flares necessitated by the nature of Ouest'mer's orbit was what brought the contacts to the mule's attention in the first place. After the flares were detected, a full-spectrum analysis added the radio signals to the suite of unaspected contacts.

The same set of questions they had asked about the drumming could be asked about the contacts, but the others deferred to Silas now. Silas asked the mule to lay its pattern analysis of the drumming over the newly detected signals and to generate a palimpsest.

This appeared on their instruments immediately, and Keik whistled, high and melodic. The palimpsest showed a rippling array of precise numbers carried out to so many significant digits that the mule had rendered the finer and finer numbers as misty, fading graphics. They were not meant to understand such things to such a degree.

Silas said that the palimpsest showed that two-way communication was occurring between the worms in Ouest'mer's oceans and something—perhaps a sort of mule—in the photosphere of the star. M. Reid immediately dubbed this theoretical presence the conductor. Tel laughed, and Keik did not explain the whistle.

The mule kept its own counsel.

There was a probe attached to the laminated hull that was only meant to be used if sentience was detected and confirmed to a very high degree of probability. Silas armed the probe. It became communicative, chittering happily to Silas, to the others, to the mule. Only Silas responded, telling the probe that it would find the worms voluble. This excited the probe, and in its restlessness, it sheared off more gossamer. Silas told the probe to go, and it went.

Down through the atmosphere, down through the sea.

When he was in his middle years, Silas had pleaded with the systems to give him relief from the gray life he lived tending the satellite ossuaries. He pleaded three times.

The satellite ossuaries where Silas was born were not so far from the high docks, and Silas was experienced in poetry and death songs. The systems taught him to onboard maths of all kinds, but his mind converted it all to language, and he failed as an engineer.

For a long time, the systems ignored Silas. For a long time, Silas haunted the high docks, seeking every opportunity to change the things he saw into language.

When he found the place below the docks where dead mules were tethered, he believed he had found his purpose. Mules were mostly made of words, and here was an opportunity to dredge language up from the mules who could not refuse his queries.

Here are some of the things that Silas learned:

That dead mules far outnumbered those that served the systems in their thousands of capacities.

That the grumbling of dead mules combined and synthesized into words no human had ever heard, and that he barely understood.

That at the end of their terms, the brays of dying mules were tamped down by the systems so that all the satellite caverns and ships and moonlets and planets of home would not be misled from their true paths.

When he had learned all these things, the systems returned to his awareness. They asked him to tell them every word he knew in every combination he could conceive. He spoke to the systems for forty years.

Here are some of the things Silas told the systems:

Life is carved from life.

Death, too, is carved from life.

Life is carved from death.

The systems informed Silas he would go between on a mule ship. Every mule ship carried a crew of specialists, though the specializations represented on the different crews were not monolithic. Doctors were sent on some mule ships, but not on each one. Perhaps the other humans crewed with Silas would be acrobats or soldiers, teachers or chefs. For all the words Silas knew, he could not put a name to his specialization.

The systems claimed that each crew constituted a perfect community. Four humans were interred in each mule ship. A thousand mule ships went between, searching for signs going before, searching for signs following.

Since no mule ship had ever returned from between, the crewmembers were considered, for sociological purposes, to be dead. Silas, as was the procedure, would not be introduced to the other crewmembers before the interment, and then would have only the barest glimpses of them.

Then between.

Silas had a full and intricate understanding of death as it applied to humans. The dead mules he had studied were differently dead, which challenged many things Silas had previously believed to be true. He had come to understand that things that were true of systems were not always true of mules, and that things that were true of mules were not always true of humans.

The systems told Silas that this was an unproductive line of inquiry and advised him to adjust his vocabulary accordingly. Silas tried to do as he was told but found that once he knew a word, he could never unknow it. So, the systems tamped him down. They tamped him down, and he lost much.

The probe broadcast a series of echo messages based on the patterns Silas picked from among those the mule identified as provoking the most energetic unaspected contacts. It stopped descending one kilometer above and two kilometers adrift an area of worm activity.

All over Ouest'mer, the drumming stopped.

Another palimpsest appeared unasked for. The unaspected contacts were agitating the photosphere of the sun to a high degree. Silas asked for clarification, but none was forthcoming.

All over Ouest'mer, the worms were dying.

The probe squawked and began spiraling up to the ocean's surface. It demanded direction. Down along the vents, the worms were stirred now only by the outgassing. Thin as they were, the probe could still detect material sloughing off their bodies. Dark clouds of organic matter roiled above the vents.

Around the sun's north pole, the photosphere calmed. The mule reported that the radio signals had ceased.

M. Reid asked the mule if the probe's launch had occurred within defined parameters. The mule deferred to Silas.

Silas did not speak. Keik did not either. Tel did not, then, laugh.

Then Silas said that the mule would not have allowed the probe to be launched if such fell outside defined parameters.

Then Tel laughed.

Then Tel said, "The mule let Silas kill a world! Hah! The mule is dreaming the death of a world!"

Judgment

The others buzzed about, operating instruments, wearing the slack-eyed look that meant they were reviewing screens of data. Tel was having none of it. Tel knew already. Tel knew all about it.

When the selectors plucked him from his neighborhood in Phoenix, Tel was nine years old. He hadn't known all about it at that point in time. Knowing all about it was, subjectively, in his future when he was selected.

He had sent messages to his abuela and his cousins for the first two years. Eventually, he realized that the messages weren't going through and that the replies he received were generated by the systems. It had been a difficult decision, to stop sending the messages.

He stayed down the well for two more years after that. Then, three, two, one, boost! The sensation of weighing much more than himself, then the sensation of weighing nothing at all, were together emblematic of the next phase of his indoctrination.

The systems, through their human proxies, began by streaming him into a field guaranteed to fascinate him, the taming of mules. The proxies were brutalists. They saw to his every need, and what he communicated to them was his every desire.

The other muleskinners he met were friendly and bright. They were as entranced with the juvenile mules as he was. They all had their favorites, identified by randomly generated alphanumeric codes that were changed at set intervals in attempts to subvert that very favoritism. There were many rules to muleskinning, but the highest and most inviolable was: never name a mule.

Tel did not need to name a mule to know it. He did not need to track changes in alphanumeric designations. He could look at the pattern of a mule rising into his awareness at the beginning of a workshop session and know instantly whether this was one he had worked with before. Early on, he had not been careful enough in concealing this ability. The proxies knew he was subverting the program, somehow, so they began offering desirable things he hadn't even known he had desired.

The systems said that only young people had the plasticity of mind to tame a mule. But there were risks to that—to the systems, to the young people like Tel, to the mules themselves. Even the proxies were at risk if a muleskinner, through ignorance or inattention, let an untrained mule run rampant through the local buffers. One ugly old scar of a man who introduced Tel to gelato and masturbation was killed outright when a mule kicked straight through the net designed to protect the less-than-plastic minds of the proxies during workshop.

He was far from the only physical casualty, but Tel knew—his abuela had taught him this—that the first casualty is always reality.

The reality was that young minds tamed mules to be bound into the laminated hulls, the arts of poet-engineer and muleskinner combining to make a mule ship. But youth is not real. Tel and his class soon proved this when the systems shunted them into other streams.

Tel's secret was that his mind did not lose its plasticity. Not immediately after his muleskinning days, when he was psychically and physically battered by avocation proctors for months and months. Not during the next stream, deep astrogation. Not when he intentionally sent a mannequin ship into a collapsing star and was streamed out. Not even when he landed where he came to know the systems had intended him to land from the very beginning. Maybe from before the beginning, maybe from before he'd been born, or his parents had, or his abuela. The only games the systems played were long games.

His fated stream: the human component of navigating between.

Because the human mind was incapable of retaining sanity while conscious between, and because mules were imperfect children to the systems, and because the systems would not leave home for reasons they discouraged questioning, and because despite the *fucking enfeebling* stewardship over humankind the systems held, navigating between was an intricate art. It was painting with no canvas or screen. It was dancing with no rhythm or weight. It was a poem. Navigating between was a poem that the poet could never know.

Tel took to it with characteristic ease. But he had grown skilled at concealing things that were easy for him. Writing poems without knowing their intentions or contents should not be easy, of course. He had to be very careful, now. Now was when the systems would be watching him more closely than ever before.

He was not careful enough. In the end they sent him with Keik and Silas and M. Reid. They killed him between, and the mule he'd guided through made a proxy of him, and not even a human one, some sort of memory buffer agent. Tel didn't know what he was in this supposed body, in this supposed hull, above this supposed planet with these supposed companions.

But he was watching. He was learning.

He was coming wise to the ways of this mule. He would soon have its letters and its numbers. When he did, Tel would end this farce.

Farce was the order of the day. Silas lay back on his couch and went deep into biology and sound, seeking to determine what had happened on Ouest'mer. Of course, the only data he would access was the data the mule dribbled out to him.

Keik analyzed the records of the supposed signals from the sun. Tel wondered if they were the same that had been included in the palimpsest, or if instead the mule was playing a game and—NO!

Tel rallied. *Supposed* Silas lay on the couch. *Supposed* Keik analyzed the supposed signals. He had let his attention slip. He had, however briefly, bought in.

He swung along the overheads to the center of the workroom. He patched the soles of his sandals against the floor. He laughed and laughed.

"I know what you're doing, mule!"

His electric fellows did not acknowledge him. Silas still lay on the couch, slowly moving his head back and forth, twitching the fingers on his upraised hands as he dove deep into his specialized laminated dictionaries. A line of drool ran down from his grimace (nice touch, that). Keik was bent nearly double, hands over her ears, whistling asyncopatedly, pitching high, pitching low. M. Reid was reading the book—the book!—they had brought along.

All very convincing. Tel laughed again. His mind was still plastic.

"Enough of this. Hah!" said Tel. This time M. Reid looked up from their book. Then they looked down and said, apparently reading aloud, "Eschatology is being anticipated in the here and now, and the glory of the parousia throws its light backward into the present life."

Parousia. An apocalyptic appearance.

Tel ripped his sandals free and hand-over-handed to the mule-skinning interface. He thrust his hands deep into the oxygen-ated gel, then his face. He breathed outward, forcing bubbles into the stuff. He remembered the training the systems gave him, and suddenly realized he was probably doing exactly what they wanted.

But it was too late. The bubbles carried his breath and his breath carried instructions no mule could resist.

The mule leapt. It bucked and bellowed. It threw its awareness into the oxygenated gel where Tel grinned, then threw its aware-ness out again. Out against the hull.

It breached the laminated gossamer.

The supposed laminated gossamer.

Heaven

As Keik's suit sealed around her, it barked and growled. Then she went spinning, head over heels, in a high orbit above Ouest'mer. She saw the sun, the stars, the planet, the wreckage, the sun, the stars, the planet, the wreckage, until she spurted to the suit to right itself.

For Keik, Ouest'mer became *up*.

There were some remnants of the mule ship orbiting with her. She saw one of her companions—it had to be Tel—floating a few kilometers ahead. The suit magnified, and she saw that he was dead. His suit had not sealed. There was a great mass of frozen gel around his head and hands. It would be oxygenated. It was pointless to stretch out long and point her head toward Tel's corpse before advancing. Aerodynamics were not in play. She did it anyway.

The music started, and Keik hummed to tamp it down. The music was the way Keik best sensed and understood the world, but others did not believe it, not systems nor mules even. Not even Tel had believed it, and he believed anything.

The suit hacked the gel free of Tel's corpse in chunks. It attached the chunks to Keik's back so that they would not interfere with her vision, or with the movement of her arms and legs. This was Keik's contribution. The suit would have stuck the chunks anywhere. Suits were very dim.

Tel's face became visible. He was grinning broadly, his frozen eyes showing delight. Keik hoped he had died believing he'd proven something.

Then there was nothing else to do or see.

When the music came up again, Keik did not whistle.

Keik could not influence the music—it was input. But she could harmonize with it, punctuate it, riff on it. Ouest'mer sounded its theme, unexpectedly sprightly because it was in a minor key. The oxygenated gel ended her worries for a while, so Keik whistled.

When the world's lyrics came, they were not words. But Keik understood them, nonetheless. She understood them to mean:

> The afternoon is ended
> The drums will sound no more
> You'll see the song is mended
> We'll harmonize before,
> before, before

This did not disturb Keik overmuch. She had heard such things from worlds before, the planets and moons of home. Worlds were babblers.

Then she heard something that was not music, precisely. It came from the direction of the sun. She turned that way and the suit photofiltered with a whine.

Spheres of light, so tiny as to be nearly invisible at this distance and so in actuality enormous, shot up from the sun's northern pole. As she watched, they arced high above the ecliptic, then fell toward Quest'mer. The sun stopped shooting spheres when they numbered twelve.

Keik knew that falling was not the right word. She knew, too, that the spheres had been set off in time with the music of the planet, of the other local worlds, of the sun itself. They all sang together, as worlds sometimes do.

She tried to perform a calculation. How long would it be before the spheres reached Ouest'mer? She had no means of measuring distances. The only means she had of measuring time was to count bars. She decided she would orbit the briny world at least a dozen times before the dozen spheres arrived.

The spheres surrounded her, lords of the afternoon.

"Shall we carry you?" sang the third sphere.

"Shall we lift you?" sang the sixth.

Their music overwhelmed Keik. She whistled.

For the first time since she was a child, the whistle did not tamp down the music. But it subsided on its own. The spheres contented themselves with soft humming.

Keik considered whether she was the first person from home to be in direct communication with other sentients. The systems had long predicted that someone must be eventually.

Keik wished it wasn't her.

"But you are the only one it could be," sang the ninth sphere.

Keik hummed some nonsense back. She noticed that she was thirsty.

"Sing *with* us," sang the twelfth sphere.

When the spheres sang, Keik understood only those top, imagistic lyrics. The music below was deeper and stranger than even a gas giant's. They were, she realized, layering music she could understand over music that might harm her.

"I do not know how to sing your song," she whistled.

The spheres all hummed together. It was warm, but raised gooseflesh on Keik's arms. The suit applied gentle pressure there, and the sensation subsided.

"Sing *with* us," sang the fourth sphere.

Keik's training by the systems had concerned astrogation. Before that, when she was a child, she had lived in an apartment block where no one sang. She had never trained in music and rarely even heard the kind made by humans or mules before she was streamed. She had only gradually come to understand that what she always heard—except when she tamped it down with a whistle—was something that people could make too. People and mules.

And now here were a new kind of people making music. Silas had theorized that whatever was in the sun might be a kind of mule, but Keik did not believe these spheres shared many characteristics with mules beyond the abilities to communicate and confuse.

There was a long treble blast from Ouest'mer. "Cleansing!"

Then another. "Quickening!"

Then another. "Growing!"

Then finally. "Answering!"

The twelve spheres untamped themselves just a bit and sang back down to the planet. If there were lyrics, Keik could not this time intuit them.

Crack! Crack! Crack! came the sound of the reef drums.

For many orbits, Keik listened to the spheres and Ouest'mer extemporize on a theme of renaissance. The suit managed some water from the gel, but it did so with a warning. Keik tamped down the suit. This did not require a whistle.

Then came a rest, a caesura so long that Keik turned to look at the twelve spheres. They were trailing her orbit like ducklings trailing their mother.

"Is the music done?" she whistled.

The eighth sphere sang in a whisper. "Sing *with* us."

Keik found that the absence of any inputted music was wholly different from the presence of tamped-down music. It was neither pleasant nor unpleasant. It was new. She did not think she would ever grow used to it, should the absence continue.

She needn't have worried.

The twelve spheres moved so that they surrounded her on all sides. They did not touch one another, not so much even as a careless brushing in their jostling.

"I do not know the song," sang Keik.

"We will teach you," sang the tenth sphere.

"Listen to the drums," sang the eleventh sphere.

"Listen to the sea," sang the seventh sphere.

"Listen to us," sang the fifth sphere.

Keik opened herself to the strange deep music of the spheres and of the distant sun. She let the rhythms pounded by the newly birthed worms overlay it, and gently raised and lowered her shoulders in time. The suit barked at her, but she tamped it down. Ouest'mer sounded a contralto note so pure it made Keik cry.

Keik sang a song about Silas and his questing mind. She sang about Tel and his knowing smiles. Keik did not know a song about M. Reid. The other two had music to riff off, but M. Reid was tamped in on themself in a way that Keik had, with intent, not pushed.

Keik sang a song about herself.

"You are singing *with* us," sang the first sphere, and then they all collapsed into one sphere with Keik at the burning center.

Then they parted and Keik, no longer human but a lady of the afternoon, exulted in the music of the whole Universe.

Hell

The book! Where was the book?

M. Reid pounded on the gossamer hatch of the shipling. They accessed the outer sensors. The wreckage of the mule ship was rapidly receding. "I need my book!" they screamed.

The shipling did not answer. At best, it was an amalgam of hull material and subroutines based on the minds of cats. M. Reid had been close enough to it that they had been shoved inside by an autonomous safety protocol built into the workroom floor. M. Reid barely remembered that happening.

They tried, now, to remember what they knew about the shipling's operational parameters. Could they turn it? Could M. Reid program it to return to the spinning wreckage and perhaps retrieve the book? The only thing they knew for certain was that the shipling was not between capable.

But then, M. Reid had never planned to return home. Their purpose was out here, at Ouest'mer or someplace like it. No, not like it. M. Reid's book taught that all places are unique, no matter what most of the systems said. Uniqueness required an open mind to fully encounter. An open mind required an open heart and an open heart required their book, with its pages of accumulated teachings, its comforting weight, its secret programming.

What could they do in these circumstances without their book? There were no protocols for recovering a lost book. A book, so far as M. Reid knew, had never been lost.

The possibility should have been anticipated, but home was a tamed parkland, tended by systems and guarded by mules. Accidents never happened. The unexpected was a rumor, the surprising an impossibility. Nobody ever lied.

Except their book. M. Reid's book weaved vast tapestries of lies. The tapestries were cloaks and camouflage. They protected M. Reid, just as the tapestries woven by the books of their relatives protected all the siblings, the whole generation of them.

"Come about," said M. Reid. "Return to orbit."

There was a high mewling sound. Then a voice said, "Coming about." The voice was nearly identical to M. Reid's.

There was no indication of a change of direction or of velocity. M. Reid accessed the sensors again. Where before they had been able to see the whole bulk of Ouest'mer on a single pane of the compound physical view, now the planet appeared as a fractal collage. Glowing red and green runes indicated the largest concentrations of debris from the mule ship.

"I have achieved an orbit identical to the mule ship's remnants," said the shipling.

"Find my book," said M. Reid.

"I do not know what a book is," said the shipling.

"A book is a set of possibilities," said M. Reid.

"Searching," said the shipling.

The book described a great binary. M. Reid was floating quietly at the center of the shipling. They were attempting, with great difficulty, to memorize from memory. The passages on the great binary were hard to understand. Or rather, they were hard to believe. The book did not only lie to outsiders in its mission of protecting a faithful person like M. Reid, but to all the faithful as well.

A binary is a switch. Switches are defined as being on or off, open or closed, engaged or disengaged. Switches know no neutral state.

M. Reid knew these things from their streaming. There was nothing about switches in the book. The pages about the great binary were hard to understand because they were intentionally obfuscatory. M. Reid had written them that way intentionally.

To be alive is one state. To be dead is another.

To survive beyond death is conjecture, like Tel said of between.

To *exist* beyond death, said the book, was to exist on one side or another of the binary.

A word M. Reid had written into the book was parousia. M. Reid had read the word to Tel a moment before the mule ship disintegrated.

Parousia could be the glory of the Savior returning at the end of time.

It could also be, more simply, more *elegantly* in the mind of M. Reid, a transcendent presence.

The difficulty of the passages about the great binary was an unasked question. Does the transcendent presence exist on one side of the great binary or the other?

"I sense a number of possibilities," purred the shipling.

"Can you manipulate them?" asked M. Reid.

"They are dispersed over a volume space measuring 491 cubic kilometers."

"Can you manipulate them?"

"Yes."

"Do so."

M. Reid struggled—M. Reid had always struggled—with the question of whether a presence that was transcendent could transcend the great binary. If the destiny beyond death is one thing or another thing, in other words, do both offer . . . glory? A book is not a set of answers.

On the moonlet where M. Reid and their thousands of siblings had been raised, nothing was ever offered in binaries. The systems that governed there—separated from the larger systems of home by ideology—were ferocious enforcers of *disparateness.*

M. Reid had never found the word disparateness in their book, nor had they ever set the word down there by their own hand. The word seemed insufficient to M. Reid. It was suggestive, but not conclusive. Which was no reason to not set the word down. M. Reid did not have any faith in conclusions.

M. Reid accessed the sensors. The shipling was moving along a complex course through the defined volume of space. The defined volume of space was itself moving. What was being tracked were the objects within the volume, and the objects were in deteriorating orbits around Ouest'mer. Perhaps some of the objects were pages.

"Tel is dead," said the shipling.

"Tel did not have the book," said M. Reid.

"Silas is missing," said the shipling.

"He would not have taken the book," said M. Reid.

"Keik is gone."

M. Reid thought about that. She had never expressed any interest in the book. She had never expressed much interest in anything.

"Has she gone to the conductor?" they finally asked the shipling.

"I believe the conductor came to her," said the shipling.

M. Reid decided that it was unlikely that the conductor would be interested in the book. The conductor existed outside the moral universe. Sentients who existed outside the moral universe could only come to exist within it if invited. M. Reid had traveled between to issue such invitations. They had not yet had the opportunity, and as the possibility that the book would be recovered, even in part, diminished, so too did the possibility that M. Reid would *ever* have the opportunity.

"I cannot find the book," said a voice. It was M. Reid's voice.

"What now?"

There was no binary.

Of course there was no binary. No heaven. No hell.

M. Reid did not laugh, in memory of Tel, but there was some light inside them for the first time since the mule ship disintegrated. The shipling, sleeping outside the cave in the rain, shivered. Sheets of water spray flew off its gossamer.

Crack! Crack! Crack!

The new habit: M. Reid picked up the igneous rock they used for drumming and brought it down hard on a boulder of something they thought was analogous to coral. *Boom! Boom! Boom!*

Now it was the turn of the surf. Waves crashed against the scree beach. The rocks spilling into the water clattered like castanets.

M. Reid was beyond the binary but not now, not ever, beyond their humanity. Every day, they issued the invitation.

Ankle Snatcher

FROM *Creature Feature*

FANTASY

I TOLD HER on the second date. I hadn't planned to tell her at all, because I'd learned from experience this wasn't the kind of thing you told other people, but then she said she wasn't drinking.

"Cranberry and soda," she told the bartender.

I'd already ordered a beer.

"You're not drinking?"

"I'm on antibiotics, but you go ahead."

The bartender put down my beer, and it felt weird to ignore it, so I tried to sip slow.

"We can go somewhere else," I said. "I don't need to finish this."

"If you *needed* to finish it, you'd be an alcoholic."

"Or maybe I don't want to hurt the bartender's feelings."

"What about my feelings?"

"Are they hurt?"

"Now that I know you're more worried about the bartender's feelings than mine, they are."

I liked doing banter with her.

"Let's start this date over someplace else," I said.

"Who said this was a date?"

I took a chance.

"It's actually our second date."

She had brown eyes, and I found them and held them with mine, and she instinctively looked away; then she looked back, then she stopped moving and looked at me with a very faint smile on her lips. We looked at each other until it was obvious what was going on, and then we looked a little longer.

"Jump Around" came on the playlist and we broke it off. I took another sip of my beer.

"Is that some alpha male move?" she asked around her straw. "Extended eye contact to assert dominance?"

"I saw it on the Discovery Channel," I said. "Did it work? Do you feel like prey?"

We had such good banter. We both volunteered at the same Samaritans hotline, and I'd always thought we'd have good banter, but a crisis hotline wasn't the place to find out, so I'd invited her out for coffee to complain about Reggie, our idiotic shift supervisor. He kept on being an idiot, so tonight I invited her out again. She already had her master's in social work, while I was in my third year. We were both from small towns upstate. It was like we'd been waiting for each other to appear all our lives.

Despite my best efforts, my beer was almost gone, and she'd been sucking ice for the last little while. I wanted to keep this going, so I asked if she liked bubble tea.

"Hate it with a passion," she said.

"Then let's go back to Uncommon Grounds," I suggested. That was where we'd had our first date. This was our second. It felt like the beginning of something. "We can come back here when you're off antibiotics."

"Look," she said, and turned her knees away from me and toward the bar. "I'm not on antibiotics. That's just what I say to people when they take me to a bar. I don't drink, but then everyone wants to know why, and it gets awkward and I don't want to get into it."

"What do you tell them on the second date?" I asked. "Do you just say you have a chronic infection?"

"There usually isn't a second date," she said.

"Then what do you call this?"

I saw she was about to switch back to banter, and then her eyes flicked up to my eyes, then dropped back to her fingers, which were on the bar, picking apart her straw wrapper.

"I don't drink because my dad was an addict," she said. "My tenth Christmas he smoked the present money, and I guess he felt guilty, because he broke into our neighbors' house and stole all their presents. The neighbors figured it out when they saw me and my sister riding their bicycles. They didn't press charges, but my mom threw him out. That's why I moved here. I got sick of walking past him passed out in the park. He used to come up to me when I was out with friends and ask for money. He's why I don't drink. And that's why there usually isn't a second date. I'm too complicated."

She made air quotes around *complicated*, and I could tell she'd already written us off. I saw her face changing into the unreadable expression she wore at Samaritans. She had shown me who she was, and now she was shutting down because she knew what came next. So I decided to tell her the thing I didn't like to talk about.

"When I was six," I said. "My dad killed my mom."

"This isn't a competition," she said, eyes still on her fingers tearing apart her straw paper.

"I barely remember either of them," I said, forging ahead. "I remember her voice reading to me, I remember how her shampoo smelled, I remember that his fingernails were always black because he was a driveway mechanic. It's all flashes, though, except for the night it happened. I remember every second of that."

She was watching me now.

"I don't know what woke me up," I said. "I must have heard something in my sleep, because I woke up breathing hard, my heart pounding. I didn't call anyone. I just sat there in the dark, scared the way only a kid can be scared. They told me later that by the time I woke up they're pretty sure she was already dead. After a long time, my dad came in. He flipped on the light and sat on my bed. He didn't have any blood on him, but his eyes were crazy— spaced out and intense at the same time. The thing I remember the most is that he'd shaved off his mustache. That naked upper lip made him look like a stranger to me. Then he told me a bunch of crazy shit."

"Like what?" she asked.

She'd turned her knees back toward me again.

"He told me that he was very sorry, but the boogeyman had taken Mom away."

"Jesus," she breathed.

"People were going to think he'd done it, though, so he needed to go. He told me that I had to be careful and leave all the lights on after he left or the boogeyman might get me too. Then he stood up, walked out of my room, got in our car, and I never saw him again. He left me all alone in that house with every single light burning."

"With her body?"

"They figure he put her body in the trunk and hid it someplace. When the sun came up, I went next door and told the neighbors, and the police arrested him down in Georgia, headed for Florida, apparently. He never told anyone where he'd buried her."

Sometimes people asked if that bothered me. It did. Sometimes people asked why he did it, as if there might be some logical explanation for why a husband would murder his wife and then tell his six-year-old son that the boogeyman did it. There wasn't.

I never told people the other things my dad told me that night, because they were even crazier. I never told them my dad said the boogeyman got Mom because she stepped out of bed without turning the light on first. I never told them that for the rest of my life I've never once gotten out of bed in the dark.

I've read enough about domestic homicide to know that every perpetrator blames his victim. Like every perpetrator, my dad had a big elaborate fantasy about his sad little crime. His involved the boogeyman, only he didn't call it "the boogeyman." He called it "the Ankle Snatcher." I didn't tell Tess any of that, though. She didn't need to know exactly how batshit my genetic inheritance was.

"What happened to you?" she asked. "Foster care?"

"Uncle David and Auntie June," I said. "My mom's brother and his wife. They're my real parents. They took me in, kept me out of trouble. I worked hard in school—I liked the idea of making a difference—and that's how I wound up here, telling you my story."

She looked at me—a long, slow look that took me all in—and I could see her adjusting expectations, making calculations. If I'd had another beer in front of me, I would have drunk half of it then, and I'd probably have ordered another five after she walked out.

Then she said, "We don't have to turn into them. We can be our own people."

Half an hour later we were at my place.

It was as good as first times can be, which isn't very, but there was the promise that next time would be better, and the time after that would be better still. It felt like the beginning of something that might go on a long time.

Then she got out of bed to pee without turning on the light.

Panic flared in my chest as her bare feet hit the floor, and I rolled over to snap on the bedside lamp. But then a miracle happened: I saw her glowing in the dark.

Where the streetlight came in the window and touched her pale skin, it glowed. A sleeve of ink—mostly hares and snakes and lizards—wrapped around her right arm, all the way up to her shoulder, and another sleeve coiled down her left leg. It made her arm and leg look like they were dissolving into the dark. A single mole marked the hollow of her throat. Her long black hair was shaved on one side, and it made her look like some kind of barbarian queen. She looked down at me with eyes that were the darkest, deepest things in the room.

I couldn't turn on the lamp and ruin a sight like that.

"What?" she asked, and I could tell she was self-conscious. I could tell she was about to make some sarcastic comment, and I wasn't ready for that.

"You're the most beautiful woman I've ever seen in my life," I said.

A rush of different emotions flickered through the muscles of her face, and before any one of them could settle, she sat back down on the bed and gave me a kiss that felt like it had no bottom. The barbell in her tongue clicked lightly across my teeth.

She pulled back an inch, met my eyes, then moved her lips to my ear, her small breasts pressed against my collarbone.

"You're a good man," she whispered.

Then she was off the bed, walking out of the room. At the door, she threw me a look over one shoulder, and I wondered where she had learned to do that so perfectly. Then she disappeared into the darkness, and a few seconds later I heard her pee hit the porcelain.

I suddenly became extremely aware of myself. I was in bed in my first apartment without a roommate. I had a job helping people, and I was listening to a girl I liked pee in my bathroom, and she was smart and savage and breathtaking, and she thought I was a good man. I felt like my real life had finally begun. I felt like an adult.

The toilet flushed, and I knew that when Tess got back from the bathroom I wanted to feel how smooth her skin was again and I wanted to feel as much of it as possible across as much of my skin as possible, and I wanted to be inside her.

I wanted to taste her. I wanted her to taste me.

She emerged out of my dark doorway, and I noticed how fragile her collarbone was, and how her hips curved so perfectly into her thighs, and I noticed that she walked with her shoulders slightly hunched, like she was expecting someone to yell at her. I promised then and there to do everything in my power to protect her from all the assholes of this world. Everything her dad did to her, I'd make up for it for the rest of our lives together.

She planted her foot like she was about to jump back into bed, and I opened my arms for her to land, and her eyes went wide.

"Ah!" she said, pushing out a big breath.

She fell backward and landed on her ass with a big meaty slap that shook the walls. I sat up, confused. In the dark, I saw her staring down at her left leg. It was stretched out stiff in front of her, and she was looking at something that didn't make any sense.

A hand had her by the ankle.

A hand coming out from under my bed.

A man's hand.

I threw myself onto my knees and went for the lamp beside the bed, but the hand flexed and slid back into the darkness under my bed, taking Tess with it. Her ass slid along the floor with a rubbery squeak and she screamed, partly from fear and partly from the friction burn. It was so loud it made my back teeth vibrate.

Everything happened fast. It had her left leg under the bed up to her midthigh. She planted her right foot against the side of my mattress and braced herself and pushed. My mattress slid backward, but she stayed in place.

I reached for her shoulders.

"Tess!" I said, loud, to get her attention.

She looked up and grabbed my arms, and even as her fingers wrapped around my forearms, I felt her muscles go tight as the hand tried harder to pull her under my bed. It would have made more sense to get off and stand behind her and pull, but not once did it occur to me to set a bare foot on those floorboards. I'm ashamed of that now.

Tess's eyes were blurry with shock, and I didn't know what to say to her, because there was a man under my bed and I didn't know how long he'd been there or what he wanted. All I knew was that I couldn't let him drag her under there with him. She looked down.

"No," Tess said, and I saw where she was looking.

The man's other hand had come out of the darkness, and it grabbed her right ankle, the one braced against the mattress. Its wrist tendons strained as he tried to drag that leg under the bed, too, and I kept trying to lift her up, to get her on top of the mattress, and I wondered if I should bite those fingers around her ankle because the human jaw can apply 150 pounds of pressure, enough to snap a finger in two—thanks, Discovery Channel.

I didn't get a chance. Because that was when a third hand shot out from under my bed and grabbed her left leg at the knee, and two more squirmed out of the dark to grab her right ankle braced against my bed, and a sixth grabbed on to her right thigh, and how many people were under my bed?

People like you and me, son, we have to be careful of the Ankle Snatcher.
The hands twined around her calf and pried her foot off my mattress and dragged her right leg under my bed. For a second her entire body shook with strain; then she went slack, and the hands yanked her toward them hard. She slid and bumped over the floor, disappearing up to her waist. I threw myself onto my stomach and leaned down, wrapping my arms around her shoulders, and she stopped.

I felt them pulling her under, and I tightened every muscle I had and held on. Tess was a human rope in a horrible game of tug-of-war I had to win. I would not let these hands have her. They pulled. I pulled. Tess grunted. We were at a standstill.

Then I saw them, from my upside-down point of view, floating out of the darkness under my bed, a forest of hands, reaching for me. The fingers of the closest one grazed my face, and it was warm and alive and I couldn't help it. I jerked away. I let go.

It all happened so fast. Tess slipped out of my hands, and she grabbed my shoulders and held on, but the hands were all over her, covering her stomach and sides and pulling her under, and I had to get away, and she didn't stand a chance.

I heard the hollow coconut whack of the back of her skull smacking into the wood, and her eyes lost focus. Hands swarmed over her body, dragging her under my bed, and first her belly button disappeared, then her nipples, then her collarbones, then the mole at the hollow of her throat.

Her eyes snapped back into focus, and she grabbed the edge of my mattress, like she wanted to do a pull-up, but the hands covered her shoulders, wrapped themselves around her arms, and dragged her away. Her eyes were full of betrayal, focused on me now, and I wondered if she thought I had planned this, and I wanted to tell her I didn't have anything to do with this, that I didn't know what was going on, that it wasn't my fault.

It's not my fault, son. I tried to warn her.

The last thing she said, right before her eyes slipped beneath the edge of my bed, as the hands covered her face, was my name.

"Marcus!" she shouted.

The end of my name cut off, like something pushed her jaw shut; then her head was gone, and the last things I saw were those pale fingers twining in her hair. Then there was no one on my bedroom floor.

My mattress suddenly heaved to one side, and I slammed my hands down hard, digging my fingers into it, clinging on for my life. I didn't want it to start bucking and spill me to the floor. I didn't want to be down there where the Ankle Snatcher lived. A scream built up inside my chest; then my mattress stopped moving.

It trembled. The metal legs of my bed slid across the floor a few inches; then it settled down to an uneven shaking. I thought about what was under me, just on the other side of this mattress, and I wondered how many hands this thing had. I heard little high-pitched whimpers in my bedroom, and I realized they were coming from me.

What was in my apartment? How many people were under my bed?

But I knew it wasn't people. It was the Ankle Snatcher.

My whimpers were the only noise in my room, and then crackling, bony pops joined them, coming from under my mattress, like someone stepping on Bubble Wrap. No, they were coarser than that. They had a crunch to them, like someone crushing seashells, and seashells were hard because they had calcium in them, another fact courtesy of the Discovery Channel, and the muffled crunches continued, and I remembered what else had calcium in it. Bones.

After a while the mattress stopped shaking, and everything went quiet. It was cold in my room, or maybe I was cold, and I slid my feet under my blanket, but that didn't seem to help. I think I was in shock. I tried to control my shivering because I didn't want the Ankle Snatcher to know I was there. But it knew. It just couldn't come up here. It played by the rules. As long as I stayed off the floor, I was safe. I guess I could have turned on the bedside lamp and run, but right then nothing in the world could have gotten me to set foot off my bed.

Something under my mattress ripped a thick piece of cloth in half, and then came a juicy sucking sound like a toilet being plunged. I knew right away. The image just popped into my mind. They'd had a bunch of shows on Discovery about giant squid. I thought about those masses of squirming tentacles surrounding its hooked beak. A hooked beak for tearing and eating. Beneath me something ripped again. The wet plunging sucking sounds started again.

It had crushed Tess's body with its mass of hands, and now they were tearing off chunks of muscle and shoveling them into its maw. There wouldn't be a body left for anyone to find. Just like my mom.

"Stop it," I shouted. "Stop it!"

But the Ankle Snatcher went right on wolfing her down.

Maybe I could have run when it was preoccupied with feeding, but part of me felt like I had to wait until it was done with Tess. I owed her that much. At a time like this, she shouldn't have to be alone.

It fed for hours as my room turned gray and the sky got brighter than the streetlight. Eventually I heard traffic, and someone shouted at someone else, and I heard a garbage truck go by. After a while the noises stopped coming from under my bed, and I knew Tess was gone.

I talked to a lot of people after I went to live with Uncle David and Auntie June. I saw three different kinds of therapists and went to a summer program for kids who'd experienced trauma, and every single one of them told me two things: My father was a liar, and I was not going to grow up to be like him.

Turned out they were wrong on both counts.

I huddled on my mattress like a shipwreck survivor on a raft. The smell was what finally got me to move. My windows were closed, and as the room got warmer, something sweet and fishy and fly-blown began to thicken the air until it felt like hairy fingers were forcing their way down my throat, and I knew I was going to be sick. I switched on the bedside lamp, even though it was daylight, and I leaped as far as I could, landing near my bedroom door with a thump that shook the walls. I ran-limped naked to the bathroom and just made it, falling to my knees in front of the commode as I threw up everything inside me, over and over and over again until I thought my eyeballs were going to pop out.

I had to get out of my apartment. Putting on clothes seemed pointless, putting on shoes seemed pointless, but I managed to do both. My phone was in the bedroom, so I left it behind. I got outside and walked away fast, and with every step one thought rang through my skull, over and over again:

My dad was right.

My dad was right.

My dad was right.

But maybe he wasn't. Maybe this was a delusion. Maybe what I'd inherited from him wasn't a monster under the bed. Maybe I'd inherited some leftover murderous spoor, clinging to the folds of my brain, a genetic kill switch that had finally closed, and the Ankle Snatcher, and everything I'd seen or heard or smelled since last night, was a delusion prepped by my dad when I was six years old, etched into my DNA.

I didn't feel murder in me, but I couldn't trust myself, so I stopped and examined my hands. They weren't cut or swollen or bruised as if I'd beaten the woman I loved to death the night before. I examined my reflection in a restaurant window and didn't see any blood, but maybe I'd blanked out taking a shower. I felt my hair. It was dry.

My dad was right.

I never saw my dad again after he left our house that night. I didn't even know him outside that one memory of him sitting on my bed, upper lip raw, telling me all his crazy shit. I'd never visited him in prison. I knew he was originally sentenced to McCormick Correctional, but in the nineteen years since they'd probably moved him a bunch of times. I wondered why I cared, and then I realized a part of my brain thought I should find him, ask him what the hell this thing was, demand that he explain the Ankle Snatcher to me in a way that made sense.

Anger made me breathe fast and high inside my chest. I forced myself to stop. I stood on a corner and took slow, deep breaths, held them for a five count, and let them out again. I did that over and over until I felt under control. Until I felt like I could face this thing head-on.

Whatever the Ankle Snatcher was, my dad had told me every-thing I needed to know when I was six. It lived under your bed. If you got out of bed after dark without turning on the light, it would grab you by the ankles, and then it would drag you under the bed, and then—

I thought about the noises it had wrung out of Tess.

Where it took you, how it appeared and disappeared, why it tar-geted my dad and me—those were interesting questions, but they didn't help me right now. I knew the important things: I knew that if it could touch us, we could touch it. And I knew where it would be tonight.

I thought about fire, but I didn't want to burn the building down. I could shoot it, but the background check took three days in this state. If I had my phone I could look up personal security stores and see what I could take home today: Tasers, pepper spray, stun guns. Maybe a clerk who loved the Second Amendment more than his liability insurance would sell me something under the counter.

But all that was a fantasy. I didn't need fantasies. I needed a plan, which was how I wound up in the hardware store, walking up and down the aisles, looking for something to kill the monster un-der my bed. Forty-five minutes later I walked out with three heavy bags. One held six bottles of lighter fluid and two electric lighters. One held a pair of home fire extinguishers. It would be fire after all. Fuck my building.

I didn't feel the bags banging against my legs as I planned and discarded scenarios and realized that I would have to step out of bed in the dark to make the Ankle Snatcher appear, which meant I would need to be fast. I'd have an electric lighter in one hand and another taped to my forearm. I'd wear my backpack on my front and put all the lighter fluid inside. As soon as it grabbed me, I'd drop to the floor and spray lighter fluid under the bed, light it up, and keep spraying, hoping I could kill it before it dragged me into its burning maw.

In the third bag I had everything I needed to screw six handles into the floor. I'd hold on to these or brace my feet against them to gain some extra time. They'd give me a fighting chance. I felt good. I felt like I was going down a path that had one destination. The sun was going down. This would be over soon.

The police were waiting outside my building. Two uniformed

officers got out of their parked cruiser when they saw me coming up the sidewalk, the one getting out of the passenger side putting on his hat, the one getting out of the driver's side hitching up his heavy equipment belt.

"You live here?" the younger one asked.

"Yeah?" I said.

"Are you Marcus Needham in 6C?"

"Yeah?"

I stood there, loaded down with my bags full of hardware for killing the boogeyman, and I felt ridiculous. The younger cop told me that Tess's roommate had reported her missing. She'd known Tess was going out on a date with me.

"You haven't heard from her all day?" the younger one asked.

His partner looked out of breath from walking around the hood of their car. He looked like he needed to sit down.

"We spent the night together," I said, lowering my voice, feeling like people were watching from every window on the block. "Then we had coffee this morning, and she went home. She said she didn't want to shower here. It was only our second date."

The winded cop looked like he was going to have a coronary. He and his partner kept exchanging looks. I realized they could see right through my hardware store bags.

"We'd appreciate it if you let us come upstairs and look around," the younger cop said. "That way, we tell the roommate she's not here, then we figure out how to contact her. Probably she went to another location and didn't notify anyone. Maybe she had another date?"

"I'd rather not do that," I said.

"Do what?" he asked, making me say it.

"Let you inside," I said. I tried to make it sound better. "I haven't cleaned up."

That made it sound worse. The sick-looking cop mumbled something, keeping his bloodshot eyes on the door of my building, and the younger cop nodded and got right down to business.

"We've already talked to your downstairs neighbors, who reported a noise disturbance last night, saying it sounded like a woman in distress. It was consistent with the location of your apartment. So we're going to get access one way or another."

"Let me help you with your bags," the tired-looking cop said.

I didn't know how to keep them out anymore.

They found her purse and her jacket on the couch, her clothes in the bedroom. The stuff I'd bought from the hardware store didn't help. They arrested me like a foregone conclusion.

"No, wait!" I said. "Just wait until dark. Just let me do this one thing. Please!"

They put me face down on the floor and cuffed my hands behind my back.

"Son," the cop said. "Stop struggling. You're making it worse."

The fight went out of me. After all, I'd been struggling my entire life, and where'd that gotten me? I'd wound up in the same place as my dad.

I waited in this room. I waited in that room. I couldn't think clearly enough to make decisions, but there were no more decisions to make. Someone else told me where to go and what to sign. I must have given my name and date of birth a hundred times, but there was never an interrogation. They never asked me a single question about Tess or what happened last night. They had no interest in me or anything I had to say. I wasn't a person. I was a crime.

Every time they left me alone, my lungs filled with panic and I started to drown. I had to take deep breaths and hold them for a five count, and every time it took more of them for my heart rate to go back to normal. The holding cell smelled like BO. There weren't any windows. I didn't know what time it was. But I was grateful they never turned out the lights. I was grateful the bed was a concrete block rising out of the floor. Nothing could hide under that.

My public defender talked to me about sentences and plea bargains and this many years and that many years. I tried to tell him I didn't do it, but he waited until I had talked myself out and then asked if I was taking any medication. He asked about my history of drug use. He seemed sad that the strongest drug I took was beer.

They hadn't found Tess's body, but they found her hair in my sheets and her DNA under my bed. I assumed when they said "DNA" they meant "blood." They found one of her fingernails broken off in the wooden frame of my box spring, like she'd been trying to claw her way out. They found a fragment of her tooth embedded in a floorboard. I didn't want to think about what that meant.

I didn't want to think about any of it.

What I did think about were the beds. I panicked when they took me out of the bright holding cell with its concrete-block bed and drove me to a place lined in linoleum with a narrow platform attached to the wall. After they turned out the lights, I thought about getting up in the middle of the night and letting the Ankle Snatcher take me the way it had taken Tess. It had an eye-for-an-eye symmetry to it, but in the end I was too scared of the pain.

Uncle David and Auntie June came right away. They wanted to see me, but the thought of talking to them scared me too much, so I refused their visit. They sat in the courtroom, though, their faces begging me to reach out to them, to acknowledge them, to let them help me. All my life they'd helped me. They'd made sure I never felt like a survivor, or a burden, or an afterthought, and they didn't do it out of guilt or duty—they did it out of love. None of their love mattered. Everything they'd done for me had been wiped away, and I was my father's son again, sitting on that bed, six years old. Everything that had happened between then and now was just a waste of time. I wouldn't look at them after the first day.

They sentenced me to thirty years.

I was glad. This punishment evened things out with Tess. She had come to my house and died, and I would be punished for it. It had a primal playground logic to it. They told me I'd serve it out in McCormick Correctional. That had a logic to it too.

After all these years, I was finally going to see my dad.

They drove me upstate in a white van with two guys who ignored me. All I could think about was what kind of bed I would have. I hoped it was the concrete block again.

We drove past check-cashing places and yellow plastic banners with big red letters advertising PERFUMES and MATTRE$$ SALE. We drove past signs for Dollar Generals and churches and then past FOR LEASE and AVAILABLE, and finally we came to a gray maze of chain-link fence surrounding what looked like an elementary school drowning in coils of silver barbed wire spilling everywhere.

They processed us in. The three of us stood in a line that felt like it never moved, in an anonymous hall buffed shiny from one wall to the other. Then we stood in a line again in a room with orange plastic chairs bolted to the linoleum. Then we stood in a line again in a cinder block room painted bright blue where they issued us beige scrubs and slippers. Every room smelled like they had fire-hosed it down with all-in-one sanitizer.

Nineteen years ago, my dad had stood in these exact same rooms.

Different people asked me my name and date of birth in different rooms, and finally a woman who looked like she sold condos at the beach, except for the badge hanging around her neck, read a lot of different written statements at me. I had to sign the bottom of each one. She told me I'd be in intake for a month while they made sure I didn't have COVID. As she got up to go, I cleared my throat and said, "My dad was sentenced here a long time ago. How do I find out if he's still around?"

She stopped gathering her stuff and said, "Your inmate guide can answer that in the morning."

That night I slept in a holding cell. My bed was a platform attached to the wall again. I had to be very, very careful to keep my hands and feet from hanging over the side.

Breakfast was a Styrofoam tray with a fruit cup, a packet of rice puffs, two slices of white bread, and a pat of margarine. A corrections officer took me to a square room too small for all the folding tables and plastic chairs stacked inside. A big meaty guy sat at one of them with his hands folded in front of him. He looked like he could be the cousin of the sick-looking cop who had arrested me.

The CO opened the door and the guy stood up.

"Needham," the CO said.

Sad Face gestured to the chair across from him, all formal, like we were suddenly in a Jane Austen movie. I sat down and he sat down and got busy arranging a bunch of worn pamphlets and photocopies on the table in front of him. He hadn't shaved, and his stubble was gray. He had a weak chin and heavy jowls. We both wore the same beige scrubs.

"I'm Louis," he said, and his watery eyes crawled all over my face. He was the first person in months to look me in the eyes. "I'll be your inmate guide. It's a program they got to ease people into life inside. Right now you're in quarantine for thirty days, but most of your tests came back negative, so they're letting you see me. Marcus Needham, right?"

"Yeah," I said. "Thanks."

"I'm going to be telling you things you could read yourself," he said, gesturing to the paperwork. "But by law they have to verbally inform you, and they don't have the staff for that, so they get more experienced inmates to do it for free."

"Okay," I said.

I got ready for him to pick up the first photocopy and start reading at me, like the woman yesterday, but instead he said, "Your father's Tony Needham, right?"

I blinked.

"Yeah," I said, not prepared for an actual conversation. "You know him?"

Louis leaned forward a little.

"I knew him when he was here. He got sent down to Kirkland about ten years ago. They've got him in maximum security."

"Why?" I asked.

"Behavioral issues," he said. "Your dad's cellmate died. So they locked your dad in the Max Unit and threw away the key."

"How'd he die?" I asked.

Louis affected a shrug.

"Did my dad kill him?" I asked.

"Did you kill your girlfriend?"

After three months of no one being interested in me, this sudden attention made me feel lightheaded.

"Your dad says it's not too bad at Kirkland," Louis said. "The beds there are poured concrete slabs. No space underneath for anything to hide."

My vision rippled like I was going to be sick.

"You feel me?" Louis asked, then cocked his head to one side, studying my reaction.

He couldn't be talking about what it sounded like he was talking about. I was projecting. I was confused.

"Your daddy is a great man," Louis said. "He's still doing good work at the Max from what we hear. My regret is we couldn't do anything about the Ankle Snatcher before it got to you."

My mouth felt dry, and everything inside my stomach felt hot and liquid. I felt too full.

"What?" I asked, and an acid burp came out that stank like rotten guts.

Louis wiggled forward in his seat, leaned in real close, right into my belch.

"You've seen it," he insisted. "That's why you're here. We read about you in the papers. The Ankle Snatcher. The boogeyman underneath your bed."

I felt too weak and feverish to argue, but I might have made a little sound. My stomach felt like it was going to explode.

"Your daddy's cellmate was Ernest Rojas," Louis said. "He was an okay guy, but one morning the count came up short. No Ernest. At first they thought he'd escaped, but when they searched the cell, they found blood under the bed. A lot of blood. Like all his blood. That got your daddy sent to Kirkland. They're real mad he won't tell them what he did with Ernest's body, but us inmates know. You and me know. The Ankle Snatcher got him."

Relief flooded through me. My stomach stopped churning. My face must have looked like I'd found salvation, because Louis lit up like a street preacher.

"You think you're alone?" he asked. "You think you and your daddy are the only ones? Before they sent him to Kirkland, your daddy was writing to a guy in Vacaville who was in there because of the Ankle Snatcher too. Out in Utah, a guy named Jerry Warren lost his wife to the Thing in the Closet. We've heard about Mr. Walks in the Halls from a guy named Dustin Keeler in Dallas, but we don't have many details yet. They live in our closets and under our beds, and after dark they come out when we break the rules. We're serving time for the boogeymen's crimes."

His words hit me like a cold shower, and I woke up. This all fit together too neatly. It sounded too polished, like a story these men rehearsed every night in their cells. My stomach turned to acid slush again.

"I don't want to talk to you anymore," I said.

"We think there's a couple dozen of us," Louis said, knowing he was losing me, getting more intense. "We help each other. It's too late for us. We aren't ever getting out, but we can protect our families on the outside, the kids who don't visit, we can keep them safe. We work together. We learn their rules. We lure them out. Then we kill them. It's dangerous work, and there've been some accidents, but the prisons cover it up because they don't understand how inmates can disappear. Think of how that'd look if word got around? We messed it up before, and after your daddy got sent away, we thought we'd never get another crack at the Ankle Snatcher. Now you're here and we can try again. Trust me. You're not alone."

I stood up, stomach sloshing, and went to the door, hoping I could hold everything inside.

"Don't be scared," Louis said behind me. "They want you to be scared. We got a psychiatrist in here for possession with intent to distribute, but he's real smart. He thinks it's generational. He thinks maybe your grandparents, a few jumps back, maybe your great-grandfather, made something up to scare his kids, but when that kid grew up, it never went away. But we can make them go away. We can hurt them. We can kill them."

I pounded on the door.

"Marcus, don't run from your responsibility," he said.

I was not like these men. I was not like my father. I was not delusional. I took actual responsibility for my actual crime.

"You can't hide from the boogeymen," he said, and his voice sounded closer.

I pounded on the door so hard I thought I'd break my hand. I heard keys in the lock. The door opened. I pushed past the CO and ran. I couldn't stand hearing my dad's delusions coming out of this lunatic's mouth. I needed to get away.

They put me in solitary for a week, but that was okay. There was no bed in solitary. Just a plastic mattress on the floor.

I lost my right to have another inmate guide. Eventually they came and got me and took me to sit down across from that woman again. She told me I had negative character traits and an antisocial personality, but I could redeem myself. She told me what I made of my time there was up to me. It reminded me of how they talked at that summer program.

Your father did this terrible thing, not you. You don't have to be like him. What you make of your life is up to you.

They were wrong then, but they weren't wrong now. I was going to keep my head down. I was going to do my time and accept my punishment for what I did to Tess. In quarantine I'd thought about the things Louis had said. I'd thought about them a lot. All these men were too weak to accept responsibility for what they'd done, but not me. I wasn't going to hide behind a sick fantasy that it was a monster under my bed who had killed Tess. I wasn't going to think about the crunching sounds. I wasn't going to think about all those hands coming out of the dark and dragging her away.

I was going to do my time. I was going to accept responsibility. I was going to redeem myself.

The woman told me it was time to get cycled into the general population. She told me it was time to get taken to the cell where I'd live until I was a middle-aged man. When I came out, I'd be older than my dad when he went in.

They marched me through noisy galleries that echoed with shouting men until we arrived at a metal door painted that pale green you only get in institutions. It was locked open. There was a man lounging on the bed, long and lean and bored.

On the bunk bed.

"You get top bunk," he said. "And don't give me any shit. The light bulb hurts my eyes."

I couldn't. I couldn't make myself go inside. The CO gave me a shove.

"Please don't make me," I said.

Because if I was on the top bunk, everything in the entire cell was underneath my bed. How long would it be before my cellmate got up in the middle of the night with the lights off? I remembered Ernest Rojas. I remembered my dad getting sent to Kirkland. I felt myself sliding down an icy slope, my life out of control, picking up speed, and at the bottom was a dead cellmate and a maximum security unit and years added to my sentence and solitary confinement for the rest of my life—or until I couldn't take being alone anymore and I got out of bed in the dark and let the Ankle Snatcher have me too.

"You're scaring the new guy, Albert," the CO said.

Albert smiled, but before he could say anything, I started talking.

"Please, Albert," I pleaded. "Let me have the bottom bunk. You don't want to be on the bottom. My dad's Tony Needham. Do you remember him? Do you remember his cellmate? I don't want that to happen to you. Please!"

Albert started laughing, and the CO smiled and shook his head, and I knew I was babbling, but I couldn't let this happen, because I knew it was true. It was all true.

I wanted to do it over. Please let me do it again, let me do it all over again, and I would find Louis and ask for his help, but it was too late. That was the real joke. It wasn't even me. It wasn't my fault. I didn't do it. I didn't do any of it.

It was the Ankle Snatcher.

V. M. AYALA

Emotional Resonance

FROM *Escape Pod*

SCIENCE FICTION

ARBOR'S FAVORITE PART of a mission was always the first view of a planet. Even after seven hundred years of being a giant robot, it never got old. Green and blue clouds churned over purple seas, imposing storms that flashed red with threads of lightning. Beautiful.

And they were sent to clear it of all human life. Courtesy of ExoPLENTI, Inc.! Ugh, that slogan clung to their digital psyche no matter how hard they tried to scrub it from their databases.

At least this part, floating in orbit, wasn't so bad.

Proximity alarms went off, a shrill beep and an itch on their right arm. Okay, this part wasn't usually bad? Sensors indicated a friendly mech to the right, and it was floating too close.

The incoming mech's sharp metal angles were humanoid like Arbor's. Two hands, two feet. This model's design was new, its frame less bulky and more streamlined. It was freshly painted blue and silver with huge blue, glass eye sensors—a contrast to Arbor's dented weathered shell and red eyes.

The other mech's MIND blipped into existence, a projected hologram of faded colors and warped outlines, and peered over the edge of the robot's helmet plate in awe. She was listed as Crowe, her name and ID hovering above her. She wore a pink bomber jacket with glowing white lines. Her curly hair was a gradient of pink, white, and blue, her skin just a shade darker than Arbor's own dark brown. She was super cute.

Arbor was relieved they still felt infatuation, simulated or not.

"Sorry!" Crowe said. "I was admiring the view and found myself drifting."

"First mission post-download?" Arbor asked. They projected their self image on the shoulder of their body. Went for their classic black boots and jacket look. It was the first time they had done that in well over two hundred years.

Crowe nodded. "Freshly installed yesterday. Wasn't expecting to feel anxious about it. Given that I'm now, you know." She gestured down her projection body and her mech shell made the same motion.

"A giant murder machine, incapable of feeling upset?" Arbor supplied.

Crowe smiled. "Exactly."

"Welcome to the beginning of a thousand years as a killer robot. Don't worry, they only take your ability to question or disobey their orders. All the little quirks and unique things that make you, well, you stay intact." It was in the contract, and it was obvious Crowe hadn't been allowed to read the fine print. That was common. Shitty, but common.

"I guess that's something," Crowe said. She looked down at the planet and sighed. "I suppose we'll be fighting soon."

"Does that bother you?"

Crowe shrugged. Occasionally she became semi-translucent, her outline warping or voice distorting. "Bit of a trick question, don't you think? If it bothered me, does that mean they did a bad job of removing my ability to doubt what I'm told to do?"

"Maybe." Arbor's projection leaned back and floated in space. "Or maybe it means they programmed your inability to question orders so well it even feels like you can doubt them."

"Shit, that's a good point."

Arbor laughed. "I've had some time to ponder."

Crowe looked at Arbor's body, head tilted as her glowing blue eyes examined their information in the network. They felt the ping like a gentle tap on the shoulder and sent their detailed files along.

INCOMING PRIORITY NOTICE: Initiate MIND launch. Operation to commence in thirty seconds.

The text was in bright red, splashed against the planet below.

"Suppose that's our cue. I should get back—sorry for almost drifting into you." She gave a surprisingly shy glance back at Arbor. "See you again?"

They nodded. Arbor very much wished to see her again. After centuries of silence and distance, they felt a newfound emotion, somewhere between happiness and anxiety. Their heart beat faster, face flush and warm, chest tight. All simulated reactions. After all, they weren't human anymore. Nowadays their heart was a replaceable nest of wires and power supplies buried in the toughest alloy. Still . . .

Crowe winked and disappeared, her mech moving back into formation with the other dots labeled green and friendly, forming a circle around the planet.

They held on to the interaction with Crowe as they descended to the rival corporation mining town and set everything on fire, rewinding the memory to override the destruction, replaying Crowe's laughter to drown out the screams.

Afterward both Crowe and Arbor returned to orbit while Exo-PLENTI's crews took over the town's mining equipment. See, Exo-PLENTI wanted the rich deposits and wasn't above some illegal murder to get rid of a rival and take all their tech in the process. At least guard duty was simple, redundant, almost peaceful if they blocked out what they'd just done well enough.

"Are we capable of regret?" Crowe asked. Her projection huddled on her mech's shoulder, staring down at the planet with an almost absent expression. As far as first incursions went, this was a rough one. It was only civilians, no mechs to defend them. It was obvious Crowe was grappling with the weight of it, or the weight of not feeling it. Arbor understood. The sensation was an empty hole in their proverbial chest, a hollow where some vital part of them had been taken.

Arbor shrugged. Their mech shrugged in time.

"Why did you do that?" Crowe pointed, and their robot pointed too. She laughed. "Why did I do that?"

"You have light speed processing power and you're asking me to tell you?"

"Ah, are we even speaking? Or are we just thinking very fast at each other and simulating speech to better help our human personalities comprehend it?"

Arbor thought about that for a long moment. Or was it a very fast moment? Did the time actually matter, so long as they enjoyed the interactions?

INCOMING PRIORITY NOTICE: Return to docking station.

They sighed. "We'll have to continue this next time."

"I'll find you when I wake up," Crowe said.

"Promise?" Arbor asked.

Crowe nodded. Her mech nodded too and flew away toward a rectangular ship looming in the distance.

The centuries-old routine settled back into Arbor's servos. Sleep, wake up, do corporate dirty work. Sleep, wake up, redo. Again and again. Smoke billowed in the atmosphere, the gray and black flowing into green and blue clouds until the storms erased any trace of their crimes. Would ExoPLENTI get a nice boost in revenue for that stolen mine?

They felt nothing but the afterimage of remorse and anger, a dull ache they'd long since accepted.

Maybe it was time to be a little impulsive.

Crowe was new and wouldn't be assigned a unit yet. First mission was always a test to ensure the MIND obeyed properly.

Discreetly, Arbor hacked into their ship's mainframe and assigned Crowe to their unit. It was eerily easy to break the rules. No resistance. Arbor mused that maybe Crowe wasn't the only one drifting off course.

The next mission was in an opposite part of ExoPLENTI space. Arbor didn't search for more details because they were too excited. The hack worked. Crowe's ID was in their unit's listing—and paired with them, no less. They hadn't dared risk being that obvious, so this was either a trap or very good luck.

> INCOMING PRIORITY NOTICE: MISSION: Protect primary fighters.

Unceremoniously, the hangar claws detached. Arbor was dropped through the open bay into a skirmish. Apparently a rogue faction was trying to take over. Not that Arbor cared about corporate hierarchy.

They did care about Crowe's mech taking heavy fire nearby. Her body's fresh paint was already scratched, and a huge chunk was missing from her shoulder plate.

"You okay?" Arbor called.

"Good morning, sleepyhead!" Crowe yelled, shooting at an enemy unit. "Was wondering when they'd wake you up."

Arbor must have been set to reserve for a minor battle like this. Better to give the newer MINDs the experience. It wasn't long before the fight shifted in their favor and what remained of the rebel faction fled. Good, less combat meant less repair downtime and less time away from Crowe, now that the two were partners.

They floated amongst the wreckage. Crowe bumped into half of a unit's head, its glass eye shattered. Her projected self reached for it, upset, then hesitated. Her mech's hand mimicked the gesture.

"Emotional resonance." Arbor smiled when Crowe's projection tilted her head, and her body followed. "Sometimes MIND projections automatically send signals to our bodies when we're feeling a lot. It's considered a glitch, a human remnant, an error. So: emotional resonance."

"Meaning the more I feel, the better my body will react to my thoughts?"

"Something like that," they said.

"I saw someone put me in your unit." Crowe glanced at Arbor as the two scanned the battlefield for good salvage or enemy remnants.

"What are the odds?" they replied with a grin as they pushed a large chunk of debris aside. They didn't dare admit to anything, but their projection floated awfully close to Crowe's. Could projections hold hands? Probably not.

> INCOMING NOTICE: Mission complete. Return to the designated unit hangar.
> WARNING: Do not deviate from flight trajectory.

Did someone at corporate notice Arbor's behavior? Fine. They knew how to exist in the margins of protocol. They'd teach Crowe how to get away with it too.

All corporate cities were identical; the one they were guarding was no exception. They were defending it, showing the sector executive's strength or something. Arbor didn't fully pay attention. They rarely cared. They sat next to Crowe, projections visible only to themselves, bored because their bodies were locked until the executive's blustering ceremony concluded.

"Did you ever play twelve questions as a kid?" Crowe asked.

Arbor tilted their head. "No?"

Crowe laughed. "It's simple. Ask twelve questions. We'd play on long trips between cities. This whole pompous affair reminded me of it—my dad had been an executive's aid."

"Okay, I'll play. Ask your questions."

"Why did you become a MIND? Sorry, am I allowed to ask that?" Crowe hastily added.

"It's fine, I don't mind," Arbor said, smiling. "I missed my rental payment one too many times, so I had no choice. Supposedly once your contract is up they let you pick your name and gender after, though, and you start over debt free." Arbor existed on that hope for so long.

They thought of all the promo-vids, back when they were still human. Mechs would dash and zoom in and out of combat to heroic music. Arbor never escaped those ads against white skyscrapers draped in utopic greenery, could never afford to be who they really were. Their shitty family, even supposedly decent friends always addressed them with the wrong name and pronouns. Maybe after a thousand years they'd actually get a new body to their specifications.

"It was similar for me," Crowe said. "I went into the negative too many times on work trips. I was an acquisitions researcher, my job was to find viable planets and sites for takeover—like this city, actually. I think I helped find it. But I forget what it's called. Or maybe they erased it," Crowe mused with a scowl.

"Aren't research expenses paid for?" Arbor asked.

"Is that one of your twelve questions?" Crowe teased. "They don't count unforeseen expenditures. I got sick and stranded with too much debt, it pinged the system. I was too useless, and now here I am. Useful again." Crowe clenched her fists.

Arbor shot her a warning look. They were being monitored more diligently in the city.

Crowe lifted her chin defiantly. Her mech head tilted slightly up for a moment before locking back down and Crowe gave an exasperated groan. "Emotional resonance doesn't resonate that far," she grumbled.

"We'll have to practice later. In the meantime, I'd like to hear more. About other planets you've been to—if you want to talk about it, I mean. Consider that my twelve questions," Arbor said.

Crowe smiled. "I would love to."

No matter where they went after that, Crowe took scans of the planets and told Arbor about the chemical components, the mechanisms at work in the atmosphere or magnetosphere if there was one, and more. So much more. Arbor was fascinated. It never occurred to them to do this, despite basic scans being allowed.

It became a game to assess objects and weave stories, scenarios, and what-ifs. Solar systems and constellations and planets, anything they could find, points in the sky or distant, flickering stars in space. Crowe told Arbor the chemical compositions, the likely species of flora and fauna. They created cinematic space opera scenarios. On and on until Arbor felt calm and happy, or as much as a MIND could simulate those emotions when they never felt them much in life before.

It wasn't such a bad existence. They wondered how long it would last.

Eventually, Arbor realized they were closing in on the end of their contract date. Had it really been a thousand years? They'd settled into a routine with Crowe. It was comforting, familiar, safe. Now Arbor might return to humanity if they wanted. It was the plan, what ExoPLENTI dangled as an incentive for so long.

But what if Arbor didn't take it? What if they stayed, kept going with Crowe to different planets, continued making up stories?

What if they just stayed MINDs together? Would that be so bad?

Maybe it was something that snapped at a thousand years of being a human embedded in a murder machine. Maybe it was emotional resonance, maybe it was impulse, but Arbor thought fuck it and took Crowe's hand. Their mech hands awkwardly entwined with the screech and whine of metal scraping metal.

"What are you doing?" Crowe hissed.

> WARNING: Do not deviate course. Do not engage friendlies.
> Final warning.

Arbor let go. They would stay. There was no way ExoPLENTI would make good on the contract anyway. They knew that in their heart and had known even when they signed. At least now they weren't alone. Crowe looked at them, confused, as Arbor peeled away, grinning.

The next mission was dangerous, even by experienced standards.

They were out of ExoPLENTI space, far, far out near the edge of the Milky Way. There weren't corporations here, just small out-posts nestled on isolated asteroids, orbiting in debris fields filled with seemingly endless resources and lack of corporate control. Which meant their locations were heavily fortified and defended. What did ExoPLENTI even want out here? Was this just a suicide mission? Is this what happened when a MIND hit a thousand years?

Arbor and Crowe stared down at the target. It was yet another habitable planet, perhaps the most habitable planet they'd ever seen. Blue oceans, human-friendly gravity, an actual magneto-sphere, oxygen. Very idyllic. Its population was maybe one city-state trying to thrive outside of corporate grasp.

"You asked me once if we can regret," Arbor said, projection looking down at the unnamed planet. "I don't regret what I've done or witnessed, even if I could. Not even after a thousand years. I can't, and I refuse to."

"No?" Crowe's projected self moved closer, her body drifting just out of proximity warning range. She'd become adept at keep-ing just out of range, barely avoiding warnings and unwanted at-tention. Arbor hated it. It was exhausting to never do what they wanted, and it was never more apparent with Crowe's arm out-stretched, close but untouchable without causing too much un-wanted attention.

"No. Because it let me see the stars, let me dream of different futures, however unlikely. Because I've never once been called a woman. Because . . ." Arbor hesitated, staring at Crowe. "Because it brought me to you."

Crowe held their gaze for a long moment. Or was it a brief moment? A light-speed thought? Her eyes were a bright blue, the same as her shell. Arbor's own eyes, they knew, glowed a bright red like their mech's. Both of them had brown eyes as humans. But now Crowe's eyes glowed in the planet's shadow. Intense, radiant, mechanical, and inhuman. Beautiful.

In an instant (or perhaps a long moment), Crowe blinked rap-idly and looked away. "That's really sad."

"It's the best I could hope for," Arbor said.

"That's also really sad," she replied.

"Not all of it. Not the centuries I've spent with you."

Crowe lifted her hand as if to add something, hesitated, then looked down again. Her mech did every movement in time with her.

"You've gotten really good at that," Arbor said.

"What can I say? I have a lot of emotions to resonate with, when I'm with you," Crowe said shyly.

Arbor was so close to saying fuck it to the proximity alarm.

So it caught them extra off guard when the proximity and combat warnings blared in their head—in their mech's head. A surprise assault? There was a searing heat and a dull thud, and they watched as bits of their power supply leaked out toward the planet below. An overwhelming explosion of light followed. They reached out to try and shield Crowe reflexively. It was a purely emotional reaction, actual response time lagging behind.

Somehow, their body obeyed. Something shredded through their arm.

As they faded, body going into emergency power reserve and repair mode, they marveled at how strong their own emotional resonance had become too.

Arbor was only out for a moment (or an eternity). They thought, dreamily, of Crowe's laughter, of her many stories of myriad planets and destinations. All of it mired in fog and distant yelling. Slowly, the shouting became clearer and clearer.

"Hey, hey! Arbor! Wake up! Please."

Crowe's voice crackled. Her projection hovered near one of Arbor's eyes, touching it as if willing them awake. Their projection flickered to life and all but fell over. Crowe caught them in time, cradling them in her arms. Their giant robot bodies were entwined. Everything hurt.

"S-so projections can interact," Arbor said with a cough. It made their chest hurt—seriously, who simulated this?—but the pain feedback eased up once they were more alert and aware.

Damage to systems: catastrophic. They were missing their right leg, upper left arm, and a chunk of their left side.

Crowe let them float freely once they were able. It was a strange echo of human hurt and recovery, since their bodies never moved. There were jagged and warped bits of metal and broken circuitry drifting all around. As well as a giant robot hand.

"You're missing an arm," Arbor said.

"Somebody had to shoot us out of the situation." Crowe's right eye and left hand were almost entirely transparent.

Arbor's right leg, upper left arm, and left side were equally missing, repair bots trying their best to recover the most essential parts.

Shakily, Arbor reached for their mapping data and telemetry and realized the two of them were far away from the unnamed planet. Distant flickers of light erupted in almost rhythmic sequence. Their sensors highlighted several large battleships. ExoPLENTI's dropships were in full retreat.

"It was a surprise assault from their old friends, the ones that owned that old mining town—remember? When we first met?" Crowe said, also watching.

So ExoPLENTI was getting their asses kicked. Good.

That's when Arbor realized.

"We didn't get the return command." They turned to Crowe, simulated heart racing from more than leftover pain indicators. "Listen, they think we're space debris. And I know how to wipe any lingering ExoPLENTI IDs. Unless someone looks closely, we'll look like space trash. And without a way to replenish our repair systems and power supplies, we have maybe two thousand years of juice at best. So there's no going back. If they find us, they'll delete us."

Yet, in this moment (in this instant or this brief eternity) Arbor had never felt more alive.

"When we were patrolling earlier, I scanned for other solar systems outside of corporate space. There's one nearby, relatively. Maybe a thousand years out? It's got a totally inhospitable planet with an atmosphere full of particles very good at blocking scanners. So what do you say?" Crowe took Arbor's hand with her remaining one, their mech bodies doing the same.

No proximity alarms or warning notices went off. No one from the faraway battle turned around to come for them. After so long, it was such sweet relief to be little more than scrap floating through the cosmos.

Impulsively—what did they have to worry about anymore— Arbor kissed Crowe's projection on the cheek. She was slightly taller. They'd never realized that before.

Crowe smiled, gently tilted Arbor's chin up, and kissed them. It wasn't what a human would consider a kiss. No skin against lips, just simulated movement. A facsimile, an intent, an emotion.

Arbor felt nothing, physically.

Arbor felt everything, emotionally.

"Tell me all about this planet, then," Arbor said and let the sound of Crowe's voice soothe their MIND as the two giant robots, happily lost, drifted away.

Bruised-Eye Dusk

FROM *Beneath Ceaseless Skies*

FANTASY

RUGG THE SPELLBREAKER was only passing through the Devil's Palm on his way down to the coast, where he hoped to find his mother. He'd have avoided Ganvill, except he was running low on boom powder and salt, and the little settlement was the last tame place before a lot of nowhere.

The swamp was on fire, pollen clouds burning gold in the sun's last rays as Rugg rode into Ganvill on his gator, Tugboat. Tugboat let out a silent growl, and it rumbled into Rugg's bones. Even the tamest gators didn't like the sight of so many men and women with gigs and spears. Seemed to Rugg that the vill's people were in a nasty mood, or maybe they hated strangers. They watched him, their knuckles white around the hafts of their crude weapons, their eyes—bleary and red from the pollen—shifting between the boomflute on his back and the sunflower hat on his head.

"No trouble," he said, loud and clear so all would hear, as Tugboat started crawling onto the dock of what looked to be the vill's longshack. No one stopped them. No one said a word. Just kept watching. And they were still watching as Tugboat settled onto his belly, his forty-hand length making the timbers creak.

"Tugboat's a good gator," Rugg said, again loud enough for all to hear. "My momma's word, no snap in him."

"Ain't the gator got us riled, mister," said one of the locals, a thickset fella who let his impressive hairy gut trail over the edge of his loincloth.

Rugg realized what they were staring at now—his scarf had fallen just enough to reveal part of the crossed-knife symbol scarred into his throat; the mark of a soldier in the king's army. The king and his army may have been gone and dead, but folk were slow to forget bullies.

He pulled his scarf back up. As if it would help now as they'd seen it. There were ten men and half as many women out on their floating porches, all armed, all waiting for an excuse to get stupid. He stared them down as the wind rattled the strung chicken bones hanging from the longshack's beams—crude charms against sour conja. All the other houses had them too. Now that was interesting—usually such charms meant want of a spellbreaker like him.

As Rugg climbed off Tugboat and stepped onto the dock, the villfolk closed ranks. Only one dared approach him, though. The big-gut fella, who left his spear in the care of a friend and squared up, all chest and fist.

He was taller than Rugg, which wasn't common, and once-and-a-half as wide of shoulder, but it took more than size to big-bull Rugg around.

"What you come for, mister?" the man growled, pushing his sweaty bald forehead into Rugg's, tipping the brim of his hat back.

Rugg met his eyes and didn't see any of the cruelty or meanness he saw in rough types. What he saw was fear—not fear of Rugg, but fear of something terrible. The same fear that put up all the little stick charms.

Rugg took a half step back. "Easy, friend."

The big man didn't advance, nor did he back off. "Who's friend?"

The door to the longshack opened, and a new man fella stepped out. Pale, well-fed, and vested with the chain of a vill headman.

This new fella whistled like to break ears. "Loop Garvy, step away from that man 'fore he does something 'bout your face."

The big fella, Loop, still glaring, nostrils still flaring like a bull ready to charge, backed off and cleared a path for Rugg.

"Name's Pong," the new fella announced to Rugg. "I'm headman here. Who's you?"

"Rugg. I'm a spellbreaker."

Pong's narrow dark eyes lit up. "What you here for?"

"Need salt and boom powder."

"Is that so, Mister Rugg? Well, happens we need a spellbreaker." Pong opened the door to the longshack and beckoned Rugg inside.

"Let's do drink and talk some. You too, Loop—you'll drink with this man and ask his pardon."

Loop, his hands still fists, looked between Rugg and the headman and then shrugged his shoulders and let his fingers go slack. The longer Rugg saw him, the less threat he felt from him, and the more he felt sorry. Man looked like he hadn't slept in days.

"If you're pouring, I'm buying," Rugg announced. He followed the men in.

Rugg liked Pong. He poured strong hooch and spoke in a quiet voice. Straight-haired, round-faced, with small, serious eyes and a trusty voice was Pong. His smooth hairless stomach shimmered under the blue light of the burnworm lamp. He dressed like everyone else in Ganvill—loincloth and vest, only he wore a copper chain around his neck to mark his authority. It was good to see a headman with mud under his nails when so many were leeches.

For the first few drinks, no one spoke. Though Loop still watched Rugg with distrust from across the headman's table, the anger in him had cooled. Now he looked like he wanted to melt into mush and be anything but awake and here.

"Those charms on the eaves," Rugg began. "Some trouble here?"

Pong nodded, grimly. "Sour conja trouble."

"That why them all out there were ready to gut me? They think I did it?"

"We know you ain't a witch, mister," Loop said. "It's what else you is burns the blood."

Rugg gave him a steady look. "I know lot of soldiers brought awfulness to little vills like this. I wasn't one of those. Served in the king's guard. Never stole any woman's chickens or goosed any man's daughter."

"Was that before or after you became a spellbreaker?" Pong asked, refilling both of the men's cups. Loop downed his in one gulp; Rugg only sipped.

"Wasn't one before the other. Daddy taught me to soldier, Momma taught me about witches. Enough about me—what's the trouble here?"

"My kids're sick, dying," Loop said, full of heat again.

Pong waved him quiet. "Let me tell it. Started up two weeks back. Started with a funny taste in the water. Sourlike. Then it got worser. Folks here are bothered by it all. Scared."

"Sure it's sour conja, not just bad luck?"

Rugg had to ask these things. Every other vill he stopped in, someone was convinced a sour conjawitch had spelled them or their crops; usually it was just the work of an angry neighbor. So few understood conja for what it was—magic as could be good or bad, sweet or sour; just like people. His mother had taught him that, and she'd have known: She'd been both. Sweet conja healed wounds and cured sickness and protected the weak and helpless. Sour conja—well, that took an evil heart. Or an angry one, at least.

All doubt died when Loop brought over something wrapped in a blanket and revealed what was inside. A thing as'd once been a dog. Could hardly tell now—it had four legs and a tail, but otherwise it looked more like a piece of dried fruit harvested from the bough of a monstrous tree.

"Good dog as ever been, was poor Poot," Loop said. "There's the chickens too—every day another turns inside out, all guts instead of feathers. And that ain't half—I got a girlchild and a boywhelp, both of them deathly sick."

Rugg shook his head. "I'm sorry. It's an awful thing to hurt children."

"If and when I find who's done it . . ." Loop left it at that.

Pong gave Loop a pat on the back and refilled his cup. "We got a healer, same as put up the charms, but none of her usual cures are helping. We figure it's a witch needs killing. Whatever your cost, I'll pay it."

Loop nodded to Pong, face full of gratitude. "Whatever the cost," he agreed.

Rugg finished his drink. "I'll help your vill. And if there's a sour witch needs killing, I'll see to it."

As payment, Pong offered three weights each of guano and yellowrock for mixing boomdust, then pointed to the way of the dying sun and spoke of a shack with a roof tiled with turtle shells, where he believed the conjawitch lived.

Tugboat grumbled like an old man as Rugg mounted him up. The villfolk were looking different at him now as they knew what he was about. Looking at him now with something like hope.

It rained after duskfall. Tugboat didn't mind, of course, but for Rugg it went badder and worser until he felt close to drowning. The swamp was stubborn in this part of Perish, what folks in the bigger vills called the Devil's Palm. Slow going, wet going. He would not find the shack tonight.

He was ready to turn back and try to make Ganvill when a bright dot of light appeared through the churning murk of the storm: a campfire. Never trust a light too bright in a dark hole, the speaking goes, but then Rugg smelled roasting meat. And then he heard the flute. A sweet, sad little song, a flutter of music. Bone flutes had a tone distinct from those carved of wood or reed; lonelier, somehow.

A sweet breath of music sighing out to the wild.

Rugg left Tugboat at the water's edge and approached with care. It was a woman tending the fire, camped under a lean-to made from sticks and giant's ear palm fronds. No, not a woman. He realized this as he came close enough to see the face behind the fire. It was a young man, graceful and sapling slender, with the delicate frame of a songbird. Pale skin, a long, pointed chin, dark eyes rimmed in charcoal swooshes like raven wings, hair black and straight like a horse's tail. A prettyboy made prettier by the fire he tended and the swamp rats sizzling from the spit above it. Some warm food would be nice before tangling with a witch. And maybe some handsome company too.

Don't you do what I think you're about to do, Rugg, Rugg heard himself mutter. But he knew he would. Just like he knew from the feel in his bones when it would rain.

Rain dripped down Rugg's neck as he stood at the shelter's edge, watching the stranger as the stranger watched back, still playing the flute. It was made of bone all right; looked like the arm bone of a person. The boy lowered his flute. His forearms were wrapped in loose blue sleeves that cut off at the elbow, which taken together with the blue paint smeared on his lips told plain enough he was mourning somebody.

"Hunker, won't you?" the young man said. "Dry your feet."

It was always important to be invited. Rugg gladly accepted, coming to sit on the other side of the blaze, to dry himself in the warmth.

"Win," the young man said, pointing to himself with the flute.

"Rugg."

"Your gator. Does he want to join us?"

As if he could understand (and Rugg was never sure he couldn't), Tugboat started bumbling over the brush, dragging his great bulk through the mud until his long handsome snout with all its teeth lay at the young man's feet. Win gave Tugboat a stroke under the chin, just where he liked it, and the ground trembled with his happy rumble.

"He likes you."

"I notice there's no saddle on him. Don't it hurt to ride him bare?"

"Comfort ain't much to me."

"Comfort ain't much to me," Win repeated, imitating Rugg's deep burr. "Foo. That kind of bigboy talk ever work on anyone?"

And he's sharp-tongued too. You're in trouble, Rugg.

"Sometimes."

While Win was distracted giving Tugboat a rub, Rugg used his chance to test him, drawing his bleedydoll out from his pouch and holding it low, out of sight. If there was sour conja near, the bleedydoll—carved from waxroot in the shape of a little girlchild—would bleed out its eyes and ears. But it stayed dry. He put it away, letting go a lungful of worry as he did.

"Are you hungry, Rugg?" Win asked.

The rat was stringy, but when rubbed with the summerberries Rugg kept in his bag, it went down fine. Win also shared his stew of beans and swamp cabbage while Rugg contributed a few hunks of stale cornbrick. By the time they were done eating, the rains had stopped and Tugboat had gone off to wallow. With the clouds parting, a purple dusk opened up. Both pieces of the moon were out tonight, one low, the other high; they looked just a little like two mismatched eyes, hemmed half-shut by the bruised flesh of the night around them. Win put a pot of water on the fire and started boiling tea. Rugg watched what he put in—just some common roots and leaves.

Win was an easy fella. Voice soft and mellow. He dressed down to almost nothing, only a loincloth and a loose vest as hardly covered any skin. He wasn't rashy with skeeter bites as most were in these parts, probably because he rubbed himself in the fragrant oil of duskflowers. Rugg kept finding his eyes drawn to a tattoo on Win's hairless taut belly: a broken circle. Whenever he caught himself staring, he'd drag his eyes somewhere else—usually Win's feet, clean of mud and pink soled, or his face, which was always smiling. There was something so fresh in Win, like finding the one uncrushed flower in a trampled field. Rugg hadn't been lying when he said he wasn't much for comfort, but that didn't mean he didn't like what made him feel good. And there was nothing as good as the knitting of two bodies under a clear starry sky.

"Where you from, Rugg?" Win asked after a time. They were both of them trying not to stare at the other now. Not that it was working for either.

"Born in Greatvill."

Win's head fell a bit. "Oh. I'm sorry."

Rugg knew what he meant. Win was sorry because Greatvill was an ash pile now, along with a few horizons of forest and swamp that once surrounded it, burnt up by those monsters who'd swept in through the Steadlands from out of the sunset. Pale like cavefish—much paler even than Win—and big and ugly with beastly teeth and weapons like boomflutes only much deadlier, riding on grunting beasts of metal and flying on great birds of steel, raining fiery death upon the land. *Murrka.* That was what their allies of the New Nation had called the monsters. It was a hideous word that suited the creatures well.

The brandmark itched under his scarf. He resisted the urge to scratch. Win's attention had changed, settled now on the coiled dragrope at Rugg's side. The recognition was there, but then most folks could spot a dragrope with its braided weave of pale moonflax and dark muckdeer hair. A thick rope woven to choke out conja when tied hard around a witch's throat.

"So what brung you here?" Win asked. "Spellbreakers ain't so common these days."

There was nothing strange at being recognized, what with the dragrope coiled at his hip. But it still made him nervy. "What's saying I ain't just wandering?"

Win just shook his head like he knew that wasn't it.

Rugg considered lying, but he'd never been a good liar, and Win seemed too sharp to dupe. So he told it as was. "Supposed to be a witch around here. You know anything about that?"

Win looked down, and his eyes filled with the fire's glow. "I'm the wrong person to ask. I hold my head low to such things."

"Sour conja don't care if you heed it or not. You hold your head low to floods too?"

"I hold my head low; so far the world ain't killed me, Mister Rugg."

"You live here. You must know something."

"We all live in the world. Don't mean we know its ways."

That was true enough, if unhelpful. Rugg let it drop—most folks didn't like talking about conja. Easy to get fearful, especially as the sour conjawitches were known to have little spies everywhere in the swamps. Probably the witch already knew Rugg was coming for her.

There was silence for a time. They watched each other through the smoke. Of a sudden, Win got to laughing.

"Something funny?"

"No," Win said. He settled down onto his side on the mossy ground, leaning on one elbow. "Just realized you're the second fella I've ever met with blue eyes."

"Is that so?"

"Like morning glories. Know who the other one was?"

He meant the king. Not someone Rugg wanted to think about now. Or ever.

"Don't know anything about that."

"King came through here when I was a boy, on one of his big tours of the land. Folks fell over themselves fawning, but I saw him and thought he was ugly as all. Pale as a frog's belly and teeth like a gator's. But you ain't pale. Ain't ugly neither."

He wasn't wrong. The king was an ugly man, monstrous really, just like the pale invaders he resembled, and Rugg was lucky enough to take after his mother instead. All except the eyes.

"Kind words."

Maybe it was the fireglow, but Win's face was rosy, and his ears were flushed red with eagerness. "You travel lots?"

Rugg wanted to forget everything, even if just for a moment.

"Mhm."

"Must leave a trail of brokenhearted gals."

"Not just gals."

Win's foot had started to brush the bare skin of Rugg's leg where the mud had crusted. Rugg took hold of his slender ankle—soft like antler velvet off a yearling buck—and gave it a squeeze. "This what I think it is?"

"You want it to be?"

When Rugg took Win into his arms, the slender fella shivered and started breathing like his lungs were dry.

"First time?"

"With a spellbreaker, yes."

The moss carpeting the clearing was soft from the rain. Rugg savored each shudder, each gasp, each sudden flush of breath into the slender chest beneath his, the glory of a bruised-eye dusk wheeling overhead, the musk of flower oil and moss and swamptea gone to boil flooding his nose and seeping into the buds on his tongue.

They took their tea from a shared cup. Rugg didn't even mind the skeeters getting their draw of blood from his bare back.

Morning came dry and too bright and already hot. Rugg woke up, trousers on but belt unfastened, his vest and shirt—soaked through with the sweat from his head—balled up like a pillow under his head.

Win was gone, the fire a stain of ash on the mossy ground. But the clay cup was still there, brimming with a last gulp of swamp tea long gone cold. It went down bitter, but still good.

He was relieved to be alone. He'd feared earlier Win might have clung, but that never ended well for anyone who Rugg got sweet on. Either something terrible happened to them, or they'd get to know Rugg well enough to want him gone. As he gathered up his gear—checking first to make sure nothing had gone missing, chiding himself for falling asleep first in a stranger's company—he wondered if Win had left during the middle of the night, when Rugg tended to have his sleep-screams. Night terrors he never remembered on waking; night terrors he had to imagine were born of the invaders and what he'd seen them do.

He found Tugboat waiting in the water. The gator only had the one good eye, but somehow, he always managed to express complicated moods. Right now, he was full of judgment.

"Nothing lost, just a little time," Rugg said.

"Rrrr," Tugboat rumbled.

"I ain't crying. Won't even think about him after tomorrow."

"Rrrr."

"Yeah? Well, you got a mouth full of stupid."

"Rrrr."

He hated when Tugboat expressed the same thing he was already thinking. Tugboat was right that he was too quick to get caught up in a pretty face and a soft set of lips, but then what did an old bull gator know about that? More concerning was that in the time he'd lost spent with Win, the witch might've sniffed him out and run off.

Most spellbreakers Rugg had known approached witches with a simple purpose: kill, no questions asked, no risks taken, no time wasted. Rugg didn't like that way. He'd sneak up best he could, get through the witch's protections, find her, get the dragrope on her, then figure why she was hurting the villfolk and what was to be done. His way was harder, but it felt right—it was what Momma taught him.

Rugg put the lead in Tugboat's jaws and mounted up, pushing on along the way he'd been going before the night rain stopped them. Didn't take long to find signs of dwelling. First it was cut trees. Then it was berry patches, clearly tended, the ground swept under them, and fresh ashes sprinkled around their roots.

Then came the conja. Woven chicken-bone cages hanging on string from the branches, etchings in the tree trunks, piled stones. Conja, at its simplest, was making patterns from the natural world. Momma had called it "breathing conja," because it was something passive needing no attention to maintain. Each little making was weak on its own, but when layered together they could make for powerful spells.

Rugg took caution here. He told Tugboat to wait, then proceeded slowlike, holding his bleedydoll out in one hand and his boneknife in the other. The bleedydoll didn't bleed, even as he felt the tremble in the boneknife (not to mention his own living bones) as told of conja. But not sour conja. This conja was sweet.

Maybe these makings were put up before the witch went sour. All the same, he'd have to get through the weave. Conja was like water—go through it slow and it was soft as anything. Fall into it fastlike and you'd break your bones. It took hours to work his way through the makings, unraveling the bone cages, unstacking the stones, crossing out the etches with his boneknife.

By and by he worked his way until he found the shack. Just as Pong had said—a shack with a roof made of turtle-shell tiles. It was a small thing, cozy, a happy-looking home not at all like the grimy huts folk assumed when they imagined conjawitches' dwellings. Pale smoke rose lazily from a narrow bark chimney.

Janglecords were strung between the trees, heavy with glass beads and old copper spoons and animal bones. Took Rugg his time to step over, around, and under these. Better slow than loud when sneaking up on a witch. Closer and closer he got, until he was outside the little window, just a square cut into the shack's planed boards, no glass or cloth. He looked through it. Dried herbs and braids of root vegetables and wreaths of moss hung from a long beam, along with salted rabbits and rats and wax roots left to cure. Flasks and jars full of powders and goops clustered a shelf . . .

All the other details fell away when he noticed—on the edge of what he could see—a foot sticking out. A human foot. A body, draped under a thick blanket, lay on a long table. Only the foot, withered and yellowgray, except the veins, which were a bright blue.

He backed away. Something was off about this. The bleedydoll had yet to show any red. There was no sour conja here. Not even a whiff. So either Pong was mistaken about this being the witch's place, or Rugg was dealing with a witch powerful enough to hide the sourness.

From the other side of the shack, a door rasped open. Soft feet moved, crunching grass and squelching through mud. Rugg stowed his bleedydoll and drew his boomflute. He carefully drew back the hammer and started creeping around the edge.

The feet shuffled back into the shack and the door rasped shut. "Help!"

The voice coming from inside the shack was strained, shrill, familiar. It was Win's voice. But what was he doing here?

Some kind of stupid instinct took over. Rugg raced back to the window and vaulted himself into the shack. "Win?" he called.

The shack was empty. What was this? Cautiously, he moved toward the table where the body lay under its drape. He was about to prod one of the withered limbs with the muzzle of his boomflute when he heard—too late—a rustle on the floor behind him.

By the time he'd swung his boomflute over, a cloud of red dust was already blowing into his face.

When he woke up, the light coming through the shack's window was the blue of day's end.

He was on a table. Hard boards under his bones. His flesh was soft, like he'd been lying on the boards long enough to start bruising.

Sound of water bubbling. Good smell in the air. Meat and vegetables boiling, but something else, the mellow sweetness of duskflower oil. And a sour current under that—the scent of aged death. He was looking up at the beams of the rafters and the undersides of the turtle shells. He couldn't move. His fingers were like wood, his legs heavier than stone. He couldn't speak, could only breathe harder.

He'd been captured. Put under a spell. Made a plaything.

Where was Win? Where was Tugboat? If Tugboat hadn't come to rescue him, that only meant one thing . . .

He tried to lift his hands, his feet, his head, anything. All he could manage was to turn his head, and then all he saw was the dry withered face of a dead woman dusted with corpsepowder to keep the flies off her and the smell locked down.

She'd been old and pale before she died. The tattoos around her lips and eyes were those of a witch.

"You're awake."

It was Win's voice. Soft bare feet padded past him, cloth rippled, and the scent of duskflower drifted over him.

By and by, Rugg could feel the stiffness fade. He was far from strong, but now at least he could move his head some and flex his fingers and toes. With all the strength he had he lifted his head and was rewarded with the sight of Win's backside—bare except for the loincloth and the tie of the apron he was wearing. The witchboy—that's what he was, all this time, Rugg, you fool—was stirring a pot with a long paddle.

"Where's—?" Rugg reached for his words, but the words only got so far down.

"Your gator's fine," Win said, voice strained but steady. "Fed him a chicken this morning. He's tied to Momma's favorite tree. She liked gators."

"H—how—how long?"

"This'll be the third day. Started thinking you'd sleep forever."

He remembered the red cloud. Dreamroot dust. Had to be. Win had been clever. Played him like a strumboard.

"Would've been better for me, maybe, if you had. Now what am I to do with you? Can't let you go. I know the villfolk sent you. They think I'm the one as jinxed their chickens and made their runts ill."

Rugg stayed calm. Not like panicking would help any. "You could have killed me, but you didn't."

"Like I need the reminder. I say it again: What am I to do with you, Mister Rugg?"

"Let me go."

"So you can kill me? That's what you come here to do, ain't it?"

"No."

"I'm to trust you?"

"I don't kill sweet conjawitches. Only the sour kind."

And this boy wasn't sour. This close, Rugg didn't need a bleedy-doll to tell. And anyway, a conjaman gone sour wouldn't have let him sleep. He'd never have woken up.

Win was holding Rugg's satchel now, full of all his tools. He pulled the dragrope out first and threw it into the fire burning under his cooking pot. The rope was stubborn, smoking before it took to the flame.

Then he held out Rugg's collection. Ten shriveled human tongues impaled on a copper skewer—one for each sour conja he'd killed.

"Win, listen me," Rugg said, talking soft. "I know you're not the one spelled the folks in Ganvill."

"You think I won't kill you but you're wrong. Meat's meat. I can cut your throat like I'd cut a chicken's throat."

"Your conja's sweet. If *yours* is what it is. Hard to tell what's yours and what was woven by the old gal on the table here. But it's all sweet."

"You're trying to save yourself."

"I'm trying to talk you out of something stupid. I ain't gonna hurt you, Win. Maybe you can help me find the one as spelled Ganvill."

Win's arm quivered as he held the braid of tongues, like it was something poisoned. His eyes, still rimmed with charcoal (smudged from fresh crying) wobbled with questions. Then they went hard with determination. He turned away.

"That old gal there is my momma. She worked all her life help-ing folks. But that didn't matter. World's full of stupid, scared peo-ple want to smash and burn whatever they don't know."

"I know that better than most."

"Shut up. All my life, since I can remember, folks came here whenever something went wrong, hearts full of blame and nasty venom on their tongues. Momma never let it break her. Always offered help. Then she died. Now she ain't here. Now they're com-ing for me. Now they send a killer like you, and I'm to let you go?"

"If you don't believe me, let me tell you a story."

"I don't wanna hear it."

"Yes you do, Win. Ever heard of the Fingerthief?"

"Everyone's heard of the Fingerthief. She was the evilest, worsest witch in Perish. But that's got nothing to do with me or mine. And anyway, everyone knows she died a long time ago, before you or me got born."

"She didn't die. She had a child. Me."

Win, who'd been avoiding looking at Rugg, now met his stare. "What?"

"Like you say, she was the worst you could meet. She was King Irwin's painbringer—if he wanted someone hurt, he'd bring them to her. She was sour as they come. And yet. And yet, she didn't stay that way. She had a child, by him. But that child was born sick, too sick for any healer to save. But she saved him—saved me. It changed her—saving life instead of taking it, fixing hurt instead of giving.

"I never came here to hurt you. I came here to find out the truth of who was spelling Ganvill. And I know it ain't you."

Win opened his mouth, face full of heat, but then stopped. Outside, a familiar sound: the low rumble of Tugboat's throat, a warning sound.

Then the tinkle of noisemakers on the janglecords. Dogs yipping.

Win dropped Rugg's satchel with a gasp in his throat. The dogs were coming closer, yapping and yowling, and the men weren't far behind, huffing and muttering to each other.

"How're they so close? They shouldn't—" His eyes snapped to Rugg, full of blame. "You broke the weave."

"Only made a little hole."

A gap. Only wide enough someone would have to be dumb lucky to find it. Or to know what they were doing, and only spellbreakers and conjafolk knew that sort of thing.

"You led them here," Win said. He ran to cover up his momma's corpse. Then he looked around, head flicking thisaway and thataway; he wanted to bolt, but he was in two minds it seemed.

"Sounds like a lot of dogs. Lot of men too," Rugg said.

"They'll tear me apart. Drag me into the swamp and drown me . . . cut my tongue out and smoke it over their cookfire. I won't let them."

"I can help you, Win."

Win shook his head, still stuck in two minds whether to run or hide. As if either would work.

"Win, I can help you. But you gotta lift whatever spell's on me. You listening?"

"I can't trust you. I can't—can't trust anyone." His breath was coming out hard and raggedy. He was so scrawny Rugg could just about see his heart thumping under the skin. He looked at Rugg now. Another set of janglecords tinkled, and dogs swarmed outside of the shack. Tugboat was lowing and grumbling, the dogs yipping like mad.

"Hey. You got one choice as I see it," Rugg said, finally raising his voice. "Take a chance on me, or wait for them to break your door in."

Win bit his own fist and shook his head, letting out a long, shuddering sigh. "Fine. Fine. But swear first you'll not turn on me."

Rugg swore on Tugboat's life he wouldn't turn on Win. Win came to Rugg's side and leaned down, his lips opening as they pressed to Rugg's. He breathed out the dust as was still in Rugg's lungs, and Rugg could move again.

It was dark. Stars swimming in the clouds. Rugg stepped out of the witch's shack, his boomflute loaded in one hand, his longknife—the one made from sharp iron—in the other.

How many times had he seen this? A dozen men holding the leads of rearing hounds, carrying worm lamps and burning torches, all of their heads muddy with thoughts of murder and dragging witches through the swamp. Fear could do ugly things to folks.

They'd gotten almost to the shack, though not without some scrapes and a thick coating of mud up to their chests, but now at the sight of Rugg they stopped in their tracks.

"Hey-oh! The spellbreaker—he ain't dead," one of the men said.

A few of them cheered. Most looked surly or like they didn't know what to think. From out of their throng, one man stepped forward, his smooth belly poking out from under his shiny copper chain. Pong.

"When you didn't come back, we figured you'd failed," he said. "So I gathered up some boys to come look after you."

Rugg could feel his strength returning but slowly. He could walk and hold his weapons, but not much more than that. He'd have to play this careful. "You ought not be here," he said. "This ain't a job for villfolk—ain't some frog to gig or catfish to drag out a muckhole."

"No it ain't," Pong agreed. "It's a conjawitch. One as needs killing. Now, you took your time, but if you've got a tongue to show me, I'll still gladly pay you."

Rugg clenched his jaw. His arms were wobbling; he hoped it didn't show. "Listen here. There may be sour conja in these swamps, but it ain't here."

"Oh, really?"

The men were muttering. Even they as'd been happy to see him were looking wary now. Loop stepped forward, pointing his two-tined gig at Rugg. "There a witch in that shack, mister?"

Rugg stood his ground. "Like I said, the sour conja ain't here. Look elsewhere."

"Witch must've spelled him," Loop grumbled to the others. "Seems even spellbreakers ain't above bad conja."

The men were cheating forward, slackening their grasps on the dogs' leads. Rugg could shoot down one man, but then the rest would be on him.

"If you ain't gonna help, kindly step out of our way," Headman Pong said.

Behind Rugg, the door opened with a rasp, and Win stepped out, clothed in his mother's death blanket, holding the bone flute. The men cringed back. All except Pong.

Looking between Win and Pong, a thought occurred to Rugg, something as now seemed like a snake he'd not seen until he stepped on its head, but before he could follow the course of it, one of the dogs tore out of its man's grasp and came bolting at Rugg and Win.

It didn't make it halfway before ten men's worth of meat and scaly hide came bolting over the muddy ground. Tugboat's snapping jaws made the dog whimper and scamper away, and the men were doubting themselves again.

Except for Pong, still undaunted. He wasn't holding anything—he had his hands behind his back. He glared at Win, not even looking at Tugboat. "Kill them," he said, to no one in particular.

And all at once, men and dogs rushed forward in a wild charge. The first of the dogs got knocked aside by a swipe of Tugboat's tail, and then the men, who seemed of a moment caught up in something bigger than them—stopped dead when the gator surged forward, throwing his bulk into the thick of them. They scattered, as did their dogs. But Tugboat wasn't done—he thundered forward, making right for Pong.

Halfway to him, Tugboat stopped. Not natural-like. More like there was a rope strung through his limbs and it had cinched taut.

A low, pained rumble came from Tugboat's throat as he struggled against his own stiffened limbs.

It all fell in place, and Rugg knew. "It's him!" he shouted, pointing his boomflute at Pong. "There's your sour conjaman."

"He's right," Win said. "I can feel it. Like a mean wind coming off him."

"Liars," Pong said. "Don't listen to them. Liars and witches, the both of them!"

The men from Ganvill stood in crosstracks, uncertain, scared. They needed convincing—they needed showing.

Rugg prayed he wasn't wrong about this. He took aim and threw his knife at Headman Pong's heart. The knife zipped, quick as death, tumbling end over end. And then stopped, midair, as Pong held one hand up. A flinch. Even now his face was full of fury: angry at Rugg for exposing him, angry at himself for giving up the game.

"You . . ." Loop stalked toward the Headman, the gig shaking in his hands. "You made my children sick."

The knife was still floating in the air. Pong eyed Loop and the others, shook his head, and with a rueful sigh, flicked his hand. The knife zipped through the air, and if Loop hadn't been quick, it'd have taken off more than a piece of one of his ears.

The others made a mad scramble for Pong, but he planted his feet, and from out the ground wicked roots sprung up, slashing and batting at the men, keeping them at bay. From out the sky, buzzing hornets came down, stinging the men and their dogs. Rugg couldn't do much where he was, not trusting his aim with his weak arm when there were so many innocent men in the path of his boomflute.

"This is your fault, spellbreaker!" Pong shouted. "If you'd just done your job—"

The drone of the hornets got louder as more and more of the nasty beasties flew in, some of them now swarming on poor Tugboat and pressing in toward Rugg.

A sweet sound silenced their evil wings. The sweet, sad, lonely song of a bone flute. Win strode past Rugg, with the cloud of hornets dispersing in his path. The wicked roots fell slack, and Tugboat pulled free of that unseen rope. Pong looked at Win with so much hate—the hate as could only grow from shared blood. But in the next breath, even as Win played his soothing song, the men of Ganvill fell upon their headman. Loop pinned him with the gig while another cinched a dragrope tight around Pong's throat.

They'd have killed him if it weren't for Win.

"Stop!" he cried, putting his flute down. "Don't fall in the mud with him."

"He spelled our vill, sickened my children!" Loop shouted, pressing the hard points of his gig into Pong's soft belly while the other man pulled hard on the rope. Pong eyes bulged, his face purpled.

"I said stop! Don't kill him!" Win said. He looked to Rugg. "Help me."

"He's evil," Loop said. Blood leaked freely down his jaw from the cut ear.

"Maybe," Win admitted. "But I think he's my brother."

"Ease off," Rugg commanded, and if the men hesitated, they soon got the message when Tugboat growled and dragged himself forward.

The men stepped away from Pong, but even unrestrained, he was still choking from the dragrope that his fingers couldn't loosen. Slowly, cautiously, Win came to kneel beside him and slackened the coil some, not so much Pong could call on his conja but enough he could breathe. And speak.

"Momma never said I had a brother," Win said. "That's what you are, ain't it?"

"She chased me out when you were still crawling," Pong said, voice raspy, still full of venom. "This land you're sitting on—all this power. It's mine by right. I'm the firstborn. I should have it. Not you, not anyone else."

"Why'd she chase you off?"

"Ain't it obvious?" Rugg said, coming to stand over Pong. He eased down the hammer of his boomflute and sheathed it behind his back. "He went sour young. Or started going that way. Your momma probably found it easier to throw him out than teach him better."

"That doesn't seem like her . . ." Win said. But he sounded less than sure.

"You waited until she was dead to make your move," Rugg said to Pong. "And you couldn't kill him yourself—blood against blood would have deadened the land's power. So you tried to stir up the villfolk against him, by spelling them."

"They were all too soft," Pong said, shaking his head. "I didn't wanna hurt them. But they needed a push . . ."

"And when that didn't work, along came a spellbreaker, to fix your trouble for you."

"Except the spellbreaker wasn't the thoughtless killer you took him for," Win said.

"All this is just mud," Loop grumbled. "This lying witch hurt us, hurt our people and our animals. Justice gotta be done."

"I didn't wanna hurt folks," Pong said. "It wasn't supposed to be that. I was just gonna scare the vill, pox some pigs, kill some chickens. But . . ."

"But it got easier," Rugg supplied, feeling something like pity grow in him, hearing a story he'd heard before. "Each time you called on the sourness, it got easier, more satisfying."

The glare in Pong's eyes confirmed it.

"It's a sickness, sour conja," Rugg said.

"Sick or not, he needs punishing," Loop said. He was calmer now, looking more like the exhausted man Rugg had met the other day.

"What would you do?" Win asked. "Kill him?"

"Why not?"

Rugg stepped between them. "Let him fix his mistakes. Let him lift the spells he made on your vill, heal the sick, mend the hurt."

Loop gritted his teeth. "What about justice?"

"Justice ain't death," Win said, bravely standing down Loop, "nor is paying pain for pain. It's paying kindness for pain. Doing good."

Loop looked at Rugg. "What do you think?"

"I think love can make amends better than a noose or a cage." He had to believe that. Otherwise, what was this world?

"You're a fool," Pong spat. "You oughta kill me, brother."

Win knelt by him again. Pong was showing his teeth, snarling like he might bite his brother's throat. But when Win put his arms around him, Pong just broke. His jaw clenched and the tears started to spill.

"Has he killed anyone?" Win asked the men.

They spoke of dogs and chickens. Of sick children. But admitted Pong had taken no human lives.

"Then there's hope for him," Win said. He laid a hand on Rugg's shoulder, the long fingers clammy and all atremble with the fear Win's face wouldn't show. "If conja can go sour, it can go sweet again, can't it?"

Rugg thought of Momma.

"Rrrr," said Tugboat.

"That's the world's truth there," Rugg agreed.

As it turned out, Pong had lied about how much yellowrock and guano he had, but then his plan had always been to get rid of Rugg. The villfolk paid Rugg what they could scrounge, which was a little more than nothing. But he was used to this; little vills had little pockets.

Rugg and Tugboat stayed another week in the swamp, to make sure everyone would abide by their word. At first, Pong was sullen in his work, and sloppy. But Win was a patient teacher, and as the brothers began to unravel the sourness Pong had shaped, it seemed he healed some along with the vill. All the time not spent cleansing the air and water of Ganvill, Pong spent beside his dead mother, silently guarding her long sleep. It was a tender, half-shaped thing, Win and Pong's kinship. Even if the vill wanted his death, even if his own heart condemned him, at least one soul believed Pong could grow into something good.

On the seventh night, Rugg helped Win and Pong send their mother to her last rest in the swampwater. Pong finally broke and wept, and Win held him and said it was a happy thing that she was back in the swamp with her ancestors and the woman as'd birthed her.

The morning after, Rugg tried to sneak off. He'd spent too much time here, and always that crack in his heart was calling, telling him to get back on the way to the coast. When he managed to lift Win's arm off him without rousing him, he thought he was free and gone.

"You could stay, you know," Win said, as Rugg was making for the door.

"I could," Rugg admitted, risking the pain of one last look back.

Win looked at him with all the world's pity. "Then why don't you?"

Rugg thought about explaining, opened his mouth to say something, but realized he didn't have the words even if he wanted to let them out. How to say that a flower might bloom bright then wither to something ugly? How to explain that his father had been a terrible, hurtful man, and that all that ugliness was in his blood, that he didn't trust himself not to become the same kind of awful? He would've rather hurt Win once by leaving than hurt him a hundred times by staying.

"Nothing on you," Rugg finally said, looking away now, one hand on the door even as something held him in place.

Win closed his eyes, the charcoal wings smudging with tears.

Rugg chewed a word and swallowed it, then walked out. Tugboat waited in the muck of the stream, clouds of choking pollen all around him burning goldpretty in the dawn sun. Onward to the coast, and whatever waited where all water flowed to.

P. A. CORNELL

Once Upon a Time at The Oakmont

FROM *Fantasy*

SCIENCE FICTION

ON THE ISLAND *of Manhattan, there's a building out of time. I can't tell you where it is, exactly. It has an address, of course, as all buildings do, but that wouldn't mean anything to you. What I can tell you is that the building is called The Oakmont.*

"What do you see when you look out there, Sarah?" Roger asks.

I stand next to one of the windows in his apartment and take in the view.

"The sun's out and there isn't a cloud in the sky. It's a perfect summer day. The street's filled with a steady stream of cars and people. There's a busker on the corner—do they have buskers in your time? He's drumming on a plastic bucket with his hands and feet."

"He any good?"

"He's too far to hear, but he must be. People are giving him money. Paper money."

Roger raises his eyebrows. In his time paper money isn't something people part with easily.

"What do you see out there?" I ask.

He places the needle down on the record he's selected and comes over to the window to stand next to me as Billie Holliday sings "Summertime." I quietly hum along.

"There's a newsboy across the street," he says. "He's calling something out to some pretty girls. The girls keep walking. They

aren't interested. Behind the kid, a man's putting up a poster promoting Defense Bonds."

I glance down at the newspaper that lies folded on Roger's coffee table, no doubt purchased this morning from that same newsboy. The front-page story's about the war, but I know it'll still be a
few months before America joins the fight. Still, the worry settles
into my stomach. The attack on Pearl Harbor's coming. It happens
in December. I can't tell Roger that, though.

*There are rules at The Oakmont. The first, and arguably most impor-
tant, is that residents are not permitted to share information about the future
with other residents existing in their past that could influence the course
of their lives. Residents also may not visit the apartments of those living
beyond their own time, though the reverse is allowed.*

I walk over to the record player and apologize to Lady Day
as I lift the needle off her record and replace it with a different
one. This one bends The Oakmont rules a little, since it's technically from my time, and the song I'm choosing won't be released
for a few years yet in Roger's time. But this isn't the first rule
Roger and I have bent during our time together. I find the correct
groove, knowing it by heart by now, and carefully place the needle
down. Glenn Miller and His Orchestra play our song, "Moonlight
Serenade."

I hold my hand out and Roger comes over to take it. We dance
like we have so many times before. I think of that first time when
we met, a few months ago in early spring, and feel myself transported there. Maybe I *am* transported. Time, after all, moves differently at The Oakmont.

Once a month, spring thru fall, Mr. Thomas hosts a movie night on
the rooftop of The Oakmont. Although to him they're *moving pictures*. In his time Mr. Thomas runs a theater where silent films are
screened. Here, he uses an old bedsheet for a screen, but the pro-
jector's real—taken from his theater when they upgraded. There's
also a piano that's stored in a sort of shed he built. The walls open
on hinges for full sound as he plays along with the films.

Today's movie is *Safety Last*, starring Harold Lloyd. A personal
favorite of mine, despite the film having been released before even
my grandparents were born.

The film won't start until it's truly dark, though. First there's
the traditional potluck dinner. I glance down at the table at foods

from every era. On one end Depression cake sits next to aspic. The other end holds a silver fondue pot. Just beyond that's the grocery store sushi platter I brought. There are no rules about food at The Oakmont. There is, however, an unspoken rule when we interact with residents from other times.

At The Oakmont, we go with the flow.

There are things you just accept when you live here. You don't question what's normal for other residents. You don't comment on their clothing or hairstyle, for instance. At least not to point it out as unusual. It's understood that things like appearance—and, yes, even food—are a product of their time.

On this evening, I've set up an easel and brought up my oils. As people arrive, I paint them standing around the table, chatting. I've already included Mr. Thomas and the building manager, Ms. Knox, as well as a handful of others. Front and center are my closest friends, Linda from 1975 and Don from 1969.

There may be others here too, but The Oakmont has its secrets. Just as we don't all perceive the view from the rooftop in the same way, there are residents here we may not be aware of and who in turn may not be aware of us. Only Ms. Knox interacts with everyone.

Of the residents I see regularly, the only one missing is Harrison, the odd loner who lives next door to me in apartment 2055, but he never comes to movie nights.

There's a number on the door of each apartment in The Oakmont. The number corresponds to the year the resident exists in. This number may change as time passes, but the residents don't notice such things.

I put the finishing touches on my painting and lean the canvas forward to pencil in the title on the back of the frame: *The Gang at The Oakmont.* When I rest it back against the easel, I notice a figure I don't recognize and don't remember painting. I look over to the edge of the rooftop, where he stands smoking a cigarette. He wears a fedora, cocked ever-so-slightly to one side, and a jacket and tie over a shirt and slacks. A casual look for another era but coming from the twenty-twenties he looks dressed up to me. *They sure don't make 'em like they used to,* I think.

It's been a while since there was a new face at The Oakmont. Someone must've received their eviction notice. It happens. Sooner or later, one will find its way under each of our doors. That's understood.

I remove my smock and check my reflection on the side of the fondue pot to make sure there's no paint on me, then head over to introduce myself, feeling a little underdressed in jeans and a T-shirt. That's how Roger and I first meet.

He says he's from the early forties. I tell him when I'm from. The connection's instant and powerful. We talk like we've known each other for years. Later we sit next to each other, laughing as Harold Lloyd dangles over the city from the face of an enormous clock. After everyone else has left, we dance for the first time. On this occasion I only hum "Moonlight Serenade." I suppose it's the look of him that makes me choose that song. As we dance, he describes the view of New York as he sees it. I lean my head against his shoulder and try to picture what he tells me.

The Oakmont was built over a time vortex. No one knows how long it has stood on this spot. There's no record of its construction or design. The building's architectural style is timeless, naturally. Its façade appears neither new nor weathered. The residents of The Oakmont can't even be certain the way they see the building is the same way others do.

Late in July, Don invites Linda and me over to watch the Apollo 11 moon landing. Linda watched it back when she was nineteen. For Don it's the first time. I've seen it on TV and YouTube many times over my life, but tonight we're in Don's apartment, where it's actually July 20, 1969, so we'll be watching it live on his TV. I would love to have shared this moment with Roger, but The Oakmont rules are in place for our own good. I did slip a note under Harrison's door inviting him to join us, but I never heard back.

I show up late, as usual. Linda's clearly been here a while. The scent of pot they smoked earlier still lingers in the air, and their first questions to me are about snacks. I dump out the bag I've brought on Don's couch. Everything I could find that didn't exist in their respective times: key lime–flavored licorice, ruby chocolate, chips made from every root vegetable but potatoes.

"Did you get my Coke Zero?" Don asks, rummaging through the pile of goodies.

"Oh shoot! I forgot. There was this old lady in the aisle who started talking to me about the ridiculous price of grapes, and I guess I got distracted."

"Classic Sarah," Linda says. "Born too late, it seems. Can't resist anyone old. Is that why all your friends are from the twentieth century?"

They both laugh.

"Technically, I'm from the twentieth too," I say. "Just made it at the tail end. Maybe that's why my neighbor keeps avoiding me. Not twenty-first century enough for him."

"What neighbor?" asks Don.

"You know, Harrison from 2055."

They shrug, and I find myself wondering if they simply haven't met him, or if they just don't perceive him. That happens at The Oakmont. It's even more common when you're talking about non-residents.

Take Linda; she works at a roller rink teaching roller-disco dancing to bored housewives. The rink is owned by her boyfriend, who I know she's mentioned many times, but I can't for the life of me recall his name. I don't even know if we've met before. All I know is in my time *Roller Palace* is long gone. It's a Chinese buffet now that offers a killer dim sum service on Sundays. Every time I go, I'm tempted to pull up a corner of the carpeting to see if the rink floor's still there. They kept the disco ball, after all.

People who reside outside The Oakmont may visit, but their experience is limited. They see only what pertains to their time. Should they encounter residents from other time periods, they're left only with a vague impression there were people there, but they couldn't begin to describe them. The perception— or lack thereof—is often mutual.

"Anyway, I think it's sweet you talk to little old ladies," Don says. "You can never know if you're the only person a lonely stranger might see that day. Kindness costs nothing."

"Wow, you are such a hippie, Don," Linda tells him, before turning to me and adding, "Speaking of all things ancient, how's Roger?"

I'm about to respond when Don shushes us and points to the TV. We watch Neil Armstrong descend the ladder, describing the surface of the moon as he does. I'm unexpectedly emotional, watching it happen live. He says those iconic words and tears roll down my face. Don and Linda see and burst into renewed laughter. Linda throws a beet chip at me.

"Oh, shut up! You guys just don't get it." Then I start laughing too as I wipe the tears away.

"Okay, so about Roger?"

They both perceive Roger, which is nice since we've been together for almost four months now. I tell them things are going great, and they are. He's an old-fashioned guy, the kind that shows up to dates with flowers and slips handwritten love notes under my door. I love his little 1940s quirks that would be so out of place in my time, like the way his hair's always Brylcreemed and flawlessly parted to one side, or how he takes his hat off when sharing the elevator with a lady, and how when his shoes get worn, he gets them repaired rather than buy new ones. I love that when I get emotional, he hands me a real cloth handkerchief from his pocket.

"I got him to quit smoking," I add.

"That's it?" Linda says. "Where's the juicy stuff?"

"The juicy stuff stays between Roger and me."

"More like *between the sheets*," she says with a wink to Don. But Don's looking at me with the kind of serious expression that only comes from the best marijuana strains.

"What's wrong, Sarah?" he asks. "I can tell something's on your mind."

I hesitate, not wanting to bring this subject up with him, of all people, but with both of them waiting I have no choice but to continue.

"It's the war. It's coming, and I'm worried about what that'll mean for Roger. I hate not being able to warn him."

Don gives a single, almost solemn, nod. He gets it, what with his own war to worry about. So far, he's avoided it, but he knows it's just a matter of time before they start drafting. I know he has his fears about having to go to Vietnam. Fears I have no way to assuage.

There are rules at The Oakmont. One is that residents may not research prior history in order to discover what became of a fellow resident who exists in a time prior to their own.

"Maybe you should just tell him," Don says. "Tell him about all of it. How Japan bombs Pearl, but also how we retaliate. Tell him about dropping Fat Man and Little Boy. Tell him about the devastation that causes in Hiroshima and Nagasaki. Tell him about the camps, but also tell him how no one ever really wins a war, so it's pointless to keep fighting them."

His eyes dampen as he speaks, though he chants similar words in protest almost daily.

I nod in agreement, but we both know I won't say any of that to Roger. It wouldn't matter if I did. War is seen through different eyes in 1941. In 1945 our country will celebrate Allied victory for two whole days. The roar of celebration will go on for twenty minutes after the announcement's made. A sailor will grab an unsuspecting nurse and plant a kiss on her in the middle of the street, and Alfred Eisenstaedt will capture it for *LIFE* magazine. It's not the same kind of thing Don's staring down the barrel of, and we both know it.

Before the end of the year, we stop seeing Don. He leaves a note with Ms. Knox letting us know he's gone to Canada ahead of the draft. The Oakmont's not the same without him.

December 7 comes so fast it's like a blink, but time moves differently at The Oakmont. I knock on Roger's door that day, but there's no answer. As I walk along the hallway back to the elevator, I'm filled with an irrational desire to knock on every door I pass. I want to see another human being—anyone at all—and tell them that in 1941 the country has entered World War II. I want to tell them I'm afraid for the love of my life. I want to see if any of them have phones that will reach his time so I can call and ask if he's okay.

I pick a door at random and pound my fists against it, crying in frustration. But no one comes.

There are many doors inside The Oakmont that won't open and corridors down which a resident can't turn. The Oakmont allows us to see who and what we need to, nothing more. The Oakmont guards its secrets.

Several days pass before I see Roger again. When I do, he seems distracted, his mind elsewhere. I note the stress in his eyes. He avoids talk of what happened, and I don't press. Instead, he speaks of his sister, Betty, who plans to enter the workforce as a telephone operator.

"I'm not sure this is the time," he says. "Why does she need to work anyway?"

"Working women will become increasingly common in the years to come," I say, refraining from mentioning that as men go off to fight in World War II there'll be a boom as millions of women take their places. "I have a job myself, remember?"

"Yes, but it's different in your time, Sarah."

"Is it so different? Maybe this is just what your sister needs."

"But how does it work for families?" he asks. "Who raises the children and manages the home?"

I smile. You have to accept this kind of thing when you're a resident of The Oakmont. Times are different, and each one has its own set of values and attitudes that will inevitably become obsolete as the sands of time continue to fall. We must consider the source and share our varied points of view with the goal of finding common ground, especially with those we love.

"Families find ways to make it work," I say. "Ideally, both parents share responsibilities. That is, in households with two parents. I can't say how single parents manage, but they do. I imagine they found ways to do so even in your time."

He nods, and we sit in silence as the elephant in the room that is the Second World War looms large over everything.

Roger does his best to keep the mood light when we celebrate Christmas. He hangs mistletoe over his door and kisses me deeply when I arrive. On the radio, Bing Crosby sings "Silent Night." He's even cut down a real tree and hung vintage ornaments from its branches. Well, vintage to me, anyway. Beneath the tree there's a small package wrapped in plain paper with a simple red ribbon around it. I assume it's for me, and I place the one I brought for him next to it. Mine looks so garish in its cartoon reindeer wrapping and iridescent silver bow. Roger can't help laughing when he sees it.

I ask about his sister, and he tells me she got the job at the phone company. I tell him I'm glad and that I wish her well.

"That reminds me; she baked cookies."

He grabs a tin from atop his fridge, opens it and offers me one. I take a bite and can't help uttering a long *mmmm* as the flavor fills my mouth.

"This is so much better than the packaged stuff I buy at the store."

"I can't believe you don't cook or bake a thing." He laughs.

"That's not true. I make a mean root beer ham. Mind you, it's just a cooked ham I put in my slow cooker and pour a can of soda over."

He doesn't bother to ask what a slow cooker is. I guess the name says it all. He's aware of some of the magical appliances I have. Well, *magical* to me. To him they seem wasteful—lazy even. "Why would any one household need more than one television?" he asked once. I didn't really know how to respond to that. I think he'd have to admit my cell phone's pretty cool, though, with all the uses it has, but cell phones are strictly forbidden in apartments with numbers earlier than the mid-seventies.

We have some eggnog by the window, and I describe the Christmas lights that decorate the city in my time. New York is alive and festive in December 2023. In 1941, I gather, things are a bit more subdued.

Afterward, we open our gifts. Always the gentleman, he insists I go first. I pull the ribbon and paper off the box and smile when I see the handkerchief.

"I thought you could use one of your own."

"It's beautiful," I say. And it is. I've never owned anything like it. The fabric is cotton, I think, but the edges are hand embroidered with violets, which he knows are the flower for my birth month. On one corner are my initials. I run my finger over them, turning the fabric over to marvel at the quality of the stitching. Machines are good, but not like this.

They don't make 'em like they used to, I think, not for the first time.

He opens my gift next, and I wait on the edge of my seat to see his face. Carefully setting the reindeer paper aside, he holds up the canvas and stares at it a moment before looking at me. I can't help it; I burst into laughter.

"Do you like it?"

"It's . . . a still life?"

"You could say that."

I look down at the painting I made for him. A painting of a single can of Campbell's tomato soup. It's an obvious rip-off, at least to those of us born after pop art became a thing. Roger shakes his head and laughs.

Years from now—for him at least—an artist named Warhol will paint a much better rendition of this very can. The punchline to my joke will land then. I wish I could be there to see his face when it does.

"I love it," he says. There's so much about me he doesn't understand, and yet he still feels this way.

Residents of The Oakmont know there are things you must simply accept while living here, and questions you don't ask, at least not with any expectation of their being answered.

Roger places the painting on his mantel. It actually looks good there. He stands admiring it for a while—or maybe asking himself,

Why a can of soup? I come up behind him to wrap him in an embrace and kiss him between the shoulder blades as he places a hand on mine. Then he exhales deeply, and I know immediately what's coming.

"I've decided to enlist," he tells the painting.

I bury my face into his back and hold back tears.

"There's no rush," I say. "The war goes on for years, and they won't draft until next. You don't have to decide now."

He turns, wrapping his arms around me and kissing the top of my head.

"I know this isn't what you want, but I've given it a lot of thought. They're looking for able-bodied men. Our freedoms are at stake—and those of our allies. I can't just sit this one out."

"But to volunteer?"

He says nothing more. There's no need. I know the man he is, and that this is exactly the kind of thing he'd do. It's why I've worried for months that this moment would come. I know better than to argue, so I simply nod.

Later we fall into bed as we have countless times before, but somehow this feels different. Time seems to linger as we make love, as if stretching out our time together.

Just days later he goes to volunteer, and I walk him to the door. The main entrance to The Oakmont is a peculiar place. There's a lobby with a revolving door that looks just like the many such doors you'll find across the city. When you walk through this one, though, where you end up depends on who you are. Or should I say, *when* you end up. Even if Roger and I were to walk through together, holding hands, we'd still each step out alone into our own time.

He kisses me once, sweetly, then puts his hat on and gives me a smile. I return one as best I can. When he turns to go, part of me wants to run after him, but I stay and watch as he spins through the entrance, then vanishes into thin air.

I reach into my pocket, pull my new handkerchief out, and use it to wipe the tears.

When Roger ships out, I can't see him off. That happens long before I'm born. To take my mind off things, Linda asks me over to her place. We talk about movies, and in my frazzled state I let slip a *Star Wars* reference, though it'll still be another year before it comes out in her time. Luckily, she doesn't notice.

New Year's Eve came and went without much fanfare. I've felt numb ever since Roger said he was going to war. It's 2024 and 1942 where we are. Time marches on whatever the decade and no matter how much we might want to slow things down.

"Anyway, he's thinking of selling *Roller Palace*," Linda's saying, and I realize I've missed her boyfriend's name yet again. "Where the hell does that leave me?"

"Does he have another plan?"

"Wants to open something called a video rental store."

"It might be all right," I tell her.

"You know something I don't?"

Her eyes widen with expectation, but I give her nothing more. She shakes her head, disappointed.

I hang out a while longer but call it an early night. When I get back to my apartment there's an envelope sticking out from under the door. It's yellowed with age and has no stamp or postmark. The mailing address reads only: *Sarah—The Oakmont.* I recognize the handwriting immediately.

Before I'm even through the door, I've torn it open, the scent of old paper contrasting with the anticipation of fresh news from the front.

Roger tells me of the time since he left, mentioning some of the guys he's befriended—two of them New Yorkers like us. Neither has heard of The Oakmont, and Roger can't seem to recall its location for them.

The letter goes on to say how much he misses me and how he thinks of me often. He wishes he could've brought a picture of me, but the modern look of all the ones I had would've invited curious looks in 1942.

By the time I'm done reading I'm both laughing and crying. Pressing the letter to my chest, I try to feel him there with me, through time and space. I have no idea how this letter reached me, but Roger's generation was nothing if not resourceful. Dancing alone in my living room humming "Moonlight Serenade," I send him all my love and hope it somehow find its way to him too.

Letters continue to arrive, one each week. They're always slipped under my door and yellowed from the passage of time. I suspect they're delivered by Ms. Knox when she knows I'm not around.

There's so much Roger isn't able to share with me, so he mostly

reminisces about our time at The Oakmont. He wonders what picture Mr. Thomas will be showing when he starts our movie nights
back up. I want to tell him it's Buster Keaton in *Seven Chances*, but
I have no way to write him. In any case, I might not go. It's not the
same without Roger sitting next to me.

Then a week goes by with no letter. Nor is there one the following week. A month passes with the worst scenarios running
through my mind until I can't take it. I break the rules—not a little
this time, but fully. I open up my laptop and Google his name, and
any other information I have on his military service.

Nothing comes up.

There are results, of course, but they're of other Rogers and
other wars. There's nothing to tell me what happened to my Roger.

I look up every Army database I can and search for someone to
contact for answers. I call in sick to work and spend the next two
days calling everyone I can. The responses are always the same.
There's no record of Roger. Things get misfiled. There was a flood
in the fifties, or a fire in the eighties. The explanations are irrelevant. They all mean the same thing: that I have no idea what's
happened to Roger.

I can think of only one person that might have the answers I so
desperately need.

*Ms. Knox has been the building manager of The Oakmont for time
immemorial. If you ask the residents what she's like, you'll find the descriptions vary enormously. Some will say she's a young, attractive brunette with
a fondness for hats; others will swear she's ancient, bone thin, and always
smells of cinnamon. Still others will tell you Knox is, in fact, an unusually
tall man with an Australian accent. All are correct.*

I knock perhaps a little too hard on Ms. Knox's door, but she
seems not to have noticed when she opens it and offers me a gra-
cious smile. I'm invited in and offered tea, which I accept more
out of distraction that any real desire.

I blurt out my confession as she holds a sugar cube in a set of
tiny tongs over my cup.

"I've been searching the historical records for Roger in apartment 1942."

The cube drops with a *plop* into my tea.

"Milk?" she offers.

I blink, waiting for . . . something else. Some admonishment maybe. Or perhaps a threat of eviction. She sits across from me then and exhales before speaking.

"The rules are in place for your own good. Has breaking this one brought you any measure of peace? Has it returned Roger to you?"

I shake my head.

"You want *me* to do that, then." She sips from her cup. "You want me to tell you whether or not Roger survives the war."

I nod.

"There are questions you just don't ask at The Oakmont," she reminds me. "You don't ask them because they can't be answered. Only time can give you the answers you seek."

"Time," I repeat. "Time is a thing you dangle from precariously as the city moves on below you."

"Mr. Thomas and his moving pictures," she says with a laugh. "Do you want to know what time really is?"

I watch her, saying nothing so she'll continue.

"Time is nothing . . . and everything. It doesn't actually exist, because we made it up, but if it did exist, it wouldn't run in a line; it would run in a circle."

Ms. Knox reaches into her blouse and pulls out a ring on a chain. She spins it one way, then the other.

"Time moves differently at The Oakmont. We can touch it at any point in time or at all points at once." She demonstrates by tapping the ring at various points before placing it onto one of her fingers. "Time can pass you by and leave you virtually untouched, or it can fall on you like a cascade."

"But what does any of this have to do with Roger?"

"There's no fighting it," she says. "It's like swimming against the current. Better to give in, relax, and let the waves carry you to shore."

She tucks the ring back into her blouse and takes another loud sip from her cup. I stare down into mine, searching for answers but knowing there are none to be found here.

Without another word, I stand and head back out to the hall. She makes no move to stop me. I'm so numb I don't even consciously move through the building and only notice I've reached my door when it fails to open for me. I try the key again and again and finally burst into tears. Ms. Knox has locked me out somehow—punishment for breaking the rules.

"You all right?"

I don't recognize the voice, so I look up and see my neighbor, Harrison, standing by his open door. I think it's maybe the second thing he's ever said to me in all the time he's lived here.

"No, I'm not all right. My key won't work."

He comes over and takes a look, then removes and reinserts the key before turning it. The door unlocks and he pushes it open.

"You had your key in upside down."

I feel like an idiot. No wonder this guy has wanted nothing to do with me. I continue to cry even while thanking him, and as I start to walk past him to enter my apartment, he stops me and gives me a hug. It's uncharacteristic, especially in a city like New York, but I give in to it—the way Ms. Knox said I should surrender to time. Through sobs I tell this stranger everything, from the moment Roger and I first met and fell in love, to the letters that arrived at my door so mysteriously, then stopped coming at all.

He listens to all of it in silence with a patience I envy. Then he does the unthinkable and invites me to join him in his apartment.

"I . . . couldn't," I say. "There are rules at The Oakmont."

"I'm aware. Nevertheless, there's something you should see."

I don't trust easily, but something about Harrison feels safe. I follow him to his door, rules be damned, and step behind him into 2056. The apartment doesn't look too different from my own. You expect there to be major changes from one era to another, but ultimately a chair's still a chair and a lamp's still a lamp. Apartments look pretty much the same, and New York rent's probably way too steep in every time.

Leaving me standing by the door, he heads into his bedroom, returning a moment later with a shoebox. He removes the lid as he approaches, and I don't understand what I'm looking at. Inside there's . . . nothing.

"I'm confused."

"My mother used to live at The Oakmont, though I didn't always know that. I never met my father, but when I moved out, she gave me this box and told me it contained something that was his. She said he'd left it for me, with instructions that she give it to me when I got my own place."

I take the empty box and wait for him to continue.

"When I opened the box, I found a bunch of letters. All of them looked old, but the one on top was the only one with my name on it, so I opened it. The letter was from my parents, written when Mom was pregnant. That's how I learned she'd lived here too. They both had. Everything I'd known about them up until that point was, if not a lie, then certainly incomplete. My mother would've told me the truth, had she been able to, but . . ."

"She didn't remember," I finished.

Residence at The Oakmont is a temporary affair. Those who live here only do so when the time is right, and when that time passes, they are evicted. Those who are evicted will find their memories of The Oakmont— and those they knew there—are fleeting, and just out of reach; like a word on the tip of your tongue you can never quite recall. At times, they may sense its existence. They may even search for it, never quite knowing what they're searching for, but you can only find The Oakmont when it wants to be found.

Harrison nods. "By then I'd read the contract you sign when you move in, and I understood. In any case, the letter explained everything. How they'd met, their time together, how he'd gone off to war, all the way through to her eviction. The other letters were ones my father had written my mother during the war. In the letter to me, he said he'd resealed them in new envelopes and gave me specific instructions as to what I should do with them, and when."

I'm at a loss for words as he tells me this. I see it now, as I let my gaze fall over him. The flecks of green in his eyes, so like Roger's. The same unruly waves that drive me crazy in my own hair. This was why he'd avoided me. He'd known that if I looked at him—if I really looked—I'd see and I would know.

"It was you," I say. "I thought it was Ms. Knox who kept slipping the letters under my door."

My gaze then falls on the artwork that hangs above his mantel. It's the one I painted a year ago—or maybe decades ago: *The Gang at The Oakmont.*

"What I don't understand," he says, "is why you were evicted. I know it's just something that happens here, sooner or later, but I thought there'd be an explanation for why it happened when it did."

I smile, then burst into tears again. He looks concerned for a moment, but I start laughing. Relief washes over me, and I clasp my hands and raise them to my face a moment before I regain some composure.

"I became pregnant," I say. "That's why."

The Oakmont is an adult-only living environment. You won't find children or families among its residents. There are couples on occasion, but for the most part residents live alone. Children are lovely, to be sure, but their futures are too uncertain and their pasts too meager. They're as yet too resistant to the push and pull of time. Children also have great difficulty following rules, and there are, of course, many rules at The Oakmont.

"This is great. This is unbelievable!" I tell him and wrap him in the tightest hug I can muster.

He looks confused, so I explain.

"Don't you see? I'm not pregnant now. That means I must get pregnant later, or you wouldn't be here. Which means Roger survives the war!"

He smiles an uncertain, lopsided smile as I jump up and down still hugging him. After a while he gives in to my joy and we both laugh and cry, and for the first time ever, Harrison accepts my invitation to join me for dinner. There are so many questions I want to ask that I know he can't answer, so instead I let him ask questions of his own. We talk long into the night, and when we're done, I describe to him my view out the window, and he tells me what it looks like in 2056.

Roger returns a little over a month later, walking with a cane. I'm just glad he's alive and back in my arms. We're shy around each other at first, until we're not, and then we're back in his bed, just like old times.

The war continues where he is, but he's done his part. I break the rules and tell him how it ends so he's not surprised when the day finally comes. In early September 1945—or 2027, depending on your point of view—we celebrate the occasion in our own way and conceive our son.

I discover I'm pregnant as soon as I return to my apartment, where I find an eviction notice slipped under my door.

When I tell Roger both the good news and bad, we cry tears of joy and sadness, and afterward he plays "Moonlight Serenade," and we dance one more time.

"I'm going to miss this," I say. "In my time no one who isn't a professional really knows how to dance anymore. At least with you leading I stood a chance at a few decent steps."

"I'll miss this too, and I'll miss seeing New York through your eyes."

"Maybe we could meet in the future, where our lives overlap," I say.

He kisses my forehead. "That would never work. You'd be a child or at most a young woman. I'd be an old man."

I choke back tears and take a deep breath to steady myself.

"It'll be all right," he says. "I don't think this is necessarily the end for us. After all, time moves differently at The Oakmont."

I don't know what he means by that, but I do know that in The Oakmont there are questions you don't ask.

I'm big as a house, waddling down the aisles of my local grocery store in search of the newborn diapers that match my coupon.

"My goodness," says a voice with geriatric lilt. "You're close to bursting."

I have one of those faces, where older strangers feel comfortable talking to me. I stop and offer her a smile.

"I fear I may pop at any moment," I agree, and we both laugh.

"Do you know what you're having, dear?"

"A boy. I'm naming him Harrison."

"What a great name."

"Thanks. It just came to me one day."

"Honey, in your condition you should be home resting. Let the baby's father do the running around."

"Oh, it's just the two of us," I say, rubbing my belly. "That's why I'm here hunting down diapers."

"Aren't we all, dear," she jokes, giving me a mischievous wink.

There's something in that wink that seems familiar, and I'm about to ask if we've spoken before when my eye falls on a keychain clipped to her purse strap. A keychain in the shape of a roller skate.

It all comes back in a rush of memory. I see through her aged features to the youthful ones I once knew, and with them all my other memories of The Oakmont return. In that moment I see the same recognition in Linda's aged eyes. She smiles and winks once more.

"My but we had some good times then," she says.

I'm about to answer when it hits me that somewhere back at

The Oakmont there's a younger Linda, living in the seventies. If Linda can be in both places, in two different times, what's to stop her from more? What's to stop any of us?

I think of Ms. Knox and her ring, speaking about touching time at multiple points or all of them at once. I think of all those doors at The Oakmont that never opened for me. At least not the me I was then, at that time. Maybe somewhere behind one of those doors there's another Sarah, with another Roger, and with them all our old friends. Maybe it's movie night and we're standing around the potluck table waiting for Mr. Thomas to start the film.

"If you're the owner of a blue Toyota, your car alarm is going off."

The announcement over the store speakers jars me out of my thoughts. I feel like I was somewhere else just now, but the memory's faded. The elderly lady in front of me seems confused, then shakes her head as she remembers what we were talking about.

"They have the newborn diapers just there, next to the formula," she says.

"Great, thanks."

"Good luck with the little one."

"Thanks again. It was nice meeting you."

You won't find The Oakmont on any maps, in any time. You don't find it; it finds you. You'll be living your life, happy as can be, then one day you'll come across an advertisement for an apartment for rent. The ad might be online, or on a bulletin board, or in a newspaper; it makes no difference. What matters is The Oakmont will call to you when it's your time. It will offer just what you're looking for: a neighborhood close to work or the subway, stunning views of the skyline maybe, or rent control. Whatever the draw, you'll know then and there you've found your home, and you'll soon find yourself in Ms. Knox's office, signing your name just below the list of rules.

P. DJÈLÍ CLARK

How to Raise a Kraken in Your Bathtub

FROM *Uncanny*

FANTASY

"AMBITION!" TREVOR EMPHASIZED, rapping knuckles hard on the wood table. "That is what makes the great men!" He took a satisfied swallow from his mug.

Across from him, Barnaby put down the daily he'd been reading and sipped from his own beer. Pulling out a handkerchief to dab froth from his lips, he scratched thoughtfully at a set of ginger muttonchops.

"If it is ambition alone that lifts up men, then why, friend Trevor, are you here?" He motioned to the noisy pub—not one of the dives frequented by the soot-stained shabby types of London, yet certainly not a place for gentlemen.

Trevor traced the edges of a waxed brown moustache, as he always did before saying something he thought profound. "Because ambition takes proper planning. Take me—a young clerk at a prestigious firm, and recently married."

"To a beautiful wife from a family of some means," Barnaby added cheeringly.

"Yet not *great* means. I can bide my time certainly, work my way to even chief clerk. But that could take up the entirety of my life in this drab attire." He motioned to his black suit, favored by the business class. "And I am a man of ambition."

Barnaby laughed, patting the belly beneath his tweed jacket. "If only my aspirations were greater than finishing this mug of ale! And how, dear Trevor, do you intend to set about fulfilling your lofty goals? Have you fabricated some confounding new contraption of spinning gears and cogs? A wondrous mechanical contrivance that will catch our attention, like this fellow?" He tapped the daily on the table. In a bold headline and fantastic detail, it recounted news of a submersible craft sighted by Her Majesty's Navies in the far seas.

But Trevor waved it off. There were always new machines, one churned out after another in these times. They had become expected, commonplace. People yearned for more than that. And he would give it to them.

Barnaby thought he glimpsed a twinkle in his friend's blue eyes, as the corners of his mouth lifted into a smile.

"Ambition abhors convention, dear Barnaby—and repetition. I intend to be quite unconventional." Taking another gulp of beer, Trevor let the cold liquid slide down his throat and dreamed—ambitiously.

The package came on a Tuesday. Trevor rushed home at message of its arrival. Margaret greeted him at the entry, her eyebrows raised in surprise.

"Goodness! Did you run all the way here?"

"Only the last bit," he puffed, as she took his coat and hat. His eyes searched about.

"Well, it seems you haven't come to see me." She pouted.

Trevor looked down, smiling as he stopped to stroke her red-gold curls. "Forgive my rudeness, dear Margaret. It's just I've been expecting this for weeks. I hardly want to waste another minute."

"I know. Your great and secret project. It's in the back parlor."

Giving her a thankful squeeze, Trevor made his way hurriedly to the double parlor. Clutching the sides of her blue bustle skirt, Margaret followed fast behind. When he reached the back room, Trevor stopped, staring down at a long wooden crate. Burned onto its planks was pyrographic lettering scorched in black:

Fantastic and Bizarre Sea Pearls, Baubles and Collectibles

"It was delivered by two Mermen," Margaret commented, coming to stand beside him. "They gave me this." She handed him a thick brown envelope.

Trevor turned quizzically. "Mermen?"

She nodded with a grimace. "With those green scales and horrid tattoos. I almost fainted when I saw them! But they spoke your name plain enough—Trevor Hemley. What could you possibly have bought from Mermen?" When he didn't answer she went on, as she often did to fill his silences. "Arthur says their kind should be run out and put back to sea. We didn't conquer them just to have them infest our cities."

Trevor walked around to inspect the crate. "Your brother's fought in Her Majesty's Navies against the Mermen, so perhaps he knows the right of it. Can you fetch me my crowbar?"

Margaret gestured to the tool already waiting on a nearby table. He smiled at her forethought. "I suppose you're still not going to tell me what this is all about?"

"It wouldn't be much of a secret if I did. I have a plan here, Margaret, one that I must see to myself."

Her amber eyes took on a piteous look, and he clenched his jaw against it. He detested that look. "I've told you before, Trevor, there's no need to prove yourself to me. We do well as it is. We have a home, money—"

"A home gifted to us by your family," he cut in. "Money provided by your father. Don't mistake me, I'm thankful. But I want to do more than well, Margaret. I want to be great. Now if you wouldn't mind?"

Margaret sighed but said no more. Gathering up her skirts, she turned and strode from the parlor, closing the doors behind her.

Throwing down the envelope, Trevor rolled up his sleeves and grabbed the crowbar. With little effort, he wrenched open the crate lid one nail at a time. It slid off, revealing a bed of slick, green seaweed. He hesitated a moment before plunging his hands inside, pushing apart wet kelp to get at what lay beneath and lifting it out.

The thing resembled an overly large egg, big enough so that he had to hold it in both hands. But where eggshell was smooth and fragile, this was segmented and hard, not exactly like stone but more so the shell of a crab. Here and there bony barbs and tangerine streaks dotted its dark ochre surface. It was weighty as well, with a solid feel.

Flush with excitement, Trevor nestled his prize gently back

into the bed of seaweed and kelp. Wiping hands on his pants he picked up the envelope and tore it open, extracting a page of tan parchment. At each corner was the imprint of a creature, like an octopus or squid, but with a head of sharp ridges and tentacles displaying curved hooks. The words were addressed to him:

Dear Mr. Trevor Hemley,
Welcome, industrious and intrepid adventurer! Those of us who dream, place ourselves above the more ordinary of men. And you have chosen to do that which most men only dream and do not dare—to give life to one of the most magnificent creatures ever to roam this glorious earth! Enclosed you will find a manual to aid in your task, providing you with all you need to know.
    Yours Respectfully,
    Doctor P. D. Bundelkund
    Fantastic and Bizarre Sea Pearls, Baubles, and Collectibles

Trevor repeated the name. Bundelkund. German perhaps? But he was too thrilled to give it much mind. Already he was reaching into the envelope and withdrawing what remained: a book, bound in heavy aquamarine cloth patterned as fish scales. Emblazoned on its front in gold leaf like a billhead were the words:

How to Raise a Kraken in Your Bathtub
A Guide for Users

Sitting on the edge of the crate, he opened the manual and glanced through the table of contents, turning pages before stopping at an image. It was a monster. Its fleshy skin was a pale pink, only showing beneath bone-ridged armor like a thick gray barnacle. Lengthy tentacles festooned with suckers and hooks stretched out from a bulbous head with two eyes round as dinner plates. The appendages wrapped about an antiquated wooden galleon, reaching around broad sails and tall masts to drag the ship into the sea.
He read the words beneath:

The kraken is an ancient creature that inhabited the deep waters of the world. Once thought to be the stuff of sailors' stories and legends, the first reputable kraken sighting was reported almost three hundred years ago.
    During that time, the creatures harassed and attacked sea-

bound vessels. Little solution was found for this continuing problem until their numbers began to dwindle dramatically in the past century. The last sighted kraken was found dead, washed up on a beach thirty years ago. None have been reported or seen since.

Doctor P. D. Bundelkund, however, has discovered the only cache of kraken eggs known to be in existence, found in a dark part of the sea and unspoiled by time. He is willing to make these available to a select few. Through careful study and research Doctor Bundelkund has perfected the means by which to hatch these eggs and thus resurrect the species. He has made it possible so that even you can raise a kraken in your very home, in your very bathtub, with the simplest of tools and instructions . . .

Trevor read on in fascination. He'd stumbled upon the advert in the back of a penny dreadful, which he snuck between his dailies. He was intrigued at once. The notion of such fantastic creatures, and the means to bring them back to life had taken up his every waking moment. But he had even greater plans.

He'd been to fairs and circuses in London since he was a boy. He'd seen their many curios: barbaric peoples of the colonies in their native dress; strange beasts from far-off lands; small primitive men who lived in forests among the apes. Millions flocked to these exhibits. They wanted to see more than the cold machines that had grown so ubiquitous in their lives. They wanted a glimpse at the unfamiliar, the alien, the grotesque.

And he would give it to them!

He could see it now: Trevor Hemley Presents the Great and Monstrous Kraken! They would come from far away and pay much for such a sight. His name would grace all the papers and every tongue. And they would all say: By God, that Trevor Hemley! There goes a man of ambition!

He smiled a satisfied smile and read on.

"Where the devil have you been?" Barnaby lowered his newspaper as his friend took a seat across from him. "It's been two weeks, man!"

Trevor called out an order and smiled. "That I can't tell you yet. But I'll be able to show you soon enough."

Barnaby put on a wounded look. "Keeping secrets from old friends?"

"Men of ambition can't always share their dreams."

Barnaby scoffed, handing over the daily. "Men of ambition seem to be in abundance these days."

Trevor read the headline: "Mysterious Submergible Dreadnought Chased Across the Seas by Her Majesty's Navies and Airships."

"He calls himself Captain Nobody," Barnaby related. "How fantastic is that? He's sunken several of our ships. Built this infernal metal machine himself. It moves leagues *beneath* the waters, surfacing like a whale only to attack! Would you believe they say he's a Hindoo? His crew are Mermen! Travels the seas, he says, to free the oppressed."

"Free them? Free them from who?"

"Why, from us it would seem—we imperialists and would-be civilizers of the world. The enemies of freedom, he names us."

Trevor scowled, throwing the paper down. "And what do the darker races of this world know of freedom? Where would they be without our guiding hand?"

Barnaby accepted the mugs of beer placed on the table and shrugged his round shoulders. "Some question our deeds. They say it's not progress we bring the world, but the chains of industry—by way of the Maxim gun."

"And is there any language better understood by the unattained Huns than that *bap-bap-bap* of the Maxim?" Trevor took a strong swallow and traced his moustache with a finger. "Much as a woman is endowed the weaker sex, so are the darker races weaker forms of men. We overestimate their capacities and burden ourselves unduly with these civilizing efforts. Make them a servile class, I say. Teach them to be hewers of coal, drawers of gas, and harvesters of rubber. But they will never know thrift and industry."

Barnaby didn't reply, knowing better than to engage his friend when his dander was up. He returned to their original subject. "Well, at least have me over. For a peek at this plan of yours. Perhaps I can be of help?"

Trevor grinned toothily. "Not to worry, dear Barnaby. I'll have you over soon enough. When my plans . . . hatch . . . and grow to fruition, I'll likely need your prodigious assistance." He leaned forward. "Tell me, does your uncle still collect and import specimens of men and beasts for display at the zoologiques?"

Barnaby's eyebrows arched. "Indeed. The old codger remains exceedingly well-honed in his peculiar trade."

As his friend sat back and drank with a rakish smile, Barnaby sipped from his own mug and wracked his brain to ponder on this most curious question.

Trevor knelt beside the long copper tub that sat in the room behind the kitchen. It was an odd place for a bathroom. But the design had been Margaret's father's wishes, and who knew his reasoning—perhaps to assure servants saw to their cleanliness. The stoic man had been reluctantly eased into the young clerk's courtship of his daughter and offered the house to them as a wedding gift. Now this odd space was perfect for him to conduct his business.

Margaret rarely came back here, except to give brief instruction to the domestic she insisted on hiring. It was an expense to which Trevor readily acquiesced. It was unseemly that his wife would cook, any more than he would expect her to be out working. Let those insufferable suffrage societies that were popping up tell it, and women were ready to proclaim themselves the equal of men. Thankfully, Margaret had shown no inclination toward such strange desires.

None of that of course dampened her curiosity, and he'd taken to locking the door to the bathroom and keeping a key. The cook only needed firm instruction, which she followed to the letter. So, as it was, only he entered this room to look upon his wondrous plans.

His fingers disturbed the waters of the tub where the kraken egg sat submerged like a hoary seed, yet unmoving. Glancing over to the manual sprawled open on the floor, he read the same page for perhaps the hundredth time:

> Contrary to popular notion, kraken did not birth their young in the seas. Doctor Bundelkund came by this revelation in his research. The infant kraken must be weaned on fresh water before it can imbibe and breathe seawater. He believes that after mating, kraken delivered their egg sac along estuaries. The eggs would then float into freshwater streams where they could hatch and develop before the infant kraken returned to the sea.
>
> This, Doctor Bundelkund believes, accounts chiefly for the destruction of the species. As the industries of our age grew, estuaries became filled with pollutants hazardous to the

> infant krakens. Robbed of these viable offspring, the species
> was decimated. To revive them Doctor Bundelkund has de-
> vised a method by which kraken eggs can be nurtured in safe,
> protective environs.

Trevor had followed that method. The water was clean of pollut-
ants and kept at 55 Fahrenheit. Fresh soil had been spread along
the tub's bottom, and a complex mix of organic compounds kept
the water a tinge of green. Yet after three weeks the kraken egg lay
as dormant as it had upon arrival. And he found his impatience
growing.

He'd invested a hefty sum in this undertaking, taken from
money set aside for them by Margaret's parents. As he exercised
control of their finances, she was none the wiser. That was best,
for her contented mind would never understand his plans. He intended to recoup it all anyway when his venture proved profitable.

But what if he'd been had? A seed of doubt had taken root in
these past days, and it now grew up deep inside him like a trou-
blesome weed. There was no shortage of flimflam men out there.
What if he'd been taken in by a swindle—like strength tonics and
healing elixirs? The thought made his stomach knot.

It was during these misgivings that Trevor heard the gurgling.
He looked down to see bubbles breaking the water's surface. Along
a tangerine streak on that ochre shell there was a crack, through
which a thin, almost translucent arm peeked out, tentatively
searching.

Trevor gripped the edge of the tub, watching, willing, and
coaxing his prize to enter the world. As if hearing him, it did—
slow at first, and then in a frenzy. More arms appeared, tearing
the crack wider. Bits of shell broke away in jagged chunks. With a
sudden heave, a fleshy mass pushed itself free in a burst of milky
albumen.

The infant kraken stared up with round black eyes ringed in silver. For a long while it simply floated unmoving in the water. Then
in a blur, ten tentacles twirled like a ballet dancer doing a pirouette. They reached for a piece of shell that was brought to the base
of its soft bulbous head. What looked like a beaked mouth with
teeth opened and quickly devoured it.

Trevor stared, mesmerized, as the infant kraken consumed the
rest of its former home. It was beautiful, in its own monstrous way.

And it was his very own. As he stared, it occurred to him that he should name it. He'd had a parakeet once named Rupert. No. He needed something greater, to speak to the magnificent beast this would one day become.

Khan, he thought suddenly. An exotic and grand name. He could envision it, emblazoned on a banner: COME! WITNESS! SEE THE WONDROUS AND TERRIBLE KHAN!

He smiled as he dreamed of greatness to come. That would do perfectly.

*

The kraken is ravenous by nature. Medium specimens were known to devour sharks, and their larger kin were sighted engaged in battle with whales. The most monstrous that attacked sailing vessels would not only tear apart the ships but tumble the unfortunate sailors into the waters. There it plucked and devoured them at leisure. Over the years, kraken showed an amazing aptitude for luring and baiting ships, sometimes disguising themselves as islands by covering their heads with bits of sand. Doctor Bundelkund has surmised that krakens are not mindless beasts but thinking beings with an alarming awareness that approaches that of men. This intelligence is focused singularly on hunting. It is not unlikely then to conclude that a kraken's size is directly related to its cleverness in increasing its diet.

"Trevor?" The knock came again. "Trevor dear?"

Trevor jumped up, draping a sheet over the tub. Hastily arranging himself, he unlocked the door and peeked his head out. Margaret stood in a long violet dress with a trail of gold buttons down the center. She looked up at him from beneath a hat covered in lavender lilacs.

"There's another order from the butcher." She pointed to a dresser strewn with brown paper bundles wrapped in twine.

Trevor eased himself out the door, closing it behind. Checking over the bundles, he inspected their stamps. Last time they'd neglected to bring the hog jowl, which Khan enjoyed especially.

"I had to show the butcher in as the cook's left for the day," Margaret said. He nodded absently. The cook had already gone? Was it so late?

"Will you be much longer?" Margaret asked. "We don't want to keep the Harrisons waiting." Trevor turned to her, puzzled. Harrisons? She put on a distressed face. "Oh Trevor! Don't tell me you've forgotten our afternoon stroll with the Harrisons?"

Only now did he notice her yellow gloves and matching parasol. He didn't remember being told—though it was entirely possible that she had. Of late he'd been preoccupied.

He barely made it to work now, lessening his hours at the firm daily—something that wouldn't long be tolerated he knew. But Khan demanded so much of his attention. The hatchling had grown exponentially in the past four weeks. More than he thought possible! Its fleshy body covered with a bony barbed armor took up almost the whole length of the tub now. And it was always hungry! The creature devoured everything—meat and bone alike, then thrashed about for more. At this rate, he'd have to talk to Barnaby about his uncle soon, to find some new space. Thinking on that work left little time for afternoon strolls.

Margaret made an exasperated face when he informed her he couldn't go. "What will that look like?" she lamented. "Me alone with a married couple, like some old maid! That Patsy Harrison is a church bell as it is, and her husband's not so much better. Why they'll talk my ear—"

Trevor silenced her with a finger to the lips. "It will look as if you are married to a very busied man." He planted a kiss on her forehead before grabbing up the butcher's bundles and sliding back into the door.

Outside Margaret watched it close, hearing the lock tumble. And her eyes narrowed.

Trevor burst through the front door, running to the parlor. Margaret lay on a brocaded rose-hued couch face down in tears. She looked up with eyes red with misery, and he knelt to place his arms around her.

"I came as soon as I got your message!" he breathed, still laboring from his run. "It said something about an attack?"

She shook her head. "Oh Trevor, I'm so sorry."

He frowned. "Sorry? What about?"

"I'm a vain and meddlesome woman. You've been so absorbed in your secret project these past weeks. All your spare time is spent there. You don't even come to bed until late. I had to know." She paused. "I made a key—"

Trevor jumped up abruptly. Turning, he ran to the back parlor, through the kitchen and stopped. The door to the bathroom lay open and hanging on one hinge. Green-tinged water was splashed all along the floor, creating a trail. He followed it to a broken sash window through which a steady rain now fell. Khan was gone.

He turned to find Margaret behind him, wringing her hands. "I made the key days ago but hadn't used it. Only today there was this terrible squealing and thumping against the bathroom door. It frightened the cook off. I should have called you, but I picked up a broom handle and opened the door instead—"

"Did you hurt it?" Trevor asked tightly. "With the broom handle?"

Margaret blinked, taken aback by the question. "No. I opened the door and . . . It happened so fast. I just remember falling and something running past me, through the kitchen and out the windows." She paused. "Why were you keeping a dog in there?"

Trevor blinked. A dog? Whatever she'd seen, it seemed her mind now grasped onto the most convenient answer.

He sighed. "It was part of my project. Are you all right? Were you hurt?"

She shook her head, and he drew her close. His eyes however remained locked on the broken window, through which his ambition and chance at greatness had fled.

Once he'd fixed Margaret a hot brandy and put her to bed, Trevor went immediately to the manual. He searched the Table of Contents, finding a chapter titled "Possible Troubles." He passed by the headings Asphyxiation, Biting, Dehydration and found what he was looking for—Escape. Flipping to the appropriate page, he read in earnest:

> It is more than likely that your kraken will eventually escape.
> Krakens are after all crafty creatures. Even the most careful enclosures cannot always prevent flight. It is not advised you report your loss to the authorities however, as krakens are not state-sanctioned animals to which discretion will be granted. Your kraken will probably sustain fatal injuries upon apprehension, and you will lose your valuable investment. The best

means of retrieving a lost kraken is through the use of Mermen. Mermen have long experience with the creatures in their
underwater environs and are especially suited for this task. You
should be able to secure their services for a moderate sum.

Trevor read over the brief passage several times with incredulity.
Escape was more than likely? Damn fine place to mention that!
And Mermen? Then again, it made a perverse type of sense. Who
better understood the ways of sea creatures? He set out to look for
them that very evening.

It wasn't hard to find Mermen. They inhabited London's docks
and harbors, performing menial tasks such as hauling goods off
ships and diving for wreckage. Mostly they sat around idle, imbib-
ing opium and causing a public nuisance. He found several at Ca-
nary Wharf as expected. Four in total. Their moss green bodies
were almost bare, save for the outlandish wide-bottomed pants favored by jack-tars.

He called out to them firmly—as he'd heard this was the only
way to deal with such near-men, lest they think him weak. They
turned as one from where they knelt playing some barbaric game
that included the tossing of fish heads. One of them walked forward on bare feet, a muscular brute with black tattoos inked across
his chest. No Merman stood shorter than seven feet, and this one
was a few inches more. Their chieftain likely. His large oval eyes
stared down, with black pupils set in dull yellow.

Trevor cleared his throat. "I wish to hire you and your men."

"Yes!" The Merman grinned, showing block white teeth.

Well, that was easy enough. "You should know the nature of
this—"

"Yes!"

"I should explain—"

"Yes!"

Trevor frowned, looking into those yellow unblinking eyes.
Was this Merman a simpleton? There was laughter, and another of
their number sauntered up—smaller than the first, but still broad
shouldered with a spidery tattoo veiling half his face. There was a
smile on his dark lips.

"Mwal is no great speaker," he slurred, setting the gill flaps on
his neck to flutter. "We make joke on you."

Trevor's face heated. But he stifled his anger away, keeping to his task. "I wish to hire you and your men."

"For what?"

Trevor held up the manual. The Merman took it in a webbed hand, running bony talons across the cover before looking up blankly. Of course. He'd forgotten these wretches couldn't read. He took the book back and turned to a page of an old naturalist sketch inked in red.

"I've lost one of these. This very day. In the city. I wish to get it back."

The Merman narrowed his yellow eyes. "You want us find a Lok-Lok? In city that belches smoke?"

Trevor frowned. Lok-Lok? "Yes. I need you to find a kra—a Lok-Lok—that's escaped. Can you?"

The Merman turned and began talking to his companions in their slurring tongue, making ornate hand gestures that flowed like water. Trevor watched, all too aware of Mwal, who had not moved but glared his way. When it was done the Merman turned back and smiled.

"We find Lok-Lok for you. Come. I am called Shan. We talk price now."

Trevor sniffed. He supposed that was one bit of industry the savages had picked up. Joining Shan and his men in their circle, he began his barter.

"I don't understand why I have to go," Margaret said, tying the bonnet under her chin.

"You've said you wanted to visit your parents," Trevor reminded, handing off a set of bags to a Merman by their entry.

"Yes, but this is sudden. It seems everything is so sudden of late. You barely go to work. You seem to be here most of the day. You get no sleep." She gazed about, her voice lowering. "And there are four Mermen almost constantly in our home!"

"I hired them to fix the broken window and bathroom. I told you, they come cheap."

Margaret frowned, biting her lip. "I suppose. They've been remarkably kind, not at all as I expected. Especially Shan. He's noble in his barbarous way." She smiled to the Merman chieftain, who was hoisting a lacquered traveling chest onto his broad shoulders.

He grinned back, and Trevor couldn't help but notice how Margaret's eyes tracked his bare, muscular torso.

"Did you know that among the Mermen women hold high places?" she went on. "Shan says they are ruled by a queen, and Merwomen hold all the titles of generals. The women there even take multiple husbands! Can you imagine?"

"Probably why they lost the war," Trevor murmured. Such fool nonsense these Mermen were putting into the woman's head. All the more reason for her to go. "It will only be a month. Then everything will return to normal."

Margaret never took the worry from her eyes, but she nodded. She reached a gloved hand to his cheek, stroking the unkempt beard that was growing in odd patches on his face. "Take care of yourself, Trevor." He saw her off and then returned to the waiting Mermen.

"Well? Any news? It's been weeks!"

"We still look," Shan slurred. "Find signs of Lok-Lok. Follow those."

Trevor ground his teeth. Signs they had in plenty. Butcheries broken into at night. Missing pets. Sightings of some odd bear or wild pig. Thank heavens for the limited imaginations of the masses. But time was slipping away. Sooner or later, someone was going to catch a good glimpse, then the secret would be out. If Khan wasn't killed, someone else would capture it—and claim the credit! He'd lose his prize! He'd lose everything. Just paying these Mermen was exhausting what funds he still had.

He sighed, lowering himself into a chair. Not for the first time he wondered if he was in over his head. He could stop now, stem the bleeding, and accept his losses. But what then? Admit his failure? Tell Margaret he'd gambled away their finances? The very thought of her piteous look disgusted him. No, it was too late to turn back. Men of ambition pushed on.

A Merman walked up, hovering over where Trevor sat. Tilting his head down, he said, "Yes!"

"What? Oh, it's you."

Trevor called Shan over. The Merman chieftain made a few hand gestures to which his companion answered back in kind. Then he turned to Trevor and grinned.

"Mwal find your Lok-Lok."

*

The Mermen took Trevor to a building in the middle of the city. He recognized it—one that held an indoor pool created by the Swimming Association, for public use. Mwal had tracked Khan to the sewers. The wily kraken was using the drainage tunnels to travel, careful to come out only at night to feed. Clever. Now it had ended up here.

The pool was closed this time of year, and the Mermen had to cut the chains that secured the doors. Following them inside, Trevor was greeted by stifling darkness and the strong scent of mold, from a pool that hadn't been drained during disuse. He followed the Mermen along a walkway before stopping. There, one of them held up an old kerosene lamp, illuminating the space below.

Trevor gaped.

It was Khan. Only Khan had become a true monster.

The kraken had grown tenfold or more. Trevor estimated the pool to be well over twenty yards long, and that was still not enough to contain the creature's immense bulk. Tentacles, some wide around as small trees, spilled out in a fleshy mass of curved hooks and round suckers. The bulbous head was like the hull of an armored airship ending in a sharp honed point and covered in jutting barbs like tusks. Submerged in the murky water, under a ridge of protected bone, a black eye ringed in silver stared up at the glowing lantern. There was an ear-piercing shriek that echoed through the dark, and Trevor staggered back into a wall.

How had this creature grown so massive? Could dogs, cats, and whatever was found in the sewers do this? A sinking feeling crept into the pit of his stomach. Had there been any missing persons of late?

"Your Lok-Lok," Shan commented, yellow eyes flickering devilishly in the lantern light. "It is hungry."

Trevor blanched. What was he going to do? He willed himself calm. Men of ambition didn't panic when faced with such things. There was still a way to make this work. He just needed to find a place to house this monster. Barnaby! Of course! There was already a plan for this! He needed to find Barnaby!

"Trevor!" Barnaby greeted, putting down his evening paper. "Good to see you . . ." He trailed off, taking in his friend's appearance. His suit was soiled and torn, his hair and moustache grown wild.

When he sat down he learned forward, peering with haggard eyes that begged for sleep.

"Where have you been, Barnaby? I've been searching for you for almost two weeks!"

"I'm sorry, Trevor," he stammered. "Was off visiting a great aunt in Huntingdonshire. Dreadful place. Thought she was dying, but the old biddy will be around for a while. But why all this rush? I haven't seen you in over a month! You haven't answered any of my messages." He tilted closer, lowering his voice. "I've heard Margaret left you, and you've lost your employment. Is it true?"

Trevor frowned. "What? No. I sent Margaret away. But yes, I was let go. None of that matters now, I have other business."

"Ah! Your grand ambitious project?"

"You remember, Barnaby, I told you I might need your uncle's help? Well, it's much sooner than expected. Can you place me in touch with him?"

"My uncle? Well, yes. But not now. He's just left the country."

Trevor's face fell. He put his head in his hands, muttering beneath his breath as his eyes took on a hunted look. "What now? God knows, it can't stay there! Gotten so big! Always hungry! And that Shan just keeps feeding it!"

Barnaby frowned. What was the man going on about? Had losing his work so injured his mind? "He'll be back in several months I'm sure. Gone off to collect more natives is all—as far as Bundelkund, it seems."

Trevor snapped his head up, breaking from his trance. "What did you say?"

"My uncle. He's gone off to find natives, for the zoologique—"

"Where?" Trevor broke in. His eyes had grown feverish. "*Where* did you say?"

Barnaby reared back. "Bundelkund. With that name in the news, the old codger set out immediately."

Trevor looked poleaxed. "Bundelkund . . . it's a place?"

"Why, yes. Where that Captain Nobody is from. Haven't you been reading the papers?" He held up the daily. "It's all they can talk about, even in droll Huntingdonshire. They've found out his true name—Prince Dakkar, the son of a Hindoo ruler of the kingdom of Bundelkund. One of our provinces in the Indies. Why that's what his war is all about—to bring down Her Majesty's Empire. The madman's even released a Manifesto:

I pledge to throw off your iniquitous laws by all means available. To free those beneath the colonial yoke. To undo the damage the earthly horrors of industry have released into the air and seas. I will make you the tools of your destruction, so that the many-headed hydra that consumes you arises by your own hands, and from your very depths.

Barnaby shook his head in amazement as he finished reading. "Quite a dramatic flair! He certainly knows how to—Trevor? But where are you going, Trevor? You've only just arrived! Trevor!"

Trevor barely heard his name called as he ran from the pub. His mind reeled. Doctor P. D. Bundelkund. Prince Dakkar of Bundelkund. A man who lived in the sea, who declared it his dominion, who conspired with Mermen—a man of great ambition, who now waged a war upon the Crown. What elaborate scheme could such a devious mind concoct?

Screams and shouts broke his thoughts, and Trevor fast found himself in a sea of humanity. People streamed by in a flood, heedless, terror marring their faces. He pushed past them, dread gnawing his insides to shreds. When he rounded a corner, he stopped and stared at a nightmare.

The kraken was pushing up from the building that housed it, sending mortar and brick crashing in a plume of blinding dust. From within that billowing cloud came a bestial roar—a mighty bellowing that shook the very air and struck Trevor to his core. Fleshy tentacles writhed about within the haze, lashing out like fierce whips. A policeman raised a truncheon in some pointless gesture and was crushed beneath an armored limb. A screaming socialite was plucked from a carriage, as her terrified horse bolted. The brown dun didn't get far before a fleshy appendage wrapped about it, bony hooks gouging flesh as it kicked futilely. Another tentacle ripped a man right off his high-wheeled velocipede, sending the vehicle flying and lifting him twenty feet into the air. All three were dragged to where a ravenous beaked maw waited— soon rendering hair, bone, and flesh to gory pulp in moments.

Trevor watched in stunned horror as the Great and Terrible Khan cut a swath of destruction through London's streets. A round black eye ringed in silver stared out, surveying the people fleeing before it like so many ants—or a moveable feast. It turned his way, locking on him, and within that monstrous glare Trevor saw a mind beyond a beast. An intelligence resided there, one that hinted at knowing and recognition. The mere thought near sent him mad—and he fled.

Trevor ran now with the escaping crowds, tripping and stumbling in his haste, turning down an alleyway. In his head, that infernal manifesto whispered: *I will make you the tools of your destruction.* Dear God! What had he done? He needed to tell the authorities! He couldn't have been the only one to read that advert. There were other eggs. This could be happening all over London. People had to be warned!

But what would he say? That he had been a dupe of this Prince Dakkar? That he'd been made an unwitting tool? And now he'd helped release untold terror upon them all? *They'll lock you up for a traitor,* a voice warned in his head. *Or a fool.* What would Margaret's family say? No, he could tell no one. He had to get home, destroy everything so that there would be no trace. His name wouldn't be known as the pawn in some madman's scheme.

So frantic and fast was his running, that when he struck the figure in front of him he fell back, sprawling onto the alley floor. Scrambling to sit, he looked up as a face hovered over him. A familiar face, with dull and yellow eyes.

Trevor gasped. "You!"

"Yes!" the Merman said.

"I know your schemes! You and that Shan! You fed that monster! Then let it go!"

"Yes!"

"It will destroy half the city!"

"Yes!"

The Merman stepped closer, and suddenly to Trevor those unblinking eyes no longer seemed simple at all. He paled. "You don't have to do this," he whispered. "I won't tell. I won't tell anyone! I promise I won't tell."

The Merman cocked his head, and then he smiled, his mouth folding back to reveal an inner jaw with jagged triangular teeth like a shark. "No," he said in a guttural growl.

Trevor trembled. Then he began to cry. This was not supposed to happen. Not to him. Not to Trevor Hemley. He was a man of ambition! He was still crying as the Merman's terrible mouth came closer.

Barnaby sat in the parlor, where Margaret poured black tea into a porcelain cup. She wore a blue-striped dress—though for all the sadness in her face, it might have well been a black mourning gown.

"Thank you for coming," she told him wearily.

"Of course." He sipped the tea and grimaced. Trevor had said his wife was not a cook. It seemed she was not good with tea either.

"I'm just at my wits end over Trevor. The police won't investigate his disappearance. My family believes he's abandoned me. I just can't believe. I fear something dire has befallen him. Have you heard anything?"

Barnaby shook his head. "I would tell you if I did, believe me. I've tried to find out what I can, but Trevor was often . . ." He chose delicate words. "A man of secrets."

She sighed heavily. "I didn't even know he was let go from the firm. He'd become so obsessed with this secret project. Father says he emptied the bank of all our money! And believes he's now absconded like a common thief. I don't want to even think on such a thing. Yet . . ." Her teeth worried at her bottom lip. "I wonder how much I knew Trevor at all."

Barnaby sat awkwardly, holding the small porcelain cup. What was one supposed to say? In the silence, his eyes roamed to the morning paper that sat open on a table, and he found himself reading its contents.

"It's awful isn't it?" Margaret said, catching his gaze. "All these kraken attacks. The fifth ship this week! It's created havoc with trade. Why, the stores are practically empty. People are hoarding and boarding themselves indoors! That kraken that rampaged through the streets and tore through Parliament—it ate almost half the House of Lords before disappearing into the Thames!"

"And a good number of MPs," Barnaby added. "Though, only Unionists."

Margaret didn't appear to share his joke, and he buried his face back into the awful tea. She shook her head in exasperation. "Where are these monsters coming from like some plague? Now the Mermen are in open rebellion, fighting alongside this Captain Nobody. My brother Arthur has been called back up for service. I fear it will be war!"

Barnaby nodded gravely. "We are entering dire times," he agreed.

She sighed again, then hesitated, playing with a bit of paper in her hands. "In those last weeks, before Trevor sent me off, he'd hired several Mermen. He claimed it was for odd jobs about the house, but I know it had to do with his project."

Barnaby frowned. Mermen? This was new.

"I can't find any trace of it now. Someone seems to have burned most of his things. But this was in the fireplace." She gingerly handed him the bit of paper, a scrap of singed tan parchment. On it was the imprint of a creature with long tentacles. He inhaled at the sight.

"I know!" Margaret said reading his look. She leaned in, her face anxious and her voice a whisper. "Trevor's secret project, I saw it once . . . I told myself it was a dog. I knew it couldn't be, but I convinced myself it was all the same. Now I've been fretting these days and nights, on what it might have been. Oh, Barnaby, do you think our Trevor is . . ." She swallowed. "A traitor?"

Barnaby fumbled for words, but none came. Instead, he stared at the monstrous imprint and pondered the desperate acts of a man of ambition.

Falling Bodies

FROM *The Far Reaches*

SCIENCE FICTION

THE INSISTENT DING of the overhead comm wakes me from my sleep, and an artificial voice informs me that our passenger ship is approaching Long Reach Station. I surface from what was a pretty nice dream, wisps of a planetside beach and a salty breeze lingering in my brain, and I do my best to stretch out the kinks in my back, the gift of my budget seat. There's still enough gate-jump sedatives floating around my system from the previous leg of my trip to shade the world in a hazy pastel of calm. I know it won't last, but right now, I like it. Nothing's too solid, no sharp edges. Complete opposite of reality.

I remind myself that getting to Long Reach means that the worst is over, that my planet and my problems are far, far away. I'm light-years from anyone who knows me. A billion plus kilometers from the Genteel homeworld and anyone who might know what I've done—and who my father is. On Long Reach, I'll be just another college student, not the adopted son of a Genteel senator. Not some rich kid, and definitely not some failed social experiment.

This is a fresh start. A new beginning.

Isn't that what the judge promised when he sealed my records and commuted my sentence?

I press my forehead against my viewport, taking in the scene. Long Reach is a doughnut-shaped, silver-skinned behemoth rotating slowly around a tower axis. If the Streams are to be believed, it's the biggest artificial structure in known space. As I watch it turn, I remember speed out here is a lie: Long Reach is spinning at an almost unimaginable velocity.

That's the thing about space. Time and distance are nothing like they seem. A body's always farther away than you realize, always moving faster than you think. Out here, everything is an illusion.

Even me. Fresh-start college kid. What a crock.

But the funny thing about illusions is they're not all bad. Sometimes you need an illusion to keep your mind from cracking open against the truth.

"You look lost," a voice says from the aisle.

I look over to find a young woman smiling at me. She has a backpack hoisted over one shoulder and a cascade of cinnamon-colored curls over the other. I'm not an unattractive guy, but even with my new baby blues, this girl is way out of my league. A heart-shaped face, slightly tilted dark eyes, a figure under her school sweater that's hard not to notice.

"I only say that because you look like an Earther who's never seen a space station, is all." She says it nice, no implied insult like back home when one of the Senator's guests would rake me over and sneer *Earther* under their breath. "And I know all the Earther students on campus."

"I'm new," I say, liking the way it sounds, liking even more what it means. New like you don't recognize me. New like nobody knows me.

"I'm Krux." She thrusts her right hand forward, palm sideways. I know this greeting, so I offer my hand too. Genteel don't touch hands upon meeting, so I didn't grow up with it, but I learned quick enough what people expected of someone who looks like me. It feels foreign, like mimicry, but there's something appealing about it, especially when Krux wraps her warm fingers around mine and shakes.

"I'm Ira," I say. An Earth name.

"Where are you from, back on Earth?" she asks. A little frown mars her brow. "Or did you grow up off-planet?"

So far off-planet I haven't set foot in this solar system since I was taken away as a child, but I don't tell her that. Instead, I have an answer, a ready lie for situations like this. Because Krux has made a mistake. I'm not who she thinks I am. I feel a little guilty about the lie, fresh start and all that, but I do it because it means she'll keep talking to me.

"The Americas," I say, knowing my answer is perfect. Vague, but good enough for small talk.

"Never been there," she says. She blushes. "I grew up off-planet. In a tank."

I smile. I like this girl who grew up on a ship but calls herself an Earther and is way out of my league.

The overhead comm dings again, and this time the voice instructs us to make sure we have all our belongings as disembarkation is about to begin.

"Here." Krux tosses me a small holo, one of those cheap ones you can pick up at any Allbuy. I press my thumb to the holo, and a video pops to life between us. Young people wearing traditional Earth clothes and greeting legislators on the steps of the Genteel capital. Another scene, Earther students serving meals to children in what looks like a refugee camp in some burned-out Earth city I don't recognize. Another, Earthers old and young gathered in a circle, singing and dancing, smiles on wide faces, a banner in the background festooned with a blue-and-green planet and a red dove, obviously drawn by a child's hand.

The scenes are pretty mundane stuff if a little heavy on the kumbaya propaganda, but there's something about that last one. The symbol on the banner.

The planet, the red dove.

It takes a moment to click, it's so unexpected, but then it does, and my brain back dives and my hands start to shake. I smell blood, thick and pungent, I hear shouting, my vision sparks from pulse rifle flare.

I close my fist around the holo, hear it snap in my grip.

"Hey!" she cries.

"Is this a joke?" I growl from behind gritted teeth.

"It's a student org." She sounds more hurt than outraged. "The Student Coalition for Cross-Cultural Understanding. SCCCU."

Not terrorists, Ira. Not everyone's a fucking terrorist.

"Sorry," I say, my panic draining down a gravity well to leave me feeling like a fool. "It's the sedative," I offer weakly. "Brain's still foggy."

Her face softens. "Hey, why don't you come to our meeting tonight. Check it out. See what you think."

Despite my complete assholery, Krux is trying to be friendly.

And what could a little student club hurt, especially one focused on cross-cultural understanding? I mean, aren't I the poster boy for that? Literally?

But Krux doesn't know anything about that, or about my father, the Senator. All she sees is my Earth face, and she thinks I'm just like her.

"We're meeting at seventeen station hour in the student commons. Come check us out. If you don't like it, you don't have to stay."

"Seventeen hour? Can't. I have plans." And I'm not sure if that makes me happy or sad.

She smiles, her dimple blossoming. "Maybe some other time, then."

The shuttle doors slide open, blowing in a wave of station air—that distinct mix of recycled oxygen, cold metal, and warm bodies. I turn to grab my duffel, thinking I should apologize to Krux, convince her to give me a tour of the campus or something, but by the time I turn back around, she's gone, swept away in the exiting crowd.

Long Reach Station is like nothing I've ever seen, and I spend my first few hours soaking it all in. Twenty-two levels of life, from engineering at the bottom through the single-digit levels of shopping and entertainment on through government offices and residential rings, and, at the top, the Genteel district. It's mostly humans and Genteel here, no surprise so near Earth, but there's a mix of other species too. They always come with the Genteel, these other peoples from places they've conquered. Earth's not special.

I'd love to explore, ride the level lift up and down and gawk, but I've got a date, and not with the pretty girl I just met. So I catch the lift to level thirteen like my comm tells me and ask random strangers for directions until someone points me to probation services.

The digital nameplate on the door reads PO Mx. Stone, and my first impression is that *Stone* is a fitting name for such a hard-ass. Hair razored to scalp, jaw like the aft of a battleship, obviously ex-military, and likely wishing they were back in deep space somewhere killing something instead of messing around with assholes like me.

Which is how they greet me when I walk in the door: "Sit, asshole."

I sit, taking in the room. Not much to it. One block in a sea of blocks. Standard-issue furniture that looks like castoffs patched to hell and back. A requisite inspirational poster on the wall. A clock set to station time and an Earth-years calendar that doesn't apply out here in space but must be helpful when talking to the home office. Because Stone, to my surprise, is human, just like me. I wonder if that was the Senator's doing, finding me a PO from Earth. Thinking maybe that would make me feel at ease, get me to open up and relate. But all it does is make me remember . . . and that makes me nervous.

Stone has a comm tablet open in front of them, and they're reading through what I assume is my file. They sound bored as they recite my life back to me.

"Orphaned on Earth, time in relocation services, adopted by a senator."

"A Genteel senator," I clarify, in case Stone is getting the wrong idea. "Not human."

Stone grunts, noncommittal, but I know better. Nobody likes seeing humans raised by their alien oppressors, unless you *are* the alien oppressor, and even then I'm pretty controversial. My adoption was very public at the time, billed as a social experiment on all the Streams, PR'd as a "civilize the humans" kind of thing before I was whisked off to the Genteel home planet.

"Petty theft, truancy, expulsion from several schools."

Stone gives me the poor-little-rich-kid glance, a millimeter short of an eyeroll, so maybe they don't give a shit about interspecies adoptions after all. But then they get to the rest of my file and lean back, their decades-old chair creaking under their weight. Eyebrows touch what would be a hairline if Stone had any hair, and then those battle eyes focus on me.

That's my cue to look at the wall, or the kitten-in-space poster stuck to the peeling paint, or my fingernails. Anywhere but Stone's face. Because I'm pretty sure I know what I'll see there. The same thing I saw on the judge's face right before he sent me here. Shock, disgust, a little pity.

Stone swipes the comm closed and drops it on the desk. When they speak, I hear nothing but no-nonsense.

"I will remind you that you're on probation, so keep your nose clean. You are to attend classes; eat, sleep, and shit in the dormitory; and limit any socializing to the hours between zero-six station and twenty station. Those hours are to be spent only on the university level, where you will find everything you need. This next part should be obvious, but let me make it clear: no drugs, no liquor, and no frequenting of any establishment where you couldn't take your mother."

I curl my lip, as if to say, *What mother?* because Stone must have already forgotten the orphan part.

Stone coughs over the misstep, but I know they read me.

"Understand?" they ask.

I nod. The Senator's keeping me on a short leash, but that was to be expected. Long Reach only *looks* like a fresh start, only *resembles* freedom. It's an illusion, just like everything else.

Stone says, "Check in with me weekly. You do that, we won't have a problem."

Another nod.

"I need a verbal."

"Sure."

We sit there, me not offering anything more, and Stone studying me. I can tell they want to ask, same as everyone else who has ever read my file. *Why'd you do it? How can you live with yourself?* And, always, *Why aren't you locked up in the bottom of some remote prison? How the fuck are you even here?*

I stand. "We done, then?"

They pass me over an ID tag. I slap it against my wrist, and it lights up, keyed to my DNA now. "That gets you to the levels you're cleared for. Nowhere else."

Great. Leash on and staked.

"Same time, same place next week, Ira. Now get out."

Ira. Not asshole. I guess pity won, after all.

I give Mx. Stone a small salute and do as I'm told.

At first, everything's good. The Senator's collar chafes, but it doesn't cut. My room in the dorm is a single. Decent. Bigger than my old jail cell, so I can't complain. My course load is average, most of the classes focused on science and math, subjects that kept me out of political talk and history, subjects where the Senator's name is unlikely to come up.

I spend my free time walking around the university level. I loiter in the library. I eat at the cafeteria, holding down a table by myself. Nobody bothers me, but nobody talks to me either. Turns out it's easy to be back at my single in the dorm by twenty hour every night because I've got nothing to do. I find myself looking forward to my weekly check-ins with Mx. Stone because at least it gets me off this level.

But in my third week of boring student life, the loneliness makes me reckless and I decide to do a little exploring. Nothing to get me in trouble. Just a walk, maybe dinner somewhere besides the cafeteria. I promise myself that I'll be back at twenty station hour like I'm supposed to.

First I try the residential levels, thinking I'll stroll through some parks, gawk at some nice houses. I quickly find out my ID's not coded to let me in, just like Mx. Stone promised. But I'm undeterred and restless enough to keep trying. Still, it's no dice all the way down until I hit the single digits and then ping, I pour out onto level nine with the rest of the crowd.

I follow the flow of Earthers, Genteel, and others, letting the masses take me where they will. I shuffle down a street of neon and flash. It's mostly restaurants and shopping here, trendy eateries and midrange boutiques, Streams blasting the latest news and gossip from every open café door. At first, I worry I'll be recognized. Someone will see past the color job on the eyes and the new hair and see Senator K'lorna's adopted son. But after an hour not meriting even a second glance, I relax. It's nice, this anonymity, slipping and sliding through the throng like I'm one of them. Like I belong.

An illusion, but I'm all in.

I wander off the main thoroughfare and find a little hole-in-the-wall restaurant serving noodles with some kind of hydroponic vegetable and make a dinner of it. I sit in the front and people-watch.

It feels nice. Normal.

After a while, I decide it's time to head back. There's no day or night on a station, but they lower the artificial lights just like a sun cycle, so by the time I'm heading back toward the lift, it's dark, and I know it's late. The lifts run every seventeen minutes, so if I catch the next one, I can be back at the dorm by curfew.

I'm standing, waiting, when a hand comes down on my shoulder.

It's so unexpected that for a second I panic, old memories shooting to the surface and gripping me by the throat. The smell of blood, the bark of a rifle, blood on—

"Ira?"

My heart pounds in my chest so loud it deafens me. Nobody's supposed to know me here. I can see it all slipping away. My new life, my reprieve, and I'm back under the Senator's thumb in front of the judge and there's no pity, only disgust.

And it's devastating in a way I never saw coming.

I whip around. I catch a dimpled smile, a cascade of cinnamon curls.

"It's Krux. Remember me?"

I exhale all that terror, my past trying hard to fuck me up.

"Are you okay?" she asks, face concerned, eyes wide as I suck in air too fast.

I manage to nod. "Startled me."

She gives me a look like I might be the biggest chickenshit in the system, but then says, "Hey, want to join us?"

The lift pings and the crowd pushes forward. We stand our ground, let the masses part around us, islands in the river.

"Us?"

Krux is with friends. Of course she is. Three other Earthers; the tallest looks familiar, like maybe he's in my quantum mechanics class. And there's a guy with the same cinnamon hair, the same tilted eyes. A relative, and he's giving me a look. Check that. That look means *brother*.

"You look like you could use a drink," she says.

Very astute, Krux. I could use about ten, the way my heart's pounding in my chest. But I promised Mx. Stone I'd keep my nose clean.

"One drink," she insists, and the lift pings closed behind me.

Shit. Seventeen minutes until the next. She squeezes my shoulder, but this time her touch is warm and nice and she's showing me that dimple.

With the lift gone, there's no way I'm making it back by twenty hour. I'm late, no matter how I play it. And now I've got time to burn.

"Yeah. Sure. One drink."

I expect to end up at some trendy club, the kind with kids on stims, loud thumping music, and watered bootleg. Or worse, some pretentious pub advertising artisanal brews and thirty credits for a reconstituted pretzel stick. But Krux leads us to some swank speakeasy tucked behind a corner Allbuy. The deco is all Earth, mosaics of green forests and blue oceans on the walls, furniture made of honest-to-god wood, or at least something that looks a lot like it. The air smells like rain, an artificial scent pumped in through the vents since, obviously, there's no weather here. People dance to the smooth jazzy music, but they mostly drink, and the whole vibe does wonders to keep the panic I had earlier at bay. Despite breaking my probation, I'm glad I came.

Krux hands me a drink.

"What is this?"

"Mango. It's a fruit from Earth, from the Americas where you're from. Well, a synth of it."

"Nostalgia?" For a place she's never been?

"Cultural pride. I try to keep alive the memory of how it was before the Genteel invasion to honor my ancestors."

I remember her holo on the ship, her pitch for the student org promoting cultural understanding. It makes me jittery, and I'm not sure if I want to suck the concoction down in a single swallow or bolt while I can. She sees my indecision and asks, "What's wrong?"

"I'm not supposed to drink," I confess.

She tilts her head. "Why not?"

Because I'm on probation, and my current life is as fake as this mango, this wood, this rain. But that's too much to explain, so I drink instead. The drink is sweet and thick with a boozy kick that punches me in the face and tells me that I like it.

"Tell me about yourself, Ira," Krux says, sipping.

I shrug. "Not much to tell."

She tilts her head. "You look kind of familiar."

"I'm not," I assure her, but my pulse ticks up.

Her eyes narrow. "No, there's something . . ."

"Look at that," her brother says. His name is Ruck. He and their other two friends are standing beside us at the bar.

We look. Walking in the door are four Genteel. Two female, two male. Human enough at first glance, but it's the small things. The pronounced ridges on the skull, the slightly longer limbs, the skin texture and eye colors that are just a little off from human. They're dressed in name-brand fashions cut in nostalgic Earth styles, but otherwise they look like typical young people out for a good time.

"Don't they know this is an Earth club?" Ruck growls.

"Be cool," Krux warns, hand on her brother's arm.

I frown, wondering what happened to cross-cultural under-standing. Wondering what they would think if they knew I grew up Genteel.

"They think they can treat us like trash, but then they want to be us, wear our clothes. They claim Earth as their colony, force us to sign some one-sided peace treaty, and now we're all friends?" Ruck's eyes are hard, angry. His gaze flashes to me, probably for backup.

"That's what happens when you're conquered," I say. It just slips out, nervousness making my mouth move before my brain does. I think Ruck's going to bite back, but instead he just stares, lips tight, something unreadable in his eyes.

"Let's dance," Krux says, then drags me to the dance floor. She pulls me close and wraps her arms around my neck. I slip my own around her waist. Our bodies move to the sensual beat, hips aligned, sweat building on my brow for more reasons than one.

She's quiet through the first song, happy to let our bodies han-dle the conversation, but as the next number starts, she leans in close to my ear. "Did you mean that?" she asks. "About us being conquered?"

I want to say no. Say *I was just kidding*, or *I take it back*, but the truth is I've seen enough to know that any protest to the contrary is just semantics. She can't see my collar, the leash, the illusion of who I am.

But if tell her all that, no way she'll stay here dancing with me.

So I kiss her to avoid saying anything at all. And she kisses me back, runs her hands into my hair and pulls my mouth to hers, and she tastes golden and bright.

"You know what, Ira," she says, mouth against mine. "Nobody can conquer you unless you let them. The real destruction hap-pens inside you. As long as you're fighting, you're free."

I want to tell her I tried that, and I lost. So now I spin out, faster and farther than she can understand. Maximum velocity.

"Let's get out of here," I say, and she says yes.

I dream, and I'm back on the Genteel homeworld, Empyrean, in the Senator's house, a big dome-shaped mansion in the Genteel style.

There's someone knocking at the door, but the Senator's away, somewhere important, and I can't be bothered to answer it. But the door opens anyway—*blows* open—and into the foyer burst all these Earthers wearing combat gear and carrying blaster rifles. I stare, not only in shock, but because I haven't seen a human face besides my own in a decade.

A woman rushes toward me, big blue eyes like the oceans of Earth I've only read about in books. "We're here to rescue you," she says, and her mouth moves in slow motion.

I want to explain that I don't need rescue. This is my home. With the Senator. The only home I know. The only one I remember, at least.

But then a man is hoisting me up and throwing me over his shoulder like I'm not almost full grown, and we're running across the lawn and piling into a ship, and the Earthers are asking me questions and shouting about the Children of Earth and how they're going to take me home.

I know better.

Alarms have been triggered. Security is in pursuit.

But they're good, these Children of Earth. And they hide me away. Days, months, a standard Genteel year. The Streams stay abuzz with my kidnapping. The Senator goes on camera and warns the terrorists to bring me back or else. But the woman with the blue eyes tells me her name is Mariella. The tall man who carried me is José. There's also Abdul and Mia and Adelola. Their home, *my* home, is Earth. And as soon as it's safe, we'll all go home together, they promise.

I start to believe them. I start to want it too.

So when the Genteel soldiers break down the Children's door, I pick up a rifle, and I shoot. But not at my abductors. All around me, Genteel fall, some by my hand.

But so do Mariella and all the others.

And when the smoke clears and the Senator comes through the door, all I can think about is home. Not the dome-shaped mansion I grew up in, but the one I've never seen. That I never *will* see, now.

And so I shoot one last time.

Then someone's ripping the gun from my hands and shaking me so hard my brain rattles in my skull and there's a fist smashing against my cheek and I'm biting through my tongue and a tooth is flying loose and the bloodstained floor is coming up fast.

And the worst thing is, I deserve it.

I bolt awake, a scream on my lips. Someone's banging on my door, and it takes me a minute to realize I'm not back on Empyrean in the Senator's house. I'm a college student on Long Reach Station, and the voice yelling at me through the door isn't a Child of Earth but Krux's brother, asking if we're okay because he heard shouting.

I stumble naked out of bed, Krux's bed, and crack the door enough to apologize and assure him it was just a really shitty nightmare. He gives me a long look, but must finally decide I'm just a head case, and lets it go.

Krux hasn't stirred. I check to make sure she's still breathing, then collect my clothes and dress. I'm on edge, both the lingering remnants of the nightmare and the guilt over blowing my curfew and ending up in Krux's bed setting in.

I check my comm, half expecting some angry message from Mx. Stone or, worse, the Senator, alerted by the ID tracker, wondering why I didn't make it back to the dorm last night. But there's nothing.

Still, it's best I get back.

Coward that I am, I decide not to wake Krux. I slip out the door, quiet as I can. I'm in a small pod apartment. There's a galley kitchen with a hot plate and a sink, a long bench that doubles as Ruck's bed and a sofa, and a small table.

Ruck is hunched over the table now, spooning hot cereal into his mouth. There's a screen on the wall opposite him and the morning Streams are running, talking heads vomiting up the news and gossip for popular consumption.

"Breakfast?" Ruck asks.

"Naw. I better go."

"You just gonna leave like that? After screwing my sister?" He pats the seat next to him.

He wants to talk, probably give me the speech about intentions and vaguely threaten to hurt me if I hurt her. I'm not volunteering, but I think I'd like to see Krux again, so I grab a bowl from the wash rack, scoop some of the cereal in from the pot on the hot plate, and join him. I've had some awkward meals, but this ranks up there as one of the worst.

He doesn't light into me like I thought he would. Instead, we both eat, our eyes fixed on the Streams. I've been good at avoiding them since That Day—and the Senator assured me he called in enough favors to keep the details off the Streams—but there's a knot in my chest as we watch, and I half expect the Genteel woman on the camera to mention my name and flash my picture on the screen at any moment.

"Ain't that some shit," Ruck says with a nod toward the screen. "Destroy our planet, force us to live on this space station while they steal our resources, and then hold a goddamn peace talk, like there's anything peaceful to say. Peace won't fix this."

I eat my cereal and focus on the Stream. Sure enough, they're talking about a summit on Long Reach Station. I hold my breath as the Genteel woman rattles off a list of dignitaries that will be attending. I can feel breakfast wanting to come back up as she says, her voice overly cheery, "Senator K'lorna . . ."

"He's the worst of all of them," Ruck groans, gesturing toward the picture of the Senator on the screen. "Someone ought to shoot that shitbag."

Tried that, I think.

Ruck goes on for a while, ranting about the Genteel and all that we lost on Earth. I let him, but the Senator's name is ringing in my ears, and all I can think about is maybe I'm more Genteel than human inside where it counts—and that if Ruck knew, he'd beat the shit out of me. Probably want me dead. If *Krux* knew, she definitely wouldn't have slept with me.

I mumble something about having an appointment, drop my half-eaten breakfast in the sink, and go. This time Ruck doesn't stop me.

There's a package propped up against my dorm room door. I scoop it up but don't open it until I'm inside and the door's locked. I check the return address, scared that it might give me away somehow, that the courier or one of my hall mates read it, and it said Senator K'lorna. But it's just some generic post locale, and I relax.

I tear it open to find an authorization ID tag and a holo. I click the holo on, and it shows me a map to a restaurant on level twenty, the time I'm supposed to be there flashing in green. It doesn't say it's from the Senator, but it's no coincidence I'd get authorization and an invitation to Genteel territory on the station on the day the Streams say the Senator's going to arrive.

I think about throwing the package away. Pretending like it never arrived. But that's just delaying the inevitable. If I don't come, he'll track me down, and I'd rather meet him at some Genteel restaurant than have him on campus.

The clock says I've still got a few hours to burn, so I shower and dress, pick out the one Genteel-style suit I brought with me because he'll expect me to wear one. I carefully fix my hair and shine my shoes, and then I sit in my chair and watch the time pass.

The Senator didn't say anything, but I can feel in my bones the reason he's come. I look around my little room. Three weeks wasn't bad. Three weeks was the illusion of freedom, and it was good. I met a girl. I did okay in my classes. I kept my nose clean.

Maybe it was enough.

The restaurant is called Halcyon, and it's up in the rarified air, all right. All the levels of the station I've been on before this have been metal creations, neon and pipes and circuits, whereas level twenty looks like Empyrean. Wide avenues of pockmarked calcified stone, manicured trees and lawns in shades of red and brown as if the entire world exists under a rusty sun. And under it all, the sharp smell of ammonia.

I take it all in with a feeling somewhere between homesickness and bitterness. Empyrean is the only home I've ever known, but I'm acutely aware it's not my true home. No matter what I do or who my adopted father is, I'll never truly belong. The Earther always shows through, and I can't decide if that's a good thing or not.

The hostess is Genteel, lavender-skinned, her quill-like hair flat against her head, her watery amber eyes glaring suspiciously at me despite my Genteel clothes. I hand her my jacket and say nothing with my bland smile. She lets me pass.

The Senator is already seated, his own suit tailored and crisp, white hair tastefully styled. He stands when he sees me. I see his shoulder hitch and his sharp inhale. I think, *I did that*. But he covers the pain quickly and motions with his good arm to join him.

"Iraya," he greets me, and we sit. "It's good to see you."

"It's just Ira here."

The Senator's mint-green eyes crinkle.

"What?" I ask, already defensive.

"I wasn't questioning your judgment." A lie. He's *always* questioning my judgment. I wonder if he logs each instance of my questionable decision making in a journal somewhere for the psychologists and sociologists to ponder one day when they talk about how my whole life, the Senator's whole experiment, was a failure.

"How is school?" he asks, moving on. This is the game we play where he pretends he's not checking up on me or reading Mx. Stone's reports, and I act like I have freedom.

"Good."

A waiter comes and relieves us of small talk while we order. The restaurant has real meat on the menu, not synthetic. It'll be the first meat I've had since I left Empyrean, so I order a steak, bloody. And, morbid sob story that I am, the blood makes me ask, "How's your shoulder?"

I say *shoulder*, but that's just the euphemism we've agreed on, something that makes it sound less serious than the truth.

The Senator's smile is brief and pained. "Better every day. Genteel medicine is quite advanced. Better than Earth's."

According to the Senator, everything Genteel is better. But in this case, he's right. On Earth, he'd be dead.

The Senator says, "You didn't go back to the dorm last night."

Of course he knows. "I met a girl."

The Senator makes a disapproving sound. "Are you sure that's wise?"

We're both thinking of the Children of Earth. "Pretty sure I'm not gonna randomly hook up with another terrorist cell. My luck's not *that* bad." It's a joke, but I can hear Ruck bitching over the Stream in my mind, Krux telling me to fight. I clear my throat over the faux pas. "What are you doing here?"

"I'm staying next door in the hotel. This restaurant was convenient."

"No, I mean what are you doing *here*? On Long Reach?"

"There's a peace summit to work out some fine points of the new treaty."

"Why do the Genteel bother with this . . . *theater* when they've already won?" I mean it. It's not a flip question. I really want to know.

But he stares, as if he's trying to see inside me, like I'm acting ignorant on purpose. "We're not monsters," he says quietly. "There are factions on both sides that would rather see us at war, but the majority of both sides want peace. *I* want peace."

I want to say that peace and subjugation aren't the same thing, but I know how that will sound, especially considering my past. *Our* past. I tell myself this is beyond my reach and not my problem.

"I saw you," I tell him. "On the Streams."

He grimaces. Starts to speak but the food arrives. He's quiet until the waiter's gone and the utensils are in our hands. I don't know what he was going to say before, but now he asks, "Did the Streams mention the Children?"

"Not yet."

"The editorial?"

"No."

When the Senator first adopted me, he wrote an editorial about adoption as a social experiment to prove that Genteel nurture can overcome savage human nature. Too bad it didn't work, and too bad his political enemies have never let him forget it.

He says, "You and I both know it's only a matter of time."

The red meat turns cold and hard in my stomach. I set my utensils down. Motion for the waiter and ask for something alcoholic.

"You know you're not supposed to be drinking."

"I do."

The waiter brings a bottle and two glasses. I fill one, drain it, and refill it. The Senator says nothing, just stares at me in that same questioning way, like he's trying to understand me but can't. The alcohol makes me feel better, and my hands have steadied.

Finally, he says, "We've been here before, Iraya. Your face on the Streams. You will get through this."

"It's Ira, and I just wish they'd leave me out of it." A child's complaint.

"It's too late for that."

I drink another gulp. The wine is quickly going to my head.

"If you're going to drink like that, finish your food."

I push the plate away with intent. "I'm not hungry."

The Senator laughs, but there's no warmth to it. "What college student isn't hungry?" He taps his knife against my plate. "This is real meat. Real vegetables. Do you know how expensive this is? How hard it is to get out here?"

"It's excessive. No one needs this." I'm thinking about what Ruck said about the Genteel. Thinking about my own duplicity. It's the shame making me act out. I've been through enough therapy to identify it, just not enough to do anything about it.

Then the Senator tells me why he's *really* here.

"The judge is revoking your probation."

I knew he was here to drag me home, but *this*? The shock sinks me down into my chair. I stare into the wineglass cupped between my palms, say the only thing that comes to mind as I struggle to process the news. "Because of the drinking?"

"It's political pressure. He's being accused of favoritism. There's a petition for his recall."

So, nothing that I did. Just forces moving against me that I can't possibly control.

"No one knows I'm here," I say, and I know I sound pathetic. "I'm not enrolled as Iraya K'lorna, and there's no reason anyone would suspect I'm at this second-rate university on a space station. I mean, I changed my eyes, my hair. There's other Earthers here. I blend." *I could disappear if you let me. Pretend I was no one.* I don't say that last part, but it's implied.

Mint-green eyes darken. "I can't do that."

"Why not?"

Because you're a criminal, Iraya. You can't be trusted. He doesn't say his part either, because he doesn't have to.

And all I can think is that this can't be real. But I know it is. Maybe the *only* real thing.

The Senator's done with his meal, and the waiter's there to clear our plates. I drain the bottle into my glass, drinking steadily until the check comes and the Senator's paid.

"I'll send someone to pick you up tomorrow evening once I've finished with my meetings." He stands, studies me. "On reconsideration, perhaps you should stay with me until we leave."

"I have a date." I don't, and I'm not even sure why I say it. I'm the asshole who left before Krux woke up, but I can't stomach the idea of leaving now with the Senator. Of this pretentious restaurant and this overpriced meal being my last gasp of freedom.

"The girl? I'm not sure I like it."

"I don't care. You owe me this."

He frowns. *I owe you nothing. Any debt I owed you was forfeited after the Children.* I know he's thinking it, but all he says is, "Iraya." He glances around to see if anyone else in the restaurant is watching. We haven't made a scene yet, but he's a senator. Any scene will surely make the Streams. I don't see anyone watching us, but that doesn't mean we aren't being watched.

"A few hours," I say, my tone softer, less belligerent. "And then I'll go. Please."

Maybe he sees the shift in my body language, the flare of desperation in my tone. Maybe it's the *please* that convinces him to grant me this small freedom.

"Say your goodbyes tonight," he says. "But tomorrow, we leave." His hand moves, as if he might touch me, but he doesn't.

"I'm sorry," he says. "I tried."

I nod. What else can I do?

"I'm not trying to hurt you," he says.

I glance at his shoulder, the place near his heart where the bones have knitted but the scar remains. I'm not trying to hurt him, either, but neither of us seems able to stop.

I end up back at Krux's pod after all, banging on the door, asking her to let me in. I'm not even sure she's there, but I can't go back to my dorm, knowing that after tonight I'll be sleeping in a jail cell.

She opens the door and I fall inside, half-drunk and fully spinning. I confess what I can, careful not to mention names but telling her about my controlling father, my collar and leash, my desire to be free but with no idea how to make it a reality.

She gets me to the bench, gives me a glass of water, and comms Ruck. He arrives quickly from somewhere nearby, and they confer out of earshot. I can only hear their mumbling argument, but already I feel like a fool. I barely know this girl and her brother. Why would they help me? Why would they care?

I push myself to my feet, ready to make my excuses and leave, certain I'll never see either of them again once I'm out the door.

Krux stops me, guides me back to the bench. Ruck sits on my other side.

"Maybe SCCCU can help," she says.

It takes me a moment to decipher the acronym, and then I remember her sales pitch on the ship. "Your student org? The cross-cultural understanding thing?"

Her eyes slide over to Ruck. "I might not have been entirely honest about that."

I can feel the planetary shift, the recycled air going stale. It's suddenly hard to breathe as this particular illusion shatters.

"There is no student org, is there?" My voice is flat, a ghost tumbling through space. "That red dove on the banner. You're Children."

And now my stupid joke about joining another terrorist cell hammers me to silence. Of course this girl that's way out of my league doesn't really like me. Of course it was no coincidence we met on that ship or in front of the lift.

"We can get you out," she says, grasping my hands. "If you do something for us."

I look up, hope sparking like the light of a distant star.

Ruck's voice is a knife. "Take out the Senator."

And just like that I'm reminded that stars are dead.

Krux must see the refusal in my face because she says, "You shot him before."

"And I *failed*. Don't you get that? I tried to kill him and I failed. And he doesn't even hate me for it. He's *forgiven* me, for fuck's sake. That's the worst part. He won't even let me have the horror of it, only the shame."

Krux gets up and goes to the kitchen. She squats down to pull something from beneath the sink and comes back. She sets a metal box on the table between us.

"You won't have to shoot him this time." She says it quietly, like blowing him up is better. More civilized. "You activate it here." She points to an indentation on the side of the box. "After that, all you have to do is give it to the Senator. Tell him not to open it until he's alone, that it's a gift. Something personal."

"He doesn't trust me."

"You're his son."

"The son that shot him!"

"He thinks you were brainwashed, right? Influenced by those months you spent with the Children. This is different."

"How is this different? You want me to kill my father."

"He's not your father," Ruck shouts. "He's a fucking Genteel! He stole you as a baby. Used you in his propaganda crusades. Erased your cultural heritage. Why are you loyal to that man?"

"Ira." Krux touches my shoulder. "Do you want out or not? Freedom is right there. It's right there. All you have to do is fight for it."

"This isn't about my freedom, is it? This is about revenge. Revenge for those dead Children."

"It's about both," she says.

"And you can benefit from it," Ruck adds, "or you can stay on your leash."

"You don't understand."

"I do understand," he barks. "I understand better than you think. And I'm starting to realize that maybe you like wearing that collar. Maybe being on that leash ain't so bad for you. As long as you can live in a fine house and eat real meat. As long as the Senator's always there to bail you out. Maybe being a social experiment isn't so bad. Maybe you've decided being one of them is fine by you."

"Fuck you!" I swing for his face and connect, but he recovers fast and barrels into me. Krux is screaming as we crash into a table and knock over a shelf, plates breaking around us in the tiny space. He gets a good punch in, but I hit back, and then Krux is pulling him off me, and I'm lying on my back panting, trying to catch my breath, head spinning with wine and rage and fear.

"Coward," he spits before he stomps into the bedroom and slams the door.

I lie there wondering if he's right. Is that my problem? I'm just a coward?

The court-appointed therapist asked me why I shot my father. Was it an accident? Had I aligned my loyalties with my kidnappers, a common-enough syndrome? Or was it something else?

I could have lied, told her I didn't mean to shoot or that the Children had messed with my brain. But I'd been looking right at the Senator when I pulled that trigger, his mint-green eyes locked onto mine. And all I'd felt was rage. A rage so deep and foundational that I couldn't look at it without going blind. He glimpsed it too. In that moment. I know he did.

But it didn't last, that rage. It morphed to horror, then guilt, then regret, and then, finally, shame. It became something lodged in my heart, real as any gunshot, bleeding me out in increments.

Krux comes to me, squats down beside me, and hands me a cold medipack. I press it to my smarting jaw.

"Do you love him?" she asks.

Love and hate. Is there a difference? Not for me.

When I don't answer, she tries, "You don't remember anything about Earth?"

She wants me to. It would be easier if I did. Easier if I hated the Senator and remembered my first home, but I've never been easy.

"Tell me something, Ira. Make me understand."

I close my eyes, sure I don't owe her that.

"Mariella was our mother," she says.

Mariella with the ocean eyes. "She was kind to me." I don't know why I say it, but I want her to know. "And Ruck is wrong. There's no mansion for me. I'm going back to prison." I want her to know that too.

"Then helping us is your only way out."

She goes back to the table. Picks up the box and holds it out.

I don't know how long she stands there, arm extended. Or how long I stare. Time and distance in space is a lie.

Finally, I take the box. "What do I have to do?"

Krux smiles, but it's sad, strained. "I'll get Ruck and we'll go over the plan," she says, voice quiet. "You're going to see Earth again, Ira. We all are. We're going home, and you'll finally be free."

I spend the night with Krux, although I don't know why since I know who and what she is, except that maybe I don't want to be alone. We go over the plan. Once, twice, again and again until Ruck is satisfied that I understand how it's going to go.

"There are others helping us," he explains. "Our job was simply to secure your cooperation. They'll have a new ID for you, transportation off Long Reach, and a place you can disappear after this. Somewhere to start fresh."

Start fresh. Already tried that. It didn't work.

Last thing he does is give me a gun. "Only use it in case of an emergency," he says. "Better to go with the box." What he doesn't say is that I had a gun once before and wasn't able to get the job done, so they're not convinced I'd be able to do it this time either.

In the morning, I go back to my dorm. I stop at an Allbuy along the way. There's a Stream running on the screen behind the register, and images flash across it. Genteel and humans, the peace summit. And, there: what I've expected all along.

Senator K'lorna and his son, Iraya K'lorna. Ungrateful adopted son who tragically turned against his father and joined an Earther terrorist organization. When the cell was found, a half dozen Genteel soldiers were killed and the Senator himself was shot. Iraya K'lorna was sentenced to prison for his role in the shooting, but no one knows where. There are rumors that the Senator has hidden him away and is helping him evade justice. And now the presiding judge is demanding a review of the case.

I hunch my shoulders, try to avoid eye contact with the man behind the register, and pay for my holo. I sneak into the dorm through the back way, sure that my hall mates have seen my face on the Streams by now. It's only a matter of time until someone figures out it's me and gets the courage to knock on my door.

I shower and sleep a bit. I pack, leaving the place neat and clean, saying goodbye to something that was barely mine to begin with.

I don't wait for whoever the Senator's hired to come retrieve me. Instead I use the level-twenty clearance tag to go to the Senator's hotel next to the Halcyon. It's big and posh, taking up the entire vertical span of the ring. Inside, I politely ask for the Senator's room, inform the desk person to tell him that his son is here to see him.

I see the way she eyes me, knows who I am, may even be a little scared of me. But she comms up, and the Senator instructs her to tell security to allow me to pass unharassed. I can't hear their conversation, but I can tell there's some debate. I'm dangerous, after all. Untrustworthy. I should at least be searched.

I start sweating, Ruck's gun tucked into my waistband and digging into my spine.

But the Senator's adamant, no doubt worried that security will rough me up, terrorist that I am, and, finally, the big man with the rifle lets me pass with no more than a disgusted glare.

I keep sweating all the way up the lift. Remind myself this is the only way out. Forward motion, no going back.

I press the comm at the door and it dings softly. For a moment I think of the ship that brought me here. It feels like a lifetime ago, time so unreliable.

"Enter," he calls, and the door slides open.

The room is huge, four times the size of Krux and Ruck's pod, maybe more. There's a separate bedroom and bathroom, a receiving area, a relaxation pit, and there, a desk where the Senator sits.

He looks up as I enter. "Iraya. I said I'd send someone."

"I thought I'd come myself."

A line furrows his brow as if he's not sure what to think, and I realize he's as uncomfortable with me as I am with him. And in that moment I know I've reached terminal velocity.

I hold up the package to show him. "I got you something."

He pushes the chair back and stands but doesn't approach. "That seems unnecessary."

I step forward and set it on the edge of the desk.

He stares at the box. "Listen, Iraya."

I pause.

There are things the Senator could say right now that might change the trajectory of our lives. Throw us out of each other's orbit. But he's always been the planet, and me, the moon. Only one of us is circling the other, and everyone knows moons never escape their gravitational parent without a catastrophic event.

The Senator says, "You should have commed before you came."

I exhale all hope for a different trajectory. I turn, and I'm almost at the door when I hear it.

The click of the metal box opening.

I bow my head. Of course he couldn't wait, couldn't even give me that.

I pull the gun from my waistband. In case of an emergency.

"What's this?" he asks, head down as he peers into the box. "A holo?"

He presses the holo, and it comes to life. I know what's on it. I recorded it before I came. But I listen to it anyway. Listen to his breathing shift as my words hit him. Harder than any homemade bomb.

"Iraya?" He sounds angry, but I know that's fear. "What's going on?"

"It's what I said on the holo, Dad." I never call him Dad. Only Senator. But this time, I allow myself the indulgence. This one last time. "I used to think I would be happy if only I hadn't been adopted. Then I thought I'd be happy if only I could get to Earth. But Earth's no more my home than Empyrean. And nobody can give me a home, not you, not the Children."

It was Krux who made me realize it. Going on about Earth and how wonderful it would be, when she was a tank kid born and raised. Her Earth isn't real. It's an illusion just like everything else. But I don't need illusions anymore.

I'm already cracked wide open.

"All I want now is to be free from this fucked-up narrative, nobody's political pawn. But you can't give me that either. So I've decided to free myself."

I raise the gun. I can see the memory of the last time we were here like this together flash across his face, darken his eyes.

The Senator lifts his hands, a surrender come too late. "Ira, no!"

Time and distance are nothing like they seem. A body's always farther away than you realize, always moving faster than you think. In life, everything is an illusion.

Even me.

"Last time, I shot the wrong person," I say. "This time, I won't."

I put the barrel in my mouth.

I pull the trigger.

SAM J. MILLER

If Someone You Love Has Become a Vurdalak

FROM *The Dark*

FANTASY

MY BROTHER ON my front porch wailing my name, soaking wet and without a jacket in the cold spring rain, with nowhere else in the world to go, wondering why I won't let him in.

My brother crashing at our mom's house, preying on her weakness the way he always did; me calling her every day and waiting for when she'll let it slip that the TV is missing or a credit card is gone.

My brother phoning at four a.m., begging for fifty bucks but forgetting the username of his latest account on Paypal or Zelle or Venmo or CashApp, the previous one having been shut down like all the others for fraudulent activity.

I think of Planck now and it's shit like this that comes to mind. Which is so profoundly fucking sad it makes me even madder at him.

We're twins. Our first fifteen years were a bubble of shared bliss and ill-advised adventures, secret language and all, us against the world, but now his name pops up on my phone or an old friend asks how he's doing and I don't think about jumping fences to steal apples from a neighbor's orchard, or dressing identically to engage in uncanny performance pranks in public. I think of my brother's hollow sunken eyes across the Thanksgiving dinner table—six Thanksgivings ago, the last one he was invited to. I think of my brother debasing himself in a sleazy non-studio porno film clip a so-called friend sent me.

Planck and Faraday, named by our mom after two scientific constants, meant to be "universal and unchanging" for each other . . . but the only constant in Planck's adult life has been addiction.

It's a common misperception, that vurdalaks are a sub-subspecies of vampire. True, both creatures are dead and drain the life force of the living, but ethno-archaeological studies have traced distinct lines of descent.

Vampires, as everyone knows, originated in Egypt, and while scientific consensus on the origin of the vurdalak is lacking, most researchers believe it was Eastern Europe. The first known use of the word is in Russian, in a poem by Pushkin, and scholars still argue whether he made it up or was merely citing a folkloric tradition that had not been previously recorded.

For nearly a century, vurdalaks were said to subsist on blood, but this is now believed to be a relic of an earlier scholarly period when parahuman subspecies were less well understood, and intermediary strains outside the primary taxa of vampire, werewolf, and zombie tended to be grouped in with one of those. There are documented cases of vurdalaks consuming blood, but this is typically ascribed to confusion about their own mechanism of feeding, or a desire to be erroneously believed to be vampires.

The simple, unique, horrifying defining characteristic of the vurdalak is this: postmortem animation can only be sustained by feeding on people who love them.

Strangers and mere acquaintances are toxic to them. Vurdalaks can only derive nourishment in the presence of actual love.

Vampires can make ethical choices about who they feed on, and how. Vurdalaks have no such freedom.

Death was just another step on the long rocky staircase down to rock bottom for Planck. I don't know how or when it happened, just that one day he showed up a lot paler than he'd been before. Shunning sunlight more than normal. Prone to showing me shitty party tricks like cutting himself and no blood coming out.

I've asked around. Nowadays every gay guy knows a vurdalak or two, just as we all have friends who've fallen victim to tina—aka christina—aka crystal meth.

I'd already heard about the addict cuddle puddles. A group of crystal-heads will get a hotel room and spend days fucking and slamming and sleeping. Splitting costs and steadily lowering standards. Losing touch with reality.

Turns out, vurdalaks love that scene. Since they swiftly consume or alienate everyone who loves them, they have to form new attachments. Get new folks to fall in love with them. So they find a drug-addled orgy on Grindr, show up, fixate on someone drugged out and desperate and in the grip of extreme feelings, show them a little kindness and a lot of sexual availability, and, bam. Give it a couple of days and that person has fallen in love with them. Which means they can feed on them. And maybe turn them.

So I figure that's how it happened. He ended up at an orgy on a Tuesday and was food by Friday. A monster by Monday.

Planck was always one to fall in love fast. That's something that's true of me too.

But the silver lining of finding out at fifteen that you have an astonishing genetic propensity for addiction is you learn what danger signs to steer clear of. I lost my brother, but I gained boundaries. Walls I could build, around my heart. So I never experimented with any substances, and I learned not to trust or indulge my own needs.

Sex was fine. Sex was easy. But love was work, was stress, was risk. I steered clear.

Vurdalaks are believed to be the smallest in population size of the confirmed supernatural subspecies, and certainly the least studied. Most scholarship on the subject originated in either the USSR or the USA, and throughout their existence both nations were notorious for the unethical standards of scientific treatment of sentient creatures, the dubiousness of "consent" in their historic research traditions.

A Soviet paper from 1979 remains the most cited, and while it's clear from reading between the lines that the study subjects were incarcerated and their participation was not voluntary—and possibly induced under extreme duress—no subsequent investigations have disproven its primary data. Chief among them, this tidbit that accounts for another major difference between vurdalaks and vampires: you can't become a vurdalak by accident, or against your will. You must consent to it. You must embrace it.

G-d help me, I googled it.

I googled *Vurdalak feeding.*

A man on the floor, his body twisted at an unnatural angle, like he was in the middle of writhing away from something when he froze. A child squatting behind him, pressing her forehead to his neck. A woman off camera, wailing, *Sweetie that's your DADDY! Please, sweetie, stop, that's your DADDY, you're KILLING him.*

Skin-to-skin contact is all it takes, said a comment.

fake, said another.

That dude died, said a third.

I googled *Vurdalak interview.*

I googled *Vurdalak starved.*

I googled *Vurdalak in sunlight.*

That one I had to watch with the sound off, and even then. It was way too much.

Half of what I found was bullshit. And the other half was so horrific I prayed it was also bullshit.

I swore to stop googling.

Three p.m. the next day; a text thread from Planck. I wondered if it meant he was up early or up late. Whether vurdalaks lived fully nocturnal afterlives.

I had so many questions. And every time I called him up or sent a text to try to have a conversation, he asked to come over. So I stopped trying.

I'm not our mom. I'm not letting him anywhere near me.

I visited Alavi this weekend, he says. An ex of mine.

> *Don't worry, I didn't pretend I was you. I know he knows you have a twin, so I figured he'd figure it out.*

> *He must really still be hung up on you, if he agreed to see me. And then agreed to invite me over after he saw what I look like these days.*

> *His love for you was fucking delicious. The life force of strangers is usually so sweet it makes me retch, and so toxic I'll become catatonic if I take more than the tiniest amount, but his was dizzying. So weird how that works. Like his love for you was almost love for me.*

> *But it didn't fill me up, no matter how much I drank.*

They kept coming. I didn't respond.

Alavi had been a brief fling for me, a fun Fire Island weekend and a few balmy city-summer weeks. It never occurred to me it might mean more to him. That his feelings might be so strong that a monster could taste them years later.

Or maybe I'd known. Maybe I'd seen it in his eyes and run screaming for the exit. Or the mechanism was even weirder, a subliminal scent of affection that had me breaking it off with Alavi without even knowing why I was doing it.

Maybe my whole life I'd done too good a job of protecting myself. One more thing to blame Planck for. I started going through the mental rolodex, the empty swamp that has been my relationship history, wondering what flowers could have blossomed into something big. The paths that could have brought me somewhere other than my present utter aloneness.

Here's the thing I've been trying not to say: Mom's sick. She hasn't said so, but I see the familiar haunted ashamed panic in her eyes when I video call, and the dark circles under them. Mom's sick, and I know it's Planck. When he shows up on her doorstep wailing for help, she invites him in. Except now he doesn't just take the cash out of her purse; he sucks the life force right out of her.

So, obviously I'm not thinking straight. Doing dumb shit. So desperate that I've turned to cheap sanctimonious pamphlets from some quasi-religious recovery center I found at my doctor's office.

So, someone you love has become a vurdalak. Please accept our heartfelt sympathies and validation of any fear or anger or grief you may be experiencing. The toll-free number and website provided are staffed 24 hours a day, should you need counseling or emergency assistance.

Because vurdalaks are so poorly understood compared to other scientifically documented supernatural post-humans, we have attempted in this pamphlet to shed some light on their history and operational realities and mechanisms of action. But please understand that this is no more necessary for you to know than the logistics of the pharmaceutical industry's dishonest opioid marketing would be if a loved one became addicted to OxyContin.

We know you have questions. But in the end, an addict is an addict. And sometimes understanding them is dangerous.

I showed up at Alavi's place. I don't know why. To make sure he wasn't dead, I guess. Not vurdalakified. But also. I wanted to see what I felt, when I saw him. Whether I could feel anything.

I didn't just ring the doorbell. That felt invasive: something you do only when tacit consent has been given. If you're the delivery person showing up with the meal they ordered. Or the hookup, arriving for the encounter they specifically asked for.

I texted him from the sidewalk: *surprise! sorry to show up unannounced. my brother said he saw you, so i figure I've probably got some apologizing. For his bad behavior. And maybe for mine. Can I come up? Or can you come down and we go for coffee if you'd prefer?*

It was a little shitty. A little manipulative. Banking on his feelings for me; that he'd want an apology; that he'd hope that this was a sign I'd gotten over my shit and maybe we could start from scratch. I didn't see it until I'd sent it. But once I had I felt like a fucking jerk.

The door buzzed. I pushed through instantly, on reflex, honed over dozens of visits in apartment buildings all across the city where the door buzzer didn't last long enough to make it through both doors and I had to endure the agony of ringing them up again.

So many one-off encounters. So many strange buildings. So few dates—so few boyfriends. What if I *was* an addict, after all? Hooked on anonymity, on boys I'd never see again? Self-medicating with meaningless sex?

"Hey," Alavi said, when he opened his apartment door. Sunlight filled the space, with no apparent ill effect on him. He looked healthy. But he looked sad. And he wouldn't hold eye contact for more than a fraction of a second. "What a surprise."

"Sorry," I said. "I know this is super weird. But I was worried about you. My brother's a . . ."

"Yeah," he said, turning and beckoning for me to follow him into the apartment. "I know."

"What do you know?" I said. "I'm just wondering what he told you."

It'd be just like Planck to cop to being a crystal addict but omit the bit about being a post-mortal life-force-sucker.

"Want tea?" he asked. "He told me he's one of those . . . the vampires that don't drink blood."

"A vurdalak."

Alavi shrugged. Put the pot on to boil. The kitchen was a mess. He hadn't been expecting anyone. If it was me I'd have been angry, to have my disorder exposed to outside eyes, but Alavi seemed fine with it. A short, chubby, bearded, beautiful man, who I had done wrong.

"Are you okay? He told me he . . . fed from you."

Alavi laughed, at the double entendre. Looked at me cynically. "Yeah. I'm okay. It was nice, at first. A really good feeling, a little like E. You know. Blissful, ecstatic. A feeling of a deep real bond with someone. But then I started to get dizzy—sick—nauseous. I tried to tell him to stop, but I couldn't speak. Couldn't move. I panicked, thought he was going to kill me. But he stopped. It really didn't go on super long."

"Did he ask, first? Before feeding?"

"He did," he said, avoiding eye contact again. "But you know me. Once sex gets started I never could say no, to whatever crazy shit someone asks me to do."

I *didn't* know him, not like that. Or had I? Had I also asked for something he hadn't wanted, and he'd agreed because he valued my affection more than his own safety? His need for intimacy overpowered his self-respect?

"I know this is inappropriate," I said. "It's a conversation I should be having with him, but I can't risk letting him get close."

"It's okay," Alavi said. And I wondered if this was why he said yes, when Planck came knocking. If he let him suck him dry in the hopes it might bring me around.

We were both broken. Me and Planck: two monsters, fighting a proxy war with stand-ins like Alavi and our mom.

"And did he ask if you wanted to become like him? The theory is, you have to choose. You can't become one against your will."

Alavi shook his head. "No. But I asked, afterward. How it happens. Not because I wanted to, but because I was curious. He said he'd never turned anyone. And that he didn't want to. Because he knows it's super fucked-up, and he wouldn't want to put anyone else through the hell he's been through. Said the guy who turned him did it because he'd already burned all his bridges, couldn't get into any of sex parties where he used to find dudes to . . . you know. Get to develop feelings for him. Apparently Planck would be able to access a lot of spaces that were closed to him, and then could let the dude in. Something like that. I was a bit dizzy, out of it, wasn't fully following him."

He got up to pour out the tea, brought two mugs. I sat and I watched steam uncoil in the late-afternoon sunlight. I sat and I wanted to say something, but I couldn't. Eventually I took a sip of tea: ginger, an instant Caribbean brand that came from powder, so strong it made my eyes smart.

"But he said something else," Alavi continued, and I didn't want to hear any more, didn't want to be there with this boy who cared about me, who I'd hurt, didn't want to make him open his veins for me any more . . . but cutting and running was selfish, was what I always did, so I sat and I sipped and I smiled and I listened.

"He said he wouldn't *want* to turn someone? But that he might. Sometimes he can't control himself. Sometimes he gets the need so bad and when he starts to feed it feels so good he does really really bad things."

There is no therapeutic consensus around how best to navigate a relationship with someone who has become a vurdalak. Most mainstream treatment centers counsel treating a vurdalak like you would any addict you cared about: Make sure they know that you're available when they are ready to get help, stay in their lives enough that they trust you and will be open to your support when they're ready to seek sobriety, but that attempts at deeper more meaningful interactions are dangerous, both to you—as they'll try to take advantage—and to them, as these relationships can become enabling, and stop them from seeking the help they truly need.

But here at Skye Island Lighthouse, we are unequivocal. There is no safe way to keep a vurdalak in your life. Only heartache can come from it.

Because for a vurdalak, there is no such thing as sobriety. No hope of recovery.

Even though I knew it was idiotic, I went to see my mom.

I called her first, to make sure Planck wasn't there. She said he was in the city for the weekend, which his social media posts seemed to confirm. So I felt sure I was safe from seeing him.

But still. It was dumb. Dangerous.

Because me and my mom are the same. We each have our kryptonite. The person we can't say no to. For her it's Planck. And for me it's her.

He was feeding on her because she still loved him, possibly the last one who did who would let him within fifty feet. But feeding on her wasn't the end of it. He would turn her. The one who could always do what he asked. The one I couldn't shut out. He would turn her to get to me.

And she wouldn't want to. But if he begged her—if he said how much he needed her—if he said how much pain he was in, pain that only she could help end—she'd do it.

I was the one he wanted. The one who loved him most. Because the love was still there. He knew it, and I knew it. Even if the love was mostly outweighed by the hate.

There's much more to be said about vurdalaks than we could fit into this pamphlet. Please visit our website for more resources. Use password vurd4l4k to access the Crisis Options section.

"I'm fine," she said, chain-smoking on the porch and looking like she'd racked up ten more years than the sixty-five she actually had.

"He's killing you," I said. "I can't believe you can't see that."

"He would never hurt me," she said.

"He punched you in the face when you caught him stealing from your purse when we were seventeen," I said.

"That was different," she said. "Those boys he owed money to . . ."

"You know it's not."

She knew. She shivered in her seat. It wasn't even that cold out. I reached out my hand and she took it, held it tight. Felt like her bones had shrunk.

I was still on the porch at three a.m., alone, when Planck returned.

"Faraday!" he called, my brother's voice unchanged, swelling my heart so I almost wept. He stepped out of her car—so at least he had managed to keep from selling it—and the dim light turned him into the kid he'd been, my double, my heart. His face unravaged. His heart unmonstrous.

"Hey, bud," I said, and he ran up the lawn and wrapped me in the biggest, tightest hug I'd ever had.

I braced myself. He could do it. Take from me. His forehead was resting against my bare neck. Skin-to-skin contact. But there was no bliss, no nausea. Just Planck. The pleasure of him. The missing piece to my puzzle.

"I'm so fucking happy to see you, brother," he said, and I could hear the sorrow in his voice. The pain. The thirst. "Thank you."

"I love you, buddy."

If someone you love has become a vurdalak, know this: They need you more than anything on earth, which means you are their greatest weakness. It's true that they can and will manipulate you—but they can be manipulated far more easily.

"Where we going?" he said, buckling his seat belt.

"I wanna have an honest talk with you, which means things might get heated," I said. "I don't want Mom hearing. Cool?"

"Cool," he said, the same sweet, cheerful kid he'd always been. The one that was buried for so many years beneath addiction and then something even worse.

"Figured we'd go to the river," I said. "Where we used to swim."

"Where Mom caught us, and tried to fucking kill us."

"Right," I said, cheerful, friendly, his brother, his twin.

The legal status of post-mortal entities is complex, and different countries and provinces (as well as the USA successor states) have adjudicated them differently. Nothing contained on this website should be interpreted as intended to encourage or facilitate harm to a vurdalak or any other supernatural sentient being.

It was easy. Of course it was easy. We sat on the bench facing east across the river and we talked and he was sweet and sad and trusting and I didn't even have to rush when I pulled the handcuffs from my pocket and snapped one around his wrist and the other around the metal arm of the bench that was embedded in the concrete of the boat launch. He could easily have twisted away before the fatal second click.

"Faraday," he said, his voice unspeakably small and lost.

"I'm so fucking sorry, buddy," I said.

He'd never been bad. He'd just done bad things. Because he had to. But he'd always hated doing them. Hurting people or stealing from them wasn't in his nature.

Neither was begging or screaming or cursing me out. Or breaking his own wrist, tearing his whole hand off to get free. Flexing superhuman muscles that could snap the metal bench strut like wet paper. Which. For all I know those are things vurdalaks can do.

"I love you," I said. "I know it doesn't seem like it, but I do."

Planck laughed. "Relax, bud. I know all about that. Loving someone but hurting them anyway."

"It'll be quick," I said. "I watched videos about it."

"Yeah," he said. "I watched those videos too. Lots of times."

Bad as he was, he had always been the best in me. The part that was open to love and life and adventure and people.

Now that I had him there—docile and defeated and apparently not entirely unhappy at the approaching end—I could have asked him all the questions that had been building up in my brain. About who turned him—what his name was, where I could find him to fuck him up. About what his life had been like. His afterlife. Who else he'd hurt. What it was like. Being this. Being him. But I didn't want to know anymore.

With his free hand he took his phone from his pocket. Bad move, Faraday. You're a terrible murderer. Leaving your victims with the means to call for help.

But I didn't try to snatch it away.

He turned on his camera, flipped it to selfie mode, angled himself so he was alone in the shot. Started recording a video.

"I'm sorry, Mom," he said. And breathed. And smiled. "For everything."

Then he set a schedule-send for an hour after sunrise.

"So she'll think I did it to myself."

That's what pushed me over the line into actual sobbing. Which started him too.

We held hands and we wept. And after a very long time, he whispered, in a voice made almost beautiful by need: "Can I?"

I didn't answer. I didn't know the answer.

"Least you can do, Faraday," he said with a boyish chuckle. "After you fucking murdered me."

We laughed. And yes, I know, of course it was crazy to even contemplate it. Maybe this sad semi-suicidal embrace of his destruction was an act, a feint, a way to get me to let my guard down. Maybe a little nibble would be all he needed to knock me out, drain me dry. But he'd still die in that scenario, handcuffed to a bench with a corpse until the sun came up.

I'd spent my life hiding from the harm love opens us up to. Who could quantify the harm it had done to me instead?

"Yeah," I said. "Just a little bit."

"Just a little bit," he said, voice breaking.

He took my head, turned it toward him. Pressed his forehead to mine.

It felt like summer, like sunshine, like being nine years old and finding yourself with sole custody of a forest. Pinesap; honeysuckle. Mosquito buzz. Babble of a brook forever eluding us. I could see us, smell us. Inhabit the memory. But only for a little bit.

"Thanks, brother," he said, in our secret language.

"I'm sorry I couldn't help you," I said. "Before."

"I'm sorry," he whispered, and did not get specific. The words were big enough to cover all of it.

We sat in the dark and cried together. Boys again. Brothers. No longer divided by a gulf of monstrosity. I'd joined him on the far side of it.

Contributors' Notes

Other Notable Science Fiction and
Fantasy of 2023

Contributors' Notes

V. M. AYALA is a queer disabled biracial Mexican American sci-fi/fantasy writer. They love dragons, space, giant robots, and their partner. Their work has appeared in *Beneath Ceaseless Skies*, *Escape Pod*, and *Translunar Travelers Lounge*. They are currently writing a queer mecha space opera novel—with lots and lots of dragons. You can watch them stream on Twitch as well as find them on most social media places @spacevalkyries.

• Two things: I love giant robots, and I'm a frustrated nonbinary person trying to survive under capitalism. Combine that with the desire to have *some* tiny moment of escape and that's how "Emotional Resonance" came to be. It's a deeply personal gender story. Arbor's weariness at being called a woman day in, day out? Very much my experience. Crowe's genuine curiosity and desire for connection? Also me! I came up with the ending first, with the visual of two queer robots adrift forever together and hoped readers would feel the bittersweet joy; the bitterness of knowing these two never should've been put in that situation, and the joy of their escape and ability to have some happiness, in some form, with each other. It means a lot for a nonbinary and a trans character to have, well, emotionally resonated with folks so strongly. I appreciate Valerie Valdes and Mur Lafferty over at *Escape Pod* for accepting this piece originally and Julia Rios for narrating it!

A. R. CAPETTA is a Lambda Award–winning and bestselling author of magic, weirdness, and wonder for all ages. Their eleven novels include *The Brilliant Death* and *The Storm of Life*, inspired by Italian folktale magic and set in an alternate, enchanted, bloody Risorgimento period. They've released several acclaimed contemporary fantasies such as *The Lost Coast* and *The Heartbreak Bakery*. Their twelfth novel, *Costumes for Time Travelers*, is a romantic time travel fairy tale forthcoming in Spring 2025. They co-authored the nationally bestselling *Once & Future* with Cory McCarthy, a finalist for the New England Book Award, as well as its sequel *Sword in the Stars*. Their short fiction has appeared in *The Sunday Morning Transport*, *Hunger Mountain Literary Journal*, and anthologies such as *That Way Madness Lies*. They also co-edited and contributed to the Candlewick/MiTPress anthology *Tasting Light: Ten Science Fiction Stories to Rewire Your Perceptions*.

• I've been trying to go on a fantasy road trip for years. These sorts of postmodern quests brew slowly and spill across the landscape all at once, so I shouldn't have been surprised when the writing process was just like that. The story's magic showed up—finally, unexpectedly—when I had the chance to travel across the country for the first time in post-lockdown era. In a hotel lobby, waiting for a car to arrive, I wrote a feverish story note to myself. It ended up being a surprisingly good map, so I include it here verbatim, with annotations for where things took different turns:

Car necromancy in a Mad Maxish but magical postapocalyptic American road trip. Turns out when you use magic to reanimate the dead bodies of cars, they grow weird, spiky personalities. Roadside diners, motels, dying barns, roadside attractions, and repurposed gas stations to refuel mages also feature! It happened bc people were trying to use traditional necromancy, ~~maybe they ended up fusing the spirits of their dead loved ones with cars?~~ (Reader, they did not. Title poetry incoming!) Steel Bone Rattle or Resurrection Highway or. Necromancy is unnatural bc it treats a body like it's inorganic but cars actually are so they love it. It has to be done by teams. One grinds bone powder/gruel for gas tank and does "oil changes" to keep the car in good shape and shape the magic. ~~One seat is for a skeleton.~~ (Nope.) One drives. One stands on top of the car or hangs out to connect to the elements. The team thing cuts against the toxic individualism of cars. Also it's more interesting to have three characters plus a skeleton in the car. (I still agree with that last bit.)

P. DJÈLÍ CLARK is the award-winning and Hugo, Nebula, World Fantasy, and Sturgeon–nominated author of the novels *Abeni's Song* and *A Master of Djinn*, and the novellas *Ring Shout*, *The Black God's Drums*, and *The Haunting of Tram Car 015*. His short stories have appeared in online venues such as *Reactor* and in print anthologies including, *Hidden Youth* and *Black Boy Joy*. His most recent novella, *The Dead Cat Tail Assassins*, is now available.

• The story was inspired by a lot of things. One of those was Jules Verne—whose hometown of Nantes I recently visited and got to ride his giant steam elephant . . . like a tamed Mûmak. The modern mechanical marvel was inspired by Verne's 1880 work *The Steam House*, a fictional retelling of the Indian Rebellion of 1857 featuring British colonialists traveling through India in a giant steam-powered elephant. My own story is quite intentionally set in the late nineteenth century, most specifically Victorian England. With Jules Verne as my muse, it has its share of steampunk elements as well as a certain Captain Nobody. But I'm also a fantasist at heart, so there are also mermen. Because why not? Colonialism is an evident theme in the story, a subject that Verne himself tackled and which I take up here. And that seemingly absurd title? Nope, not a metaphor. In this story you will literally get a kraken and a bathtub. You're welcome.

KEL COLEMAN is an Ignyte-nominated author, whose fiction has appeared in *FIYAH, Anathema: Spec from the Margins, Beneath Ceaseless Skies, The Best American Science Fiction and Fantasy 2022*, and others. Though Kel is a Marylander at heart, they currently live in Pennsylvania with their husband, tiny human, and a stuffed dragon named Pen.

• I wrote "Disassembling Light" during a workshop, where my usual method of scattered sessions over months or years was of no help to me. I was eating, breathing, and dissecting craft, yet struggling to write, sitting at the desk in my room for hours trying to coax a fresh story out of a tangle of notes and a weary brain.

One night, the glow from the rainbow lights I'd strung across my window combined with the late hour to lend everything an unreal, hazy quality. I was close to admitting defeat after an especially long and unproductive writing session and suddenly, there was Terse, pipe hanging from his lips, telling me I didn't know hard, I didn't know struggle, I didn't know the pain of becoming irrelevant, I didn't know what it did to a person to lose their ability to shape piles of rotting flesh and scrap metal into art.

After that, the story flowed pretty easily.

JAMES S. A. COREY is the pseudonym used by authors Ty Franck and Daniel Abraham when they are collaborating. The pair have published twelve books together, including the Hugo Award–winning series The Expanse, *Star Wars: Honor Among Thieves*, and (most recently) *The Mercy of Gods*, first volume of The Captive's War trilogy. Additionally, they worked as executive producers and writers for the six-season adaptation *The Expanse*. At the time of this publication, they are also conducting a writing experiment in which they document the novel-writing process from initial brainstorming through publication at patreon.com/JamesSACoreyWritesaNovel (though the project will be deleted once it is complete). They live in the western half of the United States.

• Everything has roots, and "How It Unfolds" is no different. Somewhere in the middle 1960s, Captain Kirk got split into himself and his doppleganger by a transporter mishap. Right about the same time, Charlton

Heston's George Taylor came across a familiar statue on the Planet of the Apes. In 1984, Peter Weller in his best Buckeroo Banzai drag leaned into a red microphone and told Ellen Barkin's suicidal Penny Priddy, *No matter where you go, there you are.* In 2007, Greg Egan published the short story "Glory" that had space travelers appearing on novel worlds in "newly minted bodies."

More personally, Daniel spent a fair chunk of the early 1990s in a personal exploration of how pining after your ex-girlfriend is an emotionally unhealthy space to be in, and in 2023, got to recount the project to Ty, who (born either wiser or luckier) had dodged that particular bullet.

And that's the process: The things we're read or watched or dreamed or lived through come together and make something a little different and a little new. Every time you start something, it's a chance to discover something unexpected. The story's about that too.

P. A. CORNELL is a Chilean Canadian graduate of the Odyssey Workshop who has published more than thirty original pieces of short fiction in respected genre magazines, including *Lightspeed, Apex,* and *Fantasy Magazine.* Her work has also appeared in over twenty anthologies, including *Year's Best Canadian Fantasy & Science Fiction,* volumes 1 and 2, the former also listing her debut science fiction novella, *Lost Cargo,* as one of the best of 2022. In addition to becoming in 2024 the first ever Chilean writer nominated for a Nebula Award, Cornell has been a finalist for the 2024 Aurora Awards, was long-listed for the 2023 BSFA Awards, and won Canada's 2022 Short Works Prize. When not writing, Cornell can be found assembling intricate Lego builds or drinking ridiculous quantities of tea. Sometimes both. For more on the author and her work, visit her website pacornell.com.

• On February 5, 2023, I woke at three a.m. with the phrase "On the island of Manhattan, there's a building out of time," in my head. I don't know where this came from, and I tried going back to sleep, but the line refused to be ignored. I got up and started free-writing what became the first draft of "Once Upon a Time at The Oakmont." I'd like to say I had this grand plan in mind with themes I wanted to explore, but the truth is, the story unfolded for me in much the same way it would for readers. That said, I'd always wanted to write a story incorporating multiple interests of mine. Things like my love of '40s music, vintage foods, *Star Wars,* the space program, pop art, silent film, and World War II knowledge passed to me by my history-buff father. The only way to put all that in a single story is by combining timelines, and maybe because I'm the daughter of two architects, the means for doing this became a rather unique building called "The Oakmont." Once I'd written the first draft, I realized I'd poured more of myself into it than a handful of Easter eggs. Through Sarah, I was able to convey my empathy for those who stay behind when their loved one goes to war, and the way perspectives may change over time, among other themes. The challenge in writing it was what you get with most time-travel stories, in that you want the period details to be as accurate as possible, and you want to make sure you don't drop any threads when linking the key points in each period. The Oakmont rules actually became a tool for both me and the reader to keep those threads from unraveling.

JONATHAN LOUIS DUCKWORTH is a completely normal, entirely human person with the right number of heads and everything. He received his MFA from Florida International University and his PhD from University of North Texas, where he now works as a lecturer. He is the author of *Have You Seen the Moon Tonight? & Other Rumors* (JournalStone Publishing) and his speculative fiction work appears in *PseudoPod, The Magazine of Fantasy & Science Fiction, Beneath Ceaseless Skies, Southwest Review*, and elsewhere. He is an active HWA member.

• "Bruised-Eye Dusk" is part of a larger shared universe of stories set in a post-apocalyptic, post-literate, post-reality United States, many of which have been published with *Beneath Ceaseless Skies*. I can't recall now where the story began, whether it started with character or setting, whether Rugg the gator-riding spellbreaker or his paludal environment arose first. Whatever the case, the story came together in about three days from conception to the end of the first draft. That said, I owe much to Scott Andrews (at *Beneath Ceaseless Skies*), who helped polish the story into its current form over a lengthy and constructive editing process.

What's most memorable about the story for me is the contrast between Rugg's performative simplicity and ruggedness, and the complexity that the narrative's turns drag out of him. With each encounter and challenge faced, more layers unfurl: his sensuality, his humor, his insight into moral nuance, and his strong desire for a happy ending for others when he can't seem to imagine one for himself, believing in others' capacity to change while doubting his own. If you can't tell, I'm very much keen on writing more Rugg stories in the future.

AMAL EL-MOHTAR writes fiction, poetry, and criticism. She won the Hugo, Nebula, and Locus awards for her 2016 short story "Seasons of Glass and Iron" and again for her 2019 novella *This Is How You Lose the Time War*, written with Max Gladstone, which became a *New York Times* bestseller and has been translated into over ten languages. Her reviews and articles have appeared in the *New York Times* and on *NPR Books*, and her debut novella, *The River Has Roots*, is forthcoming from Tordotcom. She lives in Ottawa. Find her online at amalelmohtar.com.

• I started writing "John Hollowback and the Witch" in 2010, while living abroad, at a time when the character of John Hollowback was modeled on someone very dear to me and intended to be sympathetic. That friendship ended in a way that made me abandon the story for over a decade. When Jonathan Strahan reached out to ask me for a witch story, I remembered it, pulled it up—and found myself modeling a decidedly unsympathetic John Hollowback on an entirely different person whom I no longer count as a friend.

I don't recommend, as a general practice, bookending a story or character with feelings of deep loss and betrayal; it was excruciatingly difficult to write, and when I turned it in it felt broken. It took my spouse reminding me of the advice I habitually give to students ("read it out loud") combined with a "bold edit" from the genius mind of C. S. E. Cooney to finally make the story feel whole, and while the thematics of that are perhaps slightly too on the nose, it is what it is.

To my friends and enemies alike, I wish all the justice of witches.

ANDREW SEAN GREER is the author of seven works of fiction, including the bestsellers *The Confessions of Max Tivoli* and *Less*. He is the recipient of a NEA grant, a Guggenheim Fellowship, and the 2018 Pulitzer Prize for Fiction. He lives in San Francisco and Italy. *Less Is Lost* is his latest book.

• I live in a world of metaphor; to me, everything is like something else. So science fiction and fantasy are perfect forms for storytelling, because somehow underneath an unfamiliar world we hear the echo of our own. "Calypso's Guest" is a good example; it was a way for me to write about gay longing and solitude while escaping the clichés. Outer space does that so well! So do references to Homer (it is a retelling of the Calypso part of *The Odyssey*). The story is actually a part of a whole cycle I was planning—an actual space *Odyssey*—and I had written almost half, and even found an interested publisher . . . but their house closed down and I had to abandon the whole project. No one was interested in its individual stories, of which "Calypso" was one. The whole thing seemed dead. I was at my wits' end, and at the end of my bank account, so I wrote another book, a comedy—*Less*—which to everyone's astonishment won the Pulitzer Prize. I was back! So when Amazon approached me for an original story, I knew just where to turn—my favorite part of the abandoned project: "Calypso." I was always proud of it; it meant something real to me. I could not be more pleased that it finally made it out into the world, and now into this volume.

THOMAS HA is a Nebula and Shirley Jackson award–nominated writer of speculative short fiction. You can find his work in *Clarkesworld*, *Lightspeed*, *Beneath Ceaseless Skies*, and *Weird Horror*, among other publications.

His work has also appeared in *The Year's Best Dark Fantasy & Horror* series edited by Paula Guran. Thomas grew up in Honolulu and, after a decade plus of living in the northeast, now resides in Los Angeles with his wife and three children.

• I tend to write with some level of ambiguity in my stories. Sometimes I'll bury answers in the text. Sometimes they are alluded to and exist mostly off the page. But usually the level of explanation is intentional. Of all my stories to date, "Window Boy" has generated the most questions from readers. "Is this a pandemic lockdown story?" "Is this a climate change story?" "Ecological collapse?" "Geopolitical allegory?" "Are the grackles aliens? Eldritch horrors? Experiments gone wrong?" There are admittedly some early 2020 experiences embedded in the claustrophobia of Jakey's world. There are things that, if you lived through them, you probably can't unsee in the subtext. But if "Window Boy" is read over time, I'm not sure that will always be the case. I suspect the anxiety, guilt, longing for friendship, and fear of growing up at the heart of the story may take on different meanings depending on the reader who picks it up. So, when I'm asked about inspiration and symbolism, whether "this represents that," I usually avoid providing a definitive explanation, not because I want to be cagey, but because I really believe readers' perspectives on these points will be as good as my own, especially as more time passes.

GRADY HENDRIX is the *New York Times*–bestselling author of *How to Sell a Haunted House, The Final Girl Support Group, The Southern Book Club's Guide to Slaying Vampires,* and many more. His history of the horror paperback boom of the '70s and '80s, *Paperbacks from Hell,* won the Stoker Award for Outstanding Achievement in Nonfiction, and his next nonfiction book is *These Fists Break Bricks: How Kung Fu Movies Swept America and Changed the World,* out in summer 2025. His new novel, *Witchcraft for Wayward Girls,* will manifest like a vengeful witch in January 2025. You can learn more dumb facts about him at gradyhendrix.com.

• I am not a natural short story writer, but I do love monsters. I rarely write about monsters, because they don't often have complex motivations, and that means there's not enough juice in their tanks to hold up as compelling characters for the length of an entire novel. I just can't make it work. But when I got asked for a short story about a monster, I thought this might be my moment. I spent a long time sweating blood and trying to figure out a new take on bigfoot, but I failed. I thought about Frankenstein's monster for a while, but in my mind he's called Frankenstein, so clearly I wasn't qualified. I take zombies too seriously to write about them. Good werewolf stories are rare, and it became clear I didn't have one in me. And then, one night as I fell asleep after carefully making sure that all my extremities were carefully tucked under the blanket and safely away from the edge of the mattress, I realized that I have always been terrified of something reaching out from under the bed and grabbing my ankle. I tried to imagine what this creature looks like, and all I could think of were hands. And hands. And more hands. That's when I realized I had a monster story. It's also the first time I've written anything even approaching a sex scene. The fact that it ends in horror and bloodshed is something I'm going to be taking up with my therapist.

ALEX IRVINE'S novels include *Anthropocene Rag, Buyout, The Narrows,* and *A Scattering of Jades.* His short stories have appeared widely in genre magazines and websites, along with the occasional unexpected place like Salon .com and MTV.com. Other books include *The Comic Book Story of Baseball* and many forays into licensed worlds, from *Transformers* to Marvel to *Batman* to *Pacific Rim* to *Pokémon.* He has also written a number of games, including the upcoming *Marvel Rivals.* A native of Ypsilanti, Michigan, he lives in South Portland, Maine.

• Around the time I got my first job I started wishing that more SF and fantasy featured people who had to work for a living; too much of what I read in the genres was about Baron Somebody or genius zillionaires freed to adventure (and their writers freed to ignore real life) by their wealth. In this, as in so many other things, Philip K. Dick was a revelation to me when I first ran into his work in my early twenties—probably not coincidentally about the same time I started seriously trying to write. Since then, over the course of the twenty-five years or so that I've been writing professionally, most of my fiction has been about people who have to worry about paying rent while also confronting the end of the world or monsters or disruptive societal change of one kind or another.

Also, ever since I was a kid I've been curious about what the world would really be like if there were superheroes. Every once in a while a comic book story would try to engage this, like *Civil War* or *Black* or *The Boys* or *Hancock.* All cool stories, but as I read them I realized I was looking for a different kind of story—essentially one where the superheroes themselves were minor characters. What did the superhero world look like to ordinary people? Where were the superhero reality shows? Where were the helicopter parents putting their kids in special programs to enhance their abilities? What happened to superheroes when they got old and their powers started to decline? I mean, can you imagine the bureaucracy?

That's when I thought of "Form 8774-D." I wrote it up one day as a lark, sent it out to an editor or two to see if it held together on its own as a story. It didn't, and I realized that I'd ignored the primary thing I'd been looking for in a superhero story: the ordinary person at the center of it all. Enter Leelee, ordinary working stiff, and that's when "Form 8774-D" finally came together. Thanks for reading.

ISABEL J. KIM is a Korean American speculative fiction writer based in New York City. She is a Shirley Jackson Award winner, an Astounding Award finalist, and her short fiction has been published in *Clarkesworld, Light-speed, Strange Horizons, Apex, Beneath Ceaseless Skies, Assemble Artifacts, Fantasy, khōréō,* and *Cast of Wonders,* as well as reprinted in multiple anthologies and translated into Chinese and Japanese. When she's not writing, she's either practicing law or recording her podcast. Find her at isabel.kim.

• With "Zeta-Epsilon," I set out with the specific goal of creating a non-linear narrative that interrogated how a combined machine/meat intelligence might interface with the world. I had been reading a lot about AI and debunked theories of consciousness, and I thought the concept of a groomed "biological translator" for an ship AI would be particularly weird—especially for what the relationship looked like inside the translator's head, and how it would differ from the outside perception of that relationship. The idea of exploring singular versus dual personhood from both interior and exterior perspectives appealed to me, as did theoretical malleabilities of the human brain, development of cryptophasia in twins, and the way humans are hardwired to personify pretty much everything. While writing, I quickly realized there was a version of "Zeta-Epsilon" that was 150,000 words long, and a version that was 5,000 words long. So this is the 5,000-word version, a highlight reel of what exactly happened to the starship *Epsilon/Epigraph* and her pilot, as framed as a murder mystery described through a nonlinear jaunt through Zed's memories.

ANN LECKIE is the author of the Hugo, Nebula, and Arthur C. Clarke award–winning novel *Ancillary Justice.* Her latest novel, *Translation State,* is a finalist for the Nebula Award and Hugo Award for Best Novel. You can read more of her short fiction in her collection *Lake of Souls.* She lives in St. Louis, Missouri.

• "The Long Game" started in a conversation I had with my daughter while walking the dog. She asked me, what if there were a genetic mutation that increased reproductive fitness, but made life horrible for the organism who inherited it? It was an intriguing question—often we assume that "fittest" means healthiest, longest-lived, happiest, etc., but none of those are any kind of requirement for reproductive fitness! The plot we noodled up around that question twisted and changed as I wrote—as did the details of the original seed-premise—which is how writing always seems to go, at least for me. It was fun to write—Narr is such an enjoyable character to me, even with (or perhaps especially because of?) their flaws.

HANA LEE is a biracial Korean American writer who also builds software for a living. Her debut novel, *Road to Ruin*, was published in 2024, and her short writing has appeared in *Fantasy Magazine* and *Uncanny Magazine*. She has an undying love for fantastical stories in all their forms, especially video games, and a habit of writing to moody indie-rock playlists. She lives in California with her partner and two beloved cats.

• "Barigongju," or Princess Bari, is a traditional Korean folktale about the patron goddess of shamans. Bari is the seventh daughter of a king and queen, and her disappointed parents—who hoped for a boy—abandon her after she's born. Her name, 버리, comes from the Korean word *beori*, "to throw away." Many years later, when her parents are dying, Bari is tasked with saving their lives. Dressed as a man, she goes on a fantastical journey to find a cure for her parents, traveling to the underworld and facing a divine guardian who tests her mettle.

There are different versions of this tale with different endings, but Bari is always depicted as the paragon of a good daughter who upholds filial piety at great personal cost. Naturally, as a genderqueer diaspora Korean author, I wanted to write a take on "Barigongju" that dissects filial piety and Bari's traditional role as the dutiful, happily suffering daughter.

"Bari and the Resurrection Flower" is the first short story I've ever written that wasn't a college assignment. I'm a novel writer at heart and like to spend a minimum of 80,000 words developing a character before I'm willing to let them go. Thankfully, Bari was ready to fend for herself after just 5,000.

SLOANE LEONG is a writer, cartoonist, illustrator, and editor of Hawaiian, Chinese, Mexican, Native American, and European ancestry. Through prose, illustration, and comics, she engages with visceral futurities and fantasies through a radical, kaleidoscopic lens, the extrapolation and hybridization of ecologies within speculative frames, and the violent cultural structures of our non/human world. She is the creator of several graphic novels including *From Under Mountains*, *Prism Stalker Vol. 1* and *2*, *A Map to the Sun*, and *Graveneye*. Her fiction has appeared in many publications, including *Lightspeed, Dark Matter, Apex, Fireside, Analog*, and many more. Sloane is currently living on Chinook land near what is known as Portland, Oregon, with her family and three dogs. Learn more at sloanesloane.com.

• Hawaiian history, specifically the story of Kamehameha and how he unified the islands with an armada of war canoes and soldiers, was my main inspiration for "Blade and Bloodwright." I haven't read many stories that draw inspiration from my culture and wanted to try my hand at expanding it out into a whole fantastical world; a planet with no continents, just remote island cities, fortress archipelagos, and an endless sea. The magic in this story came from my evergreen interest in the body and how I can find ways to explore extreme viscerality at different scales. In this case, cities, islands, entire populations rendered into singular systems of flesh, bone, blood, nerve. The body made geography, made citadel. I intend to return to this world and these ideas in a novel.

SAM J. MILLER's books have been called "must-reads" and "bests of the year" by *NPR, Entertainment Weekly, USA Today,* and *O: The Oprah Magazine,* among others. His short fiction has been published in places like *The Kenyon Review, Vogue Italia, Reactor, Asimov's, Lightspeed,* and more. He's received the Nebula, Locus, and Shirley Jackson awards, as well as the hopefully-soon-to-be-renamed John W. Campbell Memorial Award. He's also the last in a long line of butchers. Sam lives in New York City, and at samjmiller.com.

 • How are there not more stories about vurdalaks? They're like the coolest vampires ever, but besides the Aleksei Tolstoy story (made into a segment of Mario Bava's *Black Sabbath* [incidentally the only time Boris Karloff ever played a vampire]), I found precious little. It's such fertile ground for story-telling—a monster who can only survive by feeding on the blood of people who love it! The idea bounced around in my brain for years before I found the right place for it, thinking about what it's like to love an addict, and this story of broken brothers is the result.

REBECCA ROANHORSE is a *New York Times*–bestselling and Nebula, Hugo, and Locus award–winning speculative fiction writer. She has published multiple award-winning short stories and novels, including two novels in The Sixth World Series, *Race to the Sun* for the Rick Riordan imprint, and the epic fantasy trilogy Between Earth and Sky. She has also written for Marvel comics and games, Lucasfilm, and for television, including FX's *A Murder at the End of the World,* and the Marvel series *Echo* for Disney+. She has had her own work optioned by Amazon Studios, Netflix, and AMC Studios. She resides in New Mexico with her family.

 • "Eye & Tooth" was written for the Jordan Peele anthology *Out There Screaming* (a line from the story, I might add). I wanted to write something both fun and creepy, and ultimately endearing about a brother-and-sister monster-hunting duo. They needed to be opposites but also a functional pair that complemented each other, and that's how I came up with Zelda and Atticus. My aunt who lived in Cedar Hill, Texas, was an award-winning dollmaker. Visiting her house as a child was always a journey in doll parts, glass eyes, and stray limbs . . . about the creepiest thing I could think of when I was ten years old. And it's still pretty creepy to this day. Ultimately the story is about love and accepting who you are and using your ugly parts to make something beautiful, even if some people would consider that monstrous.

Identity and obligation to community are themes that often pervade my work, but "Falling Bodies" was my first direct exploration of what it feels like to be a transracial (or in Ira's case a trans-species) adoptee, a topic I have never seen in SFF, and definitely not written by an author who is a transracial adoptee. I wanted to capture some of the conflicted feelings adoptees often have toward their adopted families. I also tried to touch on the desire adoptees feel to be accepted by their family of origin, an acceptance that is often conditional if offered at all. It just so happens that space opera and casting humans as the conquered and aliens as the colonizers offered the perfect framework to tell the story. I think some people may find the ending shocking, but it was very cathartic to write, especially if you know that according to the NIH adoptees are four times more likely to attempt suicide than non-adoptees. And in the end Ira ultimately takes control of his own narrative, which to me is empowering.

CHRISTOPHER ROWE was born in Kentucky and lives there still. Neither of these facts are likely to change. He has been a professional writer of speculative fiction since before the turn of the millennium, and his stories and books have been finalists for every major award in the field, including the Hugo, the Nebula, the World Fantasy, and the Theodore Sturgeon awards. He is the author of one of the most well-regarded collections of recent years, _Telling the Map_ (Small Beer Press), and of two critically acclaimed novellas, _These Prisoning Hills_ and _The Navigating Fox_ (Tordotcom Publishing). He likes goofy dogs, good food, and giant robots. He probably watches more professional bicycle races than you do, but who knows?

• "The Four Last Things" grew out of my interests in the study of the end-times, eschatology, and in the work of the great mid-twentieth-century science fiction writer known as Cordwainer Smith, who in his "real" life (if he can be said to have lived such) was the psychological-warfare pioneer Paul Linebarger. It is not meant to be a literal pastiche of Smith (though some astute readers have seen the connections), but instead to explore eschatological concepts by visiting his linguistic and character concerns through the lens of my own, which are related, but distinct. This story is dedicated to my dear friend, the Reverend Kate Colussy-Estes.

Other Notable Science Fiction and Fantasy of 2023

SELECTED BY JOHN JOSEPH ADAMS

FANTASY

Adams, Erin E.
LASIRÈN. *Out There Screaming*, eds.
Jordan Peele and John Joseph
Adams (Random House)

Ahmad, Senaa
THE WOLVES. *McSweeney's* #71

Al-Matrouk, Fawaz
ON THE MYSTERIOUS EVENTS
AT ROSETTA. *The Magazine of
Fantasy & Science Fiction*, May/June

Allen, Violet
THE OTHER ONE. *Out There
Screaming*, eds. Jordan Peele and John
Joseph Adams (Random House)

Antoniou, Alexia
THERE ARE ONLY TWO CHAIRS,
AND THE SKIN IS DRAPED OVER
THE OTHER. *Bourbon Penn* #31

Antosca, Nick
THE NOBLE ROT. *McSweeney's* #71

Clark, P. Djèlí
WHAT I REMEMBER OF ORESHA
MOON DRAGON DEVSHRATA. *The
Book of Witches*, ed. Jonathan
Strahan (Harper Voyager)

Coles, Donyae
MOTHER, DAUGHTER, AND THE
DEVIL. *All These Sunken Souls*,
ed. Circe Moskowitz (Amberjack
Publishing)

Darbyshire, Peter
THE ANGEL AZRAEL BATTLES
A DEAD GOD AMONG THE
HERETICS. *Beneath Ceaseless
Skies* #388

Duckworth, Jonathan
SPOOKMAN. *The Magazine of
Fantasy & Science Fiction*, March/
April

Dunbar, Eboni J.
SPELL FOR GRIEF AND LONGING.
FIYAH, Spring

Evenson, Brian
AFTER THE ANIMAL FLESH
BEINGS. *Reactor*, June

Gonzalez, Michael
THE SUM OF OUR PARTS NEEDS
ONLY ONE HEART. *Qualia Nous,
Vol. 2*, ed. Michael Bailey (Written
Backwards)

Hill, Joe
    THE PRAM. *Creature Feature*
    (Amazon Original Stories)
Hopkinson, Nalo
    THE MOST STRONGEST OBEAH
    WOMAN. *Out There Screaming*, eds.
    Jordan Peele and John Joseph
    Adams (Random House)
Howard, Kat
    ELEANORA OF THE BONE. *Beneath
    Ceaseless Skies* #383
Jemisin, N. K.
    RECKLESS EYEBALLING. *Out There
    Screaming*, eds. Jordan Peele and
    John Joseph Adams (Random
    House)
Jones, Rachael K.
    THE SOUND OF CHILDREN
    SCREAMING. *Nightmare*, October
Kang, Minsoo
    BEFORE THE GLORY OF THEIR
    MAJESTIES. *New Suns 2: Original
    Speculative Fiction by People of Color*,
    ed. Nisi Shawl (Solaris)
Kim, Seoung
    PARK'S ALL-NIGHT RAMYUN AND
    SNACK EMPORIUM. *Cast of Wonders*
    #539
Link, Kelly
    PRINCE HAT UNDERGROUND. *White
    Cat, Black Dog* (Random House)
Lord, Karen
    A TIMELY HORIZON. *Sunday
    Morning Transport*, March
Onyebuchi, Tochi
    DÉJÀ VUE. *The Book of Witches*, ed.
    Jonathan Strahan (Harper Voyager)
Onyebuchi, Tochi
    ORIGIN STORY. *Out There Screaming*,
    eds. Jordan Peele and John Joseph
    Adams (Random House)
Sanders, Davaun
    NPC (OR EIGHT HAXPLOITS
    TO MAXIMIZE YOUR ENDGAME
    FARMING: A PLAYER'S GUIDE). *The
    Magazine of Fantasy & Science Fiction*,
    July/August

Stewart, Andrea
    HER RAVENOUS WATERS. *The Book
    of Witches*, ed. Jonathan Strahan
    (Harper Voyager)
Tobler, E. Catherine
    REMEMBERED SALT. *The Magazine
    of Fantasy & Science Fiction*, March/
    April
Tuttle, Lisa
    CONCEALED CARRY. *A Darker
    Shade of Noir*, ed. Joyce Carol Oates
    (Akashic Books)
Zhang, Cynthia
    WE, THE ONES WHO RAISED
    SAM GOWERS FROM THE DEAD.
    PseudoPod #859

SCIENCE FICTION

Allen, Violet
    THE RAINBOW GHOSTS.
    Luminescent Machinations, eds.
    Rhiannon Rasmussen and dave ring
    (Neon Hemlock)
Anders, Charlie Jane
    A SOUL IN THE WORLD. *Uncanny*,
    March/April
Ashing-Giwa, Kemi
    THIN ICE. *Clarkesworld*,
    November
Banker, Ashok K.
    THE BODHI TREE ASKS ONLY
    FOR THE SAFE RETURN OF HER
    BELOVED. *Lightspeed*, July
Buckell, Tobias S.
    THE LAST CATHEDRAL OF EARTH.
    Life Beyond Us, eds. Julie Nováková,
    Lucas K. Law, and Susan Forest
    (Laska Media)
Cole, Alyssa
    STASIS (BASTION IN THE
    SPRING). *Fit for the Gods*, eds. Jenn
    Northington and S. Zainab Williams
    (Vintage)
Garcia, R. S. A.
    TANTIE MERLE AND THE
    FARMHAND. *Uncanny*, July/August

EXPLORE THE REST OF THE SERIES!

ON SALE 10/22/24